Sweep Me Up, Baron

A Very Fine Muddle
Book Four

Kate Archer

ARE YOU SIGNED UP FOR DRAGONBLADE'S BLOG?

You'll get the latest news and information on exclusive giveaways, exclusive excerpts, coming releases, sales, free books, cover reveals and more.

Check out our complete list of authors, too!

No spam, no junk. That's a promise!

Sign Up Here

www.dragonbladepublishing.com

Dearest Reader;

Thank you for your support of a small press. At Dragonblade Publishing, we strive to bring you the highest quality Historical Romance from some of the best authors in the business. Without your support, there is no 'us', so we sincerely hope you adore these stories and find some new favorite authors along the way.

Happy Reading!

CEO, Dragonblade Publishing

Additional Dragonblade books by Author Kate Archer

A Very Fine Muddle
Romance Me, Viscount (Book 1)
Be Daring, Duke (Book 2)
Stand With Me, Earl (Book 3)
Sweep Me Up, Baron (Book 4)

A Series of Worthy Young Ladies
The Meddler (Book 1)
The Sprinter (Book 2)
The Undaunted (Book 3)
The Champion (Book 4)
The Jilter (Book 5)
The Regal (Book 6)

The Dukes' Pact Series
The Viscount's Sinful Bargain (Book 1)
The Marquess' Daring Wager (Book 2)
The Lord's Desperate Pledge (Book 3)
The Baron's Dangerous Contract (Book 4)
The Peer's Roguish Word (Book 5)
The Earl's Iron Warrant (Book 6)

PROLOGUE

So many young ladies of the *ton* find that their road to love is not the easy stroll they had imagined it would be. Perhaps there is resistance from one set of parents which must be overcome. Perhaps the lady goes for some weeks unsure of her dashing fellow's feelings and intentions, until he finally declares himself. It might even be the case that there is some disagreement regarding the marriage contract that must be settled.

All nerve-inducing problems for the gentle young lady, to be sure.

The Bennington sisters took a somewhat different approach to love. Theirs was no hiccup or small delay or wistful week of wondering. The Bennington style of traveling to an altar was more akin to climbing a Swiss Alp by one's fingertips, ignoring all signposts warning to turn round, teetering at the summit, flying blind down the other side on the wings of an avalanche, and somehow surviving the inevitable crash into a ravine.

These startling adventures were all led forward by Miss Eloise Mayton, the matron who had come to the aid of the earl and raised his daughters ever since their own mother had died in childbirth.

Miss Mayton was an original sort of person. She favored dressing in widow's weeds, though she had never married. Her stories of past tragic romances were even worse (and probably less true) than the dreadful literature she favored. She insisted on being addressed as "Miss," though her age gave her the right to "Mrs." and one would have thought a lady dressed in widow's weeds would prefer it.

The lady was so loosely related to the earl as to make it almost undiscoverable—everyone having settled on her being a very, exceedingly, astoundingly, incredibly distant cousin of some sort.

But then, as the earl found out when he'd spoken with some of his closer relations, it would require an interesting sort of person to agree to shepherd five young girls through their youths. The prevailing opinion on such things was that one youth was tolerable, two of them was barely tolerable, three was beginning to be a burden, four had definitively arrived at burden, and five set one looking for rooftops to fling oneself off of, thereby mercifully ending it all. So, eccentric Miss Mayton might be, but she had a certain grit about her for blithely taking on the task.

Prior to coming to the earl's house all those years ago, Miss Mayton claimed to have suffered several tragedies of the romantic variety while living on the continent. Nobody quite understood what she'd been doing roaming round Sweden, France, and Italy in the first place, and even less why she'd ever traveled to Transylvania, but everybody could agree that her time there had gone abominably badly.

The young Bennington ladies were raised on Miss Mayton's poignant tales of lost love and they were inspired to have such abject devotion for their own. An outsider might find themself faintly alarmed to hear the details of these tragedies. One after another of Miss Mayton's would-be suitors had somehow come to an unfortunate and final end—mistaken hangings, untimely blows, foolhardy poisonings, an unnecessarily dramatic impalement, and even a regretful leap off a cliff.

The young Benningtons were able to overlook the more gruesome details of these various demises and only felt the romance of it—all of those fellows were overcome and finally defeated by an overwhelming passionate love. How they should like to inspire that sort of passion in some gentleman!

Though it must be said, they were determined to keep the overcome and passionate fellows alive so they might marry them. *Threats* to do a violence to oneself would be entirely sufficient in proving one's devotion.

Passion aside, the sisters had other standards they would insist on. Each knew just the type of gentleman she sought out and was determined to have him. Beatrice's list of requirements turned out to be so long that the fates had finally just thrown up their hands and delivered Van Doren.

Rosalind had been insistent on courageousness, and if she had to arrange her own kidnapping so that the duke might prove his own courage, well, these things happen.

Viola had one thing on her mind—loyalty. If her lord had eventually noticed that loyalty had led him to standing on a green for three duels on the same morning…that really could not have been predicted.

Fortunately, it was Cordelia's turn at a season and her necessary quality was far more straightforward. She simply wished for a man of action. She wished for her very own Corinthian.

He would do everything expertly, of course—hunt, box, sail, race, fence—all with the greatest of ease and aplomb. She would wave to him from a window as he rode off to do some sporting thing, then he would return home victorious. Of an evening, he would relax in a chair, bone tired, while she entertained him with her scene from *Othello*, that poignant moment when all is lost for Desdemona.

He would be soothed by it, rediscover his energy, sweep her into his arms, and carry her up the stairs.

In fact, he was always carrying her about the house and she would begin to wonder that her own feet still worked, so little did he allow her to use them.

What a glorious life they would have—she, his own dramatic actress, and he, the sportsman extraordinaire.

She must only find him.

CHAPTER ONE

The Lamb at Hindon, 1805

CORDELIA VIEWED THE months in Somerset between the London seasons lively indeed. They had all together had a jolly time in Scotland for Viola's family elopement with Lord Baderston and then waved them off to their own estate in Sussex before returning home.

The Earl of Westmont's house, which had in the past only been filled with the sounds of five young ladies, had changed its tone entirely.

It was true that Beatrice, Rosalind, and Viola had married and left the house, thereby removing their vocalizations from the sounds of the place. But it was also true that their trips to London invariably brought them into contact with some poor creature who needed a place to call home.

They had begun with four cats, then added the dog Bess and one of her offspring. Then, last year, they had taken in darling Chester—a scarlet macaw who had a lot to say for himself. Between cats hissing and dogs barking, Chester would shriek the word "murder" which, unfortunately, he thought meant "almonds."

If someone were looking for peace and quiet in the country-side, they would be well advised to trot by Westmont House at a brisk pace.

Amidst all the barking and hissing and screeching, there were trips through the wood from Westmont House to Faversham Hall. There, they would find their eldest sister Beatrice ensconced in the nursery with her infant daughter Lily. Often, they would find Van Doren there too. The cranky viscount had already been defeated by Beatrice, and now he appeared to be clay in his daughter's pudgy little hands too.

Rosalind and the Duke of Conbatten came for a fortnight's visit and had thrown the house into a delightful topsy-turvy. The duke's valet, Henri, had arrived a full five days ahead of time to ready things for Conbatten and his duchess, and it was well he did. It was no easy thing in a country house to assure that a duke had accommodations that included an attached room for the location of a tub that would be filled with water heated to precisely ninety-eight degrees. He liked to bathe with his wife, she only wearing jewels and a tiara, and he had very specific standards on how it was to be done.

They'd had hopes that they might entice Viola and Lord Baderston to come for a visit, though they were so recently married. As it happened, Viola was up to her eyes in things to do at her new house. She was determined to manage the dowager, a project that seemed well underway, and she was equally determined to keep her lord safe at home after rescuing him from three different duels.

Their absence was thought to be no great matter—they would see Viola in Town.

The family had since set off for Portland Place, leaving Beatrice, Van Doren, and the menagerie of animals behind. Darling Lily was too young to travel, so Beatrice would spend a quiet few months watching her grow and smiling at Van Doren as he mooned around the nursery.

Their own cats and dogs were comfortable where they were, roaming the estate and coming in when they were tired or hungry.

Chester, their very charming parrot, had proved himself to be a terrible traveler—regularly falling off his perch and seeming as if he was dead. However, he had also proved himself exceedingly fond of Clara, a housemaid who would stay behind and look after him. Chester would shout "murder" and Clara would laugh and shout back, "Murder yourself, you wretch."

As Chester did not understand the words comprising the sentence, but only the friendliness of the tone, he was delighted with Clara.

The earl's carriages had meandered and detoured and stopped and started in their usual roundabout manner, arriving at The Lamb at Hindon six days after they set off.

It might have taken them even longer, but they had finally devised a method of ensuring that Juliet's book of odes did not get left behind everywhere they stopped, as had been the usual situation. Van Doren had taken the book after she'd left it in the drawing room, drilled a hole in the corner of it, and slipped a ribbon through. Now, Juliet might carry it on her wrist and had only lost track of it twice.

Cordelia was rather surprised by the scene that met her father's carriages at the innyard of The Lamb. It was usual that when they arrived, they were the largest party going, and perhaps the party thought to have the deepest pockets. These two ideas generally resulted in all hands very quickly at their disposal.

That was not the case this time. A party had arrived before them and seemed to take everyone's attention. It was only one carriage, and it seemed it only carried one lady and her maid, but whoever she was, she was making an outsize impression.

Finally, a groom had been convinced to provide his service to the Benningtons, though he'd seemed loathe to part with the mystery carriage.

Cordelia wasted no time inquiring of him. She leaned out the window and said, "Young man, who is that lady, if you will?"

The groom looked at her in some surprise, as if it she were rather dim to ask it.

"That is Mrs. Jordan. Mrs. Dorothy Jordan, you understand.

At *our* inn, staying the night. Dorothy Jordan prefers *our* inn."

Cordelia sat back. Dorothy Jordan was one of the great actresses of the age! How fortuitous that they should encounter one another. They must meet. What with Mrs. Jordan's experience performing on the stage and her own experience performing in the drawing room, they would have much to talk about.

Of course, being an earl's daughter, Cordelia herself would never tread the boards at Drury Lane, but that did not mean she could not have the beating heart and emotional soul of an actress.

How many times had she entertained her family with Desdemona's last dying words? She had perfected it, she thought privately. Shakespeare would be proud of her interpretation, she thought very silently. She made it a point to look as if she were surprised by the applause at the end of one of her performances, though she really was not.

"Cordy," Juliet said, "wait until Mrs. Jordan understands there is another actress at the inn. You might act out Desdemona for her."

"I am sure she would be delighted with it," Miss Mayton said.

"I'll not argue it," Cordelia said, "but first we must be introduced and then invite her to dine."

They watched the lady descend from her carriage. She was a striking personage and wore a hat sporting several exceedingly long ostrich plumes. It was the sort of hat that waved to the world and proclaimed, "I am not afraid to be noticed." This would be a bold thing on a usual day but was perhaps even bolder now. The lady was visibly with child.

Naturally, nothing would be mentioned regarding her expanding waistline. For one, it was not a thing that was ever mentioned between strangers. But for a very important two, there was no *Mr.* Jordan who might be comfortably responsible for such a state.

If there were a baby on the way, that baby would be the Duke of Clarence's issue. Mrs. Jordan had long lived with the duke at Bushy Park and their children were too numerous to count.

Cordelia put all those ideas aside. Whatever was Mrs. Jordan's personal life, she was an actress first. She was an actress in her heart and soul.

Miss Mayton called to the groom. "Do let us down," she said. Turning to Cordelia and Juliet, she said, "Come, my girls, we do not have a moment to lose."

Out of the carriage, they hurried across the innyard to come upon Mrs. Jordan just as she was being led into the inn by the innkeeper himself.

"Maisie dear, is that you?" Miss Mayton said, reaching Mrs. Jordan's side.

The lady turned and said, "I am afraid you are mistaken, my good lady."

"Heavens, so I am," Miss Mayton said. "I haven't seen my dear cousin in years, but you are so like, I hardly imagined there could be two such beauties in England…"

Mrs. Jordan, and Cordelia supposed every other lady in the land, was not immune to such a compliment.

"You are very kind, I'm sure," Mrs. Jordan said smiling.

Miss Mayton dramatically staggered and cried, "Wait! I know who you are. How did I not perceive it at once?"

This was taken as a further compliment, and Mrs. Jordan nodded condescendingly.

Miss Mayton turned to Cordelia and Juliet and said, "This is the esteemed Mrs. Dorothy Jordan of the stage. The greatest comedic actress who has ever tread the boards."

Cordelia and Juliet curtsied very low.

"Really, madam," Mrs. Jordan said, "you are too effusive."

"Not at all," Miss Mayton said, shaking her head. "I am rather known for not passing about unearned flattery. If I say a thing, I *mean* a thing."

"I see," Mrs. Jordan said, appearing very pleased to hear it. "And you are?"

"Miss Eloise Mayton, and these are the Earl of Westmont's

daughters, Lady Cordelia and Lady Juliet."

"Charmed," Mrs. Jordan said. Cordelia could not help noticing Mrs. Jordan's eye taking in Miss Mayton's widow's weeds and then hearing that she was a "miss." People who were unacquainted with her aunt's tragic past romances always did wonder about it.

"If I am not being too forward," Miss Mayton said, "we would ask you to dine with us this evening. The earl will not wish to miss a chance to meet the great lady herself."

"Oh, I…"

"Please do, Mrs. Jordan," Cordelia said. "Papa should be heartbroken if you do not."

"Well, I *am* traveling with just my maid…"

"Our father does admire you so," Juliet said, "he often mentions it."

"It cannot be comfortable to dine alone," Miss Mayton said, "and we always do make up a very jolly party."

Mrs. Jordan nodded her acquiescence, and the thing was settled. Cordelia Bennington was to dine with the greatest actress of the time.

Was not life marvelous?

PERCIVAL GRANGER, BARON Harveston, reread the note he'd just opened. Were someone to have viewed him as he did it, they might describe his expression as a unique combination of dubiousness and dread.

As the founding member of *The Society for Serious Literary Examination*, or the *SSLE* as it was called by longstanding members, he was often in receipt of odd communications.

There were those gentlemen all across England who sought to make their mark as an intellectual. They'd drum up an original idea and then closet themselves in their libraries trying to prove it by hook or by crook, no matter how tenuous or outlandish the alleged proof seemed to be. These various theories eventually wended their way to his door, hoping they might garner an invitation to become a member of the *SSLE*.

He had only last week received such a theory from Sir Lawrence Veld, proposing that Shakespeare was actually two people. Twins, in fact. Sir Lawrence gave as his evidence that Shakespeare wrote both comedy and tragedy and no writer could do both. He supposed that the writers were twins because their styles were similar—one preferring serious and the other preferring light. The further evidence that they were twins was there for anybody to see—all known portraits of the bard were very like.

It was preposterous.

Sadly, it was not as preposterous as the note he just read.

Lady Rawley, a lady who every year took one of Shakespeare's plays and rewrote the ending to suit herself and then performed the ill-advised results for her friends, wished to join his society.

Her theatrical evenings had gained a following of sorts, not because there was anything worthy in them, but because so many viewed them as delightfully ludicrous.

Last season's offering had been *Much Ado about Nothing*, in which Hero lost her mind, murdered Claudio at the altar, and seemed none the worse for wear afterward. He supposed she ought to have retitled that one to *Much Ado about Something Very Bad*.

There had been others, of course. Romeo and Juliet living happily ever after and naming their firstborn Romiet had been much talked of.

He did not himself attend the evenings, his excuses getting ever more creative with each passing year. Lady Rawley was under the impression that Baron Harveston carried a heavy weight of duties upon his shoulders, all tied up with ancient traditions that must be seen to on his estate in Kent. The last had been a "spring steward's ceremony," whatever that was supposed to be.

Fortunately, she never inquired into the details.

Unfortunately, Lady Rawley also happened to be his aunt.

He read the note again, searching it for any escape tunnel he might slip down or a secret door he might use as an exit to this untenable proposal.

My darling boy—

I, of course, know how devastated you are to always miss my theatrical evenings. (A baron is called to take on so many responsibilities, my departed earl was never so busy!)

I write you to tell you that I have had a smashing idea—I will join your society of literary people. In fact, I thought I would invite my entire acting troupe as it is only a handful of ladies.

This year's offering at my little theatrical soiree will be Othello *and we will be glad to hear the various opinions of your members on how I intend to improve on the ending.*

All my love,
Aunt M

Improve on the ending of *Othello*? Good Lord, what would the members think of it? And then, not just his aunt would descend upon him, but her collection of ridiculous ladies who join her in her fever dream of improving Shakespeare's work?

Worse, there was another letter in his pile and it was from his mother. He was very afraid it would be some directive to humor his aunt's latest bad idea.

He dug it out and tore it open.

Percival allowed it to drop from his hand and flutter to the desk. That was exactly what it said. Couched among the sentiments of the importance of family and supporting one another, there it was. His mother would be most appreciative if he would welcome Lady Rawley into his little club.

She'd called it a "little club."

He felt a heaviness descend upon him as he contemplated his very near future. Lady Margaret Rawley, butcher of Shakespeare, was to join the SSLE.

The first salon of the season was next Tuesday. Did she know it? Would she just turn up?

Could he ignore the letters from Lady Rawley and his mother and blame it on the post?

Makepeace softly knocked and entered the room. "My lord, do you require anything?" he asked.

Percival sighed. He would have to break the news to his butler. Makepeace was an intellectual in his own right and a longstanding and valued member of the SSLE.

The society did not discriminate against any man—a man's mind was what was evaluated. A pirate or a grocer might gain entry, if there were such a man of suitable knowledge and discernment. Makepeace might be a butler, but he was a learned fellow with a razor-sharp intellect and insightful opinions.

Having been well acquainted with Lady Rawley over the years, Makepeace would take it as a heavy blow.

"My aunt has decided to join the SSLE," he said.

Makepeace staggered just the smallest bit and then steadied himself by putting his hand on the mantel.

"Lady Rawley?" he whispered.

Percival nodded.

"But, my lord, an offer of membership to the society is extended to one who has proven...and it is presumed all the members see the value...a person cannot simply *decide* to join."

"My aunt has very conveniently overlooked that point, as has my mother."

"We do not even have any lady members, but for Madame d'Arblay, and that lady only sends letters from Paris. We have never had a woman at a salon, in the actual room, in person."

"That is the least of our problems. Should a lady be of a refined and educated mind, I see no reason why she should not attend my salon. Lady Hightower has always been welcome to join, if she ever chooses to do so."

Makepeace nodded. Lady Hightower was indeed an intellectual, but she liked to read and study in a solitary manner and had no interest in talking about it at a club.

There were a few others, too. There were two matrons in particular who he would have welcomed, but they had no interest in it. As far as Percival could tell, they had both allowed their husbands to imagine that they were the brains of the operation and did not wish for the illusion to be shattered.

Someday though, he would encounter a lady with a keen intellect who was the right age and not yet married. He looked forward to that day and he would not hesitate in his pursuit of her. He was determined to marry such a lady.

After all, how else could it be? He must marry his intellectual equal and when he did so, he would afford her every opportunity to pursue her educated interests. Theirs would be no ordinary dining table, but rather filled with interesting and erudite conversation.

He had not met such a lady yet, but he was confident that he would. Each year, ladies as yet unknown to him arrived to Town to take their place in society. Perhaps she was even now in a carriage, poised to enter his life.

"Does Lady Rawley know about the salon next Tuesday?" Makepeace said quietly.

"I do not know, but there is worse news," Percival said.

"There cannot be," Makepeace said, thereby summing up his opinion of Lady Rawley joining the society.

"Oh, I can assure you there is," Percival said. He handed Makepeace the note to read for himself.

His butler read the missive and Percival noted perspiration spring upon his brow.

"She brings her *troupe*?" he said.

Percival nodded sadly.

"She rewrites the ending to *Othello*?" Makepeace whispered.

"Indeed," Percival said. "So, perhaps Desdemona does not die after all."

"Lord help us."

"I certainly hope so," Percival said, "as I do not know who else could help us."

CHAPTER TWO

CORDELIA HAD SOUGHT out her father and he'd been apprised that the famed actress Mrs. Dorothy Jordan was to dine with them that evening.

He did not meet the idea with the same unbounded enthusiasm that everybody else did, but then he did not fight against it either. The Earl of Westmont was a comfortable and calm sort of person and unless something was on fire, he was not likely to be unhappy. He had long operated on the idea that once a thing his daughters thought up got going, turning it round again would be as pointless as Sisyphus pushing his boulder.

The earl's butler, Tattleton, had been at the earl's side when the news was relayed, and that person had rather stronger feelings about it.

Tattleton had gasped and whispered, "An actress!"

But then, poor Tattleton had seemed to grow more tremulous year by year, so Cordelia could not take the sentiment too much to heart. None of them knew what affected him so, but their relocation to Town always seemed to bring on his frayed nerves.

Cordelia thought perhaps the noise and bustle of the town was too much for his constitution.

They were already seated in a private dining room when Mrs. Jordan was escorted in by what seemed to be half the staff of the inn.

They'd since had a jolly dinner and Cordelia thought her father enjoyed himself more than he thought he would. Mrs. Jordan, being of a comedic bent, was a wit of the first order. Her repartee flew like lightning seeking ground.

The dessert course came round and the innkeeper brought in a bottle of port for the earl.

"Ah, Mrs. Jordan," the earl said, "shall you take port? I ask because we did dine with a French lady once who indulged in it. One never knows what various people's habits might be—I suppose the theater has its own traditions."

"The Frenchwoman was Madame Tussaud," Juliet said for further clarification. "You might have seen her wax figures at the Lyceum two years ago. She was very fond of port and drank three glasses in a matter of minutes."

Mrs. Jordan said, "I am not opposed to port on occasion, but whenever I am…in a certain condition, I lose all taste for it."

This silenced the party, as nobody wished to inquire into the Duke of Clarence's whereabouts while his mistress traveled the countryside alone.

"Mrs. Jordan," Miss Mayton said, always willing to step into an awkward breach, "you are in for quite the treat this evening. We will have a very special surprise, but first I will read aloud from a novel we have just begun."

"It is *The Dreadful Doings of Dembric Dale*," Cordelia said. "It begins with a duke hopelessly in love with his gentle governess. Her father, Mr. Denbrow, lives in the dale and refuses to sanction the marriage. We were entirely surprised by that turn of events because her father is the poorest man in the county and the duke is the richest."

"That does seem surprising," Mrs. Jordan said.

"Doesn't it just?" the earl said. "But then we discovered that Mr. Denbrow was willing to part with his daughter for all the money the duke had—making *him* the richest and the duke the poorest."

"The duke has agreed to it," Juliet said. "What else could he do, he is so in love."

"But there is one thing that troubles Mr. Denbrow, who is now very rich," Cordelia said. "The duke would only agree to the idea if he were named Mr. Denbrow's heir."

"Ah, very sensible," Mrs. Jordan said. "The duke will get his money back in the end."

"Yes, but when is the end and how is the end?" Miss Mayton said mysteriously. "This is what lingers in Mr. Denbrow's mind."

"He's terribly tortured over it," Juliet said happily.

Miss Mayton nodded. "All right, chapter three."

Mr. Denbrow should have been a happy man. He had entirely transformed what had been a ramshackle hovel into a place of luxury and comfort.

And yet, there were ideas that insisted on troubling his mind and disturbing his sleep. He knew that the duke and his own daughter lived in poverty now. They still had a grand house, but they'd had to fire all the servants and they now lived exclusively in the drawing room to save on firewood. They had to chop the wood down themselves these days and neither of them were very good at it.

While the duke seemed satisfied with the arrangement, his daughter appeared rather less sanguine to find herself a duchess with nothing to show for it. Her unhappiness was nothing, though, compared to the duke's fired servants.

More than half the village had been employed in that house and the stares and threats Mr. Denbrow got from those persons were terrorizing. More alarming, the duke was named his heir. He almost got the feeling that somebody might murder him to get their job back.

It was beginning to drive him mad. At night, he could not sleep for the imagined footsteps outside his window. During the day, he hardly dared to venture out, as some disgruntled person might catch him alone and unawares.

It was such a burden to be rich!

His kitchen maid hurried in with a note. "This just got slipped under the door," she said. "Probably another one of those notes about how you're gonna die."

"Stop saying that, you wretch!" he said, ripping the note from her hands.

The kitchen maid shrugged and left him alone. He tore open the note and was despondent to see that the kitchen maid had been right. It was another message about how he was going to die. This time, somebody proposed that he would be tied to a tree and covered in honey near a beehive and then after he was stung so many times that he was weakened he would be thrown down a well.

Miss Mayton closed the book. "So, now we wonder, will Mr. Denbrow be murdered and if so, will it be a villager or perhaps even the duke himself?"

Mrs. Jordan snorted. "That is…a unique piece of literature. It is difficult to know if it is a comedy or tragedy."

"All these books do end happily, if that is a clue," Juliet said.

"Happily for who?" Mrs. Jordan asked.

"The romantic couple—the duke and his gentle governess," Juliet said, seeming faintly surprised that she would have to explain that point.

Mrs. Jordan laughed and said, "That won't do Mr. Denbrow much good."

"We cannot fathom how it will all play out, Mrs. Jordan," the earl said. "The books Miss Mayton finds for us are always so filled with twists and turns. I quite lose sleep over them sometimes."

Mrs. Jordan nodded to the earl, looking vastly amused.

"Now we come to the special surprise I mentioned earlier," Miss Mayton said.

"There is another story even more surprising than Mr. Denbrow's difficulties?" Mrs. Jordan asked.

"Ah yes," Miss Mayton said, "and it is a story you will know well. Our Cordelia, and this is the great surprise, is *also* an actress."

Mrs. Jordan turned to her. "An earl's daughter? On the stage?"

"Gracious no," the earl said. "I would never allow such a

thing."

"I only perform for the family," Cordelia said. "But I do it often," she added for further clarification.

"She's Desdemona," Juliet said. "You will not believe your eyes."

Cordelia rose and attempted to ignore the fluttering in her stomach. She was not at all nervous as a performer, but this *was* Mrs. Dorothy Jordan.

"Now, what I have done, Mrs. Jordan," Cordelia said, "is refashion poor Desdemona's tragic death scene by removing the other actors' parts in it."

She noted Mrs. Jordan's brow wrinkle, so Cordelia hurriedly explained, "As I am always my entire troupe and do not have other actors to employ."

"Ah, yes, I see," Mrs. Jordan said.

"Also," Juliet added helpfully, "it's faster and more exciting without having to listen to Othello drone on and on."

"Yes, it would be," Mrs. Jordan said, a smile playing at the edge of her lips.

Cordelia walked to the fireplace and draped herself elegantly against the mantel. "Alas!" she cried. "He is betrayed and I undone! O, banish me, my lord, but kill me not!"

She raised her head and took on a faraway look, as if she were viewing the afterlife ahead of her. Cordelia raced across the room, stopped dramatically and turned to her audience. "Kill me tomorrow, let me live tonight! But half an hour! But while I say one prayer!"

Cordelia viewed Mrs. Jordan and became very encouraged; the lady was leaning forward in her chair. Now, it was time for the final poignant moment.

She ran to the inn's window and banged dramatically on it. "O, falsely, falsely murdered! A guiltless death die I! Nobody, I myself. Farewell! Commend me to my kind lord. O, farewell!"

Cordelia slowly sank to the ground and lay still.

Among the loud applause from her family, Mrs. Jordan roared

with laughter.

Cordelia opened one eye. Mrs. Jordan was clapping along with the rest, but she was laughing too. What did it mean?

She scrambled to her feet. Mrs. Jordan rose and walked to her, grasping her hands. "That was astonishingly good, Lady Cordelia. It is a shame you will never walk the boards of Drury Lane, you have a natural gift for comedy—you could have been one of the best."

Cordelia was nodding and smiling, but thoroughly confused. How on earth had Mrs. Jordan taken Desdemona's tragic death as comedy?

The lady turned to the table. "Earl, you have a charming family. I greatly appreciate the entertainments you have provided this night, it is so rare that I am ever truly entertained. I bid you all a fond goodnight as in my condition I do need my rest."

She curtsied to the earl, blew a kiss to Juliet, patted Cordelia's cheek, and swept out of the room.

After the door closed behind her, the earl rose and said, "Well done, Cordelia. Now, I think we should follow Mrs. Jordan's lead and retire so we are fresh in the morning."

As Cordelia fairly staggered up the stairs to the bedchamber she would share with Miss Mayton and Juliet, her sister patted her arm and whispered, "I am afraid Mrs. Jordan is not very familiar with *Othello*."

"Even so," Cordelia said, "how on earth could she think it a comedy?"

As they entered the chamber and Lynette shut the door behind them, Miss Mayton said, "It occurs to me that while actresses can seem as if they have so many original ideas, they are only reciting what they have memorized. They need not have the slightest bit of real intelligence."

"So," Cordelia said slowly, "you think Mrs. Jordan did not understand my interpretation of Desdemona because she is stupid?"

"Well, I do not see what else it could be," Miss Mayton said.

"Really, it is the only explanation that fits, Cordy," Juliet said.

Cordelia nodded, somewhat soothed over the idea that Mrs. Dorothy Jordan must be a dolt.

PERCIVAL HAD TAKEN Pericles to the park, which would suit them both.

His horse was a bay stallion descended from Highflyer and would not tolerate being exercised by grooms for too many days together. On the few occasions he had been, he'd been known to kick down a stable door or buck off his rider.

As for himself, Percival found riding alone very conducive to thinking. Pericles' steady gait soothed him and allowed him to examine whatever matter was on his mind.

They both preferred the early afternoon, before the crowds streamed in for the great parade of the *ton*. During that time-honored tradition, gentlemen would showcase their horsemanship in a ridiculous fashion, no doubt annoying their horses. Ladies would come dressed in their best while pretending they did not think they would encounter anybody on the outing. Conversations about nothing of import would be had and gossip would be traded like tea from the Far East. He found the whole thing tedious.

In the relative quiet before the rush, he was pondering his opinions on the SSLE's current salon topic—what was the real relationship between Shakespeare's lost play *Cardenio* and Theobald's play *Double Falsehood*? Had Theobald ever really had *Cardenio* in his possession and edited it to become *Double Falsehood*?

He expected there to be wide-ranging views on the matter, which was excellent. An intellectual salon was not very interesting if all parties agreed on a topic.

As Pericles followed the carriage road without requiring

direction, Percival's thoughts meandered through everything he knew or suspected on the subject.

From somewhere outside himself a voice clamored for his attention.

"Percy! Percy, dear!"

As if being pulled by a rope, he was instantly yanked from his pleasant reverie and into the present day of the park.

And his aunt's carriage.

And his aunt hanging out the carriage window and waving to him.

She was directing her coachman to approach him. What could he say to her? He had not answered her letter about joining the SSLE. He'd planned to, but he'd found it impossible. He did not want to be unkind and tell her to stay away, and he did not want to be a liar by telling her she was welcome.

He'd wished the whole thing would just go away on its own. After all, Lady Rawley was a flighty sort of person, might she not have changed her mind and decided to try out hot air ballooning instead?

"My dear nephew," she said.

"Aunt," Percival said. "You are early to the park."

"Yes, well you see, I went to your house and was told you were here," Lady Rawley said.

"Makepeace told you?" Percival said, working to keep the surprise from his voice. He would have thought his butler would have closely guarded his location from his aunt.

"Goodness, no," Lady Rawley said. "You know Makepeace— grim as an undertaker as always. I sent him into your library to fetch a book I wished to read. It's called the *Dreadful Doings of Dembric Dale*. Lady Agatha says it is very good."

"I am absolutely certain no such book would make an appearance in my library."

"As I thought, but I knew it would occupy Makepeace for a suitable amount of time. He said you'd never have it, but I said you did and he must go and look. Then I worked on your footman. Goodness, the poor fellow was shaken when I threatened to dismiss him. How on earth did he think I could do it?"

"Dismiss him?" Percival asked, his incredulity apparent.

"Never mind that," Lady Rawley said, "after he told me where you'd gone, I explained I could only dismiss my own servants but never had the heart for it, then I gave him a guinea and he was right as rain."

"Aunt, I would ask that you refrain from—"

"Yes, yes, no more threatening the servants. I knew you'd say so," Lady Rawley said, waving her hands. "I really was forced to it as it was necessary that I speak with you."

"Oh?"

"You did get my letter, did you not? About your little literary club?"

"*The Society of Serious Literary Examination* is not a 'little club,'" Percival said stiffly. "It is comprised of England's most accomplished intellectuals who take an interest in literature and wish to exchange ideas with other likeminded people. We hold salons where that activity takes place."

"Excellent, the salon, just as I thought," Lady Rawley said. "It is on Tuesday, is it not?"

"Well, I…"

"Of course it is, I wrangled that out of your young footman too."

"Aunt, I really do not know if my salon is, well I'm not sure if it would be…you see, it's likely to be rather dull to someone of your temperament."

"Say no more, my dear nephew, I understand you perfectly."

"Do you?" Percival asked, both perplexed and cautiously joyful. Was the whole thing just gone away?

"I will do it, have no fear on the front."

"Do what?" Percival asked, beginning to fear on that front.

"I will keep my enormous creativity under wraps. I realize your friends are not likely to excel at imagination, being so mired in facts all the time. I shan't intimidate them with my prowess—

it's not their fault!"

Intimidate them with what? With her imagination?

Percival gripped his reins until his knuckles were white. He felt like a fish in a net fighting for an escape.

"I will even go so far as to speak to the other ladies I will bring along. After all, your intellectuals do not tread the hallowed boards as we do, allowing our creative visions to soar. You already know Lady Agatha and Mrs. Robinson of course. And then I intend to invite a certain Miss Mayton and her niece, Lady Cordelia Bennington. I'm certain they will accept."

"Miss Mayton?"

"Very helpful woman, she assisted me several times when I found myself in a pinch. But goodness, perhaps you know her already. She is Lord Darden's aunt and I had quite forgotten you were a member of that fellow's little club."

"*The Young Bucks Club*," Percival said stonily.

He certainly did know Miss Mayton. Everybody either knew her or knew *of* her. She was a spinster dressed in widow's weeds who spun outrageous tales of suicidal lotharios knocking themselves off in one absurd way after another. Nobody could quite figure out if she were senile or an inveterate liar or just liked to amuse herself by shocking people.

My God, it was bad enough that the members would be faced with his aunt and her two cronies, but Miss Mayton too! It was a nightmare playing out in real life.

"Now, what is it we will be discussing on Tuesday?"

"Whether Theobald's *Double Falsehood* is really based on Shakespeare's *Cardenio*," Percival said dully.

"I've never heard of either play, but I am looking forward to meeting all your friends. I *will* need their input for this year's theatrical! And do not tell me you cannot attend me this time—I checked with your footman and he says he's not heard of any spring steward's ceremony scheduled for this year. You are quite free, is that not delightful?"

Lady Rawley rapped her cane on the roof of her carriage and

said, "Smith, carry on!"

As Percival watched his aunt's carriage depart, he had a sinking feeling his salon would never be the same again.

CHAPTER THREE

M ISS MAYTON AND Juliet had spent the passing days in the carriage convincing Cordelia that Mrs. Dorothy Jordan was an idiot who would not know a tragic and poignant scene if it hit her over the head with her own overdressed bonnet.

Her confidence having been greatly restored, Cordelia found herself rather sanguine over the matter. For one, so many of her relations adored her interpretation of Desdemona's demise. The only person who was not bowled over by it was Beatrice's husband, Van Doren. The viscount was such a crank that if Mrs. Jordan chose to align herself with him, well that was a very unfortunate comment on the lady's judgment.

For another, they were closing in on London. Somewhere in that town was her Corinthian. Somewhere was a strapping gentleman with arms so muscular that his tailor almost despaired of encasing them in material. Her Corinthian was no doubt doing something sporting at this moment, and wondering when his lady would present herself. *He* would adore her Desdemona.

And then as a further distraction, she, Juliet, and Miss Mayton had just come upon a remarkable scene at The Angel at Hindon. The earl was still in the yard, no doubt conferring with the innkeeper regarding their dinner, while they had been drawn to the door to the kitchens over what they'd heard there.

The smallest and loveliest of gentle calls, the kind only a baby animal of some sort could make.

They peeked round the doorframe and were delighted to see an elderly gentleman holding a kid, the baby goat certainly being no older than a few days.

"Can't you help me out? His ma died this morning," the man said.

"We are not serving goat at The Angel," the cook said.

Juliet gasped. Cordelia grabbed at Miss Mayton's sleeve.

"Serving?" the man cried. "I just want some milk for it! Just enough to hold me over until I can sell the little mite."

The cook took a moment to realize that the goat was not being proposed for somebody's dinner. He said, "I see your plight, old fella, but I can't give out food and drink to everybody who comes along and asks. I'd be dismissed."

"I don't know what to do," the old man said, shaking his head. "This here is the last goat and a billy at that, all but useless as we won't get no milk from it. Aye, the wife wants to cook him up but I can't bring myself to do it. She says I'm soft and I'm afraid I am."

Cordelia looked at her aunt and Juliet. They looked back. They all three nodded.

They burst into the kitchen. Cordelia said, "Sir, we cannot allow you or that darling little baby to suffer. You must tell your wife that adorable creature has been adopted into a loving home."

"Adopted?"

"This is Lady Cordelia and that is Lady Juliet, daughters of the Earl of Westmont. I am Miss Mayton," her aunt said, "I can assure you, this enchanting creature shall live in the lap of luxury."

"Luxury?" the man asked, seeming as if he had not considered that outcome as a possibility.

"We will pay you handsomely," Miss Mayton said. She turned to Cordelia and Juliet. "Your father still gives me a clothing allowance, though I only wear the black bombazine."

"You are so good, Aunt," Cordelia said. She turned to the

elderly gentleman and said, "Tell us, what is the little fellow's name?"

"Name?"

"Goodness, he does not even have a name yet," Cordelia said.

"My own name is Jim Carpenter," the man said, doffing his hat.

"That does not help us, I do not think," Cordelia said.

"I think we should call him Lord Darling, Marquess of Basingstoke," Juliet said.

"Oh that is perfect," Cordelia said. "Lord Darling."

"Lord…"

"Here is three pounds, Mr. Carpenter," Miss Mayton said. "Now what will we require? How much milk will we need for Lord Darling?"

Mr. Carpenter took the money and handed Lord Darling into Cordelia's arms.

He was a lovely little thing, round eyes drooping with sleep and little tail wagging.

"I brought a glass bottle, works just fine, been using it for years," Mr. Carpenter said, pulling out a small bottle from his coat. "You're gonna need a mixture of half milk, half buttermilk, dosed with a bit of sugar. He drank the last of what I had not an hour ago so he should be set up for now."

The cook had been looking back and forth at the goings-on, and probably wishing everyone would leave his kitchen. Miss Mayton said to him, "Please prepare the mixture, my good sir, and have it ready for when we dine. You may put it on the earl's bill."

The cook nodded, and Cordelia got the feeling he viewed them all as eccentric. They were not though—who could leave adorable Lord Darling to the winds of fate?

"Now," Miss Mayton said, "we'd best go and acquaint your father with this turn of events."

"Poor Papa," Juliet said. "He is bound to be very surprised."

Mr. Carpenter looked alarmed over the idea of the earl being surprised. He said, "No returns!" and fled the kitchen.

Cordelia carefully carried Lord Darling into the inn, while Juliet and Miss Mayton cooed over him and petted his head.

"Papa," Juliet said, stepping in front of Cordelia just as their father came inside. "A very surprising thing has happened that absolutely could not be avoided but you are not to worry as it has all come out right."

The earl was such an even-keeled sort of fellow, but even he must show concern when a young Bennington explained that something was surprising, could not be avoided, and there was no need to worry.

"Oh dear," he said, "what has happened?"

Juliet stepped aside and Cordelia said, "This is Lord Darling. We discovered him in terrible straits in the kitchen."

"In the kitchen?" the earl said. "He is very young for that!"

If their father had somehow, and entirely on his own, come to the conclusion that Lord Darling had just been rescued from a stew pot, well, neither Cordelia nor Juliet ever liked to correct their father.

"Never fear, Papa," Juliet said, "he is ours now."

"Well, hmm, of course, I am not opposed to having a goat on the estate, there is plenty of room, but there is the matter of getting him there. We should not wish to turn back now. We are nearly at London's door and it has taken almost a fortnight to get this far."

"No, of course we would not turn round," Cordelia said. "We shall take him to Town with us. He will like the back garden, I think."

"You ought not worry over anything, Papa," Juliet said. "We have a bottle and understand the recipe for milk. We have things well in hand."

As the earl generally did not like to worry over things, his brow cleared and he shrugged. The innkeeper approached and he said, "My lady, may I take the kid to the stables for the night?"

"The *stables*?" Cordelia said, clutching Lord Darling to her breast. "This poor baby cannot sleep in the stables."

"He cannot?" the innkeeper asked.

"Certainly not," Cordelia said. "He must be kept warm and we must feed him every few hours and most of all he must feel secure that he has a new family that will care for him."

"Can you imagine what he would think if he were to find himself alone in the stables, with only horses looming over him?" Juliet asked.

"I cannot imagine," the innkeeper said resignedly. "I will make some arrangements. A basket with bedding, I suppose."

"Soft bedding, if you please sir," Cordelia said. "Lord Darling has been through it today and must rest."

Lord Darling nuzzled her and surely he knew he had been lucky indeed to come upon the Benningtons. It seemed that wherever they went, needy animals were to present themselves. They were very like Saint Francis, calling all orphaned creatures to their side.

"He will stay in the back garden?" the earl said softly. "In Town, I mean. He will not be in the house?"

"He will adore the garden, Papa," Cordelia said. "I am sure of it."

⤛⤜

THE SERVANTS' HALL of Portland Place had emptied, only leaving the butler remaining at table.

Horace Tattleton, butler to the Earl of Westmont, had spent the intervening months between the London seasons in a slow recovery from a harrowing ordeal.

Shocking rumors, three proposed duels, an elopement en masse—could one butler stand up to all of it? If that butler be in service to the Benningtons, there seemed to be little choice.

It had been usual that the quiet of the countryside would restore his shattered nerves following one of the Bennington ladies having gone through her season and then somehow got married by the end of it.

Unfortunately, the countryside was no longer very quiet, what with four cats, two dogs, and a parrot milling about the place.

Really, though, it was the parrot. He would never get used to that creature. He would never be comfortable entering the drawing room and having "murder" shouted at him.

He had been grateful to hear that they were to leave that bird to the care of a housemaid. At least he would not be shrieked at while he was in Town.

Just now, Tattleton scolded himself for his foolhardiness in thinking he was fortunate to get away from the parrot. Of course they could not possibly arrive to Portland Place without some pathetic creature in tow. It had only been his mistake to never have imagined it would be a goat!

How? How had they possibly found a goat that needed taking in?

His name was, supposedly, Lord Darling. He was, supposedly, to live in the back garden and be no trouble to anybody.

But then had come the details accompanying the "no trouble to anybody" claim. According to Lady Cordelia, the kid was too young to stay alone in the back garden just yet, would require a proper bed in the servants' hall, must be kept cozy, and would need feedings every few hours of a warmed and special mixture of milks and sugar.

Oh, no trouble at all!

He stared down at the little creature, who was just now doing something odd. It would attempt a hop and then stumble and try again. Where did it think it was going? The ceiling?

"There we are, Mr. Tattleton," Mrs. Huffson said, coming in, "everybody is settled above stairs and the maids and footmen had gone to their beds."

He nodded and poured them both a brandy.

"I suppose we must be cheerful over not having had to prepare a full-on dinner on the night of our arrival. Lord Darden is not expected back to Town until the morrow and so we have had a quiet and easy night of it. Tomorrow will be time for bustle."

"Easy, you say?" He pointed at the goat, who was just now chewing on the corner of the tablecloth. "Where do you think this is going, Mrs. Huffson? Do you believe this creature will ever really move to the back garden?"

Mrs. Huffson's brow wrinkled and Tattleton well knew what troubled her. The lady did not like to predict disaster, but she could not help facing the facts! They had a goat in the servants' hall and it was not likely to go anywhere. What it would do, as he knew from past experience with other creatures, was grow, get into things, and cause no end of trouble.

"Perhaps to cheer yourself, Mr. Tattleton," Mrs. Huffson said, "you might recall that Lady Cordelia is far less likely to get herself into scrapes than the others were. She claims that all she looks for is an athletic sort of fellow. Seems straightforward enough."

Straightforward. Mrs. Huffson was an eternal optimist. The Benningtons had never done a straightforward thing in their lives. Straightforward people did not set off for Town and then pick up a goat along the way!

"I reckon there will be no end of fellows fitting the description," Mrs. Huffson said. "All she need do is pick out the one she prefers, easy as you like."

Tattleton shook his head. "I am very sorry to say it, Mrs. Huffson, but I am beginning to think you are a touch naïve."

CORDELIA HAD LEAPT out of bed early that morning. It was her first proper day in Town as a lady who was out in society and it felt marvelous.

She'd run down to the kitchens to see how Lord Darling was getting on. Charlie, Cook's righthand in the kitchens, had taken a shine to the little lord. Of course, he would. It had been Charlie that had brought them their four kittens who had since grown into marvelous specimens. It had been Charlie that had helped Bess birth her pups when it was very suddenly realized that she was pregnant.

After seeing Lord Darling had been given his breakfast and was making determined little hops round the servants' hall, she gave him all the pets he seemed to require and went above stairs to the breakfast room.

Miss Mayton had come down early too, quickly followed by Juliet. They spent a marvelous quarter hour going through the invitations that had already arrived.

Miss Mayton suddenly exclaimed. "Oh, I knew it should be so! I just knew it."

"What is it, Aunt?" Cordelia said, leaning forward.

"Lady Rawley. You will remember that I have stepped into the breach at her theatrical evenings several times."

"You think of your triumph last season as Benedick in *Much Ado about Nothing*," Juliet said, buttering a piece of toast.

"Just so," Miss Mayton said. "Well, listen to what she writes me now."

My dear Miss Mayton—

Words cannot express the thanks I owe you for your past assistance at my little theatricals. I feel as if we are one thespian speaking to another. Who could forget your inspired turn as Benedick? Who does not still dream of your dazzling portrayal of Cymbeline—the expressions of surprise so elegantly increasing to shock and then a dramatic fall to the ground!

I pray you feel the honor of what I am now to convey to you. I would be delighted if you would consent to join my troupe of actors as a permanent member. You would attend all our rehearsals, play a part on the night, and come with us to Lord Harveston's literary salons.

We have recently joined the Society for Serious Literary Examination and we look forward to gathering opinions from those learned people. (Just a note on that, though—I have assured Lord Harveston that we will work to keep our superior creativity and imagination under wraps so that we do not intimidate any of his members with it.)

Now, I do realize you have your own duties to attend to, being chaperone to the Bennington girls. I have been told this season is to be Lady Cordelia's. Do you suppose she would not mind accompanying you to our little activities?

If you are amenable to this invitation, please do write back in all haste. The literary salon is on Tuesday and I could convey you there in my carriage.

Margaret Rawley.

"That is marvelous!" Cordelia cried.

"Just wait until she finds out you are an actress too, Cordy," Juliet said.

"Yes, indeed," Miss Mayton said. "I will write her back and make that clear. Goodness, we are to join an acting troupe."

"And my glorious Corinthian gentleman will likely come to Lady Rawley's theatrical to see me," Cordelia said. "Then, he will know what to expect when we are at home and he requires entertainments after an arduous day of sporting."

"What do you suppose you will do at a literary salon?" Juliet asked.

"Perhaps our aunt could read from *The Dreadful Doings of Dembric Dale?*" Cordelia asked. "They're probably always looking for superior literature and nobody knows how to find them as well as you do, Aunt."

"That is always a possibility," Miss Mayton said nodding. "Then of course, the members may well wish to see your Desdemona if they are in the mood for something particularly poignant."

In the distance, they could hear the front doors crash open. Juliet leapt from her seat. "Can that be Darden already? So early in the day?"

"Goodness, we did not expect him until dinner," Miss Mayton said.

Lord Darden himself came into the breakfast room and braced himself for the onslaught of sisters. It was a deal more manageable than it had been in the past, as only Cordelia and Juliet remained in the house.

Cordelia had leapt up and threw her arms around her brother, as Juliet did from the other side.

"Our dear brother."

"Dear Darden."

"My sisters, Miss Mayton, I am so pleased to see you," Darden said from somewhere behind someone's India shawl.

"How is it you are here so early?" Cordelia asked.

"I was only in Kent, and I set off before sunrise," Darden said. "I told Cahill and Dunston, we were staying at Dunston's house you understand, that my sisters were arriving and I must not tarry."

"You are a very good sort of brother, Darden," Cordelia said.

Darden laughed and said, "Now unhand me so I can be a still *breathing* sort of brother."

They did unhand him and took back their places at the table, while Darden filled a plate from the sideboard.

"Father is not yet down?" he asked.

"Not yet," Miss Mayton said. "I believe the journey tires him, though he is too good to say so."

Darden returned with his plate and sat down. "How long did it take you this time?" he asked.

"Thirteen days," Juliet said.

"Thirteen?" Darden said laughing. "From Taunton? I suppose you managed to entertain no end of people."

At that, the uncomfortable memory of Mrs. Dorothy Jordan came to everyone's mind.

"We only dined with an actress," Juliet said. "I do not know if you know this, Darden, but they can be rather stupid."

"Nothing between the ears at all," Miss Mayton confirmed.

"I suppose that's why they have such a terrible reputation," Juliet said.

Darden snorted. "Yes, that must be why."

"I wrote an ode about it," Juliet said. *"Ode to Incomprehension."*

"I see," Darden said. "Well I am surprised Cordelia did not fancy knowing a famous actress."

Cordelia took on a stoic look and said, "I am afraid Mrs. Jordan and I live in different spheres, with different understandings."

"Yes, I suppose you would," Darden said. "Any other adventures of note? I do not see any wildlife roaming about so that seems a good sign."

Tattleton cleared his throat from the sideboard. "We have acquired a goat, my lord."

"Surely not, Tattleton," Darden said.

The butler let out a long and protracted sigh to indicate his seriousness.

"His name is Lord Darling, Marquess of Basingstoke," Cordelia said, glad to be off the subject of Mrs. Jordan.

"He is not even a week old and the most charming little thing you've ever seen," Juliet said.

"I suppose he's roaming round the garden," Darden said.

"Hah!" Tattleton said, then turned on his heel and stalked out.

After the butler had closed the door rather loudly, Cordelia said, "Lord Darling *will* be in the garden when he's grown a bit and is strong enough. For now, he's in the servants' hall."

Darden nodded. "That explains Tattleton, then."

"Guess what else, Darden," Juliet said, "Cordelia and our aunt are to join an acting troupe."

"Acting? As in acting on the stage?" Darden said, his concern written all over his features. "You did not get that idea from Mrs. Jordan?"

"Do not worry, Lord Darden, it is all very respectable," Miss Mayton said. "We are joining Lady Rawley's acting troupe, for her famed theatrical evening."

"Ah, the theatrical evening…" Darden said, "I did not realize it was famed."

"And guess what else?" Juliet said. "The acting troupe is to attend Lord Harveston's salon on literature."

"The SSLE?" Darden said, seeming a bit incredulous.

"The very one," Miss Mayton said.

"We wonder if Miss Mayton will be asked to read from *The Dreadful Doings of Dembric Dale*," Cordelia said.

"No," Darden said, "definitely not. Not one of our aunt's books. Those books would not be suitable for such a salon. Really, I am not certain you should go at all. It will not be the right…environment…to showcase…oh, I don't know what I'm saying."

"The salon is on Tuesday," Miss Mayton said, "Lady Rawley has kindly offered to take us in her own carriage."

Seeing as how his reservations were entirely ignored as if they'd not been spoken, Lord Darden smiled weakly.

"I suppose you've sorted out Cordy's voucher for Wednesday, Darden?" Juliet asked.

The lord nodded. "Almack's is well in hand—vouchers secured and tickets purchased."

"Excellent," Miss Mayton said. "We feel very sure that Cordelia's Corinthian will be in attendance."

"You're still stuck on a Corinthian," Darden said.

Cordelia nodded. "Of course I must be, Darden. A gentleman such as that is, well, he is everything!"

"Perhaps," Darden said, "but there are not that many of them. Not real ones, anyway."

"Cordy only requires one of them, Darden," Juliet said, as if her brother had somehow thought she required more than one.

Tattleton opened the door and led the earl to his place at the head of the table. "What ho!" the earl said, upon seeing Lord Darden. "The errant son arrives without having to be summoned out of his club!"

"It is very good to see you, Father," Darden said. "I was in

Kent. Naturally, I set off early to be with you all."

They went on to have a very merry breakfast, with Lord Darden outlining all the activities his club had been up to. The Young Bucks Club had been founded by Darden himself, and they were now up to thirty members. They still had not figured out how to approach Conbatten about joining, but they *had* formed a committee with the patronesses of Almack's to do good works.

If Lord Darden was left to wonder why his father seemed not at all vexed over having a goat in the house or a daughter who was determined to act in a theatrical, he did not say anything of it.

CHAPTER FOUR

ERCIVAL SURVEYED THE drawing room. It was set up as it always was for an SSLE salon.

The far end wall was lined with sideboards of meats, cheeses, rolls, biscuits, cakes, nuts, and both fresh and dried fruits, alongside wine, punch, lemonade, coffee, and tea. He left the selections up to Makepeace and his butler knew what he was about.

The evening might be cerebral, but Percival had learned long ago that even a learned man preferred to be watered and fed. Wine, in particular, seemed to grease the wheels of intellectual debate.

Tables and chairs were set up in groupings of four and six, where people might settle to thoroughly discuss a point and posit their own theories and opinions.

The night would begin with a review by Makepeace of Theobald's claim, made in 1727, of having in his possession the lost Shakespeare manuscript *Cardenio*.

Did Theobald in fact base his play *Double Falsehood* on the original *Cardenio*, which was itself based on an adventure in *Don Quixote*? Then, Percival would posit his own opinion. That should spark various discussions on the matter.

He looked forward to anything new he would hear. A list of topics for the season's salons were always sent out over the summer so that there would be ample time to prepare.

If he understood his members sufficiently, research had been conducted, trips to various sites made, more than one study of linguistics concluded, and perhaps letters of inquiry sent to descendants of Theobald.

In the distance, he heard the door knocker. Who on earth could be knocking? His members were not due for another hour and they all made an effort to be precisely on time. This was not the sort of evening where one might stroll in late. And *no* evening was the sort of evening where one could stroll in early.

Well, Makepeace would handle it, whatever it was. Probably a tradesman who could not locate the servants' entrance.

Makepeace himself hurried in, practically at a run. "I have delayed them with the footmen, who are taking their coats."

"Who?" Percival asked.

His butler looked very pale to be asked. "Lady Rawley's friends," he whispered, "Mrs. Robinson and Lady Agatha."

What? Why?

Percival thought these things, but he did not say them aloud, as he well knew Makepeace would have as little idea as he did himself.

A footman led the two ladies into the drawing room.

"Lord Harveston," Lady Agatha said, coming forward. "How charmed we are to join your little society."

"So charmed," Mrs. Robinson said, hurrying to catch up to her friend.

Percival bowed. "Ladies," he said, declining to comment on yet more people referring to his society as "little."

He cleared his throat and said, "I am afraid you have been misinformed regarding the time. The salon is scheduled for eight and…it is seven."

"Oh yes, we know all about it," Lady Agatha said. "Our dear Lady Rawley commissioned us to turn up early to help you."

"Help me?"

"One understands how a bachelor host does require assistance," Mrs. Robinson said. "There is no shame in it, Lord

Harveston! You will find your bride soon enough and she will take over these duties and elevate them sufficiently. For now, you may rely on *us*."

"Goodness, where are the flowers?" Lady Agatha said. "There is not a vase in sight."

"Precisely the sort of thing we feared," Mrs. Robinson said, shaking her head sadly.

"The room is rather austere," Lady Agatha said.

"It needs a woman's touch," Mrs. Robinson said, examining papers from the Royal Society stacked on a side table.

Lady Agatha turned to Makepeace and said, "Well, let us at least have a look at the sideboard and see how far you've got on your own. We'll prop it up somehow."

Makepeace looked positively affronted. "How *far*? Prop it up?" he asked incredulously.

"Put the cook on notice," Lady Agatha said, "instructions will be incoming shortly!"

Mrs. Robinson looked round the room. "Is this really the most comfortable arrangement, I wonder?"

"Ladies!" Percival said, though it might have been closer to a shout than a said. "We really are quite fine as you find us."

"Fine, Lord Harveston?" Lady Agatha asked. "Is *fine* really what you were going for?"

"Precisely what I was going for," Percival said. "The salon members are very used to this set-up, and they should not like to experience any changes in it."

Lady Agatha and Mrs. Robinson looked at each other. It seemed as if the same idea was occurring to them both. They nodded knowingly.

"Say no more, Lord Harveston," Lady Agatha said.

"Our dear Lady Rawley did not take into consideration the state of your membership and we failed to remind her of it. That must be laid at our door, I'm afraid."

"How did we not think of it?" Lady Agatha wondered.

"Think of what?" Percival asked, though he was rather afraid to hear any more of these two ladies' thoughts.

"Our dear Lady Rawley has mentioned that creativity and imagination will not be your people's bailiwick, as it were," Lady Agatha said.

"Of course we shouldn't wonder if these people would be thrown off by any sort of change," Mrs. Robinson said. "Our dear Lady Rawley did mention that scholars have an unfortunate habit of becoming very rigid. I daresay she is right."

Percival pressed his lips together. Their dear Lady Rawley had begun as a thorn in his side, but she was speedily becoming a battalion's worth of swords in his side.

"Well!" Mrs. Robinson said to Lady Agatha. "We are here now and it would seem entirely silly to leave and come back again. I suppose we ought to have some wine and ponder literary questions?"

"Let's do," Lady Agatha said approvingly. "I've finally got my hands on a copy of *The Dreadful Doings of Dembric Dale* and I can tell you it is masterful."

The ladies set off for the sideboard. Makepeace stared at their backs and it was probably fortunate that he could not shoot arrows out of his eyes, else they'd both be dead on the carpet.

Quietly, Percival said, "I am going above stairs to change clothes. Have a footman run up a brandy. A large one."

CORDELIA HAD NOT been certain what one ought to wear to a salon and Miss Mayton had not had any ideas on the subject either, but for the notion that widow's weeds were very convenient as one did not have to decide.

On the one hand, Darden had explained to her that the evening was likely to be peopled by dry and dusty types who spent their lives with their heads in books. He did make an exception for Lord Harveston, the host of the salon, as he said that gentleman was exceedingly learned but was not always throwing it in people's faces. He was a member of the YBC and forever helpful with thorny problems around the budget.

On the other hand, this would be Cordelia's first encounter with Lady Rawley and her troupe of actors. She wished to make the best impression possible. Her aunt had written the lady that Cordelia was in fact a skilled actress and now she would discover what Lady Rawley thought about it.

In the end, it had been Juliet who had swayed her selection of a dress. Her sister had rightly pointed out that while she would meet nobody interesting at the salon, anything could happen on the way there. Perhaps she would be descending from her carriage and her Corinthian would trot by—instantly taken by the sight of her and demanding of onlookers to know the name of the lady. Perhaps they would throw a shoe and he would gallantly come to the rescue. The fates were at their work and absolutely anything might happen.

She had chosen a deep blue silk, very plain in its decoration but fitted to perfection. Cordelia felt the color did something for her hair, as did the family's modiste. Mrs. Randower said her hair was a very forward sort of color and must be managed carefully lest it present itself too loudly.

The shade was a deep and vibrant auburn and one did not pair that color with a pastel. White was fine for a day dress, but they would not venture into anything approaching a pastel yellow or pale blue for gowns. It would look clownish and Mrs. Randower could not entertain the idea of any of her dresses appearing so.

Lady Rawley's carriage had arrived after a quarter hour of Cordelia's pacing in the great hall and a quarter hour of Juliet and her aunt telling her that her nerves were for nothing. She was a lovely and talented actress and anybody must be pleased to make her acquaintance.

She'd taken a deep breath and followed Miss Mayton to the carriage.

Settling themselves in, Lady Rawley said, "How pleased I am, Miss Mayton, that you have agreed to join us. And of course, Lady Cordelia, it was an added delight to understand that you were not without your own interest in treading the hallowed boards."

"Indeed, my lady, I am most interested," Cordelia said. "My sisters and Miss Mayton have praised your theatricals to the skies."

"We are simply delighted to receive you," Lady Rawley said. "We have never had a young person playing in the troupe and I have a notion that it must add a certain charm."

There. She'd said it. Cordelia Bennington was officially a member of the troupe.

She was a professional actress. Or, if not professional, then something very close to it.

The rest of the carriage ride was not overlong, as Lord Harveston lived on Bedford Square. Cordelia was quiet for most of it, as she was delighted to listen to Lady Rawley and Miss Mayton rehash the events of last year's theatrical.

When they arrived, they found a line of carriages and Lady Rawley posited that intellectual types were likely tied to their clocks. If Lord Harveston said eight o'clock, then they would turn up at the precise time.

Fortunately, Lady Rawley had sent Lady Agatha and Mrs. Robinson ahead to arrive at seven and assist Lord Harveston's arrangements. Lady Rawley was determined to provide the lord with any little service he might find useful.

They were helped down from the carriage and Cordelia thought it was a very fine house Lord Harveston lived in—quite bigger than she would have imagined for a bachelor. She supposed it must be part of the family's estate, rather than a house rented for the season.

A rather serious-looking butler escorted them to the drawing room. "Lady Rawley, Miss Mayton, and Lady Cordelia Bennington," he intoned as they went in.

The crowd of people in the room turned like a school of fish and appeared very surprised to see them.

"Ah," Lady Rawley said very quietly, "they see they have new members and feel the compliment of it."

Cordelia was not certain what they felt about it. She was dubious over the idea that they appeared complimented. Some of them looked confused, some of them rather dismissive. Then there was the stern-looking mien of a very tall man. A very handsome tall man, were he not quite so serious.

If there were any faces that appeared unreservedly enthusiastic over their arrival, it was Lady Agatha and Mrs. Robinson. They hurried over.

"Miss Mayton," Lady Agatha said, "we are so pleased you will join our little troupe."

"And we understand Lady Cordelia will too?" Mrs. Robinson said.

Cordelia nodded. "Lady Rawley has been very gracious."

Lady Agatha leaned in close and said quietly, "Now, my dear Lady Rawley, you will know that we did as you asked and came at seven. Unfortunately, poor Lord Harveston refuses to admit that he requires help."

"He is quite stoic about it," Mrs. Robinson said, "and I think that butler of his supports his wrongheaded ideas. We did point out the lack of vases of flowers and they both looked at us as if we'd just arrived from the moon."

Cordelia glanced at the sideboard, which looked very well put together, and the general air of the room, which was perhaps more masculine than she would like but well done all the same. She could not think what the ladies would have modified beyond their idea of flowers.

"The point is, you tried," Lady Rawley said graciously. "Now, here he comes."

The "he" Lady Rawley had referred to was the tall and serious gentleman. The handsome gentleman.

Goodness, she would not have thought that was Lord Harveston. She imagined a person running a literary society and helping Darden with the club's books would be a short and bespectacled sort of person.

"Aunt, Miss Mayton," he said, delivering an elegant bow.

"Dear nephew," Lady Rawley said, "do be introduced to the latest member of our little acting troupe—Lady Cordelia Bennington. Lord Darden's sister, if you will recall."

Cordelia curtsied. She felt nervous. Why did she feel nervous?

"Lady Cordelia," he said, his voice oddly deep but with a silken tone to it. It practically sent a shiver over her.

"Lord Harveston," she said. "You are very gracious to allow us to attend your literary society."

The lord laughed just a little and said, "My aunt was so good as to simply inform me that she and her friends would be coming."

Cordelia willed herself not to redden over the realization that they had crashed their way in. From the comment, it did not appear that Lord Harveston rejoiced at their arrival.

"Pay no attention to my nephew, Lady Cordelia," Lady Rawley said. "He is a great one for jokes."

Cordelia glanced at the lord and could not at all see that he was joking.

"Perhaps you will avail yourselves of the sideboard," Lord Harveston said. "We will be set to begin in a few minutes."

Another party had come in after them, two very old and scholarly-looking gentlemen. Lord Harveston bowed and moved off to greet them.

Lady Rawley led the way to the sideboard. While Cordelia had not any intention of drinking wine this night, she changed her mind. It would be well to have something to settle her.

She felt exceedingly unsettled.

It had seemed as nothing to come to a literary society. All her nerves had been firmly aimed at impressing Lady Rawley and her troupe of actors.

The literary society was only where it would be done. She

had not given it any thought at all.

"Aunt," Cordelia said in a whisper as they moved away from the board, "look at that."

She directed her aunt's gaze to a placard set up on an easel. It read:

Tonight's debate—

Did Theobald base his play Double Falsehood *on Shake-speare's lost work* Cardenio?

"Who is Theobald? What is *Double Falsehood?* What is *Cardenio?*" Cordelia said. "The only word I recognize is Shake-speare."

"Gracious," Lady Rawley said next to them, "he told me that was the subject of debate, but I thought he was joking."

Miss Mayton squinted at the placard and shrugged. "Perhaps Mr. Theobald is here and can shed some light on the subject."

Cordelia did not answer, but she did not think that likely. There would not be much of a debate if Mr. Theobald could simply answer the question.

Though she knew of Shakespeare, as of course everybody did, and though she had perfected Desdemona's dying scene, she had not come across a play called *Cardenio.*

In truth, while she had vowed she would study all of Shake-speare's works from the moment she had become aware of Lady Rawley's theatrical evenings, she had not got as far with it as she would have liked.

Lady Rawley was in the habit of reimagining the ending of a Shakespeare play, and so Cordelia had been most diligent about studying those endings. It was just the beginnings and middles she had not got to.

She supposed it did not signify, since the debate was to be round *Cardenio* and she did not even know the ending of that one.

Lady Rawley had led them to one of the groupings of tables and chairs. Cordelia gratefully sat between her aunt and Lady

Agatha. She wished to blend in and disappear and felt more safe between the two ladies.

The truth was, she felt entirely out of her depth. All round her, she could hear snippets of conversation. Learned conversation she understood little of.

Who was Fletcher? Why had one gentleman just said, "How do you account for the lack of subplot?" Why had another said, "It's all in the linguistics!" Or another said, "Come now, the theory regarding Tonson has been thoroughly debunked."

What were all these people talking about?

Her own education, while being very jolly, had not been particularly rigorous. Her aunt had overseen various tutors, but only kept on the ones she found genial. She had also allowed all the sisters to pursue their own interests. It had resulted in a great deal of time studying the end of Othello, and the poignant death of Desdemona, but perhaps not as much time on other worthy things.

Cordelia felt she was on a slowly sinking ship. In fact, she rather wished the chair she sat on this moment *would* sink through the floor. What was she to do if someone asked for her opinion?

PERCIVAL GLANCED ROUND the room and noted that his aunt and her "troupe" had all placed themselves together.

That would be for the best. He had no idea what they would debate among themselves, if anything, but he doubted it would be of a sort that the other members would find edifying.

Lady Cordelia, though. How had that lovely lady become embroiled in Lady Rawley's theatricals?

Of course he knew how—her aunt, Miss Mayton. Everybody knew that lady had enthusiastically stepped into the breach at a few of the theatricals. Now it seemed she'd become a regular part of it and dragged her niece in with her.

Darden really had such a run of remarkably pretty sisters. One was more attractive than the last. This one had the most enchanting hair, and pretty eyes…well, he ought to stop thinking about that. He had a society meeting to run.

Percival dinged his glass. "Gentlemen…and ladies, we will commence the first society meeting of the season. I welcome you all and look forward to hearing your learned and considered views this night. As always, Makepeace will lead us through the question, and then we will debate the various answers."

Makepeace stepped forward. "In 1727, Mr. Lewis Theobald claimed to be in possession of a lost play by Shakespeare named *Cardenio*. We know that a play of that name was in fact performed in Shakespeare's time, by his own company. We also know that the play was itself based on an episode from *Don Quixote*. Mr. Theobald wrote a play named *Double Falsehood*, which he claimed was *Cardenio* edited and made better. However, though he claimed to have original manuscripts of *Cardenio*, and he claimed he would show them as proof, he never did show them as proof. Lord Harveston?"

"Thank you, Makepeace," Percival said. "I look forward to hearing facts I had not considered and am open to changing my opinion. For now, my opinion is this—Theobald did have a manuscript named *Cardenio*, I believe it was co-written by Shakespeare and Fletcher based on the similarities of writing found in another of their collaborations, *The Noble Kinsman*. I also believe Theobald thought he was improving on Shakespeare and Fletcher's work by doing away with the subplot and the usual complications associated with Shakespeare. Though, I think we can all agree that *Double Falsehood* does not accomplish the aim of improving on Shakespeare. I speculate that Theobald refused to show the original manuscripts because he was either not as confident of his work as he claimed, or that he had obtained the manuscripts in some manner less than usual. Perhaps there was even written a clue on them as to where they had come from."

Percival paused and looked round the room. It seemed everyone had settled themselves where they wished to be. The gentlemen who would have studied the linguistics were already together, those that would have raked through records and gathered correspondence had already various papers laid out, a certain group who were all friends had taken up a corner, and then there were his newest members—his aunt and her "troupe."

"Discuss and debate," Percival said, "while I circulate the room."

An immediate chatter rose up. Makepeace made his way to the grouping who had laid out their records. Percival went to the board for a glass of wine and surveyed the scene.

It was very gratifying to see so many brought together with the same thirst for knowing. It had always been so with himself. His father used to complain that most young men had to be chased into a schoolroom, while he had to be chased out of it.

There was so much to know, and one life would never be enough time to know all of it.

He smiled to himself when he thought back to how hard he'd worked to master those things the *ton* valued. He'd learned to ride creditably, and he really did enjoy it, but he'd come at it with full concentration and effort so it might be mastered in as little time possible.

Taking up a sword had been a straightforward effort, as he'd found it easy to pick up. The same with shooting bird.

He was a good shot, at least he used to be—he could not remember when last he'd bothered with it. As for hunting fox, that was where he'd put his foot down. People could be hired to do it and he thought it the stupidest waste of time in the world to go riding all over creation for a full day and usually return with nothing to show for it.

All his childhood, aside from some of his tutors, he'd been surrounded by people who did not spend much time in a library. For him, the library had been a sanctuary away from the doings of the household. It had been one of the great joys of reaching his majority to surround himself with like-minded people.

These days, he did not always closet himself away with a book. He'd learned that was not a very good way to go on. He enjoyed balls and parties as much as the next man, and he valued the friendships he'd made through Darden and the YBC, but he must have his intellectual pursuits too or life would feel very empty.

As he thought which group he might eavesdrop on first, as that was always what he did on such a night—act the magpie collecting bits and bobs of ideas—his aunt's grouping kept pulling at his attention.

He'd thought they'd all be looking around and rather lost, but they were heads together and talking.

Perhaps he had been wrong about the ladies. Perhaps he ought to be ashamed of his assumptions. He did not like to misjudge people.

He walked over. "Ladies, might I listen in on your debate?"

All of them looked up, very startled to see him. Lady Cordelia looked almost frightened to see him.

Lady Rawley was the first to speak. "Nephew, we do not have the first idea of anything Makepeace said just now."

Percival nodded, and he had to admit to himself that he'd been unfair. All the other members had months of time to look into the question. The ladies could hardly be expected to know much about it.

"This is understandable," he said. "I send out a list of literary debates over the summer and so everybody else has had ages to prepare."

He signaled to a footman, who hurried over. "James, please retrieve five copies of our schedule for the ladies."

"That is most kind, Lord Harveston," Lady Cordelia said.

He nodded, feeling somehow proud of himself, though he could not say why. "Perhaps, for this evening, you might all simply enjoy the offerings on the sideboard?"

"Oh, you are not to think we do not have our own subject to

debate," Lady Rawley said. "In fact, I'll have a look at your little list of proposed topics and see if we might fit in some of our own suggestions."

"Suggestions?" Percival asked warily.

"Indeed," his aunt said. "My dear, you must admit that this night's subject is rather…dry."

"Dry?"

"Yes, Lord Harveston," Lady Agatha said, "rather dry. Now, you are not to feel downhearted about it. A bachelor cannot manage everything on his own."

"I see," Percival said, feeling less sympathetic to the group by the minute. "And your suggestions would run along the lines of?"

"Well, take us talking just now, Lord Harveston," Mrs. Robinson said. "We are having a lively discussion over *The Dreadful Doings of Dembric Dale*."

"Is someone going to kill the duchess' father?" Miss Mayton said. "Will it be the duke?"

"It is a rather gothic romance, quite titillating," Lady Rawley said.

"What would a gothic romance have to do with a society that examines respected literature?" Percival asked through gritted teeth.

If his aunt had any notion of interfering with his society, of inserting herself and her dreadful taste in books, well, he would quash that notion firmly.

"I've had a notion," Lady Rawley said, "what if we shake the dust off this little society of yours? What if, at the next meeting, we introduce this fascinating book?"

"Absolutely not," Percival said.

The footman came hurrying back with the sheets of paper outlining the topics for this season's meetings. He handed them round.

"Come now, nephew," Lady Rawley said. "Do not be such a stick. One must be continually open to new ideas. We ought to at least try it out."

"As I said, absolutely not. Aunt, ladies, if you wish to discuss any dreadful doings in a dale, you are encouraged to start your own society. Such drivel will never darken my doors."

He turned on his heel. Before he could get too far, he heard Lady Rawley assure her friends that he was "likely to come round."

He would not come round. His mother could not write enough letters on the importance of family for him to come round. Somehow, he must get his aunt and her friends out of his society.

CHAPTER FIVE

CORDELIA FELT HUMILIATED. They had all, quite naturally, been entirely lost on the subject of *Cardenio*. They had briefly ventured a discussion on *Don Quixote*, as certainly they had all read it. But, it seemed nobody had *actually* read it, though they all owned to starting it at some point.

That result had, also very naturally, led to a discussion on what they *were* all reading at the moment, since of course it was not *Cardenio* or *Don Quixote*.

Her aunt had mentioned *The Dreadful Doings of Dembric Dale* and then to everybody's delight, it was discovered that Lady Rawley, Lady Agatha, and Mrs. Robinson were reading it too.

That had all been very wonderful. Then, Lord Harveston had joined them and was most sympathetic to their unfamiliarity with *Cardenio*. And did not inquire into their unfamiliarity with *Don Quixote*.

It had been very charming of him actually. Very kind, she thought.

If only the conversation had ended there!

It had not ended there, though. Lady Rawley had insisted that they introduce *The Dreadful Doings of Dembric Dale* to the society.

It had, at first, seemed a worthy idea. She would like very much to discuss and debate the twisting plot and the way the author made one guess at what would happen next.

That was, it had seemed a worthy idea until she saw Lord

Harveston's expression upon hearing it. He'd been outraged. He looked down upon the book, though he had clearly never read it.

It was the type of book he looked down upon.

This somehow felt a reflection on herself, and on her tastes. As if she were not sophisticated enough or learned enough. As if she were silly to countenance such a book.

She supposed a gentleman like Lord Harveston would never read such a book.

"Do not fret over it," Lady Rawley said. "Young gentlemen propose themselves to be invincible, but the truth is they have very fragile feelings. His selection has been pronounced dry and he feels the sting. Harveston will take the time to reflect on my suggestion and then he will see the sense in it."

"But Lady Rawley," Cordelia said, "he did seem so…so firm in his opinion. Perhaps the gentlemen here would not like to hear of our dreadful doings in the dale? Perhaps they are satisfied with the topics that Lord Harveston has composed for them?"

With that idea, they all looked down upon their papers.

If there were any of the ladies who understood any of the topics proposed, they did not say so. Cordelia, herself, was entirely lost.

"This might as well be written in Greek," Mrs. Robinson muttered.

"Greek would be a deal more understandable than this!" Lady Agatha said.

"It is the precise evidence proving that my nephew has gone astray," Lady Rawley said. "Certainly, nobody would wish to discuss St. Thomas Aquinas' idea that no man can be a judge of himself and how it relates to Aristotle's opinion that most people are bad judges of their own case?"

"Oh dear," Mrs. Robinson said, "I am very afraid that the people here tonight come out of loyalty to Lord Harveston, but are fast becoming bored. It is almost inevitable that they will begin dropping out, one by one—making excuses as to why they cannot attend."

Lady Agatha nodded. "One suspects poor Lord Harveston is poised to begin hearing of sick relatives and unforeseen circumstances."

"They'll wish to let him down gently," Miss Mayton said.

Cordelia glanced round the room. She felt as if she were not viewing what the rest of the ladies were viewing. As far as she could see, Lord Harveston's guests were entirely engaged.

"Perhaps, though," Cordelia said, "their tastes are just very different from our own?"

Lady Rawley held up the paper containing the topics to be discussed at future meetings. "Goodness, nobody's tastes could be *this* different!"

⇶⇷

TATTLETON NOTICED THAT it was becoming more regular these days to discover himself in unforeseen circumstances.

This evening only highlighted that idea, as when he began his career as a butler, he could not have envisioned finding himself in a drawing room with the youngest lady of the house and her newly-acquired goat.

"Now, Tattleton, I can see you are against it," Lady Juliet said. "It is written all over your face."

"I only say, my lady, that the drawing room may not be the proper place for what is, in the end, a farm animal."

"A farm animal!" Lady Juliet cried, as if he'd just pronounced the goat a criminal. "Lord Darling," she said, cupping his face in her hands, "I want you to forget you ever heard such a thing. You are the Marquess of Basingstoke and, as such, have every right to be in the drawing room."

Tattleton sighed. Lord Darling might be a new-minted marquess, but he did not seem to know anything about the use of a water closet. The room reeked of his intemperance already and that carpet would be stained forever.

"Tattleton," Lady Juliet said in a rather plaintive tone, "you do see my circumstances these days? I have always been surrounded by my sisters. Beatrice, Rosalind, and Viola have all married and left the house. Cordy is still here, but she will be out most nights and then she will find her Corinthian and marry too. I am quite alone these days."

If there could have been anything Lady Juliet might say to pull at his heartstrings, she had found it and said it.

She was alone and he felt very sorry over it. He might have lamented over her dreadful ode-writing on more than one occasion, but he always did have a soft spot for the youngest.

"You will always have Miss Mayton by your side, my lady, until you also marry and depart the house."

Lady Juliet sighed. "Oh yes, I shall find my poet. Then, when that happens, you shall only have Miss Mayton and Papa to look after."

That idea did more than pull at his heartstrings. It fairly brought tears to his eyes. What a future! Just the earl and his nutty cousin.

How had he not thought about that before?

"Let us only think happy thoughts for now, though," Lady Juliet said in an encouraging tone. "While Cordy and my aunt and Papa are out and about in the town, we shall make merry in the drawing room. We could call the footmen in and play cards!"

"The footmen? I do not know if that would be—"

"Oh, do say you will, Tattleton. I really do not like being lonely. Lord Darling does his best and he is everything charming, but I would feel ever so much better if I had company that could talk."

Tattleton was certain he ought not be playing cards with the footmen in the drawing room. But what could he do? There was already a goat in that room—were footmen so much worse?

In any case, he supposed he could not allow Lady Juliet to suffer.

"WILL YOU ATTEND Almack's this evening, my lord?" Makepeace asked as Percival thumbed through papers on his desk.

"Yes," he said absentmindedly. "It is not worth the trouble to cross the patronesses, and in any case, I do not mind it."

"Yes, yes," Makepeace said quietly, "always looking for *her*."

Makepeace of course referenced his so far unfruitful search for a lady he could call his wife. His butler knew what he looked for—his intellectual equal.

"If only Madame D'Arblay was very much younger," Makepeace said. "And unmarried. And not living in Paris."

This was Makepeace's usual comment, as if Madame D'Arblay, née Fanny Burney, was the only lady on the earth that had sufficient wit to grace his table. Makepeace regularly reread her novels and treasured the letters the lady sent to the society.

The Madame certainly did have wit about her, her letters were always delivered in some original fashion by an unusual person she'd conscripted to take on the task. As far as Percival could tell, the letters would pass through a number of hands on their way to someone heading to London.

"Shall you wish to ride to Almack's, or will you take the carriage?"

"I will ride, as I always do."

His butler had been asking him questions he already knew the answers to for above ten minutes. Now, the fellow stood ramrod straight, staring at the far wall.

"Out with it, Makepeace," he said. "What do you wish to say?"

The butler's shoulders slumped just the littlest bit. He said, "It was only that I wondered what your view might be regarding Lady Rawley and her party continuing to attend our literary society meetings."

"My view? My view is it is a dashed inconvenience, and I

would like to devise a polite way to get them out." He paused, then said, "Though I have not thought how to accomplish it yet."

Makepeace nodded gravely and Percival was certain his butler wished to acquaint him with some idea that he was not yet acquainted with.

"What?" he said.

The butler cleared his throat. "There was somewhat of an unfortunate circumstance last evening. Mr. Haventops was sadly situated close enough to Lady Rawley's grouping and was forced to overhear several things."

Silence hung in the room and Percival wondered if he would really be made to ask what the several things were.

"First," Makepeace finally went on, "there was some discussion about dreadful doings in a dale somewhere. Haventops almost believed that the ladies were discussing a fellow about to be murdered—he was most alarmed. Then he surmised it was a piece of dreadful storytelling, rather than any real dreadful doings."

"Yes, they mentioned the book," Percival said, preferring to leave out the news that they'd wanted to introduce his members to such a thing.

"Then," Makepeace said, "he overheard them discussing how they would shake up our society and make it more interesting and this was for your own good. There was also mention several times that there was a distinct lack of flowers in your drawing room."

Makepeace sighed, as if he had wrested a terrible confession out of himself and felt the lighter for it.

Those ladies were so meddling! At least, the older ones were. He could not fault Lady Cordelia too very much; she was just being swept along by Miss Mayton.

In any case, he did not suppose anybody could stay angry with *that* face for long. She really was very pretty. It was clear enough that she did not dabble in any particular intellectual pursuits, but she could not be blamed for it. She was, after all, only a product of her environment.

No, *she* was not the problem. It was the other four of them.

"As well…" Makepeace said.

"There is more?"

Makepeace shook his head sadly. "They reviewed the schedule of debates for the coming season and pronounced it Greek and unintelligible."

"I'll bet they did."

"Further, they were very afraid that all your members would quit out of boredom."

"If only *they* would quit out of boredom."

"Naturally, after Haventops relayed all of this in the hottest terms possible, I acquainted him with the idea that Lady Rawley is your aunt and had just barged in, dragging her troupe in with her and there was little to be done about it."

Haventops was a temperamental fellow, so Percival doubted he took that news with any sort of equanimity.

"Well? What did he say to it?"

Makepeace appeared grave indeed. "He said he would take steps."

"What steps?"

"He would not say. I'm not certain he knew, but I would gamble that he's spending every waking minute thinking about it."

Percival tented his fingers. "We have got to get my aunt and her friends out of the society."

CORDELIA HAD GONE straight to her bedchamber after coming home from the literary society meeting. She'd found Juliet curled up asleep there and she was certain her younger sister had made a valiant attempt to wait up, but with nobody to talk to it had been all for naught.

She and Lynette had been ever so quiet as she was undressed, so as not to wake her sleeping sister.

Cordelia would not have admitted it, but the reason she did not wish to wake Juliet was that she did not yet know how to even discuss the evening she'd just attended.

Lord Harveston had made his feelings about their troupe clearly known. They were not wanted there. Their attendance had been met with disapproval. Somehow, though, it felt as if she were the only one to have perceived it.

Lady Rawley viewed her nephew as misguided. She was determined to make his society more lively. She was convinced that Lord Harveston's subjects for debate were one long bore.

Cordelia was very afraid of where that idea would go.

Worse, she felt Lord Harveston viewed *them* as the bores.

It was very upsetting to feel as if one did not measure up. It felt as if there was a whole world she was not acquainted with, as if she were just stumbling around in the dark.

Cordelia had not ever considered the possibility that she might be looked down upon for what she did not know.

She had thought she would be judged by her looks, which Miss Mayton had told her were very good, and her clothes, and dancing, and ability to make charming conversations. Her acting out Desdemona's poignant adieu was meant to be the special surprise treat on top of it all.

Now, she was beginning to wonder about it. She was beginning to wonder what Lord Harveston would make of her Desdemona. She began to suspect that he would make nothing of it at all.

Of course, she should not mind that he thought so little of her accomplishments, such as they were. He was not her Corinthian after all. She was not at all interested in such a bookish fellow.

Though, somehow she did mind that his opinion was so dismissive.

How could she have possibly explained all that to Juliet?

She had lain awake for quite some time before finally falling asleep.

The morning dawned cloudy and gray, and she might have slept very late were it not for Rosalind slipping into the room and jumping into bed with them.

"Have you brought Conbatten with you and left him in the drawing room?" Cordelia said sleepily.

"I have not," Rosalind said. "I left him in his morning bath with Henri monitoring the temperature to keep it at ninety-eight degrees precisely."

Juliet yawned and said, "Too bad, I was wanting to ask him how much he was enjoying reading the ode I wrote for your wedding."

"He adores it, and it is hung up in our new family room. Is he not clever to think of designing a room that is for our special things? I cannot believe anybody else has such a room."

"Very clever," Juliet said, "though sometimes I wish everyone who came into the duke's house could read the ode."

"And view the wedding portrait that Viola painted," Cordelia said.

Rosalind nodded. "He insists that those private family things must stay private. In any case, it is just as well I did not bring him along this morning. There is a goat standing on a sofa in the drawing room—did you know it? It appeared to be sizing up how to climb the bookshelves. I asked Tattleton if he had not noticed this, but he only said he has given up trying to hold on to rationality."

"Ah, that is Lord Darling," Juliet said. "We found him in Basingstoke, he is a poor orphan."

"He does look darling, but how does Papa view him having run of the house?"

Neither Cordelia nor Juliet ventured an answer on that question.

"Ah, I see," Rosalind said, laughing. "Well, it is not a house-fire, so he'll not be too put out about it, I do not think."

"Lord Darling is supposed to be in the servants' quarters, as he really is too young for the garden yet," Juliet said, "but then I did find myself so lonely last evening and I brought him up. I suppose he developed a fondness for the drawing room."

Cordelia rolled over. "Poor Jules, it cannot be comfortable to be the youngest and have everybody leave you."

"Was it terribly dreary all by yourself last night?" Rosalind asked.

"I thought it would be, but then it was not. First, I retrieved Lord Darling, then I told Tattleton that he must fetch the footmen so we could play cards. Benny and Johnny were enthusiastic over the idea and we had a rousing game of lottery tickets."

"Then you shall do just the same tonight," Rosalind counseled. "Cordelia will be off to Almack's to find her Corinthian."

"Do you suppose he will be there?" Cordelia said.

"I cannot know if *your* particular Corinthian will attend, as we do not yet know in what direction your heart will go, but I know of at least one Corinthian who will be there—Lord Hamill. He is a friend of Conbatten's and my dear husband complains that the fellow never sits down. If they meet at the club for coffee at ten, Hamill has already been out riding *and* in a boxing match."

"He sounds perfection," Cordelia said, stretching out under the blankets.

"What will you wear?" Juliet asked. "I know you have gone back and forth on the subject."

"I have indeed," Cordelia said, "but it occurred to me that I ought to stop worrying over it and just take Mrs. Randower's advice on the subject. She said the green silk was the right one for Almack's."

Rosalind nodded. "I think you are right to follow her counsel, Cordy—our modiste is never wrong."

NOW, AS THE carriage trotted through the streets, Cordelia glanced down at the gown she had selected, relying on Mrs. Randower's advice. The shade was the deepest green, like moss in a shaded forest. Subtle embroidery of the same color created a vine and flowers motif on the edges of the sleeves. Other than that, the gown was unadorned, just as Mrs. Randower liked it.

Rosalind had increased Cordelia's already strong faith in Mrs. Randower by mentioning that Conbatten was very approving of the lady's designs. He was so particular with his own dress, and Rosalind claimed his valet Henri was a madman on the subject, that he must be considered an expert. Gentlemen across London, including her own brother, were always attempting to discover who his tailor was.

"I feel I have made this speech many times now," the earl said jovially, "but I will counsel you to throw off any nerves you might have coming upon you, Cordelia. They are unnecessary, as the three sisters before you have discovered."

"Just do not order someone to take you into supper like Rosalind did," Darden said.

"But she ordered Conbatten to do it," Cordelia said, "and that turned out rather well."

"It did, but could just as easily gone terribly," Darden said.

"I do not believe our Cordelia will have to direct anybody to do anything," Miss Mayton said. "Her Corinthian will see that she has arrived and that his life is to be changed forever, and he will proceed accordingly."

"Ah! You are firmly set on a sporting fellow, then?" the earl said.

"Not just any kind of sporting gentleman, Father," Darden said. "A Corinthian! I have already told her there are not that many of them banging around. It's very difficult to be good at absolutely everything."

"Rosalind says Lord Hamill is a Corinthian and that he will be there," Cordelia said. "Naturally, I cannot know if the signs of true love will strike me, but they might."

Miss Mayton had schooled them all very thoroughly on the signs of true love so that they might recognize it when they were felled by that emotion—one felt as if one's hair had been struck by lightning, and one was drowning but taking in more air, and one's heart sped up though one felt well. It was so specific that Cordelia had no fear of not recognizing the condition.

Of course, she would add one more symptom. It seemed to be a family trait that one felt ill.

"Hamill?" Darden asked. "I really do not think he is in the market for a wife. He always seems too busy and he's not said anything about it."

Miss Mayton laughed at the idea. "Goodness, Lord Darden, do you suppose poor Hans was looking for love when he threw himself off the side of a mountain? What about Gregorio or Phillipe or the Transylvanian duke? No, they were all just going about their lives before we encountered one another and then they were quite suddenly struck."

Cordelia nodded with enthusiasm. "Who knows, Darden—perhaps *you* will be struck by someone this evening."

As she knew it would, this set off a paragraph of mumbling having to do with Darden being busy with his club and of course he would get to it, but it was foolhardy to pin a date on it.

Cordelia was beginning to think her brother wouldn't pin a date on it until her father absolutely pressed the matter.

So far, the earl had been indulgent. But certainly that could not go on forever.

"Here we are!" Darden said, in a tone that was far more enthusiastic than one generally employs to announce an arrival.

CHAPTER SIX

PERCIVAL COULD NOT remember when he had ever encountered Lady Rawley at Almack's on a Wednesday. He could not remember, because it had never happened.

She was here now, though.

His aunt spotted him and was making fast headway in his direction.

Almost as if she'd been waiting for him.

He suppressed a sigh. He'd just handed off his coat and had not even got all the way into the ballroom yet.

"My dear nephew," she said.

"Aunt," he said, working to keep his tone pleasant, "I am surprised to see you here."

"You would be, I never do attend. But then, I had an excellent notion and got myself an invitation. Lady Rondeleigh secured me a stranger's ticket. What a palaver, you would think Lady Castlereagh was the queen of the world."

"You said you had a notion?" Percival asked warily, ignoring the rest of what she said.

Lady Rawley did not appear to be paying attention to him. Her eyes were on the doors behind him.

She very suddenly smiled and waved. "Ah, and here is the notion, just coming in."

Percival turned his head to see the Earl of Westmont, Darden, Miss Mayton, and Lady Cordelia approaching.

Lady Cordelia was looking rather smashing in a dark green dress. Most of the ladies in attendance were dressed in pastels and she was like a forest queen of the faeries come to have a look at her flowers.

Percival was very suddenly filled with dread, his mind catching up to his aunt's words.

She'd said she had a notion. Of course that had instantly caught his attention. Whenever she mentioned having had a notion, it was always less of a notion and more of a very bad idea.

Now he was to discover that Lady Rawley had clearly been waiting for Miss Mayton and Lady Cordelia to arrive. *They* were the notion.

Why? Did it have something to do with their acting troupe?

Would Lady Agatha and Mrs. Robinson be springing out from behind drapes, the whole company descending upon Almack's?

Had they all come here to advertise their theatrical? Or worse, attempt to perform any of it?

Both scenarios would be entirely absurd, but that would not slow down Lady Rawley. Her ill-advised notions had run far and wide for as long as he could remember. Lord Rawley used to live in terror of her notions.

Had she not had a notion to host a dinner comprised of fourteen ways to serve chicken? Poor Lord Rawley had not known of the plan so he'd ended just as surprised as his dinner guests. He'd told Percival afterward that most of the dinner conversation had run along the lines of, "Goodness, more chicken."

Then there had been the time she wished to change their name to Rawleystone, feeling it had a better sound to it. Lord Rawley had been obliged to outline the cold, hard fact that one could not just change a title.

Only three years ago, she'd paid to have her "novel" published, which turned out to be just a listing of the unpleasant qualities of one person after another that she did not like, with the names thinly veiled. Lord Rawley had scoured the town, bought all the copies, and then burnt them in the back garden.

Percival was of the opinion that her adventure in novel writing was what had finally done his uncle in.

Now, though, Lord Rawley was long gone and that meant his aunt had free rein with her notions.

"My dear Lady Rawley," Miss Mayton said. "I feel you must know the earl and Lord Darden?"

"Indeed, I do," Lady Rawley said. "And of course, the lovely Lady Cordelia."

Darden had greeted Percival and swiftly introduced him to the earl.

Then, the dreaded excellent notion that Lady Rawley had mentioned landed on the ground with a thud and began to take its shape.

Lady Rawley said, "Dear Lady Cordelia, I know this is your first outing to Almack's—nerves must be aflutter!"

Her father smiled and said, "I did tell my daughter there was no need—"

"No need, but they are there just the same," Lady Rawley said. "You are not to worry, Lady Cordelia, reinforcements have arrived! I have already arranged with Lady Castlereagh that my nephew may put himself down on your card. Naturally, he will take you into supper. It will be comforting to you to dine with a gentleman who is already known. As for the rest of the evening, I will be standing by to assist if you have the slightest need!"

Percival was stunned. Had she really been so bold as to arrange for him to take Lady Cordelia into supper?

It was not that he was opposed to the idea as a general thought, there was no particular lady he'd had in mind to ask. But she had no right to do it! It was blasted highhanded.

"Now, dear Percy," Lady Rawley said, laying a hand on his arm, "Lady Cordelia has not even retrieved her card yet. Do see to it."

See to it? Now he was to retrieve her card like a dog going after a shot pheasant?

He very much wished to pull his aunt aside and speak to her sternly regarding her audacity. However, the earl was smiling pleasantly at him and Darden looked a bit wide-eyed.

He'd have to make the best of it. For now.

Percival turned on his heel and worked to hide the fact that he was storming off, though he was definitely storming off.

After waiting in a line of people who had just come in, he finally did get hold of a card. When he returned to the party, he found Lord Hamill had joined them, looking just as strapping as he always did.

Percival had penciled his name in on Lady Cordelia's card and handed it to her as Miss Mayton said, "Lord Harveston, I suppose you know Lord Hamill? You are both in Lord Darden's club, I believe?"

"Yes, of course," Percival said. Hamill nodded his acknowledgment.

"We are so pleased to have a real Corinthian in our midst," Miss Mayton said.

Percival forced a tight smile, as clearly nobody was referring to *him* in such a manner.

It always filled him with irritation that men such as Hamill were given all the glory. Hamill raced around, hunting, sailing, boxing, driving, and was said to be extraordinary.

What did the fellow have between his ears though? Percival had once had a passing conversation with Hamill at the club and asked him his opinion on Wordsworth's new poem. The man had claimed he "left reading to his sister."

"I hardly lay claim to any title of the sort, Miss Mayton," Hamill said.

He said it with ridiculous modesty that nobody was meant to believe, in Percival's opinion. If Hamill was not a Corinthian he would like to know who was.

"I have heard from my sister Rosalind," Lady Cordelia said, "that Conbatten becomes tired from just hearing what you've accomplished before ten in the morning."

Hamill laughed. "I like to be up with the sun and the duke does not, surely that is no great accomplishment."

"I suppose you must be quite tired after a full day's exertion," Lady Cordelia said.

Why was she wondering if Hamill were tired at the end of the day? Was all the world to be fascinated by a sporting fellow?

"I am never too tired to dance, though," Hamill said gamely. "May I, Lady Cordelia? Lady Jersey has given me leave."

Lady Cordelia nodded prettily.

Was she to be impressed because the man left the house before ten in the morning? It seemed a rather limp yardstick.

Percival paused. Why were his thoughts running so heated? Yes, it was a constant annoyance that a gentleman like Hamill had his talents out where everybody could see them while an intellectual's accomplishments did not wave a flag for everybody to notice. However, he was not in a competition for Lady Cordelia's approval.

What care he if she was bowled over by the sportsman?

"I see you have surged ahead and secured Lady Cordelia's supper, Harveston," Hamill said.

Percival nodded. It was a small victory, but at least he'd won some sort of victory. He did not suppose he would come out victorious on any other matter when it came to Hamill, lest it involve a debate.

"I arranged it all," Lady Rawley said proudly.

And…his small victory just went up in a puff of smoke.

"Miss Mayton," the earl said, "shall we repair to the card room and trounce another couple at whist?"

"Let's do," Miss Mayton said. "I will tell a few stories from my days on the continent—that always does throw the play in our favor. Who can concentrate on the cards when they are in the midst of pondering that Gregorio dealt himself a deadly blow? I will just see that Cordelia has been taken on the floor for the first."

Though Percival might have expected any rational person to

be very surprised at Miss Mayton's mention of Gregorio and his deadly blow, the earl just nodded genially throughout.

"I should very much like to see the sideboard," Lady Rawley said, "if, Earl, you would not mind escorting me in that direction. I would not be opposed to securing a plate of sweets."

"Oh no, Lady Rawley," the earl said, shaking his head sadly.

"No?" Lady Rawley asked.

"Come, dear lady, and I will acquaint you with the offerings here," the earl said, leading the lady toward the card room.

Apparently, his aunt was not aware that the patronesses wore their poor offerings as some badge of honor. Lady Rawley would soon discover it, though.

Darden said, "Miss Mayton, I will escort you both so that my sister may be introduced to Lady Jersey. Harveston, Hamill."

Percival bowed and found himself left with Hamill.

"Very pretty little filly," Hamill said, watching Lady Cordelia stroll away with her brother.

Percival did not answer, though he could not imagine that any lady would like to know she'd been called a filly, pretty or otherwise.

"Darden tells me she's set on a Corinthian; I suppose that was why Miss Mayton had me dragged over."

Lady Cordelia was set on a Corinthian, was she? The idea was exceedingly annoying.

"Gad, though," Hamill said, "before you arrived with her card, she asked me for my views on Desdemona and whether that lady ought to have died."

"And what did you say?" Percival asked.

"I said I did not know Lady Desdemona. Do you?"

"Only at a distance," Percival said drily, "when I have seen her at a playhouse."

"Well, you won't see her there anymore. She is dead, apparently."

Percival pressed his lips together. What world did he live in that approved of a body accomplishing physical feats while the mind attached to it sloshed around its skull like thin porridge?

What world did he live in when a woman like Lady Cordelia was determined to chain herself to such a man?

Percival sighed. England's *ton*. That was the world he lived in. If one were not poised to break one's neck or be run through with a sword or have one's face boxed in, one was not very interesting.

CORDELIA HAD BEEN very confused by what had occurred upon entering Almack's. Lady Rawley had all but forced Lord Harveston to put himself down for her supper.

He'd not liked to do it, she could see that very well.

What had been the lady's aim? It had all been so awkward.

Then, after Lord Harveston was sent off to retrieve her card as if he were a footman sent on an errand, Miss Mayton pointed out Lord Hamill. Her aunt had urged Darden that he ought to wave him over.

There he was. Lord Hamill, the Corinthian.

He certainly met what her thoughts had imagined. His arms did look as if his tailor must be brought to the edge of despair in attempts to encase them. He was broad chested and it looked as if his wide shoulders strained at the seams of his coat.

He was very pleasant too.

And yet, he had seemed to think that Desdemona was a contemporary lady. He claimed he did not know her but that he was always sorry to hear that somebody had died.

Cordelia found herself disturbed by that. She also found herself disturbed to notice that her nerves were a bit shaken at anticipating dining with Lord Harveston. He was bound to talk about things she had no knowledge of. She really did not wish to be embarrassed and could not imagine why Lady Rawley had thought to arrange it.

She had then been introduced to Lady Jersey and got through

it creditably. It seemed that Rosalind having married a duke had laid a shiny veneer over the Benningtons. Cordelia was not asked anything particular about herself, though Lady Jersey was most interested in hearing of Conbatten.

Darden had since wandered off in search of ladies' cards.

Miss Mayton leaned over and whispered, "I believe Lady Rawley has had some matchmaking in mind."

"Matchmaking? With Lord Harveston?"

"Yes, I believe so. We cannot blame her, it is a very great compliment to you that she should think of it. Of course, she does not know of your proclivity for a Corinthian."

"No, I suppose she does not."

"Lord Hamill secured your first, I noticed. Very good sign."

"Yes, yes it was," Cordelia said.

She had imagined that she would be thrilled by such a development—her Corinthian approached and took her first. It was exactly what she had dreamed of.

Yet, she was not as thrilled as she ought to be.

His arms were everything perfection, just as she'd seen those appendages in her thoughts. He was exceedingly handsome, anybody would say so. But how was it that she was not stirred by him? Lightning had not struck her hair at all and she certainly did not feel as if she was drowning with more air.

Perhaps she'd only been thrown off by Lord Hamill failing to comprehend that when she spoke of Desdemona, she had meant that tragic heroine of a Shakespeare play.

It was even possible that there was a living Lady Desdemona in London somewhere, and now she had given Lord Hamill the impression that the poor lady was dead.

After all, he'd said he did not know the lady, not that he had never heard of the lady. If he had heard of a Lady Desdemona living amongst them, then it was the most natural thing in the world that his mind had gone there and not to *her* Desdemona.

"Yes, I really ought to like him," Cordelia said with resolution.

"That is good, for the musicians have done their tuning and Lord Hamill approaches," Miss Mayton said. "Now, leaving you in good hands, I will repair to the card room and join the earl. Goodness, we are on our way to another happy visit to the altar!"

With that, Miss Mayton promenaded her black bombazine across the ballroom floor and disappeared into the card room.

Lord Hamill led her to the floor and the dance began soon after.

He was skilled at it, as he must be with anything to do with movement and physicality.

He made general conversation about how excellent Darden's club was.

It was all very…as it should be?

Cordelia said, "My lord, I believe I may have inadvertently given you the wrong impression when I mentioned Desdemona's death. I was referring to Desdemona from *Othello*. Shakespeare's *Othello*."

"Ah, Shakespeare," Lord Hamill said, seeming as if the clouds had parted from his misapprehension. "I'll suppose it is not one of his comedies, as I have never seen it. In truth, I do not attend the theater very often, I get bored, as I like to be doing something, rather than watching other people do something."

"I see, yes, of course," Cordelia said.

That was something she'd not considered about a Corinthian. They would, very naturally, always like to be doing something.

She had thought that at the end of the day her Corinthian should like to relax and watch his wife perform Desdemona's death scene.

"Do you, yourself, enjoy the theater, Lady Cordelia?"

"Goodness, yes," she said, unable to resist speaking on her favorite subject. "In fact, I find acting to be almost in my blood. I have recently been invited to join Lady Rawley's acting troupe."

"Ah, the theatrical she puts on every year," Lord Hamill said. "I have never gone myself, but my father goes regularly. He says he would not miss it for the world."

This cheered Cordelia quite a bit. Lady Rawley's troupe had dedicated enthusiasts.

"He claims it is positively hilarious, and my sister seems to think so too," Lord Hamill said.

"Hilarious?" Cordelia asked, not at all sure what could be hilarious about them. According to Viola, last year's offering had been *Much Ado about Nothing*, in which Hero had murdered Claudio at the altar. Surprising? Of course. Amusing? She did not see how it could be.

"Mind you," Lord Hamill went on, "my sister is not yet out and so has not gone herself. My father goes and then describes the thing to her and they laugh and laugh. I never know what is so funny, but she says I wouldn't get the joke as I would not be familiar with the original play. Apparently, Lady Rawley takes shocking liberties with Shakespeare's words."

Everything Cordelia was hearing was most unsatisfactory. Lord Hamill was not the least interested in watching a play. Then worse, his sister was interested, only so that she could laugh at them!

But surely his sister, and his father for that matter, were misguided. Lady Rawley was so experienced in putting on her theatricals. Miss Mayton praised them to the skies. If an audience member did not perceive the true intent of a piece, then that must be laid at their own door. It spoke of a lack of understanding and finer feelings.

"I suppose your sister is also a sporting type of person?" Cordelia asked. "I suppose she is a very great rider?"

She must suppose so. It was one thing for an older gentleman to fail to be carried away by the emotion of Lady Rawley's theatrics, but she could not find anything else to account for the lord's sister not grasping the thing.

"Theodora?" Lord Hamill said, laughing. "You'll not find her atop a horse when a carriage is available. She'll happily climb in with a pile of books and then spout facts out the window at me."

"Do you say she is an intellectual, then?" Cordelia asked,

really not seeing how it could be so.

"*I* do not say it, though *she* is very free with the description," Lord Hamill said. "She claims, and we all do think it is rubbish, she will only marry her intellectual equal." He seemed to find great amusement in the idea.

"Someone like Lord Harveston, I suppose," Cordelia said quietly.

"Yes! They would make a fine match," Lord Hamill said laughing. "They might go on, both heads buried in books and never realizing there was life going on outside their doors."

Lord Hamill shook his head sadly. "Honestly, how some people choose to live, I will never understand."

Cordelia nodded to the statement but said nothing.

This was all most unsatisfactory. Nothing was going as it ought. She did not feel as she ought on her first night out on a ballroom floor. She did not feel as she ought, dancing with her Corinthian.

She felt prickly.

CHAPTER SEVEN

PERCIVAL HAD MADE his way through the evening, dancing with various ladies. Some he knew, and some he had just been introduced to as they were recently arrived.

As always, his conversation attempted to uncover how a lady's mind worked. At least, he did so with the ladies just met.

The ladies he was already acquainted with had various interests they would wish to speak about. Lady Marie wished to talk of her roses, Lady Ellen preferred guiding the conversation toward novels and possibly the weather, and of course Lady Mary had an unpleasant interest in gossip.

He was a gentleman, therefore he did his best to accommodate, though none of it was interesting to him.

With the ladies just met, he was always hopeful of uncovering an incisive mind. An educated mind. A mind that had read widely. He was certain he would come across such a lady sooner or later, though this night was not to be it.

One of them had been hardly able to answer a question and certainly had no questions of her own. How many times could a lady laugh and say, "I'm sure I do not know?" He'd been very tempted to say, "Why do you not tell me what you *do* know and we can talk about that?"

He had not, of course.

Now he was to escort Lady Cordelia to the floor. He did not know what she'd have to say for herself, but at least she was rather glorious to look at.

Further, it had begun to dawn on him that perhaps it was not a bad thing that he would take her into supper. Perhaps there was a way to plant the seeds of retreat in her mind. Perhaps if *she* thought the ladies ought to exit from the SSLE, she might plant that seed in the other ladies' minds.

After all, they had indicated amongst themselves that they were bored at the literary society meeting they had already attended. At least, according to Mr. Haventops' recounting of it to Makepeace. Certainly there might be a way to provide a graceful and face-saving slipping out of the door.

Why should she wish to go on with it anyway? It was not as if her Corinthian would be found in his salon.

He approached Lady Cordelia, who was fairly surrounded by gentlemen lamenting that they had not secured a dance and pestering her to vow that she would allow them on her card at the next ball in which they encountered one another.

The usual dramatics arisen from the minds of foolish fops.

Of course, he would not say so aloud, as some of them were from his own club. He got along famously with Darden and some others, but there were those members who were a little too happy and carefree for his tastes.

"Lady Cordelia," he said. "If I may?"

He held his arm out, gently nudging one of the fops to the side. With much sighing, they allowed her to pass and he led her to the floor.

As they waited for the music to strike up, he said, "I understand your father's estate is in Somerset?"

It was the sort of vague conversation he could use to pass the time before he found his opportunity to hint at an exit from the SSLE.

"Yes, Westmont House is just west of Taunton," Lady Cordelia said.

"That is not too bad a journey to Town, I trust it was pleasant?"

"It was most pleasant," Lady Cordelia said. "We encountered several travelers who were genial, and then dear Lord Darling was *so* genial that we've taken him into the house. Never was there a creature more aptly named—he really *is* a darling."

Who was Lord Darling? He'd never heard of the gentleman. And then how had this Lord Darling managed to insert himself into the household?

Percival began to see how it might be so. Certainly, he was some crony of the earl's.

"I suppose he's very old then?" he said. "A friend of your father's?"

"Lord Darling old? Goodness no," Lady Cordelia said. "He's young and full of fun. As for my father, he is so good-humored that he tolerates Lord Darling, but it is I and my sister who are smitten with him."

Good Lord. What was going on in that house?

"Miss Mayton does not mind?" Percival asked, working to keep the incredulousness out of his tone.

"Why should Miss Mayton mind?" Lady Cordelia asked. "Lord Darling is hardly the first we have met upon the road and taken in." She paused and then said, "Though he really is the most darling. Now, I will not say a word against Chester, but he does have the habit of screaming quite a bit."

Chester? Who were these men? What was Chester screaming about? Why did the earl allow it?

Percival was silent, attempting to make sense of what he'd just heard. One would have thought, if such scandalous things were going on, that a person would not speak publicly about it!

Of course, there had always been talk of some sort regarding the Benningtons. The eldest sister had collected a whole pile of gentlemen mooning about her drawing room, then chucked them all out and married her country neighbor.

The second sister had allegedly arranged her own kidnapping so Conbatten might rescue her, though since the queen had expressed her displeasure over the story nobody talked about it publicly.

Then the third sister had come along and managed to get Baderston engaged for three duels on the same morning; somehow they didn't come off, and then the whole family eloped to Gretna Green in some sort of mass migration.

Did any of these husbands now married to a Bennington know about Chester? Or the more recently arrived Lord Darling? They must do, one could not exactly hide a houseguest. Especially not a screaming one.

Their turn came and Percival led Lady Cordelia through the steps. She was very graceful on the floor, as all the Bennington ladies seemed to be. He could not say the same for himself. He felt rather…discombobulated.

Finally, the dancers had all completed their steps and the people in the ballroom turned as if they were a tide and headed toward the dining room. Percival never could understand why there was such a hurry to get there, as there would be nothing good found upon arrival.

They passed two of the gentlemen who had surrounded Lady Cordelia when he'd gone to collect her for the dance.

They both bowed low. One rose and said, "Until we meet again."

The other followed suit with, "I shall not sleep."

He led Lady Cordelia to open seats and motioned for a footman to bring whatever dreadful offerings were to be had.

As he did not wish to revisit the subject of Chester and Lord Darling residing in her house, he said, "I see you have now met the more dramatic fellows who haunt these halls."

"Dramatic?" Lady Cordelia said. "In what way?"

"Oh, you know, they surround a lady and pretend they will die if she takes no notice of them. Shall not sleep, indeed."

"I thought the gentlemen all seemed very pleasant," Lady Cordelia said.

It was a general sort of statement, but her tone had been rather sharp. He had only been attempting a conversation.

"Certainly, you are not offended that I characterize them so," Percival said. "You did not take it to mean any particular comment on yourself?"

"I did not take it to mean anything at all, other than you do not like them."

He got the particular feeling that she *had* taken offense, though he could not think why.

Attempting to smooth things over, he said, "I only say, a lady has to be careful of what she takes to be true. She may well be hearing a song that has been sung to many a lady before her and is only for amusement."

"I am warned," Lady Cordelia said curtly.

"Excellent," he said. Though, he was beginning to think that Lady Cordelia could be rather prickly. And unpredictable. One minute she was casually talking about two unknown men living in her house very cheerfully, the next she was irritated by a pointing out of a very obvious fact.

He stared at the sour lemonade that had just been delivered to him. He must stick to his purpose. He must find a beginning to ousting his aunt and her friends from the literary society.

"My aunt is a very interesting woman," he said. "She is always daring to try new things when others might shy away. And then, she does have the good sense to drop a thing that has not proved as interesting as she'd hoped. So many people feel they must stick with a thing, just for sticking with it. There really is only good sense in dropping a thing when it does not suit."

He waited for Lady Cordelia to answer, but she did not. Rather, she was staring at her slice of dry cake as if to crumble it with her eyes.

Finally she said, "One wonders what this mysterious thing is."

What did that mean? Did she know his meaning or did she not?

As she did not comment further, he came to the conclusion that trying to hint round the idea was getting him nowhere at all. He'd best just be direct.

"Lady Cordelia," he said, "not every club or society is meant for every person. For example, I should not fair very well at Boodle's—the country set that are so enthusiastic about a hunt or a race simply do not capture my interest. Now, I did recall that my aunt and her friends were all reading the same book. About a dale and some terrible doings there, I believe. Have you not considered founding a club to gather all like-minded ladies together to discuss it? A book club, of sorts?"

"Rather than attending your own society meetings," she said.

Finally, she had perceived his point. "Precisely," he said. "After all, people do have different abilities and proclivities. There is no shame in it."

Lady Cordelia stabbed her cake with her fork, then she laid that utensil down. "Lord Harveston," she said, "you have done everything possible this evening to make me feel small. If this is an example of an intellectual's habits and manners, then I am sure I do not know why you are so impressed with yourself. This cake is insufferable, and *you* are insufferable."

She rose and said, "I will find my aunt and Lady Rawley, they are far better company."

Lady Cordelia turned on her heel and stalked off.

What had just happened?

He was insufferable? Because he'd attempted to give her some friendly hints?

Though he did not feel he was in the wrong, his face grew rather hot. The lady's abrupt exit had not gone unnoticed. There were various people staring in his direction, not the least of which were the sharp eyes of Lady Hightower.

THOUGH CORDELIA HAD claimed she would go to find her aunt and Lady Rawley, she had felt entirely incapable of it and sought out the ladies' retiring rooms.

There, after telling the maid she needed no attendance, she found a quiet and private corner at the far end of the room, pulled the curtain, and sat down on the velvet covered bench provided for those who merely wished to rest or fix their hair. She sobbed silently, not wishing to make a sound, lest some other lady come in and hear her.

Never had she been treated so. It was not so much what Lord Harveston had said, it was what she knew he meant by what he said. She, and Lady Rawley's acting troupe, were not wanted. They were judged unworthy. Their interests were deemed stupid, *she* was deemed stupid.

In fact, he thought her to be so dense as to not understand that some mild flattery from a group of young gentlemen was not a proposal of marriage. As if the most obvious thing must be explained to her.

He found her tiresome and unaccomplished and did not even bother to hide it, as she was of so little consequence.

Then, to further heap on the misery, she'd felt nothing at all for Lord Hamill. He was genial, to be sure, but she could not be in love with him.

All in all, she felt exceedingly stung by the events of the night. Very stung indeed.

When Beatrice and Rosalind and Viola had made their debut at Almack's it had all gone stunningly well. She felt like some sort of failure that she could not claim the same.

From outside her little corner, she heard the door to the retiring room open. A lady's voice, a very commanding voice, said, "Where is she?"

Cordelia could only imagine the maid had pointed to her location as she heard footsteps approaching. Very determined footsteps.

Was it a patroness? Was she in trouble of some sort for leaving Lord Harveston alone at the table? Had she broken a rule and was about to be lectured?

She could not bear it, not this very moment.

A lady came round the corner and Cordelia instantly recognized her as Lady Hightower. She had not ever been introduced to the lady, but she had seen her in the park when Lady Hightower had inserted herself into the scene of Rosalind's pickpocket arrangement.

"I recognize you as a Bennington girl," Lady Hightower said.

"Yes, Lady Hightower, I am Cordelia Bennington," she said, attempting to hide her sniffles.

"Hah! And you will know me from the day your sister very dramatically fainted into Conbatten's arms when she lost her handkerchief to a pickpocket."

Cordelia nodded, though she was not entirely sure why Lady Hightower seemed amused by the recollection.

"My lady," she said, wishing to get whatever scolding was coming to her over with, "am I in trouble for leaving Lord Harveston at table?"

"In trouble? Goodness, no. I merely saw the state you were in when you left him and thought I ought to assure myself that you were alright."

At this kindness, Cordelia burst into tears all over again.

Lady Hightower ordered the maid to bring all the handkerchiefs in the place. She sat on the bench next to Cordelia and began handing them to her, one by one.

"That's right, cry it out," Lady Hightower said, "it never does a bit of good to hold it in and the young have a great propensity for feeling things sharply."

Though the lady had given her leave to cry as much as she liked, Cordelia did make an effort to regain her composure.

"You must think me a terrible ninny," she said.

"Well, that entirely depends on what you were crying about. Did Lord Harveston spill something on your dress or some other easily remedied matter?"

"No, of course I would not collapse over such a small thing," Cordelia said. "I really should not have collapsed at all, I do not know why his opinion has stung me so, he is nothing to me."

"And what opinion was that?"

Cordelia mopped at her eyes and said, "He thinks me very stupid."

"He did not say so!"

"Not in those words exactly, but his meaning was clear enough."

Lady Hightower sighed, and Cordelia thought it was rather a disgusted sort of sigh.

"If it will soothe you at all to know it," Lady Hightower said, "Harveston thinks almost everybody is stupid."

This idea did soothe. In truth, Cordelia began to feel less injured and more angry that he should have behaved in such a manner.

"I have observed for some time that he values pure intellect above all else. This is to his detriment, of course, as he fails to see his own failings. He has blinded himself with facts."

This cheered Cordelia even more. Lady Hightower was right—just because he'd read all sorts of books did not mean he was perfect. It did not mean he did not have faults.

Other than a propensity for rudeness, she did not know what those other faults were, of course, but certainly he had them. He probably had piles of them.

"Lord Harveston has carved out for himself a narrow lane to live his life through," Lady Hightower said. "This will be his downfall if he does not correct it. Books are always a very one-sided conversation—they cannot cheer you on, nor soothe you when you are ill."

"Yes," Cordelia said, feeling very encouraged. "Books are not everything. Lord Hamill told me he does not even read them at all."

Lady Hightower snorted. "Yes, well, Hamill is another story altogether," she said. "Now, dry your eyes, take deep breaths, and stay here. I will find Miss Mayton and the earl and tell them you have a headache. We will have your carriage called. You will miss nothing by skipping the patronesses' offerings. By the by, next time sit by me—I bring a sugar mixture to pour over everything to make it more palatable. They know it but they dare not do anything about it."

Cordelia nodded and said, "Lady Hightower, you have been most kind to put up with me."

"Nonsense," the lady said, "what is one of the oldest bats in the rafters to do if not come to the aid of a weeping young woman in a retiring room? It happens more often than you might imagine. In any case, I always do find a Bennington girl interesting."

⇢⟫⟫⟩⟨⟨⟨⟵

PERCIVAL HAD NEVER had a lady become so offended by his words. He supposed it was his hinting that Lady Cordelia and her troupe of actors ought to form their own club that had done it.

At least, that was all he and his butler could make of it. Makepeace theorized that Lady Cordelia suffered from an ailment of the nervous variety and might become upset over practically anything.

That might be true, of course. She *had* seemed unpredictable—one moment waxing on about Lord Darling and the screaming Chester, the next naming him insufferable and rushing off.

Certainly, her condemnation had not been rational. While his words might have been direct, he had not been insufferable.

No, he could not have been insufferable. He would have known if he were being insufferable.

He might have been the least little bit irritated. He supposed mention of her searching for her own Corinthian had grated, as he never did see the sense in it. Irritated, yes. Insufferable, he could not see it.

Now, Makepeace had just come in and handed him a letter that had been delivered.

Percival saw that it was from Lady Hightower and became the slightest bit uncomfortable. She had been staring at the scene when Lady Cordelia had run off. She had risen herself and followed the lady. She had stared at him when she came back.

He opened the letter.

My dear Lord Harveston—

I pray you do not view this as an intrusion, but as I have known you since you were a schoolboy and I am a friend of your mother's, I do not hesitate to write and point something out to you.

Your behavior last evening was insufferable.

Percival dropped the paper. Lady Hightower pronounced him insufferable too! But how could she know? She did not hear the conversation. She would have only been told Lady Cordelia's side of things and that lady had proved herself unpredictable.

He picked up the sheet to read the rest of it.

To have reduced a young lady just out in society to tears is outrageous. I did not need to hear from Lady Cordelia any of the details of your conversation beyond the idea that she understands you think her stupid.

Then, I knew as much as I needed to.

You have become so blinded by your perceived intellectualism that you are beginning to forget how to be a proper gentleman. What can be found in books is not all that can be found in life. Further, there are more kinds of intelligence than you are aware of. Do not become so enamored with your knowledge that you gain the reputation of being insufferable on a regular schedule.

Rectify this, Harveston.

Regards—an irritated old bat

"I cannot believe it," Percival said quietly, handing the letter to Makepeace. "Can this be right?"

His butler read through the letter and laid it down on the desk. "What does she mean?" he asked. "How does one become blinded by intellectualism? It is those who do not learn and think deeply who are blinded!"

Percival would have thought so himself.

"What do you suppose she means by saying there are more kinds of intelligence?" he asked.

Makepeace rubbed his chin. "Well, animals have a certain intelligence built into them."

"Their instincts."

"Just so."

"But why should she point that out?" As he asked it, he thought he began to get an inkling. Lady Hightower had said he was forgetting how to be a gentleman. Did she mean he was losing his instincts as a gentleman? Could that be true?

He'd thought he'd said things politely last evening, if not directly. On the other hand, Lady Cordelia had come away with the idea that he thought her stupid. He had not wished that.

He did not even think it. At least, not entirely. He thought the acting troupe silly and absurd and he thought Lady Cordelia not particularly an intellectual. But that was a far cry from stupid!

And yet, he'd made her think it. That must be laid at his door and Lady Hightower was right. He ought to rectify it.

How he would do so, he had not the first idea.

"Well, Makepeace, it seems I've made a misstep and must fix it. I cannot go about making ladies cry, it's just not the done thing. Not by a gentleman, anyway."

Makepeace sighed so long and deep it sounded like his last breath was leaving his body and he was making his journey to the great beyond. "I suppose this means they will continue to contaminate our society meetings."

"Yes, I suppose so, though I do not think 'contaminate' is really the right word. Now, I just have to figure out a way to fix this somehow, lest Lady Hightower begins writing me every day."

Makepeace sniffed. "Perhaps you ought to get hold of that book they're all so wild about?" he said, his tone dripping with sarcasm. "Perhaps you ought to look into these dreadful doings in a dale."

Though his butler said it with the express intention of throwing another condemnation upon Lady Cordelia and her friends, it was not a bad idea. If he could engage on a topic she was interested in, he might show that he had been misunderstood.

Percival tented his fingers. Yes, of course that would do it. A proper apology and then a hint dropped that he was reading a book of interest to her must fix the thing.

"Makepeace," he said, "get me a copy of that book. The dreadful doings of something or other dale."

"You jest," Makepeace said, looking as if he'd been asked to go out and hire a murderer.

"I do not. I want a copy on my desk today. In fact, get me a copy of every book that author has written. It would be well to go even beyond what would be duty; Lady Cordelia could not hold out against such a gesture. Send the footmen out in all directions."

CHAPTER EIGHT

LADY HIGHTOWER HAD been as good as her word. She'd found her aunt and her father, and the carriage had been called to take them home. Darden was left behind, as he was well able to make his own way back.

Cordelia had expected that her father would wish for some sort of explanation or assurance about her condition, but it was not so.

Lady Hightower had seen them off and Cordelia had heard her say to the earl, "Remember my counsel, my lord, do not enquire into it."

Her aunt had told her later that Lady Hightower had explained to her father that it was nothing to be concerned about, just a womanly problem.

Cordelia had thought it was only her and her sisters who used such a ploy when they did not wish to explain a thing, but apparently it was a well-known strategy amongst women.

Her dear Papa had not the slightest wish to hear of womanly problems and so did not press her for information. He'd just stared out the carriage window, pretending nothing was amiss.

Her aunt, on the other hand, would not be put off, nor did Cordelia wish to put her off. They'd found Juliet still awake and lounging on her bed. As Lynette brushed out her hair and put it in a braid, Cordelia had poured out the whole wretched story for both of them.

"You were very right, Cordy," Juliet said, "he *was* insuffera-ble."

"I am very surprised at Lord Harveston," Miss Mayton said, shaking her head.

"I am even more surprised by my own behavior," Cordelia said. "Why should I run off and cry, simply because some gentleman recently met does not approve of me?"

"It was the shock of not being approved of," Juliet said. "You have always been approved of, you must have felt staggered when all of the sudden somebody did not."

She *had* felt rather staggered. And, she was becoming aware that she had been particularly staggered because the disapproval had come from Lord Harveston.

"You see, Cordy," Juliet went on, "not every family is like ours. Just think of the Grant sisters—they are always ready to tear each other's hair out. We're different, we all approve of one another and so you have got used to it."

What Juliet said was true. She could not ever remember any of her sisters fighting with one another. She did not see why they ever would—it was far too much fun to be in one another's confidence.

"Just think," Juliet said, "when I first began writing my odes I was not very good at it. Could I ever have got to where I am now without the cheering on of my sisters? I am not sure that I could have. And what about Rosalind on the pianoforte or Viola's painting?"

"You girls are all so talented," Miss Mayton said.

Lynette suppressed a snort.

"Do not tease us, Lynette," Cordelia said. "Juliet is right, I have just been too used to being enveloped in the loving arms of my family. Not everyone can be like us."

"That is the truth," Lynette said with a giggle.

Cordelia ignored Lynette, as the maid did like to tease for her own amusement. Everything Juliet had pointed out made so much sense. Though, why should she be so struck by Lord

Harveston's stance, even though it was rude? She had not just been surprised and offended, she had actually cried. Why should his opinion matter to her?

She really had no idea.

"I wonder if we should apprise Lady Rawley of this shameful incident?" Miss Mayton said, tapping her chin with her forefinger.

"Oh, no, let us not, Aunt," Cordelia said hurriedly. "I'd much rather as few people know of it as possible."

"Well, yes, I can certainly understand that, my dear."

"But that will also mean that you both must keep attending his stupid literature society," Juliet pointed out.

That was true, and though she was rather delighted to hear Juliet name it a stupid society, she could not be enthusiastic about continuing to go. Not when she now clearly understood Lord Harveston's opinion regarding her attendance.

On the other hand, were they to be driven out? Was she to wave the white flag of defeat?

And then she had an idea. "Aunt, we were at a severe disadvantage at the last meeting because we did not know what the subject matter would be. Now we have the printed schedule."

Cordelia hopped up, wresting herself away from a sighing Lynette, and found the paper on her writing desk. "Here it is. We are to discuss St. Thomas Aquinas' idea that no man can be a judge of himself and how it relates to Aristotle's opinion that most people are bad judges of their own case."

"Ugh," Juliet said. "Two ancient fellows who could not write a decent ode between them."

"I am afraid I do not know the first thing about it," Miss Mayton said. "Did any of your tutors ever say anything about either of those two gentlemen?"

Cordelia sat back down at Lynette's urging and let her carry one with her work. She was certain that they had been told of these two fellows, but whenever one of their tutors droned on about some uninteresting person or event, it slipped out of her mind as fast as it had slipped in. Mr. Cramden used to liken her mind to a sieve.

"Jules?" she said.

Juliet shook her head. "Mr. Cramden probably waxed on about them. He was very good at finding the most boring people in history and talking about them for an hour."

Miss Mayton nodded sadly. "I did not care for Mr. Cramden, myself, but the earl was doing a favor for the vicar in employing him. I did point out, several times, that he always smelled like fried bacon."

"He used to keep it in his pockets, wrapped in paper," Juliet said. "I caught him eating it a few times."

"He used to get if from Cook," Lynette said. "He always said he felt faint if he did not have bacon and Cook did not want to find out if it was true."

"Interesting," Juliet said. "Perhaps he had a medical condition we did not know about?"

"He did always seem pale," Miss Mayton said.

"I suppose we will never know, but all this reminiscing about Mr. Cramden does not help us much," Cordelia said. "However, just because we did not learn about Aristotle and St. Thomas Aquinas then, does not mean we cannot now. We have a whole library downstairs."

"Goodness, we do," Miss Mayton said. "I always forget about that room."

"On the morrow, we will begin our studies. We will learn something about these fellows. Then, when Lord Harveston attempts to paint us stupid, he will find out otherwise."

"He will be shocked to his insufferable shoes," Juliet said, sounding very satisfied by the idea.

"And, as an antidote to our tedious studies," Miss Mayton said, "we expect Viola and Rosalind to dinner on the morrow and afterward I will read from *The Dreadful Doings of Dembric Dale*. It will be a palate cleanser after we have struggled to understand two old men and their ideas about judging themselves."

Cordelia felt infinitely better about things. She would show

Lord Harveston just how mistaken he'd been. And how insufferable he'd been, which had now been established as an incontrovertible fact.

TATTLETON HAD A vague sense of unease. Of course, there were reasons aplenty for such a feeling. For one, it seemed it was to be a regular habit that Lady Juliet called him, Benny, and Johnny to the drawing room to play cards after the earl, Miss Mayton, and Lady Cordelia had gone out.

He could not believe that the earl would be approving of it, but then he did sympathize with Lady Juliet's plight. It was just nerve-wracking when the time grew late and he must keep one ear out for the sound of carriage wheels stopping at the front of the house.

He did not like sneaking around!

It also seemed to be becoming a habit that Lord Darling, that cheeky creature, was to come to the drawing room. He attended the card games and one had to watch him carefully as he liked to make off with cards and chew them up. When he wasn't doing that, he was chewing on the curtains. How was a butler to explain frayed curtains?

It seemed Lord Darling was to have the run of the house now and putting him in the garden was looking like an impossible dream. He could not be contained and Tattleton was forever discovering him in the most unlikely places.

Whatever they set up below stairs to keep him from wandering off was soon defeated. The devilish kid managed to jump over everything.

No, not even jump—it was more like a springing straight up in the air. It defied the laws of nature!

So far, he'd found the thing standing on a sofa, attempting to balance on a windowsill, and standing on the earl's important papers on his desk in the library.

It had been no easy feat to dust off hoof prints from the earl's letters. Tattleton was just grateful the wretch had not eaten them.

And then, it had taken to chewing on things. It seemed particularly fond of tablecloths and the bottoms of curtains.

All Lady Juliet had to say of it was that he was still a baby.

Yes, he *was* still a baby. What sort of havoc would he create as he grew!

This was all disturbing enough, but something else had happened to put him on edge. Something had happened at Almack's. He did not know what, but he'd known Lady Cordelia since she was a baby. She'd been crying.

What could she have been crying about?

"There now, Mr. Tattleton," Mrs. Huffson said, "I know the little mite is a handful, but even you must admit that Lord Darling *is* rather darling when he's sleeping."

The creature was curled up on the bedding the ladies Cordelia and Juliet had set up for him. Finely-made bedding that ought to be on actual beds.

"I need not admit any such thing, Mrs. Huffson," he said, sipping his brandy.

"Well, think of it this way," the housekeeper said, "whatever Lord Darling is, what he isn't is four cats underfoot, and he isn't a dog poised to have a litter of pups, and he isn't a bird who screams 'murder' at everyone who walks by."

Tattleton was rather surprised that Mrs. Huffson would bring to his notice the creatures that had plagued him during other seasons. As if that was supposed to ease his mind!

He eyed the now-sleeping Lord Darling. Oh yes, he looked so harmless in his repose. The morning would bring a different story, though.

Tattleton sighed and said, "I would be most gratified if that creature were the only thing weighing heavily upon me, Mrs. Huffson."

"Oh dear," Mrs. Huffson said, "has something occurred?"

"Not yet, but I can only feel that something is in the offing," he said. "When Lady Cordelia returned home last night, she had been crying. Crying, Mrs. Huffson. What could have caused her to cry at Almack's? It is an esteemed institution."

Mrs. Huffson was thoughtful. "Naturally, I cannot know, but I must think it had to do with a gentleman."

"A gentleman? What has caused you to think it?" Tattleton asked.

"It is always because of a gentleman."

That was very true. It *was* always about a gentleman.

"I expect," Mrs. Huffson said, "that whatever has occurred, it will blow over."

"Blow over? Blow over, Mrs. Huffson? When did they ever allow a thing to blow over?"

It really astounded him at times how Mrs. Huffson seemed to never remember the past.

"Oh my, you do not think…they would not…surely not…"

Now it was occurring to her.

"That's right," he said, "they will devise a plan. And what do we know about their plans, Mrs. Huffson?"

"They are always bad. Very bad," Mrs. Huffson said sadly.

Tattleton nodded gravely. They were always very bad.

"And what do you think Lynette told me before she retired for the night?" Tattleton asked.

Mrs. Huffson was now looking very alarmed, which calmed him. If he were to be alarmed, it was soothing to have somebody else alarmed with him.

"What did Lynette say?" Mrs. Huffson asked in a whisper.

"They require use of the library on the morrow. They are going to study."

"*They* are? Study what?"

"Lynette was not altogether clear, she said it was something about judges. *Judges*, Mrs. Huffson! Are they planning to involve us in the courts now?"

"I do not see how they would."

"No, we never do see how it will be. It is always a shock, Mrs. Huffson. Always a terrible shock."

CORDELIA, JULIET, AND Miss Mayton had been in the earl's library for over an hour. At the breakfast table, Cordelia's father had been most surprised that they planned to spend their morning in that location. He'd been even more taken aback that they intended to embark on a serious study of Aristotle and St. Thomas Aquinas.

Darden had joked that Oxford would shudder to hear of it, but the earl had frowned at him and he said no more.

The earl had been so good as to pull all the books from his shelves that would be of interest to them, and it was quite a few books, all of them unusually heavy.

The first half hour had been grueling, each one of them squinting at the dense text and struggling through the first few pages of the book they'd picked up.

They'd speedily come to the conclusion that they could not go on in such a manner and did several things to remedy the situation. They had Tattleton send in a tray of tea and biscuits to sustain them, then brought Lord Darling in to entertain them while they worked.

The second half hour had been far more pleasant, but Cordelia did not think they made much headway in their quest to understand Aristotle and St. Thomas Aquinas.

"The problem, as I see it," Miss Mayton said, "is that these fellows write in circles."

"Yes!" Juliet said. "Can they not simply say what they mean?"

Lord Darling hopped up on the desk and surveyed the room, as if to further confirm those assessments.

"This does seem rather hopeless," Cordelia said, only three pages into the book she'd picked up. "Perhaps I *am* stupid and have no business attempting to understand Aristotle and St. Thomas Aquinas."

"Do not say so, Cordy," Juliet said. "As a writer myself, I can tell you that these men wrote like this on purpose. They do it to sound smarter than they actually are. Just like Mr. Peabody does at home. They mean to befuddle, thereby tricking you into believing they've said something remarkable."

"Goodness," Miss Mayton said, "Mr. Peabody. I do not understand half of what that fellow says."

"Because you are not meant to," Juliet said. "He hurls out a hurricane of words when three would do, all to make him seem highly intelligent."

"You might be right, Jules," Cordelia said. "The last time Viola, Aunt, and I saw him in the village he insisted on stopping us so we very naturally made general conversation as a matter of courtesy. Viola mentioned we were having rather pleasant weather."

"Oh yes," Miss Mayton said, "there we were, for a quarter of an hour, hearing about different kinds of clouds on a day there were none in the sky."

Cordelia nodded. "He walked away looking very pleased with himself. But if Aristotle and St. Thomas Aquinas worked to make themselves unintelligible, what are we to do?"

"I think we ought to come to our own judgments, just as women have very sensibly been doing since the beginning of time," Juliet said.

"I see," Cordelia said. "The question is should a person be able to judge themselves? We might just see what *we* think about it."

"That does sound a deal more pleasant," Miss Mayton said, looking rather forlornly at the book in her lap.

Lord Darling seemed to be in complete agreement with this new idea. He let out one of his interesting sounds—sort of a muffled and raspy bleat that sounded as if it were a far off cry for help.

And so, they spent the next hour discussing their ideas regarding people judging themselves, interspersed with passing rather stern and condemning judgments on Aristotle, St. Thomas Aquinas, Mr. Peabody, and Lord Harveston.

CHAPTER NINE

PERCIVAL LOOKED OVER the pile of books on his desk. Makepeace, though he'd been reluctant to do it, had secured every known novel by the author Richard Roydon.

There were *The Terrible Goings-on of Montclair Castle*, *The Awful Happenstances of Grimwood Hall*, *The Harrowing Homecoming at Harrowbridge Hall*, and finally the subject at hand, *The Dreadful Doings of Dembric Dale*.

None of the books were very long and they seemed rather cheaply produced. The publisher appeared to be a small operation in York. The descriptions were entirely absurd. Aside from the doings in the dale, the rest of them featured a duke and a gentle governess. Harrowbridge Hall even had *two* dukes. The dale had one duke and a gentle governess who was now the duchess, saddled with a father who was wondering if he would be murdered.

From the looks of it, they were all meant to have a gothic flavor to them. Shakespeare, they were not.

"All right, Makepeace," Percival said, "it will be our task to discover some redeeming qualities in these books."

"We?" Makepeace said softly, as he poured Percival a coffee.

"I cannot read all of these on my own," he said. "My head would explode in a hundred bits. No, we must divide and conquer. You take *Montclair Castle* and *Grimwood Hall* and I'll take the other two. Come back with interesting things I might say about them."

Makepeace picked up the two volumes he'd been assigned, though Percival thought he was being rather dramatic about it—he held them with his arms straight out as if they were two live vipers.

Percival ignored his silent histrionics. Then he ignored the not so silent histrionics that went on in the hall. He very clearly heard Makepeace say to a footman, "I will be in my room, reading these. If you encounter me later and I seem to have lost my wits and can no longer speak in full sentences, tell the doctor I was assaulted by crass writings."

The poor footman agreed that he would do so, and Makepeace presumably wandered off.

Percival opened the dreadful doings of the dale, feeling he might as well tackle that one first since it was the current favorite amongst the ladies.

The next hour found him rubbing his eyes to be certain he'd read what he thought he did, occasionally snorting, saying things to himself like, "Certainly not, no do not tell me, oh yes that's where it is going."

Among his thoughts on the ludicrous situations in the book, it occurred to him to wonder not just who would bother to write it, but who would bother to read it. That did give him pause, as he knew very well who was reading it. His aunt, her friends, and Lady Cordelia.

They saw something in it, but what was it?

He did not know. All he did know was he would have to find something positive to say about it.

There was a soft knock on the door and Makepeace came in looking very stern.

"Yes, I realize," Percival said, "these books are dreadful."

"Allow me, my lord, to bring you current regarding the terrible goings-on at a place named Montclair Castle," Makepeace said.

He said it in a controlled fury and Percival wondered that

there was not steam blasting out of his ears.

"Go on," he said. "I wish to know enough to be able to speak creditably on it."

"Very well," Makepeace said, hands clasped behind his back and strolling back and forth. "Though what could be creditable about it escapes me. It seems there was a one-eyed duke widower. Very predictably, he had a governess for his children. Even more predictably, this young governess is described as being very gentle, though I've never known a gentle governess in my life. The question of the story, which is repeated numerous times in case the dull readers of such books have failed to perceive it is can this allegedly gentle governess love a one-eyed duke?"

Percival poured himself another coffee, as he was fairly certain he would need it.

The butler stopped in his tracks and turned. Holding a forefinger in the air, he said, "And here is where it becomes somewhat less predictable. It turns out the duke has two perfectly good eyes and is only a madman who imagined he'd lost an eye. He's been walking round with an eye patch he does not require."

Makepeace waited for that news to sink in. Percival shrugged as there seemed to be no answer to make to such nonsense.

"Now, the unanswered question of the story whipsaws to if this allegedly gentle governess can love a madman with two eyes. Which, happily, she can. So, they go on, pleased as Punch, while the new duchess spends her days reminding the mad duke about which body parts he has, in fact, not lost. That concludes the goings-on of that particular castle. I challenge you to say something creditable about it."

Makepeace pulled the book from his inside coat pocket and dropped it on the desk. "Now, I will repair to my rooms to discover what awful happenstances have beset Grimwood Hall."

As his butler made his exit, Percival would have almost laughed at the situation. Except he really would need to pull some sort of compliment out of the air for these books.

Somewhere in Dembric Dale, there must be some little nugget of something that could be commended. He just must find it.

CORDELIA FOUND HERSELF much cheered by the time evening came. How could she not? She'd spent the day in the company of Juliet and her aunt, and this evening would see Viola and Rosalind coming. They would only be missing dear Beatrice, who was at home with her new baby and Van Doren.

Lord Darling had followed them everywhere they went throughout the day, including into the drawing room as they awaited her sisters. He was such a charming little thing, though if one looked closely, one might begin to see the wear and tear regarding his interest in chewing on the furnishings.

The earl came into the drawing room and stopped short, staring at Lord Darling.

"Now, Papa," Cordelia said soothingly, "our poor Lord Darling will be out in the garden any day now, but he is still too young and in too delicate a condition right this moment. Charlie says, and you do remember Charlie grew up on a farm, that he would catch a chill and he would not do well without company."

"I see, yes, well, as to all that I am sure I cannot say," the earl said, as Juliet gently nudged Lord Darling away from the hem of the curtains he was eyeing, "I just wonder, at least I did think, that he would be downstairs in the servants' hall."

"Of course, he is usually there," Juliet said, "but just now, with Cook preparing dinner, he would be underfoot."

"Now, I do like to be agreeable," the earl said, "but I feel forced to say that the aroma in here is rather like a barn."

"Well it would be, I suppose," Miss Mayton said. "Nothing an open window might not remedy?"

Benny hurried to the aforementioned window and threw it open.

"Papa," Cordelia said, "one of the things I find most wonderful about the Benningtons is that we are always willing to be a little inconvenienced in service to others."

Her father's brow wrinkled. "Naturally, service to our fellow man is all well and good," the earl said, "but he is a goat, Cordelia. I really feel I must point that out."

Cordelia glanced at Juliet. She said, "Though, this particular inconvenience is also *helpful* in some ways."

"Is it?" the earl asked.

"Well, I didn't like to say," she said, "as it's to do with womanly problems."

"It is?"

Cordelia, Juliet, and Miss Mayton all nodded gravely.

The earl, always helpless in the face of womanly problems, which were a series of mysteries he would very much like to remain mysteries, waved his hands. "We'll say no more about it."

Lord Darling bleated at him, as if to confirm that he'd made a wise choice.

The drawing room doors opened and Viola, now Lady Baderston, entered with her new husband.

Viola crossed the room and was with them in a trice, throwing her arms round her sisters. Lord Baderston greeted the earl. Then he said, "Gad, you've got a goat in here."

The earl looked askance at the goat. Cordelia thought that, for all his willingness to overlook Lord Darling's presence on account of women's problems, he was not that eager for his newest son-in-law to notice it.

"That is Lord Darling, Lord Baderston," Cordelia said, "as I know you to be a particularly genial and liberal gentleman, I am convinced you shan't mind it."

Lord Baderston, having been named both genial and liberal, could not of course mind it. He nodded as if it were the most usual thing in the world.

Cordelia heard more noise from the front hall—the more difficult hurdle had arrived. Conbatten.

Rosalind floated into the room on the arm of her duke. "Sisters!" she cried. "How I have longed to see you. Dear Aunt, you are looking marvelous."

What commenced over the next few minutes was a flurry of embraces, examination of dresses, interrogations regarding health and happiness, explanations as to Lord Darling's presence, and flighty giggles.

Those things having run their course, Conbatten, who stood ever so well put together and taking in the scene from under his hooded eyes, said, "I feel I should be surprised at noticing a goat here, and yet I am not."

"My darling Conbatten is so rarely taken off his guard," Rosalind said. "Just the other day, I brought home two Chartreux kittens and they very naughtily got into his neckcloths and made a frightful mess of it. He did not lose his equanimity for even a moment."

"I dared not," Conbatten said, "My valet was in a state of apoplexy and one of us had to keep our head."

"Poor Henri," Rosalind said, "Always threatening to throw himself into the Thames over the slightest mishap."

Darden came into the room and once more there was a flurry of greetings. "Well! We are the merry party, are we not?"

"We most certainly are," the earl said.

"I see Lord Darling has weaseled his way in," Darden said laughing.

"Yes, well as to that," the earl said, "it was unavoidable. Ah, there is Tattleton giving me the signal. We can go through."

DARDEN WAS OF course right—they were a very merry party. News of all sorts was exchanged, and Miss Mayton recounted the final words of Gregorio before he perished on his library floor after dealing himself a deadly blow. Neither Lord Baderston nor the duke challenged the story, very unlike Van Doren who was always trying to shoot it full of holes.

Conbatten even said, "He was admirably effusive, Miss Mayton, though his lifeblood was fast draining into the carpet."

Miss Mayton nodded and murmured, "A man in love always is, no matter the circumstance."

Cook had done a first-rate job on the dinner and Tattleton was at his stiff and upright best. Cordelia was certain they were both cognizant of having a duke in the house, especially Tattleton.

Finally, the dessert course was going round and they were coming close to when the ladies must retire and leave the men to their port.

Cordelia wished to say something though, before they must rise. She wished to ask something. The situation with Lord Harveston was like a constant little itch in her mind.

Was it a situation, though? What was it, exactly?

Cordelia was not certain. She only knew that it irked her in some fashion that he held her in disdain. It irked her that knowledge wrung from books was to be the yardstick with which she was measured.

"I would like to ask the gentlemen a question," she said. "And of course you too, Papa."

The earl smiled. "I am flattered to be named one of the company of gentlemen at table."

"Oh, you do know what I mean," Cordelia said, laughing.

"Indeed, I do, my dear."

"I wonder, is it better that a gentleman spend all his time with his nose in a book, or should he spend all his time on physical activities?"

"Must it be either or?" Lord Baderston asked.

"It is not that it *must* be either or," Cordelia said, "it is just that sometimes it *is* either or."

This did not seem to clear things up for Lord Baderston. Darden was looking just as befuddled.

"Perhaps," Conbatten said, "it would be quicker to the finish to just name the two gentlemen in question?"

She had not thought she would be asked to name them.

"It's Lord Harveston and Lord Hamill," Juliet said.

"Ah, is there a rivalry between them for your heart, Cordy?" Rosalind asked.

"No! Certainly not! I was just wondering about…the merits of the thing."

"Were you?" Viola asked. "I am surprised, though, Cordy. Lord Hamill is a Corinthian and Lord Harveston is…well, I do not know what he is. Rather serious, I'm afraid."

"Harveston is a good friend," Lord Baderston said.

"I second that," Darden said. "He is just, well he's the sort of fellow that…becomes a good friend on further acquaintance."

"And Hamill?" Cordelia asked, hoping they would tell her something that would intrigue her.

"Hamill is a jolly fellow," Darden said.

"Always good for sport," Lord Baderston said.

"If he is on his horse, I lay my bets in his direction," Conbatten said.

"I have only noticed that one of them reads everything and the other reads nothing," Cordelia said.

"There is no point in comparing them, I do not think," Conbatten said. "They are two ends of a spectrum. One somehow stumbled his way through Oxford and the other would stumble in a boxing ring."

"That reminds me, you never did say, Cordelia," Darden said, "how you and Miss Mayton made out at Harveston's literary salon."

Cordelia certainly did not know why stumbling through Oxford or stumbling in a boxing ring should remind Darden of them going to the salon.

"We were lost ducklings bobbing in the ocean," Miss Mayton said. "A Shakespeare play nobody has ever heard of, then another play by another fellow and did he have the first play in his possession? It was rather grueling until we ladies decided to have our own more pleasant conversations."

Cordelia noted Conbatten suppressing the smallest smile. In a rather defensive tone, she said, "We could not know anything about it, as we did not have the schedule of discussions as everybody else did. We are far more prepared for the next salon."

"They were in the library for above an hour this morning," the earl said, as if to back up her claim.

"Goodness," Rosalind said, "what were you studying?"

"It is not so much what we were studying," Miss Mayton said, "as it was what we decided we would not study."

"We decided to use womanly judgment," Juliet said in a defiant tone, "as women have been doing since time began. I dare Aristotle to write an ode about *that*."

Before anybody could comment on Aristotle writing an ode at this late date in his history, Benny raced into the dining room, breathless. "The goat," he said. "He's gone out the open window in the drawing room!"

The gentlemen sprung out of their seats and raced through the doors, with only the earl trailing behind. The ladies were not far behind them.

They must find Lord Darling! He might be run down under carriage wheels or stolen or lost and wandering round forlorn!

Cordelia did not stop for her cloak but ran out the doors and to the streets with Juliet on her heels.

Lord Darling was on the street and not so much lost as he was refusing to be caught. Conbatten ran one way, Darden the other way, and Lord Baderston took up the rear.

The dear little goat trotted this way and that and occasionally sprung up in the air for good measure. He seemed to look upon it as a very good game.

As the scene unfolded in front of her, Cordelia heard hoof-beats approaching from behind her.

She turned so she might warn the rider to steer clear of the chaos. Then she stopped short.

"Lord Harveston?"

HOW PERCIVAL HAD come to be at Portland Place, he could not precisely explain. He did not know anybody on that street except for Darden, nor had he been invited to any house on that street on this particular night.

Hours before, he had plowed ahead in his reading of the ladies' favored novels and even taken the second book into the dining room. There, he had read of the two dukes, one of which was an impostor, and the aged butler who thought he was dismissed but was too nearsighted to find his luggage.

As if that hadn't been bad enough, Makepeace had chosen that moment to give him his assessment of the beleaguered inhabitants of Grimwood Hall.

His butler paced the room as Percival helped himself to a plate of beef.

"The duke is in love with, guess who? That's right, another gentle governess. There is no impediment to the couple, as his original duchess is dead at the bottom of the well. Oh wait, there is the small matter of the gentle governess not being entirely sure if the duke has murdered that lady currently residing in the well."

Percival downed his wine and motioned to the footman. His glass was speedily refilled.

"Do not fear," Makepeace continued, "our gentle governess is not left to wonder long! Why, you wonder? Because the duchess is not dead at all! No, she was knocked out and left in a cave by the housekeeper who, naturally, has designs on the duke. An old crone who lived in the woods discovered the duchess and nursed her back to health. Isn't it always an old crone living in the woods? One wonders how these old crones manage to eat, living by themselves in the woods as they do!"

Percival ignored Makepeace's wonderment over the old crone. "So, at least it breaks the mold a bit, does it not? The duchess is restored and the gentle governess does not win her man."

Makepeace laughed, a sardonic sort of laugh. "How naïve! Of course the gentle governess marries the duke. How can that be? It seems the duchess becomes enraged upon discovering her duke's love for the governess, a fight ensues, and the duchess accidently goes over the side of the well. Dead at the bottom of the well after all."

"Surely not?" Percival asked, certain his butler was just making things up to express his displeasure over the assignment.

"Surely so," Makepeace said. "I feel as if my brain has shrunk three sizes in the contemplation of it. Those ladies must be driven out!"

By ladies, he was perfectly aware that his butler was not talking about the gentle governesses, but rather his aunt's acting troupe.

"But, what happened to the housekeeper who started the whole thing by leaving the duchess in a cave?"

"Nothing happened! They do not even look for her. They are in love and do not wish to sit through a trial!"

Percival had then directed his butler to take the rest of the night off and help himself to the good port amidst the snorts of the footmen. Though the footmen both admired and feared Makepeace, they could not help but find his histrionics endlessly entertaining.

Percival had spent the rest of his dinner mulling over what both he and Makepeace had read.

All he could come up with was that the plots were so improbable that one could not possibly guess where they were going.

Perhaps that was it. He might comment upon the twists and turns. They were ridiculous twists and rather stupid turns, but he need not include those adjectives.

Relieved that he had at least come up with one thing he might say, he ordered his horse, determined to ride out and clear his head.

As he walked his horse down one avenue after the next, taking in the night air, his thoughts kept drifting to Lady Cordelia's household.

He really could not understand it. Darden seemed such a sensible fellow and the earl too, for that matter. Why on earth would they allow random gentlemen into their house to stay? It was a particularly bad idea, considering there were eligible young ladies in the house.

Percival did not suppose that Chester, whoever that fellow was, had got very far if he had designs on one of the ladies. A gentleman screaming all the time would be hard-pressed to inspire any sort of feeling beyond irritation.

This Lord Darling, though. He did not know the man so could not assess his circumstances, but he was a lord, after all.

Where had he come from? Was he Scottish?

Lady Cordelia, at least, found him eminently charming. Did the earl and Darden not perceive the danger?

Perhaps not, perhaps they were encouraging a match. Still, to have the gentleman move in seemed rather…shocking, he supposed.

Unless, of course, he was some kind of relative. A distant cousin perhaps.

That must be the likely answer.

Somehow, his horse turned down Portland Place. He thought he ought to turn round, as the street was enclosed and did not lead to another.

He did, though, feel the urge to go past the Bennington's house. He could not say what he thought he would see there. Maybe he would spot Lord Darling coming or going. But what then? And why did he concern himself with it?

What he ended up seeing was not something he could have conjured in his imagination.

Lord Darden, Lord Baderston, and the Duke of Conbatten had surrounded a kid who was leaping into the air as if taunting those gentlemen. Miss Mayton stood in the doorway with the earl, cheering them on.

Lady Cordelia and another lady, who he presumed to be her younger sister stood just before his horse as he reined him in.

"Lord Harveston?" Lady Cordelia said.

CHAPTER TEN

S HE WAS LOOKING very pretty in the moonlight, dressed in a simple yet well-cut muslin with embroidered roses round the bodice. He had an almost overwhelming feeling of wishing to begin again, to erase the encounters they'd had and just start over.

Her sister turned and looked him over. "So this is Lord Harveston," she said. Her tone did not convey that she found anything good about being Lord Harveston.

He wondered what she'd been told.

Probably that he was insufferable.

"Lady Cordelia, Lady…"

"Lady Juliet."

"Good evening. I am sorry, I seem to have intruded upon…"

Lady Cordelia had turned back to look at the scene. "Ah, there. Conbatten has got him, that naughty little boy."

Lady Juliet called out, "Papa, do see that the window is closed so he cannot escape again."

The earl gamely nodded and disappeared into the doorway.

"The goat escaped from your house?" Percival said.

"Well, he would have," Lady Cordelia said, "he is our goat after all." Standing on her toes, she said loudly, "Very well done, Conbatten! You too, Darden and Lord Baderston. Well done, gentlemen."

Two other ladies raced out of the house to greet the returning heroes and Percival recognized them as Lady Rosalind, now Conbatten's duchess, and Lady Viola, just recently become Lady Baderston.

It seemed the whole extended family was in attendance on the runaway goat, but for Lady Van Doren, who he understood was at home in the countryside.

Percival began to feel as if he had intruded upon a family party, which he supposed he had. He should probably not be surprised that a Bennington family party included a goat hopping around on the street.

"What brings you this way, Lord Harveston?" Lady Juliet asked. "I presume you call on one of our neighbors."

Percival felt he was being cornered. She was rather bold for a young lady not yet out.

"I was merely exercising my horse and did not pay too much attention to where I was going."

Both Lady Juliet and Lady Cordelia looked critically at his horse, as if to ascertain how much the beast was enjoying wandering round Town with no destination in mind.

"As I have very accidentally encountered you, Lady Cordelia," he said, determined to have his say on some recent books he'd read, "I had been thinking of recommending some books—"

"Recommending books?" Lady Cordelia said, in what he was certain was an offended tone.

"We know all about your books, Lord Harveston," Lady Juliet said. "Men write in circles, hoping to befuddle their readers into thinking they've said something remarkable. A bunch of Mr. Peabodys—we'll depend upon womanly good sense, thank you very much."

Who was Mr. Peabody?

"Jules, do stop," Lady Cordelia said. Though she admonished her sister, she also looked amused.

"I was thinking of the novels written by Richard Roydon," Percival said, determined to plow ahead, "but then it occurred to me that you would already be aware of those works. I had not realized that *The Dreadful Doings of Dembric Dale* was one of his when my aunt mentioned the title to me. My butler has since brought me a copy."

Both ladies' brows wrinkled.

"Do you mean to say that you enjoy those stories?" Lady Cordelia asked.

"I say I must admire the author's originality," Percival said. "There are so many twists and turns, one can hardly keep up."

"That is what my father admires in them, too," Lady Cordelia said thoughtfully.

Good Lord, the earl read that drivel?

"Our aunt, Miss Mayton, reads them to us," Juliet said. "She's a terrific storyteller."

"Indeed, I have heard it said," Percival said. He did not mention that absolutely everybody had heard that particular thing said of Miss Mayton and the stories she told.

"Harveston," Lord Darden said, approaching them.

"Darden," he said. "I was just exercising my horse." It sounded very stupid, even to his own ears, but he felt compelled to invent some excuse for being there. He could not say how or why he'd really come, as he was not at all certain, but it seemed to need some sort of explanation.

"Lord Harveston was just telling us that he enjoys reading the same stories our aunt reads to us," the very pert Lady Juliet said.

"Really?" Darden asked, all surprise. "Dreadful doings and horrible happenstances?"

"Awful happenstances, Darden," Lady Cordelia corrected.

"Ah, yes," Percival said, wishing to show his familiarity, "the awful events taking place at Grimwood Hall. Very ironic that the duchess ends up down a well through her own doing."

"That is what my father thought!" Lady Cordelia exclaimed.

"Well, if you are such an admirer," Darden said, "you ought to come in. Miss Mayton is poised to read to us and father says we'll have our port in the drawing room so as not to delay further."

"I do not wish to inconvenience, I am not at all dressed—"

"No inconvenience at all," Darden said. "A man in his riding clothes is welcome in our drawing room. Is that not right, Cordelia? We are just an informal party tonight. If you have not yet had your dinner, I'm sure we can fix up a plate for you."

Lady Cordelia did not look particularly enthusiastic, but said nothing. Lady Juliet did not say anything either, though her expression spoke volumes. The gist of it was, "go away."

"I have already dined, and I really do not wish to—"

"Benny," Darden called to a footman, "take Lord Harveston's horse to the stables. Johnny, tell Tattleton we will need an extra glass for port."

WHILE PERCIVAL FOUND himself in the Benningtons' drawing room, he could not fathom how it had happened. He'd just taken his horse out to clear his head, then somehow turned down Portland Place, then witnessed a goat's escape and subsequent capture, and now was poised to listen to the very story that he had struggled through earlier in the day.

The goat, and he still had not been given any rational explanation as to why there was a goat in the house, had been sent to bed in the servants' quarters. One of the footmen had carried him off, his bleats eventually fading to nothing.

Though the goat was gone, his particular scent lingered on. Then, he could not help but notice that a footman had come in and used the fireplace shovel to swiftly dispose of the goat's last fond farewell to the party.

Why did they have a farm animal in the house? He could not think it at all usual!

He glanced round the room. Lady Cordelia was sitting very prettily between Lady Juliet and Lady Baderston. Lady Juliet was scribbling furiously in a diary of some sort. The duchess and Conbatten were squeezed together in an oversized chair and appeared very happy to be so. Darden and Baderston were talking of YBC matters in low tones, the earl was in his repose, eyes half closed. Miss Mayton held the book in her hands, ready to address her court.

There was no sign of either Chester or Lord Darling and no mention had been made of those two houseguests. Percival was burning to ask about them, but could not think of a way to introduce the subject.

If these gentlemen were relations of some sort, the conversation would be very comfortable. But what if they were not? How to bring up the subject without casting some sort of aspersion on the situation or hinting that it was odd or not quite the thing?

"As we know," Miss Mayton said, "the duke gave up his fortune to Mr. Denbrow in order to wed his daughter, but he insisted on being named Mr. Denbrow's heir. Now, the duke and duchess are living in poverty and, while Mr. Denbrow is rich, he is also fearing for his life. Will one of the many servants the duke was forced to dismiss attempt a murder? Or might it be the duke himself, in order to regain his fortune? The kitchen maid has just delivered another note full of threats. Chapter four."

Mr. Denbrow could not go on as he was. He rarely slept, and when he did, he had one eye open. He was exhausted and it was very hard to enjoy being rich when one was exhausted.

He was determined to get to the bottom of the threats being delivered one after another. But how to do it?

The kitchen maid came once again to his library. "Here's another one," she said, dropping it on his desk. "They's comin' in like birds to roost."

Mr. Denbrow ripped open the paper and read it. Again, another threat! This time, he would be tied to a tree and coated in bacon grease. Then, a bear from the circus would be let loose very nearby. After he was sufficiently mauled to death and half eaten, whatever was left of him would be used as fishing bait.

"Ya seem upset," the kitchen maid said.

Mr. Denbrow glared at her.

"I'm only sayin' you ought to take steps. If you was to marry and have a son, then that little fella just born would be the

heir, no matter what you signed."

"Is that true?" Mr. Denbrow asked, clutching at the idea as if it were a branch that might pull him out of swift water.

The kitchen maid nodded. "And what would you say to marryin' a gal who already proved she can produce a babe?"

The girl turned and showed her profile. Mr. Denbrow had not noticed it before, what with his own problems to think about, but she was very clearly with child.

"We hitch up at the altar and then three months later, you got a son on the ground."

"But wait, you cannot know it is a boy."

"Oh, I know it," the girl said. "I'm carryin' low."

Could that be the answer to his problems? It was not perfect, of course it was not. For one, he'd have to marry the kitchen maid. He did not even know her name, and he was fairly sure he did not like her. For another, it would really only solve the problem of the duke murdering him to get his fortune back. It would do nothing to appease the villagers who had been dismissed from the duke's service.

"I reckon," the maid said, "that you get a son and then take your piles of money and your wife and babe and move away so as nobody can touch you. I heard Spain is always sunshine, it don't hardly rain there."

Spain? That would be a nice change of pace. The dale seemed to trap clouds and rain overhead. And then, could any of these disgruntled servants chase him to the continent? He couldn't think they'd have the means to do it!

He would be free. He would be able to sleep.

Miss Mayton laid down the book. "So now we wonder, will Mr. Denbrow marry the kitchen maid and move to Spain to escape the clutches of his would-be murderers?"

Percival, of course, already knew the answer to that question. And what an answer it was.

"I'm always left on tenterhooks over it," the earl said. "What say you, Lord Harveston?"

All eyes turned in his direction. He said, "I find it simply astonishing."

"Well said," the earl answered.

Lady Juliet stood. "I suppose you'll want to hear the ode I just composed?"

"I could not rest if we did not," Conbatten said.

Percival could not tell if the duke was joking or not.

Lady Juliet held her book up to read. *"Ode to a Traveler."*

He turns this way and that with no direction in mind
Walking and trotting, through London they wind
His horse is confused and thinks 'where do we goes?'
Less confused is the gentleman, who already knows.

My God, was that about him? Did she suggest that he meant to end up at Portland Place? That it was by design?

The party clapped, and so did Percival as he knew not what else to do. Perhaps nobody had thought to connect him to the ode. That was, if naming it an ode was not too lofty for whatever that had been. Where do we 'goes,' indeed.

"Ah, that sounds very like you, Lord Harveston," Miss Mayton said. "Suddenly turning up like that."

"No, of course not, I was only wandering, I never thought to—"

"You are always welcome, Lord Harveston," the earl said jovially. "All of Darden's friends are welcome, however they end up here."

⇶⫷

THOUGH IT MIGHT not be usual that one's married sisters accompanied one above stairs, both Conbatten and Lord Baderston were not at all surprised to be left waiting in the drawing room while Rosalind and Viola went up.

The sisters had all crowded into Cordelia's bedchamber while

Lynette fussed with clothes and hair.

"What did you think of my ode, Cordy?" Juliet asked, eyeing her sister.

"I think you hinted that Lord Harveston arrived here by design," Cordelia said. "I am sure he was galled by the idea. You have managed to punish him as I could not and he seemed to know it. Well done."

"But I did not do it only as a punishment," Juliet said.

"Ah, you think he *did* mean to come here," Viola said.

"So it is not even the plot at Dembric Dale that thickens," Rosalind said. "Cordy's plot thickens too."

"There is no plot," Cordelia said. "There is no reason why Lord Harveston should mean to end in front of our house, it was just happenstance."

"Bosh to that," Juliet said. "If he were to be out simply exercising his horse, there are far better routes."

"That is true," Viola said. "He is at Bedford Square. He might have had a very pleasant ride round Russell Square."

"Yes, that is the route I would have chosen too," Rosalind said. "When Conbatten and I ride out, he always puts me just ahead of him so he might watch out for danger, so I often choose the route. Certainly, that is the way I would have gone."

Viola propped her chin on her hands as she lay across Cordelia's bed. "Conbatten is still intent on saving you from things then, Ros?"

"Terribly so. I adore him for it."

"And the baths?" Cordelia asked.

"Still precisely ninety-eight degrees with chilled champagne."

"Lovely," Viola said.

"Now, Viola," Rosalind said, "I know you have written that you get on famously with Baderston and it surely looks so, but now that we are just us sisters, how is it for you?"

"We are two peas, same pod," Viola said with the slightest blush. "He is such a loyal fellow—we really do not like to be apart."

"And your difficult mother-in-law?" Rosalind asked.

"Far less difficult. She's given up the fight and when she does not fight she is very pleasant. She often asks about Papa and I think she admires him still."

"Did I tell you I just got a letter from Beatrice? She says her comfort is still Van Doren's first concern and that Lily has him entirely conquered. If dear little Lily babbles anything even remotely sounding like Papa, he is a puddle."

"When we see them over the summer," Viola said, "I am going to paint Lily, even though Van Doren has claimed it will be over his dead body that they hang it anywhere in the house. I wrote Beatrice that I would be happy to hang it over his dead body if that was what he is insisting upon."

"Van Doren," Rosalind said, laughing, "he never changes. Thank goodness Bea is delighted with him."

"All right," Juliet interrupted, "everybody is deliriously happy and blah, blah, blah. The question at hand is what does Lord Harveston mean by pushing in tonight?"

"He hardly pushed in, Jules," Cordelia said. "Darden practically dragged him in. You were there, you heard our brother."

"He could not have been dragged if he had not been there," Juliet pointed out. "Furthermore, do you not think it odd that suddenly he is interested in the books that *you're* interested in?"

Cordelia paused. That had been a surprise, of course. She had not imagined that Lord Harveston would be the least interested in the dreadful doings in the dale.

"Perhaps I have only misjudged him," Cordelia said. "He can be terribly rude and I believe he is very impressed with himself, but it may have been wrong to jump to the conclusion that I knew absolutely everything about him."

Juliet sighed, though it was really more of a groan. "Are you all blind? He is trying to apologize for his wretched behavior. I'd lay money on the idea that the first time he picked up one of those books was today. He was very determined to work it into a conversation."

He *had* been determined. Could Juliet be right? If her sister was right, what did it mean?

She did not know, but she could not help but admit that he'd been far more pleasant this night than he had been before. And that he'd looked rather smashing in his riding clothes.

It certainly would be a lot of effort, if he'd read the books only on her account.

"Mark me," Juliet said, "Harveston has designs. That's right, I said it. Designs."

"Surely not," Cordelia said, hoping her cheeks had not gone red.

"Surely so," Juliet said. "I tell you to put you on your guard. I would not like him to trick you into something and then you wake up one morning and realize you've wed a bookish gentleman. You will not be happy unless you marry a Corinthian, you've said so many times."

Cordelia was thoughtful. Softly she said, "Do you suppose there are many more of them? Corinthians? Aside from Lord Hamill, I mean."

"Lord Hamill does not cause the signs of love?" Miss Mayton asked.

"No, unfortunately Lord Hamill does not cause the signs of anything. I cannot think why, but it is so."

"Then, we must dig up more Corinthians," Viola said. "Ros, ask Conbatten about it, surely he will know."

Rosalind nodded. "He did say Lord Jeffries was returning from South America from some business or other having to do with mining. He said the lord will require purchasing more horses and he has very specific standards. That sounds Corinthian-like, does it not?"

"It really does," Miss Mayton said. "Perhaps all this palaver that's gone on was just the fates' way of passing the time before your real Corinthian could make his appearance."

"Trust in the fates, Cordy," Rosalind said. "They always have your happiness in mind."

Cordelia felt very buoyed by the idea. An as yet unknown Corinthian was making his way to London. Surely, she would feel the signs of love when she encountered him.

Miss Mayton's maid, Fleur, poked her head in the door. "I've been given a desperate message from Johnny to deliver to you. The duke says he will do a violence to himself if he is parted from his duchess longer. Lord Baderston agreed and said he will do a violence to himself if he cannot go home to his bed."

The sisters burst into laughter. Viola and Rosalind jumped from the bed and kissed their sisters and Miss Mayton.

They hurried down the stairs to stop their husbands from doing a violence to themselves out of desperate love, desperate boredom, or a bit of both.

TATTLETON HAD BEEN accustomed to understanding his own feelings as they came upon him. In truth, his feelings had always been comfortingly straightforward. Happy, unhappy, content, not content.

What a whirl of emotions overtook him now!

On the one hand, the duke and his duchess had been to dine, a thing he might speak about in those instances when he encountered one of his peers. Cook had held up his end and rolled out a dinner fit for any palace. Tattleton had brought up the most sublime wines from the cellar.

If he were to only examine those facts, the dinner had been a rousing success.

There were other facts floating around, though.

That goat had been seen by the duke, and no doubt smelled by that illustrious personage too. The Duke of Conbatten now understood that Horace Tattleton was a butler who presided over a drawing room attended by a farm animal.

Worse, the despicable little creature had the temerity to draw attention to itself even further by leaping out a window just as Tattleton was taking round the dessert wine.

It was an affront! He'd selected a superior German ice wine with hints of apricot and honey, a choice he was certain the duke would approve of. How was a duke to approve of a butler's wine selection if he was running undignified on the street trying to catch a goat as if he were a lowly farmer?

Just now, the butler glared at the creature, fast asleep on good blankets meant for people, as if he hadn't done a thing wrong.

That goat had no conscience.

Mrs. Huffson sat down beside him, the rest of the staff finally in their beds. He poured her a large brandy.

"I understand you had a time of it tonight, Mr. Tattleton," the housekeeper said comfortably.

"To call it 'a time' is to underestimate what I have experienced, Mrs. Huffson."

The housekeeper glanced over at the sleeping goat. "The little mite made a nuisance of himself. Well, that cannot be laid at your door, the young ladies did insist on having him in the drawing room."

"The duke noted there was a goat in the drawing room. The drawing room I oversee. Then, the duke was forced to run round the street in the most unbecoming manner possible to catch it."

Mrs. Huffson nodded sympathetically. "The whole palaver makes Miss Mayton's terrible novels seem not so bad, does it not?"

"Is that what we've come to? Hoping other unfortunate circumstances seem not so bad by comparison?"

Mrs. Huffson shrugged. "What I wonder is, how did Lord Harveston end up here? Nobody just passes by Portland Place on their way to another destination."

This idea seized Tattleton's mind in the most uncomfortable manner. He was certain the ladies were up to something, they were always up to something. Earlier in the day, they spent an hour in the library, tearing half the books off the shelf only to decide they would depend upon womanly judgment when it came to intellectual questions. Then Lord Harveston, the host of an intellectual salon, unexpectedly turns up.

What was going on?

"I cannot say how or why Lord Harveston arrived at our door, but I do know that gentleman is in for a surprise. Miss Mayton and Lady Cordelia have determined that they will rely on their own judgment as it relates to the great questions being asked at his salon."

"Rely on…their own judgment?" Mrs. Huffson said, concern creeping into her tone.

"Their own judgment alone, Mrs. Huffson. Aristotle and Thomas Aquinas cannot be counted upon."

"Oh dear."

CHAPTER ELEVEN

For the moment at least, all thought of Lord Harveston and his salons and his opinions were entirely absent from Cordelia's mind. She and Miss Mayton were attending their first rehearsal in Lady Rawley's drawing room.

"Now, Miss Mayton and Lady Cordelia," Lady Rawley said, pouring cups of tea, "as my dear friends Lady Agatha and Mrs. Robinson already know, this first meeting is about concept."

"We always delight in the announcement of the concept," Mrs. Robinson said.

"We never guess where it is going," Lady Agatha said.

Lady Rawley nodded graciously. "It is very fortuitous that we have added two esteemed new members to our troupe this season, as it is a particularly special year."

"You said it would be in your last letter," Lady Agatha said, "I am on tenterhooks over it."

Cordelia could only be pleased that this year would be somehow special, though she did not yet know what the specialness might be.

"I had a notion that there is one Shakespeare play in particular that has always needed the most work. I have acted upon that notion. We will, as an acting troupe, bring our new vision of it to life. I bring you, *Othello Redux*."

Othello! Cordelia could hardly stay seated. How she longed to perform her Desdemona on the stage.

"I think we can all see where Shakespeare went so terribly wrong in this one," Lady Rawley said.

"I must admit," Mrs. Robinson said, "it is not a favorite, what with everybody dying or going to prison."

"Yes, indeed," Lady Agatha said. "Why should Desdemona die when she's done nothing at all wrong?"

"My thoughts exactly," Lady Rawley said approvingly.

Cordelia was entirely stumped. Desdemona does not die? How would she do her death scene, the scene she'd practiced and perfected, if Desdemona does not die?

"This is very exciting," Miss Mayton said, "I have never thought it possible that Desdemona does not die."

"I propose that Desdemona has been secretly in love with Cassio," Lady Rawley said. "So, when Iago plants her handkerchief in Cassio's room and arranges for Othello to discover it, he has inadvertently pushed those two lovers together. Naturally, Othello will wish to kill Desdemona, but she will be one step ahead. She announces she will drink poison. She seems dead, but it is only a sleeping draught."

Cordelia's forehead wrinkled. That sounded very like Juliet's ruse to escape with Romeo. On the other hand, though Desdemona would not die, it would look like she's dying. Surely, something could be made of that.

"Then," Lady Rawley said, "Iago's wife makes her appearance and reveals it was Iago who planted the handkerchief. Othello raises his sword, as does Iago, and they kill each other."

"Leaving Desdemona and Cassio free to marry!" Lady Agatha exclaimed.

"Just so," Lady Rawley said, seeming very pleased. "Lady Agatha, I depend upon you for Othello. Mrs. Robinson, you will play Iago."

The two ladies looked at one another. "Goodness, we're to have a sword fight!" Lady Agatha exclaimed.

"Miss Mayton, I know you shall be brilliant at Emilia, Iago's wife, who reveals the shocking secret."

"Oh, I do love a shocking secret," Miss Mayton said.

Cordelia felt her heart pound in her chest. It seemed an unreal dream that she would play the Desdemona who lived. Inspiration was flying at her from all directions.

"Lady Cordelia, you have my full confidence as Cassio. I, of course, will play Desdemona."

Cassio? She was not to be Desdemona? She was to be Cassio?

Lady Rawley's butler opened the doors to the drawing room and said, "Lord Harveston, my lady."

Lord Harveston?

Cordelia's thoughts could not keep up with the new ideas being presented. She was to be Cassio, not Desdemona, and Lord Harveston had arrived? What was happening?

⇥⟫⟫⟨⟨⇤

OF ALL THE letters Percival had received from his aunt, none had been so cryptic. His attendance was requested, no, it was insisted upon, at two o'clock. It must be two o'clock as it was of the utmost importance.

She'd not bothered to explain what was of the utmost importance, though he could make a reasonable guess at it.

He'd made Lady Cordelia upset at Almack's. Plenty of people had seen it and Lady Hightower had already made her opinion decidedly known. He supposed others were commenting on it and, if his aunt had not observed it herself, she'd since been told about it.

She wished to call him on the carpet and demand an explanation for being insufferable.

It was odd, though. Lady Rawley was pushy and intrusive, but he'd never known her to be stern and scolding.

Nevertheless, he would not make things worse by not attending her. He would simply go and explain the situation, including the steps he'd taken to remedy it.

In fact, somewhere in that conversation, he might be able to work in the idea that his salon was really not the right venue for her acting troupe. She was unlikely to take that news as the affront that Lady Cordelia had.

Lady Rawley's long-suffering butler, Jones, led him into the drawing room.

He stopped short when he noted his aunt's entire acting troupe gathered round a tea tray.

"My dear boy," she said, rising and coming to his side.

"Aunt," he said, by way of greeting.

He felt fairly transfixed where he stood. Lady Cordelia was staring at him as if he were a ghost. He rather wished he was a ghost and could float through one of the walls, making a speedy exit. This felt like some sort of trap.

Lady Rawley turned to her friends. "I have been holding this back as a surprise, but look who has come to assist us!"

Assist? What on earth was she talking about?

"My dear nephew, once apprised that we would be employing swords, could not but wish to provide instruction. I hardly needed to even ask."

Hardly needed to even ask? She had not asked at all! His mind moved at a rapid pace. What did she mean? How to remove himself from whatever she meant? Instruction? With swords?

"Swords?" he said.

"Indeed," Lady Rawley said cheerfully. "Othello and Iago kill each other, you see."

He was afraid he did see. His aunt, as had been her habit, found herself dissatisfied with a Shakespeare ending and had taken to rewriting it. He could only suppose Desdemona somehow lived happily ever after. Another of Shakespeare's greatest works was set to go spiraling down a drain in her drawing room.

"Now, Lady Agatha and Mrs. Robinson," Lady Rawley barreled on, "come to where we will have the stage and let us block out that sword fight. Miss Mayton, you had best come too, since it will be your words that set off the fight. Lady Cordelia, if you would be so kind as to pour a cup of tea for my nephew and apprise him of the plot, that would be very helpful."

It was a trap. But why? Why did his aunt wish him to assist her in butchering Shakespeare?

As he could not turn on his heel and run out of the room, though he would very much like to, he approached the table and sat down.

His aunt, Lady Agatha, Mrs. Robinson, and Miss Mayton had crossed the room and were heads together. Blocking out the sword fight, he supposed.

Lady Cordelia poured him a cup of tea and handed it over. "I am surprised, Lord Harveston, to find you wish to help your aunt with her play."

That statement felt like a trap too. If he said he thought the whole enterprise ridiculous, which he did, she would be insulted.

"I am rather surprised myself," he said, "as I have just found out about it."

"I see," she said.

It was a noncommittal statement, and Percival could not determine what she meant by it. Perhaps he could not work it out because he was spending too much of his thoughts on examining an escaped wisp of hair that rested very charmingly on her forehead. A very pretty color hair too, which prompted the outrageous thought of what it might look like if all the pins were to suddenly fall out of it.

What was wrong with him? He pinched the side of his leg to force himself back to the matter at hand.

He did feel that he had made strides the evening before to atone for his behavior at Almack's. He did not wish to slide backward now.

"Lady Cordelia," he said, wishing to get through the thing as quickly as possible, "I could not help but notice that I discomposed you at Almack's. I must apologize for my behavior."

"I was not at all discomposed," Lady Cordelia said. "I merely pointed out that you were rude. Do you make a habit of it?"

"A habit…no, I do not believe so. Though, I must think I sometimes express myself badly—I did not intend to cast any aspersions on anybody."

Lady Cordelia nodded and he got the feeling he'd got as far as he was going to get.

"I believe my aunt wished you to apprise me of the new plot?"

⇛⥼⥼

CORDELIA FELT SHE'D been left in a trap somehow. Lord Harveston had very unexpectedly turned up, at least, unexpected by her. Then, Lady Rawley had whisked everybody else to the other side of the drawing room, leaving them alone.

Miss Mayton had claimed that she thought Lady Rawley may have been imagining a match between her and Lord Harveston. Cordelia had dismissed it, but perhaps her aunt had been right all along?

But what an idea! How had Lady Rawley even thought of it? They were so ill-suited. Even his apology had been a bit of weak tea.

She glanced at him. It was not that he was not handsome, he was very handsome as it happened. He was very tall and lean, he might even be a smidge taller than Conbatten. And then, he did have a lovely smile, on the few occasions he chose to show it—his eyes crinkled in a rather delightful manner.

But his arms were quite usually proportioned, his tailor would not despair to encase them. As well, nobody talked about Lord Harveston's prowess in a boxing ring, or atop a horse in a race. He was not a Corinthian. In truth, he was not at all a sporting man, as far as she could see.

And his manner! That was another thing entirely. He was rude and condescending and full of himself. He looked down upon other people he did not deem as sophisticated as he was. It was very bad, indeed.

Of course, he had not seemed quite so bad the evening before. He had worked to make himself pleasant. And then, he had made some sort of apology just now.

A small light, like a far-off flame, lit itself in Cordelia's mind. It occurred to her that what really bothered her about Lord Harveston was that he did not admire her or her accomplishments. Even if she did not admire him, it irked her that he did not admire her.

She felt herself pink as she thought it, as she knew it was not a quality of temperament to brag of.

Now he wished to know the plot to *Othello Redux*. If felt like another opportunity for him to display a looking down the nose.

"Well," she said, "Lady Rawley is against having Desdemona die, and I really can see her point."

Lord Harveston nodded. "It was deeply unfair, as she was entirely innocent."

"Exactly," Cordelia said, feeling a little encouraged. "So when Othello very stupidly believes Iago and wishes to kill his wife for her supposed adultery, she pretends to take poison. Then Iago's wife reveals all and Othello and Iago kill each other."

"It's not the worst idea my aunt has had in rewriting Shakespeare. I suppose they both deserve it," Lord Harveston said. "Iago for his villainous deeds and Othello for not realizing he was being tricked."

"Othello could have realized it though," Cordelia said. "That has always bothered me."

"You say he should have believed his wife's denials? I am inclined to agree. Especially over a man who was a malcontent."

"It should never have come to Othello choosing who to believe," Cordelia said. "If he had understood his wife's heart to begin, there would never have been a question of believing or disbelieving Iago. He would have known the truth."

Cordelia stopped talking. How had they begun to talk of

hearts? It seemed somehow intimate.

And the way Lord Harveston was looking at her! It was very discomposing.

"So this particular Desdemona lives," he said. "Though if she did indeed love Othello, she must be unhappy at this turn of events."

"Well, no, not in this version. I mean, in the original she loves Othello and he should have seen that. In this interpretation, she has always secretly loved Cassio."

Lord Harveston's look of surprise was unmistakable.

"She would not have acted on it, of course," Cordelia hurried on. "But Iago, having planted the handkerchief, has pushed them together. And then, with Othello dead…"

Cordelia trailed off. It had sounded so much more logical when Lady Rawley had explained it.

"I see," Lord Harveston said. "I wonder if that is a common condition—a lady regretting her marriage."

"No, I cannot think it would be," Cordelia said. "As long as the lady married for love. I speak of *true* love, obviously."

"And how does one distinguish between true and not true?"

Cordelia really did not know how they came to be talking this way. It sounded almost…inappropriate. Though, she could not explain why.

"I ask because I do not know," Lord Harveston said. "It is not a thing I've learned from books."

Cordelia felt very vindicated by that statement. What he said was perfectly correct—there might be all sorts of information found in books, but the truth of the human heart would not be there no matter how long he looked.

"I think one can rely on what is being experienced," she said. "Does one feel as if one is drowning and yet has more air, and that their hair has been struck by lightning, and their heart has sped up and yet they feel well."

"I have never heard anything like that described," Lord Harveston said, looking at her quizzically.

Cordelia nodded. "It is a very difficult matter to describe, but my aunt is exceedingly gifted in putting it all into words. Oh, as well, my sisters have reported feeling a bit sick."

Lord Harveston appeared very struck by the information. Cordelia was well pleased that she'd been able to inform him of something he did not know.

"I suppose you will step forward as this new, triumphant Desdemona?" he said.

Cordelia blanched. "Actually, I will be playing Cassio."

Lord Harveston sighed. "I am sorry to say that I believe my aunt has done a little miscasting."

Cordelia would not for the world agree to such a statement. At least, not out loud. Of course, in her heart, she thoroughly agreed.

It felt very complimentary that Lord Harveston should have perceived it so quickly.

It felt somehow that there had been a warming of temperatures between her and Lord Harveston. It felt as if they were on more equal footing now that she had been able to educate him on something he did not know. And of course, that he rightly thought she ought to be Desdemona.

Perhaps he was not quite as bad as she'd originally thought.

PERCIVAL HAD NEVER spent such a strange afternoon in his life.

For one, he had somehow been bamboozled into helping his aunt with her theatrical—*Othello Redux*. As far as her usual ideas went, it was absolutely not the worst he'd heard of. However, it was not one he would care to share with any of his more intellectual friends. There was not much danger in their hearing of it, as even if they had been invited to the theatrical they never would have attended.

Though the general idea was not as terrible as it might have been, he became exceedingly alarmed when he understood the scope of the swordfight they were planning on. They wished to use real swords and hide bags of cow blood under their clothes. Lady Agatha had been strangely enthusiastic about "blood spewing everywhere to the shock of the audience."

He wondered if they would end up inadvertently murdering each other. That certainly would put the period at the end of the sentence for his aunt's troupe.

Percival would not be sorry to see the end of it, though he'd rather not get there via two dead matrons on the floor.

All of that had been alarming enough, but then there had been Lady Cordelia.

He'd felt he'd made further strides in rehabilitating himself with Lady Cordelia, though he'd also found himself uncomfortably bested by her in some manner. He'd grown used to feeling like the intellectual superior, but today she had spoken of things out of his ken.

She very glibly spoke of that whole mess called human emotions as if it were not the least thing to fear. As if putting oneself in another's power was not an exceedingly dangerous thing to do.

He knew it was though. He'd seen it with his own eyes.

His father had dallied with a housemaid and the result of it could not have been more different than night and day, depending upon what floor of the house one laid one's head.

Above stairs, everything went on as it always had. His parents were cordial to one another, but nothing more. It was very like two people who acknowledge each other as acquaintances and always put their best foot forward—painfully polite.

Though he should not have, Percival had reason to know what went on below stairs too. His set of rooms had an old staircase running down to the servants' hall. It was at the back of a narrow dressing room, behind a set of drawers and Percival was certain nobody remembered it was there.

The door in the servants' hall had been walled over so he could never have used the staircase to enter that domain. The wall was thin though, and he had taken to sitting on the bottom step and listening of an evening when he was supposed to be abed.

He was certain he should never have been eavesdropping, he knew it even then. He just could not help himself. He lived in a cold and quiet house with cold and quiet tutors and cold and quiet parents. He had no siblings he might have sought company from.

All he had was the company of the servants, even though they did not know he was there.

Life below stairs was anything but cold and quiet. It was at times raucous, other times it was complaining, other times filled with stories from the village. Often, it was a reporting of the family's doings—the mistress had ripped another hem and her maid wondered if she did it on purpose, or the baron was so out of sorts he drank three glasses of port though it did him little good.

He had even once heard of one of his own misdeeds. He'd broken a China bowl and had been spied by a maid hiding the pieces in the ash of a fireplace.

Percival had been very cheered by how sympathetic they'd all been to his crime. One of the footmen claimed he'd clear it out first thing in the morning and nobody would be the wiser.

He had begun to think of them all as friends, though they did not think of him that way.

But then one night, a pall had settled over the servants' table. The story came out in bits and pieces, and what a terrible story it was. Dora, one of the housemaids, was with child. She would have to leave service. She would go with nothing—no money and no reference. The child would be unacknowledged.

She was meant to be already gone, but the butler and house-keeper were kind people and had discussed it between them— they would hide her until arrangements could be made for her to travel.

Percival had been outraged at how Dora was being treated.

The fellow involved must be forced to marry her. That was, until he heard who the fellow was.

Dora's harsh punishments were caused by *his* father. The baron was the father of the unborn child.

And then even worse, the poor young woman's heart was broken. She was in love with his father and could not understand how he could throw her out.

Percival could not understand it either.

That was the night he'd stopped using the stairs. Instead, he'd thrown himself into his studies. They were the ideal way to avoid thinking about what he'd heard. They were a reliable excuse to avoid even looking at his father or doing the sporting things the baron liked to do. Mostly, it was an ideal way to stick to the facts and keep feelings at arm's length.

He never did find out what had happened to Dora, though when he'd inherited the barony, he'd hired a firm to track her down. All that could be discovered was that she'd first gone to relatives in York and then married and moved away.

Now here was Lady Cordelia, talking about the human heart as if it were nothing at all to fear.

She was either incredibly naïve and did not know the things he knew, or she was not naïve and she knew things he did not know.

To consider that she might know something he did not was very unsettling. He knew feelings and human behavior were a weak spot. How could they not be when he'd been determined to avoid them? He'd surrounded himself with the sort of intellectuals who would not delve into those topics either, so it had not often been brought to his notice.

He would attend Lady Hightower's musical evening this night. He dared not skip it, not after her hair-raising letter regarding his manners. He presumed Lady Cordelia would be there, showcasing whatever musical talent she'd managed to acquire.

Would she speak more about the human heart?

He was not certain whether he wished it or did not.

CHAPTER TWELVE

Lady Hightower's drawing room was filling up. Cordelia had been well briefed by her elder sisters on what was required on such a night. Play something and make it not too long, the audience always appreciated a short piece.

Cordelia was not at all intimidated by the prospect. She played perfectly adequately. She was not, of course, her sister Rosalind, and so a travel through the world of music was out of reach. But that would not be expected.

Lady Hightower had asked her outright if she played in Rosalind's style and seemed strangely reassured when she could not claim the skill.

Cordelia's thoughts on other topics were, as they seemed always to be these days, in a bit of a jumble. Mr. Jeffries, the Corinthian returning from America, was expected to attend. She could only wonder if she would feel a spark upon viewing him.

Darden said he was a jolly fellow and well-liked. Her brother was a good judge of character, so that was promising.

But then, there was Lord Harveston. Why would that fellow never leave her thoughts?

As they had talked at Lady Rawley's house, he had seemed so…genuine. Very naturally, she must feel a little sorry for him having to admit to knowing so little of matters of the heart. The poor gentleman had not even known the signs of love!

And then, of course, it had been amusing to watch him take

in Lady Rawley's ideas about the sword fight and Lady Agatha's wish to see blood flying everywhere.

All Cordelia could think of was that she would not like to be in the first row of the production, lest those persons leave with red-stained clothes on account of Lady Agatha's enthusiasm.

"Lady Cordelia, Miss Mayton," Lady Hightower said, "I would have you know Miss Bretherton."

Cordelia curtsied to the young woman.

"Miss Bretherton's father is a bishop," Lady Hightower went on, "and I must say there is something to the education of women brought up by clergy. She is *exceedingly* well read, a thing one does not often come across these days."

Cordelia smiled, but felt herself a little resentful of Miss Bretherton's excessive reading. It was almost as if Lady Hightower had spied her in her father's library, attempting to understand Aristotle and Thomas Aquinas and getting nowhere with it.

"I am sure I do not deserve such accolades," Miss Bretherton said meekly.

"Well, who can tell?" Miss Mayton said.

Miss Bretherton looked very surprised to hear it. Cordelia suppressed a giggle—her aunt could suddenly say a thing that threw a person off on occasion.

"Ah, look who we have here, Lord Harveston," Lady Hightower said.

Cordelia had the uncomfortable feeling of her heart speeding up, and at the same time wishing to push Miss Bretherton under the sideboard.

"Lord Harveston, this is Miss Bretherton," Lady Hightower said. "An exceedingly accomplished young lady—I defy anyone to best her knowledge of Royal Society papers."

Now the woman was reading Royal Society papers? Where did one even get Royal Society papers? What was in them? She had heard of the society, of course. It was yet another learned group raising questions and attempting to answer them. What the questions were, she had not the slightest idea.

Cordelia supposed she should be grateful that she at least knew what it was. When she had first heard of it, she had assumed it was a newspaper dedicated to reporting on the king and queen. Her father had corrected her when she asked how they might get a copy.

"You might even think of extending an invitation to your literary salon after she has married and can move about society freely," Lady Hightower said. "Naturally, the bishop could escort her now, as he is equally learned, but the gentleman is so busy with his duties I doubt it would suit. Even this evening, I have been tasked with acting as Miss Bretherton's chaperone. Ah, more guests arrive, I will leave you to it."

Lady Hightower drifted away. Cordelia watched Lord Harveston to see how he would react to this womanly paragon of information.

"Very good to know you, Miss Bretherton," Lord Harveston said. "Lady Cordelia, Miss Mayton, I trust you have recovered from the first meeting of the acting troupe?"

"Perhaps the better question is," Cordelia said boldly, "have *you* recovered, Lord Harveston?"

"Not entirely," he said with a laugh.

"Acting troupe?" Miss Bretherton asked, her tone faintly shocked.

Cordelia found herself annoyed over the lady's shock, as if she were inventing it to seem more principled or delicate or…something.

"Yes," she said, "My aunt and I are both actresses. We will tread the boards on the sixteenth in *Othello Redux*. Desdemona lives, by the by."

Miss Bretherton appeared further shocked, though Lord Harveston was clearly amused. He said, "Perhaps more of a clarification is in order. My aunt, Lady Rawley, puts on a theatrical every year in her private house and by invitation."

This information seemed to soothe the delicate sensibilities of Miss Bretherton. Her brow cleared. "Ah, I see. My father has often let his children perform scenes from the bible for close friends and family. Tableaus, if you will."

Tableaus from the bible, indeed. Cordelia was certain she was just as religious as the next person—she gave her full attention to the Lord when she was in church. But there was no reason to go making tableaus about it. She was certain that Miss Bretherton's tableaus were insufferable.

"We will have a swordfight," Cordelia said, "right in Lady Rawley's drawing room."

"We are hoping for a lot of blood," Miss Mayton put in helpfully.

As Cordelia observed Miss Bretherton's reaction to the idea of hoping for a lot of blood, which was predictably shuddering, a hulking sort of a man slapped Lord Harveston's back.

"Harveston!" he said in a rather booming voice.

Lord Harveston turned. "Jeffries," he said, "when did you get back?"

So this was Mr. Jeffries. Of course, she should have known it instantly. He was powerfully built, and his arms did likely cause his tailor to despair over how to encase them.

"I landed a month ago," Mr. Jeffries said. "Had to go to my father's estate and see it ticking along smooth before I commenced spending all his money in Town."

"I will introduce you to Lady Cordelia Bennington, Miss Mayton, and Miss Bretherton."

Mr. Jeffries bowed. "Ladies. Charmed. I suppose we will hear from all of you this evening?"

Miss Mayton was terribly flattered by the idea. She laughed and said, "Only the young ladies, sir."

"Then I cannot believe you will not be among them," Mr. Jeffries said gallantly.

"You are a flirt, sir!" Miss Mayton said, tapping him on the arm with her fan.

It was such a charming scene, and Cordelia could not imagine why Miss Bretherton had just grimaced.

"Now, what will we hear from Lady Cordelia and Miss Bretherton?" Mr. Jeffries asked.

"I will be on the pianoforte," Cordelia said, "and play something short. My sisters have all told me that an audience always does like it short."

Mr. Jeffries roared with laughter. "Yes, it is the sort of thing that is true, but nobody will admit it. Your sisters have very good sense. And you, Miss Bretherton?"

"I will play the harp," she said stiffly. "I will perform an original composition of *Psalm 119*."

The harp. Of course she would play the harp. It was supposed to be a very difficult instrument to master, though Cordelia could not see why. And *Psalm 119*? That could go on for a quarter of an hour!

"Well," Mr. Jeffries said, "no doubt the audience will be in the mood for longer pieces too. Especially on the harp."

Cordelia was both admiring of Mr. Jeffries' courtesy and irritated by it.

What she was not, though, was in love with Mr. Jeffries. Or even on her way there. She had no symptoms of love whatsoever. He was a genial fellow, but she was not struck by him.

"Everyone," Lady Hightower said from the front of the room, "if you will arrange yourselves. The ladies playing will be in the front, the rest of you, recall that the seat you choose does not need to be perfection. You will not be in it for eternity. I say something along those lines every year, with seemingly little effect."

PERCIVAL HAD NO idea he would be so amused at Lady Hightower's musical evening. Lady Cordelia was a bold little minx. It was immediately apparent that she did not care for Miss Bretherton and had gone about attempting to shock.

He could not be too condemning of her stratagems, though. Miss Bretherton was as so many ladies were that had come before—serious and dull. Probably a deal like himself, as he supposed he was viewed rather serious and dull too.

If Lady Hightower believed Miss Bretherton had the wits to join his literary salon, then no doubt she did. He just did not particularly wish her to. He was certain that she would find herself shocked by some of the conversations that were had. Whatever his members were, falsely modest they were not. If the decision came down to making a point or observing courtesy, well, courtesy had flown out the window more than once.

Percival paused, an uncomfortable idea arising in his mind. Had he not said a hundred times that he would only wed a highly educated lady? And now here was one dangled in front of him and he did not have the least inclination for it.

She was endorsed by Lady Hightower as having a mind sharp enough for his salon, she was well read, she played the harp, which was no small accomplishment assuming she played it well. She was modest, well bred, and every inch a lady. Miss Bretherton was precisely what he'd said he wished for.

And yet, she was not.

She played the harp just now and it seemed as if it would go on forever. His hair would gray and he would lose an inch of stature and develop a paunch, they'd be carving his gravestone in order to be ready for his imminent attendance, and here he'd still be, waiting for Miss Bretherton to finally conclude.

The idea of struggling through such an evening at home with a wife…well it did not seem very appealing.

Finally, Miss Bretherton did come to an end of her musical journey through *Psalm 119*. Gentle applause commenced, though he noticed Lord Grant had to be woken up to participate in it.

"Excellent," Lady Hightower said. "So accomplished. Now, we will hear from Lady Cordelia Bennington."

Lady Cordelia rose. As she made her way to the pianoforte, she said, "Please do not nurse hopes that I can equal that skilled performance. As it happens, I am only playing a short reel."

Upon hearing the word "short," Percival saw the many approving looks in the audience. He began to think that, whatever the deficiencies were in Lady Cordelia's education, she did have a particular knack for understanding other people. A knack he did not excel at himself.

If Miss Bretherton had been all disciplined skill and serious execution, Lady Cordelia was all liveliness and fun. People sat up straighter in their chairs, Lord Grant even toe-tapped. And, just as she had promised, it was short. The applause was distinctly enthusiastic.

He watched her laugh and curtsy, assured of her approval. The literary salon and the Royal Society might be *his* milieus, but this was *hers*. People were her milieu.

As Lady Cordelia was the last to play, everyone rose from their seats. He was seated near the back, but he was suddenly gripped with a determination to make his way to Lady Cordelia and dispense his congratulations.

He could see that Jeffries had already done so. He supposed that fellow, always so jolly, was making a good job of it, which was rather irksome.

He weaved round Lord Grant and was waylaid by Lady Hightower and Miss Bretherton.

"Lord Harveston," Lady Hightower said, "have you ever heard anything like Miss Bretherton on the harp?"

"It was very accomplished, Miss Bretherton."

Miss Bretherton blushed, as if she had not been aware that it was de rigueur to collect compliments after performing musically.

"It was just a little piece I hastily scribbled the notes to," Miss Bretherton said.

Now that was going entirely too far to be believed. Percival had not observed the work that went into that endless piece, but he was certain she'd slaved over it for months.

"Do not dim your own light, my dear," Lady Hightower counseled.

Out of the corner of his eye, Percival could see Jeffries joking with Lady Cordelia. He wouldn't mind dimming Jeffries' lights this very moment.

"Are you quite well, Lord Harveston?" Lady Hightower asked. "You seem out of sorts."

Out of sorts? It seemed that he was. What was wrong with him?

He cleared his throat. "Not at all, Lady Hightower."

Before he could make his escape, he watched Miss Mayton leading her charge out of the room. Lady Cordelia waved to him.

He waved back.

"You know," he said, hardly knowing where he was going with it, "I think I ought to escort Miss Mayton's carriage home. The road between here and Portland Place can be…unpredictable."

"Unpredictable?" Lady Hightower asked.

"Well, one never knows," he mumbled. "Two ladies on their own…"

He sounded very foolish at the moment.

"Now, I see what you say," Lady Hightower said. "Miss Bretherton's father brought her here and her maid is here as well and I was meant to take her home, but goodness I am very tired. When I think of calling for my carriage, well, I wonder if it would suit if a hansom was called and you escorted the lady home? After all, her maid will be with her and with you protecting from danger atop your horse, I am sure it would be all right."

Escort Miss Bretherton? He did not wish to escort Miss Bretherton!

"What do you say, Miss Bretherton?" Lady Hightower asked. "Do you suppose your father would approve the idea?"

"Oh, yes, I suppose so," Miss Bretherton said.

"Excellent. It is settled then. Come along, we will retrieve your maid and call a hansom and you will be on your way."

THERE HAD BEEN some delay in departing Lady Hightower's house. Cordelia and her aunt waited for a quarter hour for their carriage to come round. It was longer than usual but not wholly unexpected—one could never be quite certain what went on after a coachman let one out somewhere. Sometimes, they lined the street and were easily in view, other times they went off somewhere. Miss Mayton had suggested that the coachmen must all get together in the stables and have their own party to pass the time.

Wherever Sandren had been, it did not seem as if it had been to a party. But then, their coachman generally did sport a stern mien.

Lady Hightower had come out with Miss Bretherton and Lord Harveston. Apparently, Lord Harveston was to escort the lady home.

The idea made Cordelia feel a little sick, which was the stupidest thing in the world. Why should she be discomfited to find Lord Harveston bowled over by the educated bishop's daughter? Of course he would be, they'd probably traded a hundred facts already.

Once again, she felt she must be very conceited. What else could account for being put out that one was not admired by one who was not particularly admired? Did she suppose the whole world should be in love with her?

Cordelia paused. Where had that idea come from? Where did the idea of love come from?

As Miss Bretherton's hansom trotted away with Lord Harveston dutifully following it, Sandren jumped down from his box and a groom opened the carriage door.

They were settled in a trice and on their way home.

"You gave a wonderful performance, Cordelia," Miss Mayton said. "I was nearby Lord Grant and overheard him say to his lady, 'that young woman knows what's wanted at these sort of things.' The applause was *quite* pronounced."

"I think my sisters were right in advising me," Cordelia said, "people do like it to be short."

"And Mr. Jeffries found the idea so amusing and he was so quick on his feet to congratulate you at the end. What did you think of him? Is he your Corinthian?"

Cordelia sighed and gazed out the window. "I am afraid not, Aunt. I was not struck by him at all."

"That is a shame, but the heart will not tell tales."

"I am beginning to be worried though," Cordelia said. "Darden has mentioned several times that there are not many eligible Corinthians in the town to begin. What if I end the season without meeting that special person? The one who is meant just for me?"

"I shouldn't worry over it," Miss Mayton said, "he's bound to turn up eventually. You must simply go forward until you encounter a gentleman who occupies your thoughts."

Cordelia bit her lip. She had already met a gentleman who occupied her thoughts—Lord Harveston. Though, he occupied it for the wrong reasons.

"But do you not think that a gentleman could occupy one's thoughts for other reasons?" Cordelia asked.

"Not for long," Miss Mayton said, laughing.

Cordelia was exceedingly perplexed with herself. Or with her heart. Her heart seemed to not know what it was doing or what it wanted!

It was being so very obscure about things. Rosalind and Viola had been single-minded. Rosalind must have her duke, Viola must have Lord Baderston.

Another idea came to her. Not a particularly welcome idea. Her eldest sister Beatrice had not known her own heart for quite some time.

Of course, it was absurd that Cordelia Bennington, of all people, should not be in very close communication with her heart. She was an actress. She interpreted the words of Shake-speare to evince the emotion and make it come to life.

"You seem very tired, my dear," Miss Mayton said.

"Yes, I believe that must be it. I am only very tired and it has made my thoughts go round in circles."

CHAPTER THIRTEEN

PERCIVAL WAS FEELING very prickly as he escorted Miss Bretherton to her house. He'd wished to escort Lady Cordelia home but had been boxed in by Lady Hightower.

After the lady so recently having lectured him on the attributes of a gentleman and that he was not coming up to the mark, there had been no way to slip out of it.

Begrudgingly, he had ridden his horse behind Miss Bretherton's carriage. Until that was not deemed sufficient, apparently.

Miss Bretherton had opened a window and told him she would feel more secure if he rode next to her and if the hansom driver would slow down.

The boy hanging on the back of the hansom had snorted, the driver all but ignored her though she'd said it very loud. Percival had done as he was asked. Unlike the driver, he could not see how to refuse.

"To pass the time, Lord Harveston," she said, her head at the window, "I wonder about your views on Reverend Fordyce's *Addresses to Young Men?*"

Of course, Percival had read them, and his advice to young ladies too. He did not suppose, though, that Miss Bretherton wished for his real opinion on the sermons.

His actual estimation of Fordyce was that the fellow had looked round his own family and social sphere, thought about what annoyed him, concocted a recipe of behavior that would be for his own personal convenience, and then written it all down.

As he did not answer immediately, Miss Bretherton said, "I have not been permitted to read the addresses to young gentlemen yet, as they are addressed to young gentlemen, but my father says he will use the advice as a yardstick in measuring any gentleman who comes calling."

Percival pressed his lips together to hide a smile. If the bishop was indeed using such a yardstick, he wished for a very dull sort of person.

His hands tightened on his reins. *He* was a very dull sort of person. At least, he must suppose so. He dearly hoped that neither the bishop nor Miss Bretherton were looking in his direction.

"My father says that Reverend Fordyce rightly points out that any true gentleman does not like frittering away time on gambling or boxing or horseraces. He says that so many gentlemen pretend they like such things just to go along. But Lady Hightower tells me you do not pretend at it."

This was hitting a little too close to the mark. Had Lady Hightower been singing his praises? At least, the sort of praises that Miss Bretherton would approve of?

Why? Was it some sort of revenge for his recent bad behavior at Almack's?

Blessedly, the hansom slowed and then stopped. They had arrived at the bishop's house.

Just as he thought he might tip his hat and turn his horse round the moment he spotted a footman at the doors, a whole bevy of people descended the steps.

The crowd was led by what he assumed were the butler and housekeeper.

"A hansom!" the butler said, his voice wavering like he might cry over it.

"And who is this, Miss?" the housekeeper said, looking askance at Percival.

As Miss Bretherton was helped down, she apprised the staff of

Lady Hightower's fatigue and how other arrangements had been made. She was escorted by Lord Harveston, and it had all been very respectable.

The expressions on their faces were priceless. One sniffed, another was wide-eyed, a maid clutched at her fichu. One would have thought Lady Hightower had sent the girl accompanied by a dozen rakes on a ship to the Americas.

They then promptly surrounded Miss Bretherton and escorted her into the house. One of the footmen looked over his shoulder at him as if he might chase after them and murder them all.

He turned Pericles and urged him to a trot. He noticed he did not have to do much urging and supposed his horse was just as befuddled as he was himself.

What a household.

What a difference from the Bennington household.

Had he escorted Lady Cordelia, he might well have found the duke chasing after a goat again, as the earl looked on and cheered.

Sensing his sudden thoughtfulness, Pericles slowed to a walk.

Why had he been so determined to escort Lady Cordelia home anyway?

Her family was odd, to say the least. But then, they had something he'd never had. They were warm. Even the duke had not seemed so ducal in their midst.

For all his mother's talk of family and how they must support one another, he'd not seen much of that in his household.

Lady Cordelia herself was so different!

He was ashamed that he'd initially taken on a condescending opinion of her intellectual abilities. In her letter, Lady Hightower had mentioned that there were more types of intelligence than he was aware of. He and Makepeace could not quite work it out and had settled on instincts.

Perhaps they had been wrong though. Perhaps Lady Cordelia's intelligence was of a harder to define sort. It was not anything pulled from a book or based on a fact. It was not analytical. It was something else. It was as if she could see into a person's thoughts, though they had not spoken them.

He ought to stop thinking of the lady so much. He ought to stick to what he had planned—he would wed a highly educated lady and they would go on to have lively intellectual debates.

Though, he could not ignore that the idea of sitting across a breakfast table from Miss Bretherton, discussing Fordyce's advice to young gentlemen, made him feel a little sick. It also made him a bit queasy to think of Lady Cordelia's future.

She would end merry with Lord Darling, or even perhaps Jeffries.

Stupid men.

→≫≻≺≪←

LADY RAWLEY HAD been determined that she would once more take Cordelia and her aunt in her own carriage to Lord Harveston's literary salon.

They would arrive on the early side of things, but Lady Rawley assured them that his nephew would not mind it. In any case, Lady Agatha and Mrs. Robinson would already be there to assist the bachelor in his preparations.

Now, as they stopped in front of the house, they found both of those ladies pacing in front of it.

They hurried to Lady Rawley's carriage. Lady Agatha said, "We did as you asked and have been here for a full half hour."

"But my dear Lady Agatha," Lady Rawley said, "What do you do on the pavement? Hadn't you have been better served to be inside to examine Lord Harveston's arrangements?"

"We have been barred from the house," Lady Agatha said.

"Positively barred," Mrs. Robinson said. "I was here. I heard it myself."

"It was that butler," Lady Agatha said, huffing with the outrage of it. "He said Lord Harveston told him to not open the doors until eight precisely and he was just following his orders."

"Well," Lady Rawley said, being helped down from the carriage, "it all sounds like a misunderstanding. My nephew probably forgot you were arriving to help. After all, he has struggled on as a bachelor for the past few years. And Makepeace, he can be difficult at times."

Cordelia was not so certain that Lord Harveston *had* forgotten that Lady Agatha and Mrs. Robinson would turn up early.

Mollified, Lady Agatha said, "Now I suppose that is right. Servants *do* get it wrong so often."

"We've brought flowers, they are in Lady Agatha's carriage, just as you asked," Mrs. Robinson said. "I daresay if we can get in now we can set them up in good time."

"Say no more, Mrs. Robinson," Lady Rawley said. "I will lead the way."

Miss Mayton was helped down, and then Cordelia. Reluctantly, she followed the determined group of matrons to the doors. Lady Rawley used the door knocker very forcefully.

When there was no response, she called, "I know you are in there, Makepeace. Open this door at once!"

Slowly, the door opened. The butler stood there grave and said, "It is not yet eight o'clock."

"Stand aside, you saucy man," Lady Rawley said.

Makepeace did stand aside, though he did not look very happy doing it. They entered the house and Lady Rawley pointed at the two footmen. "One of you bring the flowers in from Lady Agatha's carriage, the other fetch every vase in the house."

The footmen looked to their butler for confirmation of these orders. Makepeace nodded reluctantly.

Lady Rawley, seeming victorious over the whole thing, stared at Makepeace and said, "Now, we will have a look at the sideboard and see what we think of it."

Makepeace had his hands balled into fists and Cordelia was certain that he'd like to throw himself in front of Lady Rawley to stop her progress if he could do so without becoming unemployed.

She sailed into the drawing room and Cordelia reluctantly followed.

The sideboard looked as it had last time—very well composed. Lady Rawley eyed it critically, while Lady Agatha and Mrs. Robinson took charge of the incoming flowers and vases.

"It will do, I suppose," Lady Rawley said.

Makepeace turned on his heel and stalked out of the drawing room. Cordelia supposed he would take himself to some far away closet, close the door, and shout for a few minutes.

"Goodness," Miss Mayton said, watching the activity around her, "that is an awful lot of flowers."

Her aunt told no tales—Lady Agatha and Mrs. Robinson had brought enough flowers to fill a farmer's cart. Lilies, delphinium, and overblown peonies dominated, though there was also a large pot of sage. Cordelia stifled a laugh, guessing sage was thought to be appropriate for an evening of sage discussion.

Lord Harveston entered, trailed by his incensed butler. Cordelia's breath sped up though she willed it otherwise. He was looking very well in his close-cut coat. His neckcloth was superbly done in an understated manner. Goodness, she always forgot how tall he was.

The lord looked about him and said, "Aunt, this is completely unnecessary."

"Nonsense, my boy," Lady Rawley said. "Just look at how much more cheerful and welcoming it is."

"It smells like a hothouse," Lord Harveston said.

"Well it would," Lady Rawley said, brow wrinkling. "It's from the flowers. By the by, Makepeace barred us at the door, Nephew. I had to positively barge my way in."

"I gave Makepeace instruction that the doors were not to open until eight o'clock. There was no cause for anyone to arrive before then."

"Yes, yes," Lady Rawley said, waving her hands, "but we are hardly *anyone*."

Before Lord Harveston could say whether he thought they were anyone or not, the footmen began to lead in guests as they arrived.

Cordelia was perhaps more astute about what she was seeing than she had been the last time. On their first attendance she'd known so little about what to expect or who would attend. Now, she could see that certain sets of gentlemen were eager to see one another.

Nobody seemed particularly interested to see Lady Rawley's acting troupe and Cordelia began to feel as if they were being treated as pariahs. That feeling was further confirmed by the various glares at the vases of flowers, which nobody seemed to appreciate.

Therefore, she was very surprised when an older gentleman who she'd taken as a bit ornery last time approached their party.

"Ladies," he said, "I will be so forward as to introduce myself. Bertram Haventops, Oxford Fellow."

Cordelia curtsied. At least one gentleman had some manners and friendliness.

"May I speak for my fellow salon members when I say we were ill-prepared for your arrival last time. This time, we hope to do better."

Lady Rawley nodded condescendingly. "You are very good sir," she said. "And we have tried to do our part by bringing in some flowers."

Mr. Haventops glanced around. "Yes, yes indeed. Now, what I would propose is that our new members cannot isolate further! We must have you integrated into our debates."

Though she had initially taken him to be mannerly and friendly, there was something about Mr. Haventops that began to give Cordelia pause. She could not put her finger on it exactly. His words were pleasant. The tone in which he spoke them was pleasant. But, there was something that made her feel uneasy.

"Mr. Haventops, you are too good," Lady Agatha said. "Now, you really ought to know everybody. This is Lady Rawley, she is

Lord Harveston's aunt, and here is Miss Mayton and Lady Cordelia, and there is my good friend Mrs. Robinson. I am Lady Agatha."

Mr. Haventops bowed. "Charmed," he said. "Now, I suggest that we proceed as follows. Lady Cordelia and Miss Mayton, you will sit over there. That is my group, we are a freewheeling set—we discuss whatever seems interesting about the topic. Lady Rawley, Lady Agatha, Mrs. Robinson, I would send you that way. Those fellows always bring along some fascinating document of some sort."

Lady Rawley said, "I do recall that last time, there was a third group. They sat over in that corner of the room. What do they do?"

Mr. Haventops said, "Ah yes, well they are all friends and a rather closed group. I do not think you would enjoy their company, as they keep very much to themselves."

Lady Rawley nodded. "Mr. Haventops, you have been *very* accommodating."

Mr. Haventops bowed. "Until then, ladies." He moved off and Cordelia felt further uneasy, noting the small smile that played upon his lips.

"It was just as I suspected," Lady Rawley said. "The poor members were so taken aback when we arrived last time. As we know, these sorts of intellectuals are not particularly good at thinking on their feet. Now they have had time to take in our presence and have nominated Mr. Haventops to do the honors."

"But Lady Rawley," Cordelia said, "I am worried about our participation. Have any of us really studied the question at hand?"

"Oh dear," Lady Agatha said, "I had presumed we would all be together in our little circle and have further discussion about *The Dreadful Doings of Dembric Dale*."

"We are as one mind, Lady Agatha," Mrs. Robinson said. "I thought the very same. I was planning to comment on the effrontery of that kitchen maid."

"She is rather forward," Lady Agatha said, "but then her idea of moving to Spain is not a bad one."

"But what about Aristotle and Thomas Aquinas?" Cordelia asked, praying that somebody knew something they might impart.

All eyes turned to Lady Rawley. She said, "I haven't thought the first thing about it, nor do I even recall what the question was."

"It was to do with Aristotle's idea that people are a bad judge of their own case," Cordelia said, "and how it relates to St. Thomas Aquinas' idea that no man can be the judge of himself."

"Cordelia and I spent an hour in the earl's library, but we could not make heads or tails of it," Miss Mayton said.

"We ended agreeing that we should be guided by womanly sense," Cordelia added. Though, it did not sound as brilliant an idea as it had when they'd thought of it.

"It is a ridiculous question," Lady Rawley said. "I propose we employ a strategy that has always worked well for me. A dodge the question sort of strategy."

Cordelia had never heard of such a strategy.

"When one is asked a question one does not know the answer to or simply doesn't wish to answer," Lady Rawley said, "one can respond in several ways. My own preferences are: 'One wonders' or 'that is a weighty question that requires much thought' or 'that certainly deserves further investigation.' I always used it to great effect with my husband whenever he inquired into a bill from the dressmaker or milliner."

"Yes, I see," Miss Mayton said. "As well, one might answer a question with a question. For example, one might say 'perhaps the more important point is, what do *you* think about it?' I also find one might almost always say to a gentleman, 'I defer to your superior judgment.'"

"Oh, yes," Mrs. Robinson said, "they always do like that!"

"Of course," Lady Rawley said, "if one finds oneself in a very uncomfortable corner, one might simply change the topic altogether. This worked wonderfully well in my marriage. My lord would be waving some bill or other around and I'd say, 'How do your hounds get on, my love?'"

Cordelia was feeling more uncomfortable by the minute. They were to speak on a subject none of them knew the first thing about by using vagaries and hoping nobody noticed? And then, there was something about Mr. Haventops' friendliness that she did not trust.

Though she told herself she was in no real danger, regardless of which way the evening turned, she almost began to feel as if they were ancient Romans being thrown to the lions.

At the front of the room, Lord Harveston dinged his glass.

"Well," Lady Rawley said, "we'd best sort ourselves into our respective groups."

Cordelia's heart sank. There was something very wrong here. She did not wish to join Mr. Haventops' group. Though, she supposed she did not have much choice.

⟫⟪

PERCIVAL, OR RATHER his butler, had been successful at keeping his aunt's friends from invading his drawing room before eight o'clock.

Not that it had not made much of a difference—the room was filled with flowers and he could see very well what his members thought of it. At least his aunt had not had time to meddle with Makepeace's sideboard.

Percival had presumed that his aunt and her friends would stay separate from the rest of the members and carry on their conversation regarding the doings in the dale.

He had even planned on occasionally taking part in the discussion as he made his way round the room. Though, beyond noting that the plot was unpredictable, which he had already said to Lady Cordelia, he had not thought of any other positive he might remark upon. But certainly something would come to him.

Lady Cordelia was looking very well this night. She wore a simple cream silk with only a thin gold chain round her neck as adornment. Her auburn hair was swept up and kept in place with a gold and pearl comb. She was very elegant really.

It occurred to him that she always did look elegant. It was as if she had the confidence of restraint. She did not add what was not necessary.

As he was admiring her person, Percival had been quietly alarmed to see Mr. Haventops approach the ladies. His alarm had been for naught, though, as they'd seemed to have a civil conversation.

Mr. Haventops could be ornery in the extreme, but apparently he'd cooled off since the last salon. He imagined the fellow had managed to recover from his initial outrage and decided to make himself pleasant. After all, he always sought connections and Lady Rawley was exceedingly connected.

At least, that's what he'd thought. Now he was not so certain.

Now, the ladies had split into two and joined two different groups. Wishing to bring them into the fold was rather too big a turnaround to be believed from Mr. Haventops.

What was he up to?

Whatever it was, it seemed to come as a surprise to the other members, who clearly were not expecting to find a lady beside them.

Makepeace ended his description of the question of the night. "As Aristotle and Thomas Aquinas theorized, is it in fact hopeless for a man to judge his own case?"

Percival said, "At this moment, I usually give my opinion on the question. Though, I am not entirely sure where I've landed on this one. On the one hand, it seems clear that a person cannot always be objective when an outcome will materially affect them. On the other hand, if one sets out clear rules to live by, then one need only follow them rigorously and that must enforce objectivity. So, I will be interested in hearing the range of debate on the matter. Begin the discussion."

Percival retrieved a glass of wine from the sideboard and drifted over to where his aunt, Lady Agatha, and Mrs. Robinson had seated themselves.

Mr. Royford was laying out various documents. Sir Frederick said, "Lady Rawley, I would know your assessment of the points both Aristotle and Thomas Aquinas set out to make."

Lady Rawley shook her fan at Sir Frederick. "Well, Sir Frederick, what *I* would know is your view on Desdemona's death in *Othello*. Was not Othello judging his own case and doing a very bad job of it?"

"One wonders," Mrs. Robinson said.

"It certainly merits further thought," Lady Agatha said.

The other members, including Makepeace, looked entirely flummoxed. As was Percival himself. How had she worked in *Othello*?

He was certain his members were about to be taken on a ride they would not enjoy. However, he was all confidence that his aunt and her two friends could defend themselves sufficiently, if not rationally.

He was more concerned about Haventops.

CHAPTER FOURTEEN

PERCIVAL MADE HIS way over to Mr. Haventops' grouping.

"May one presume that both Lady Cordelia and Miss Mayton have read Aristotle and Thomas Aquinas widely?" Mr. Haventops asked them.

"Presume whatever you prefer, Mr. Haventops," Miss Mayton said. "I always think things are made a deal more pleasant when one allows others to carry on with their presumptions."

"Do you say then," Mr. Haventops went on, "that you have or have not?"

"One wonders," Miss Mayton said.

"Yes, one *does* wonder," Mr. Haventops said.

"I say, Haventops," Mr. Genterly said quietly.

Haventops disregarded the warning. Percival could see Lady Cordelia's cheeks redden. He would have to put a stop to this.

"I am only trying to assess the ladies' knowledge of the subject," Haventops said with a shrug. "This is a salon, not a rout, and we have the right to expect certain standards are met."

"Haventops," Percival said in a warning tone. "We will follow the rules of conduct here."

It was said in a tone that meant to convey that his behavior was unacceptable and would not be tolerated. He would throw the man out on his ear if it became necessary. It was one thing to conduct a fierce, and even bordering on rude, debate with an equal challenger. It was quite another to bully a weaker opponent.

Lady Cordelia sipped her wine and set it down. She was looking less embarrassed than she had been. She was looking rather furious.

"Mr. Haventops," she said calmly, "I would be delighted to acquaint you with my knowledge of the subject. Both Aristotle and St. Thomas Aquinas are correct—a man cannot be a good judge of his own case. This revelation has crystallized for me just now, as I have seen with my own eyes when a man does not realize he is acting ungentlemanly, petulant, and spiteful. But then, one must assume such a gentleman does not have a wife or sisters at home who might point out and soften such flaws before they are advertised so publicly."

Mr. Genterly snorted. Sir Matthew said, "Touché, Lady Cordelia."

Mr. Haventops looked as if his very head would explode into bits. He stood and said, "I need not remain here to be insulted in such a manner!"

"If one does not wish to be parried, one ought not swing one's sword," Lady Cordelia said coldly.

"Yes, you did start it, you know," Miss Mayton said. "We were perfectly prepared to be civil and only say 'one wonders' or 'what do *you* think' all the night long."

Mr. Haventops turned on his heel and stalked out of the room.

Percival was rather stunned by this turn of events. How on earth had Lady Cordelia bested Mr. Haventops?

She was positively marvelous.

"Lord Harveston," Lady Cordelia said, "I apologize if I have driven one of your members from your drawing room."

Percival surveyed the group. He said, "Please raise your hand if you are despondent over the departure of Mr. Haventops."

There were some very decisive snorts, but no hands were raised.

"Now that piece of business is dispensed with," Sir Matthew

said, "Lady Cordelia, how did you know Haventops had no wife or sisters?"

Percival sat down in the chair beside Lady Cordelia that had so recently been vacated by Mr. Haventops. He was rather wondering about that himself.

While it might be his usual habit to circulate, this was far too interesting.

He briefly wondered if he ought to go and see how his aunt and her friends were faring. He dismissed the need, though. Lady Rawley was entirely capable of steering the ship wherever she was and he assumed there was far more discussion of *Othello* than anything else.

"I instantly suspected the gentleman lived alone," Lady Cordelia said.

"Oh dear, yes, I see what you say," Miss Mayton said.

What did they mean? It was as if they were speaking a foreign language only they understood.

The rest of the gentlemen leaned forward, looking as perplexed as he was.

"But then you say," Mr. Genterly volunteered, "that a man cannot be a good judge of his case without womanly intercession?"

"How else can it be?" Lady Cordelia asked. "If a man lives alone, he lives on his own mountaintop, so to speak. Everything he does and says must be right, as there is no differing opinion."

"But what if he lives with another man, rather than a woman? Say he lives with his father, or his brother?" Sir Matthew asked. "Would that not accomplish the same aim?"

Lady Cordelia and Miss Mayton looked at each other, appearing very amused by the idea.

Why were they amused? It seemed a very rational and logical argument.

"The tone in the house will not be conducive to it," Lady Cordelia said.

"Goodness, the tone," Miss Mayton said. "I'm manly, no I'm

even more manly, wait I will be manlier still! Before you know it, somebody has broken a bone or caused a ghastly offense."

Sir Matthew rubbed his chin. "I think I begin to see what you say. It has been a thing in my house that I am both cognizant of and incognizant of. I am not the same man I was when I married, though I could hardly tell you how it happened."

Lady Cordelia and Miss Mayton nodded approvingly.

"And then!" Sir Matthew said, seeming as if an idea had just hit him like a lightning bolt. "And then, there is this thing my lady says that I had not ever really noticed…but now I think of it, that phrase has guided me quite well all these years."

"What is the phrase?" Mr. Genterly said in a whisper.

"Well, I'll say something or other, some opinion, and she'll just smile and say, 'Perhaps keep that just between us.' And so I do keep it between us. Often, time will pass and I'll think to myself, *What a stupid opinion, I'm glad I didn't blather on about it at my club.*"

"Gad," Mr. Genterly said. "My wife says, 'You will see you do not mean it when you've had your dinner.' It makes me pause, even when dinner does not seem to have any material effect."

The other gentlemen nodded, as if they heard some version of the phrase in their own houses.

"So you theorize, Lady Cordelia," Sir Matthew said, "that it was never a question of whether a man can be his own judge, but that it is a foolhardy quest. Good judgment is a soup that will not come out right if it does not contain two ingredients, rather than one. It must depend upon both the male and female point of view. Or tone, as you called it."

"I fear you have said it far more eloquently than I ever could have, Sir Matthew," Lady Cordelia said. "I simply feel what I feel."

"This is a thing both Aristotle and Thomas Aquinas did not consider!" Mr. Genterly said, all enthusiasm. "How on earth did they miss it?"

How *had* they missed it? Was it true to begin? Percival

thought he had no way of knowing, as he did live alone. There was no woman in the house to tell him a phrase if his opinions had veered off the road.

What if his opinions had done just that but he was blinded to them? After all, Lady Hightower had written him a letter about it.

"Harveston," Sir William said, "will you weigh in with an opinion on this idea?"

"I am afraid I do not possess the information to fully form an opinion," Percival said. "I believe I will stay quiet and take in what I hear. Sometimes, one is the debater, and sometimes one is the student."

⇶⇜

CORDELIA HAD PRACTICALLY skipped out of Lord Harveston's house. She had been trepidatious when Mr. Haventops suggested her group of ladies be split up to join the other groups. She had not a thing to say about Aristotle and Thomas Aquinas.

She had felt a distinct and growing sense of unease regarding Mr. Haventops.

But then, a rather marvelous thing had happened. Mr. Haventops had set out to embarrass her and her aunt. She'd seen that had been his plan all along.

She'd realized that she'd known it before she'd known it. That had given her confidence to express her views, despite those views not coming out of a book.

Cordelia had been certain Mr. Haventops lived alone. No gentleman became such a curmudgeon unless left to his own devices for too long a time.

The other gentlemen had seemed fascinated that she'd known it, and then further interested in her ideas.

Goodness, they even wondered how Aristotle and Thomas Aquinas had missed such a point.

And then Lord Harveston, putting himself forward as a student ready to learn from her!

It was all very gratifying. Lord Harveston had been very gratifying.

There had even been a moment, as the conversation went on, when he'd gone to fetch her a glass of wine and their hands had brushed one another in the exchange.

It had been lightning on the horizon. That feeling when the air is filled with a charge of what was coming and the hair on one's arms stood up.

Had he done it on purpose? She could not be certain, but she knew from her sisters that it was an age-old gambit. Was he flirting?

Then, she was sure he'd nudged his chair just a bit closer to her. She could practically feel the heat from him, the vitality of him.

Now, she trotted up the stairs to her bedchamber with Miss Mayton on her heels. Her dear aunt had talked to her all the ride home, but it had been so difficult to attend to it. Her mind was full to bursting with all that had gone on.

Juliet rolled over in Cordelia's bed as they came in. She yawned and said, "I do not suppose you found your Corinthian at Harveston's little meeting."

"Not one in the whole house," Miss Mayton said, "though we did have rather a delightful evening. Your sister was an absolute triumph."

"Triumph?" Juliet said, sitting up. "About Aristotle and Thomas Aquinas?"

Cordelia jumped on the bed. "I took your advice, Jules. Really took it. I trusted in my womanly judgment."

"Cordelia spoke of the woman setting the tone in the house. Lord Harveston was so admiring of it," Miss Mayton said.

"It was as if he'd never heard of the idea before, which I really think he had not," Cordelia said. "Goodness, where would Papa and Darden be without us?"

"Positively floundering," Juliet said.

"It made them rethink their initial opinions," Miss Mayton confirmed.

Juliet narrowed her eyes. "Was Harveston flirting again?" she asked.

"Flirting? Flirting *again*?" Cordelia asked, wishing to hear Juliet's opinion before she gave her own.

"You know what I mean, Cordy," Jules said. "First he somehow magically arrives at our house though he cannot explain how, then he claims he admires the book we're reading, though I do not believe it for a moment. Now he's applauding your ideas at his salon. If that is not flirting, I do not know what is."

"I did wonder about it, actually," Cordelia said. "He brushed my hand when handing me my wine, which of course might have been accidental. But then I am sure he pulled his chair closer to my own."

"There you have it!" Juliet said. "I told you he was flirting. He has *designs*, but he is not your Corinthian."

"No, he is not my Corinthian," Cordelia said thoughtfully. There was probably no less of a Corinthian in the whole town.

And yet, she'd been so pleased that he had regarded her ideas so approvingly and he'd stayed at their group. It was her understanding that he used the gatherings to wander from group to group, he'd said so himself on that first night. He'd done that very thing on that first night.

He hadn't wandered this night. He'd stayed right by her side.

Now she felt that they were on equal footing. Firm equal footing. Because they were, were they not? She had one sort of knowledge and he had another. He had finally recognized that fact.

Or was it, that she had finally recognized that fact?

How ever it was, she was grown in confidence. He did not intimidate her now. She did not feel small or less than.

Somehow, his coming down in her estimation or her rising in her own estimation had made him more attractive.

Cordelia really could not help but be impressed with her own knowledge. She'd hardly known she had it, it had just come out.

Perhaps she knew even more that she did not yet recognize. Perhaps she might learn even more than she already had.

It was one thing to depend upon her womanly judgment, which really was turning out to be very good. Might she not learn other things?

To her surprise, she'd had no trouble at all debating the men this night. She could only imagine where she might get to if she put some effort into picking up new knowledge.

"Aunt," she said, "might we go to Lackington & Allen on the morrow?"

"The bookstore?" Juliet asked. "Cordy, do not tell me you will try to turn yourself into an intellectual on account of Lord Harveston."

"Not an intellectual, exactly," Cordelia said, "just to know more than I do at this moment. And it is not for anybody but myself."

"Books? Goodness," Miss Mayton said.

Juliet threw herself back on the pillows and stared at the ceiling. "Just remember, when it is my season, I will seek out my poet. I shan't go willy-nilly changing my mind. I shan't think well, now, that fellow has just insulted me to my shoes, I think I'll decide to like *him*."

"Nobody said anything about liking anybody," Cordelia said.

Though, she *was* growing rather to like Lord Harveston. It was a strange idea, but there it was.

✦⟫⟫⟩⟨⟨⟨✦

THE DRAWING ROOM had emptied out and Percival had taken a last glass of wine before the sideboard was cleared.

Makepeace surveyed the footmen at their work and said, "I have become a shell of a man. I am living inside a nightmare. I am awake and it simply unfolds all around me. There is no escape!"

The footmen turned their heads and Percival was certain they were laughing. He said, "Come now, your evening could not have been *that* bad. My aunt can be rather a lot to manage, but I will hardly believe she has reduced you to a shell of a man living inside a nightmare."

"You have little imagination if you do not think so," Makepeace said. "Every time we attempted to discuss the matter at hand, it was right back to Shakespeare! A whole catalog of Shakespeare's heroes judging their own case and coming out on the wrong end of the stick."

"It is a valid argument, I suppose," Percival said.

"But it was not the argument posed for the evening," Makepeace said. "Oh, and then, what did Lady Agatha and Mrs. Robinson have to add? Apparently, one is to wonder over every idea and claim it deserves further thought. How can there be further thought when there has been no thought to begin? I really wished to ask that question."

"But you did not, I pray," Percival said.

"I was the model of restraint," Makepeace said, "though I was tempted to march right out the door to express my displeasure, just as I noted Haventops did, that lucky sot."

"That was not why he left," Percival said.

This seemed to give his butler pause. "Why else would he leave?"

"He left because he was being petulant, ungentlemanly, and spiteful, which Lady Cordelia very forcefully pointed out to him. She was quite marvelous."

"Marvelous? That seems rather far-fetched. I do not suppose she had anything particular to add to the actual debate."

"She did, rather. She claimed that a man cannot be a good judge of himself and would be well served to have a wife or sisters in the house for good counsel."

"Didn't she just. Well, if ever there were a heavier hint dropped, I am sure I don't know about it."

"Hint?"

"Surely, you did not fail to perceive that boulder of a bon mot dropped on your head? A lady of marriageable age hints that you ought to have a lady in the house?"

"Certainly not," Percival said.

Lady Cordelia had not been hinting about his particular situation. At least, he did not think so.

No, definitely not.

Though, he could not escape the fact that it was an intriguing idea. He was mightily attracted to Lady Cordelia. There really was nobody prettier. And then, what a mind!

He'd been so mistaken in the beginning; he saw that with all clarity now. Really, he thought he'd been, well as Lady Hightower had said, insufferable. It certainly gave evidence to her ideas about the tone of a house.

Lady Cordelia perceived things other people, or him in particular, did not perceive.

But even if he considered a pursuit…well for one, he was not at all certain he was interesting enough for Lady Cordelia. She was looking for a Corinthian and he could not be further from that. For another, this Lord Darling character was living in her house, no doubt making himself amusing. *He* was probably a Corinthian. *He* was probably polishing his sword and talking about boxing all the day long.

At least, he supposed that was what Lord Darling was doing.

For all he knew about it, an announcement of an engagement might be in the offing.

He would like to know more about this Lord Darling and his plans.

"Makepeace," he said. "On the morrow, find me a private investigator. I would like to know more about Lord Darling."

"Who is Lord Darling?"

"That is exactly what I want to know. Is he some sort of a Corinthian? What is he doing in Lady Cordelia's house? What are his intentions? And that fellow Chester too, for that matter. That rogue might spend his days screaming, but what is he screaming about? What are *his* intentions? I want to get to the bottom of it all."

Makepeace grabbed at a decanter from a passing tray and swigged from it. "Why not? I have been dropped into a waking nightmare—no reason I shan't live in it forever. Of course we must have an investigation into the lady's household."

Having set the ball rolling regarding a private investigator to provide some answers, Percival sipped his wine.

He would have his answers.

But then, what would he do with the answers he got?

What would he do if in fact this Lord Darling was a very great Corinthian set on sweeping Lady Cordelia off her feet?

"Makepeace," he said, eyeing his butler drinking straight from a decanter, "on the morrow, find me someone who can instruct me on sporting things."

Makepeace's arm suddenly went limp and the wine left in the decanter drained out of it. "Sporting things?" he whispered.

"Yes, sporting things," Percival said. "By the by, you are ruining that carpet."

❧

TATTLETON EYED THE sleeping goat in the servants' hall. Of course it would be exhausted after the energetic day it had.

When would that creature perceive that it was living in an earl's house and not on a steep mountainside?

Only this afternoon, he'd found it balancing on top of the mantel in the drawing room. Quite predictably, everything that had been on that mantel had been scattered on the floor and broken.

How had it got up there?

"Yes, I know, Mr. Tattleton," Mrs. Huffson said, "Lord Darling has caused a bit of chaos today."

"A bit, you say?"

"I do think he is getting of an age where he might do very well in the garden."

"We are in whole-hearted agreement on that point," Tattleton said.

"Perhaps we have Charlie take him out for an hour on the morrow?"

"Or even longer," Tattleton said. "Or forever, if it please God."

"Now, I cannot think Lord Darling is the only thing that troubles you, Mr. Tattleton. You and I have been working together for these twenty years, I think I understand when you've something bothering you."

"You know me too well, Mrs. Huffson," Tattleton said, rather cheered that at least one person in the house perceived the weight on his shoulders.

"Out with it, then."

"Did you know that Miss Mayton, Lady Cordelia, and Lady Juliet went to Lackington & Allen this afternoon?"

"That behemoth of a bookstore on Finsbury Square?"

"The very one," Tattleton said. "Not only did they come back with a pile of books, but they have befriended Mr. Lackington and arranged to correspond with that gentleman. I was told by Miss Mayton that the letters would be addressed to her."

"Goodness, why?"

"That is the question, is it not? What are they trying to learn that they could not find in the earl's library and why do they need to be in contact with Mr. Lackington? And why did they steal up the stairs when they returned, taking the books up to Lady Cordelia's room with no mention of what they were? Not one word to the earl at dinner."

Mrs. Huffson's brow wrinkled and she sipped her brandy.

"You see where I am going, Mrs. Huffson."

The housekeeper nodded sadly. "Aye, if they buy a hair clip or a sheet of paper, they describe it in detail to the earl. It has always been so."

"All I know," he said, "is that up until now, they have only been interested in those dreadful books Miss Mayton finds somewhere. Now, they have secret books and a correspondence nobody knows anything about."

"Miss Mayton knows about it, at least," Mrs. Huffson said hopefully.

Tattleton sighed. The housekeeper really was so dreadfully naïve.

CHAPTER FIFTEEN

THOUGH PERCIVAL HAD ordered Makepeace to find him both an investigator and a sporting tutor, he had rethought the sporting idea.

It was not that he'd rethought his aim, but how to go about it.

An investigator could come from any walk of life, as long as he knew his business. A sportsman would be a different matter. He needed a man who could coach him on the pursuits of the *ton* and that would require that he be a gentleman.

Once that notion had settled in his mind, it was easy enough to determine who he ought to seek out—Hamill.

He would not go to Jeffries. That fellow had loose lips and a propensity to turn everything into a joke. He would not go to the duke, as he was married to Lady Cordelia's sister. He did not wish for word of what he was doing to get round. He did not wish for anyone to know anything about it.

He'd much prefer that Lady Cordelia simply discovered he was very sporting as if he'd always been so—he just did not show off.

In any case, how difficult could it be? Simply master the various pursuits as he probably should have done long ago. He would not care for them, nor would he live his life dreaming of his next boxing match or carriage race, but there was no harm in mastering such things.

The drawing room doors swung open. "Lord Hamill," Makepeace said.

"Excellent," Percival said. "Hamill, do you care for a brandy, port, claret?"

"Coffee if it is not too much trouble," Hamill said. "I am driving in a race to Brighton tomorrow morning and wish to keep my head clear, the bets are steep."

Of course he would be racing to Brighton on the morrow. What else would he be doing?

They spoke of pleasantries until Makepeace had brought in the coffee and departed the room.

Now, he must get to it. Though, he was finding it hard to actually get started.

"Now what's the lay of the land?" Hamill asked. "You seem dead serious, as if you are a second to a duel I know nothing about."

"A duel? Certainly not, I would never involve myself in such nonsense."

"Not like Baderston, eh? Three duels on the same morning? Well, it all came off in the end."

Percival nodded, as of course he and everybody else in England had heard of that situation. Baderston had wedded another of the Benningtons after she'd stopped the duels in their tracks.

"Hamill," he began, "it has occurred to me that a gentleman has a duty to be well rounded. Naturally, a gentleman will have his own proclivities—those things he is naturally good at and wishes to pursue. But can that really be enough? Is it not a responsibility to push oneself into gaining expertise on those things that the gentleman is perhaps not as interested in?"

Hamill's expression grew dark. "Have you somehow talked to my sister?" he asked. "Has she convinced you I should read all the books she keeps piling on my desk?"

"Your sister? No, I do not know the lady. I did not even think she was out."

"She is not. Who then? Who is complaining about me spending all my time out of doors rather than locked in a library? Who put you up to being a tutor I do not want or need?"

"No, it is entirely the opposite. It is I who require a tutor."

Hamill laughed. "Gad, man, why on earth would you come to me?"

"Because I require a tutor on sporting sorts of things."

"Well, that makes more sense. But why?"

"That is not the important point, I do not think. The important point is we are both members of the YBC and, as such, we are in a position to do one another favors. Someday, you will require something from me and I will oblige you."

"It's about a woman, isn't it?"

"A woman? No, there is no woman," Percival said hurriedly. Even to his own ears, he did not sound very convincing.

"It's always about a woman. I reckon it's Lady Cordelia, you did get your back up a bit when I named her a pretty little filly."

"As to that, I simply thought—"

"*And*, Miss Mayton claims the lady seeks a Corinthian! Now I see—you wish to turn yourself into a sportsman."

Percival pressed his lips together. It was very inconvenient that Hamill was turning out to be not as stupid as he'd thought.

"I really do not think it matters why I have come to this conclusion," Percival said stiffly.

"All right, never mind. How about you come along on our little race on the morrow. We leave at sunrise driving our phaetons. The first one arriving to the green at the Pavilion wins. If you can keep up, it might be something you could mention to her."

"That sounds intriguing, but I am afraid I cannot," Percival said. "My aunt puts on her theatrical on the morrow, I have promised to be there."

He did not mention that he did not in fact own a phaeton. When he wished to ride, he rode Pericles. When he wished for his carriage, his coachman drove it. He supposed he would have to remedy that.

"The theatrical is tomorrow is it? My father always does get a laugh over it. Just last evening, he was telling my sister that this year was *Othello*. They laughed and laughed and claimed Desdemona was likely to live."

Percival grimaced. Of course, Hamill was right. Desdemona would live. At least, he thought so. He had not given any particular instruction regarding the use of swords, one sportsman-like skill that he had actually mastered. His aunt claimed they'd worked it out on their own—they had blocked out each step and practiced with wooden swords until they could do it in their sleep.

He was still hopeful that he could convince them to stick with wood swords and leave real swords alone.

"I should be back in Town on Tuesday—I'll take you to Jackson's for a few go rounds, then we can walk over to Angelo's for some swordplay."

Percival nodded, though it sounded like quite a lot for one day. No wonder Hamill never had time to read.

"Very much appreciated," he said. "Now Hamill, I would ask that this arrangement remain just between you and I."

"Mum's the word, though it won't go unnoticed that Lord Harveston has laid down his books and entered the ring."

No it probably would not go unnoticed. If only the *ton* were not so set on reporting everything they see!

"We could always claim it's for health reasons—doctor's orders and all that," Hamill said helpfully.

"Yes, yes, that would make sense," Percival said. It really was the only answer. He certainly could not say why he was really doing it.

He was not so sure he understood it himself.

CORDELIA HAD BEEN very diligent with her studies and had rather surprised herself with her enthusiasm. Mr. Lackington had been so very helpful!

The gentleman had found them wandering the aisles with dazed looks on their faces and immediately took them up the stairs to a charming receiving room overlooking the square. He'd ordered a pot of tea and biscuits and asked them to explain precisely what they looked for. He was certain that, whatever it was, he could find it or order it.

Cordelia had explained that she was not, perhaps, as mindful of her studies as she should have been when she had tutors. Now, she was a member of a literary society and would like to acquire a more well-rounded education.

Juliet had jumped in with the major caveat to the idea. They had no use for literary types who took five words and transformed them into fifteen and looped-de-looped, backtracked, and went off on tangents for hundreds of pages.

Dear Mr. Lackington had laughed heartily over it. He'd seemed to know precisely what Juliet meant by it. He'd questioned Cordelia about her interests and selected a variety of works that might engage her, all written in a straightforward style.

It turned out, when a subject was interesting to her she could read quite a lot in a day. She'd just discovered that Shakespeare was unaccounted for going on seven years. Certainly, he must have been somewhere, but historians could not confirm where.

She theorized he must have been on the continent—how else could he have set his plays in those foreign places? It was very interesting to think about.

Now, though, her books had been put away and all her thoughts had gone to her upcoming performance as Cassio. It was the night of Lady Rawley's play and while she was disappointed that she would not play Desdemona, she was determined to triumph as Cassio.

She did think her costume was very good looking. She wore a tight-fitting coat with regimental braid and a skirt with braid running down the sides of it to hint at trousers. Cordelia had thought it might be something more plain, as by this point in the play, Cassio had been dismissed from his position.

However, Lady Rawley said she did not wish for Cordelia to appear drab and one of the most charming things about rewriting Shakespeare was that she could take any liberty she felt like taking.

Miss Mayton was dressed in her usual widow's weeds, which Lady Rawley thought would be a wonderful hint to the audience, as Emilia would end a widow after all.

As they approached Lady Rawley's house, she had one last look at the invitation that had gone out.

In this exciting new idea of Othello, renamed Othello Redux, *things take a surprising turn. Iago has managed to convince Othello that Desdemona has taken Cassio as her lover. Will Desdemona die, as she has a thousand times on a thousand stages? Or will she take her fate into her own hands and live on? If so, how and with who? (Heads are spinning as Desdemona races toward the fate that the fates have set out for her!) All will become known in the most dramatic terms in a final revealing moment.*

Cast: Desdemona played by the incomparable Lady Margaret Rawley
Iago played by the indomitable Mrs. Jemima Robinson
Othello played by the indubitable Lady Agatha Montfried
Emilia played by the indispensable Miss Eloise Mayton
Cassio played by the ineffable Lady Cordelia Bennington

"I am indispensable and you are ineffable," Miss Mayton said as Sandren opened the carriage door. "I feel we've done very well for ourselves."

"Goodness," Cordelia said, her nerves creeping up on her, "this is the first time I will have a real audience! People who are not a part of my family. It is rather thrilling."

Hoofbeats drew her attention and Cordelia turned.

Lord Harveston approached on his horse. He did sit a horse very well, despite spending all his time reading books. It was a rather fine horse too.

He swung himself down easily and handed the reins to a groom. "Lady Cordelia, Miss Mayton."

"Lord Harveston," Cordelia said, "I did not realize you would come early."

"My aunt requested it specifically," Lord Harveston said. "She wishes me to examine the flowers and the sideboards, so that I might pick up tips for my own entertaining."

He said it in a sort of sighing voice and Cordelia knew very well what he thought about it.

"I can only applaud your willingness to indulge your aunt," she said.

"Oh yes," Miss Mayton said, "as an aunt myself, I can confirm it is very much appreciated."

Lord Harveston appeared gratified that they understood the real case of the thing. After all, there was nothing wrong with the sideboards he'd presented so far. As for flowers, well, for a gentleman like himself, it did not really suit.

"May I escort you inside?" he asked, holding his arms out.

Cordelia took one side and her aunt the other.

He really was such a gentleman. Oh, of course, he'd not begun so pleasant, but then he did not have a sister in the house who could have straightened out his ideas.

Since then, though, he'd seemed to have straightened his ideas out himself.

"Lord Harveston," she said, "did you know that historians lost track of Shakespeare for seven years? They cannot account for where he was."

"I believe I did read that somewhere."

"I theorize that he was on an extended grand tour. That's how he was able to set his plays at such places."

"It would seem to make sense."

"Tonight, we go to Venice," she said.

"So we do, Cassio."

Cordelia felt pinpricks all over her arms. There was something intimate in him calling her Cassio. She did not know why exactly. It was not even her name.

They had entered the drawing room where the play was to take place and Cordelia realized she was disappointed that their speculations about Shakespeare's seven unaccounted for years must be cut short.

Lady Rawley came at them at a rush. "The remaining members of my troupe have arrived!" She turned to Lady Agatha and Mrs. Robinson and said, "Come, let us gather together and reflect on what we are to accomplish this night. My dear nephew, please feel free to examine the sideboards, I am sure you will get ideas."

Lady Rawley wore a billowing blue silk dress with a delicate fichu. Both Lady Agatha and Mrs. Robinson were looking rather smashing in their military garb, their hilts swinging jauntily at their sides.

Cordelia smiled as Lord Harveston made his way to Lady Rawley's multiple sideboards that seemed to contain everything that had ever been found in her kitchens. He made a very good show of looking at it all, then poured himself a large glass of wine.

"My dear actors," Lady Rawley said, "we prepare ourselves to tread the hallowed boards, shining a beacon of light into our audiences' imaginations. They shall be fascinated and engrossed and they will entirely forget their own troubles as they invest themselves in Desdemona's fate. I predict we will have several people on the edge of their seats."

Lady Rawley had a dreamy expression and Cordelia could only appreciate that the lady loved the theater and acting as much as she did herself.

"Lady Agatha and Mrs. Robinson have worked tirelessly on the pivotal scene," Lady Rawley continued. "That moment when Shakespeare's ideas go topsy-turvy and Iago and Othello kill each other."

Lord Harveston had looked up at the mention of the sword fight. "Aunt," he said, "I do hope I was able to convince you to stick with the wooden swords?"

Lady Rawley laughed. "My dear nephew, no audience would be fooled by such a childish ruse! No, we must have veracity in all things. Veracity is what will move our audience to tears of joy."

"But I really—"

"Freddy," Lady Rawley said to one of her footmen, thereby ignoring her nephew, "bring the glasses. Ladies, in a time-honored tradition, we shall steady ourselves with a glass of the noble grape."

PERCIVAL HAD BEEN disturbed that his aunt was carrying on with the plan to use real swords during the play. He thought the chances of an injury resulting from it was rather high.

He'd since slipped out to the hall and found Jones, the lady's butler. He'd requested Jones send word to Lady Rawley's doctor, explaining that the violence of the play might upset some ladies' constitutions. He could not very well say he worried about a lady being run through, as that would likely bring a magistrate too.

His aunt's physician lived in Mayfair, catering to ladies with deep pockets and deep admiration for their nerves. It would not take any time at all to get him here, and he would be directed to discreetly watch the proceedings from a doorway. Should things go awry, he would be on hand to treat the patient.

That done, his mind kept drifting to his conversation with Lady Cordelia. How lovely she'd looked in a military coat. There was something dashing about it.

Then, she'd mentioned she'd been wondering about Shakespeare's unexplained seven-year disappearance.

No, that was not it—she'd *theorized* about it.

Since when did the lady theorize? Perhaps she'd had theories all along and he'd just been too insufferable to notice?

The drawing room had filled and though Percival was irritated that his aunt still hinted that his sideboard was not up to snuff, he could not ignore how popular her own seemed to be.

Each set of chairs round the stage had a small table in front of them and people were carrying plates piled high and full glasses to their seats.

Amidst the hubbub, Percival noted Lady Cordelia's extended family arriving in force. The earl, Darden, the duke and his duchess, and Baderston and his new bride.

Where was this Lord Darling character? Did they not take him out anywhere? It did not seem so.

He would understand why Chester was forever left behind, as it sounded as if he had a vile temper, but where was Lord Darling?

Unless there was some reason to leave him behind too. Could there be a reason the man could not appear in polite society?

His investigator had written that he had "made strides" in gathering information. But the confounded fellow had not outlined what those strides were!

Percival was beginning to feel very impatient for answers.

Before he knew where his feet traveled, he was in front of the earl and Darden.

"Harveston," Darden said jovially, "I did not expect to find you here."

"Lady Rawley is my aunt," he said by way of explanation. Though, the explanation sounded rather weak, as Lady Rawley had been his aunt all the other years that he had *not* attended.

"I do not usually come to such things, myself," the earl said, "but my daughter and Miss Mayton have been so very keen on the whole thing."

"Yes," Percival said, "they are all exceedingly enthusiastic about it."

"Well, I suppose we will be entertained in some manner," the earl said genially. "And then, the sideboard looks very good. Very good indeed."

Percival nodded. Perhaps his sideboard was not quite as good as it should be after all.

He pushed that notion aside. He must find out about Lord Darling.

Boldly, he said, "Lord Darling does not attend? He does not care for such entertainments?"

The earl and Darden both laughed heartily.

"That is very good, Lord Harveston," the earl said. "Very good indeed."

"I suppose," Darden said, "Lord Darling would be delighted with the entertainment, and even more with the sideboard. What might he help himself to, I wonder? The entire sideboard, and then Lady Rawley's precious possessions, for good measure."

"Gracious, that fellow is becoming the bane of my existence—I cannot get him out of the house!" the earl said jovially.

Percival was rather stunned by these revelations.

What was he to understand of this situation? Was Lord Darling some sort of freeloader who could not be shown the door?

Percival paused. Darden had said Lord Darling would go after "precious possessions." What could be a more precious possession than a sister or a daughter!

Why did the earl and Darden just stand there laughing about it though? Why did they not take action?

He could not question them more closely about it, even if he'd known what question to ask without causing offense, as Lord Iverson was calling everyone to their seats.

As most in attendance had already claimed their spots by way of filled plates and full glasses already on tables, the operation did not take as long as might be expected.

Percival reluctantly left the earl and Darden to find his own place.

Iverson, forever admiring of Lady Rawley's productions, had long been assigned the role of introducing each new play. Or each new…whatever it was.

"My dear ladies, esteemed gentlemen," Lord Iverson said, "it is my honor each year to introduce the latest burst of originality leaping out of the nimble mind of Lady Margaret Rawley."

A burst of originality was certainly a diplomatic way to put it.

"This year, she brings you *Othello Redux*," Iverson said with his own particular brand of enthusiasm.

Lady Rawley and her acting troupe had arranged themselves on the stage, but for Miss Mayton, who stood in the wings.

Lady Cordelia looked so well! What did she face at home though? Did she have that diabolical Lord Darling trying to catch her in corners? What must she feel to have her brother and her father take so little care! And what of Miss Mayton? Would she not speak out against the rogue?

He glanced toward the door and saw Jones standing next to a late middle-aged and rather portly gentleman. Lady Rawley's physician, no doubt. Please God he was not needed.

Percival sipped his wine as the play began. He gulped it when they came to the sword fight.

Desdemona lay on the ground, supposedly dead from drinking poison but having winked at the audience to say she was not really dead. How she'd got there had been filled with rushes from one end of the stage to another, plaintive speeches proclaiming her innocence as she cradled the alleged bottle of poison, a final drinking of said poison, and a sudden collapse.

Miss Mayton had just rushed onstage, oddly cast as Iago's bride, though dressed in widow's weeds, to deliver the message against her husband. Desdemona had spoken the truth, she was innocent, and the vile plot was Iago's.

"I will run you through!" Lady Agatha's Othello shouted.

"Not before I run *you* through!" Mrs. Robinson's Iago shouted back.

Percival leaned forward. Here was the danger.

The two ladies danced round each other and then thrust their swords.

They stopped and glanced down at themselves, noticing

nothing had happened. They had not managed to pierce whatever bags held his aunt's concoctions of blood—red paint mixed with a little flour to thicken it.

They swung their swords again. This time, Lady Agatha hit her mark. The audience gasped as a sickly red erupted through the material of Mrs. Robinson's costume and dripped down in rivulets.

Mrs. Robinson sank dramatically to the floor, seeming to have forgotten that she and Lady Agatha were supposed to kill each other and *both* die.

Lady Agatha, through what Percival supposed was quick thinking, turned her sword on herself and stabbed her bag, then dropped to the floor.

"Everyone!" a voice from the doorway shouted, "stay calm and follow my directions!"

Percival turned and saw the portly physician hurrying forward. "Gentlemen, I need towels and bandaging! Ladies, this sight is too horrifying to witness—turn away!"

Percival put his head in his hands. Apparently, Jones had forgot to tell the poor fellow about the bags of blood.

CHAPTER SIXTEEN

PERCIVAL LEANED BACK and observed the debacle before him. Lady Rawley's doctor had rushed the stage.

As men were always ready to spring into action once one of them had sprung, it hardly mattered whether there was cause or not. Various of them raced this way and that.

Mr. Hemmingshaw attempted to pull down a curtain, though Percival was certain that had there actually been a need for bandaging, there would have been better options. The poor fellow had raced past a foot-high stack of linen napkins that would have done very well.

Despite the physician warning the ladies to turn away from the gruesome sight, the two women next to him were very determinedly staring at it.

One said, "It was bound to go wrong sooner or later."

The other nodded. "She took the thing too far."

Both Lady Agatha and Mrs. Robinson sat up.

"Do not move, ladies!" the physician cried. "You are gravely injured."

Percival could not hear what Lady Rawley said from her location on the floor, but her lips moved rapidly so she clearly had a lot to say to her doctor.

The poor fellow, seeming to finally understand the case of the thing, stood and turned to the audience just as Mr. Hemmingshaw was dragging a curtain to the stage.

The doctor waved him away. "Well!" he said. "It seems that was a false alarm of sorts. Now, to carry on, Lady Rawley informs me that both Iago and Othello are dead, and Lady Agatha and Mrs. Robinson are very much alive."

The fellow hurried from the stage and the last Percival saw of him, he was gesticulating to the butler.

The play carried on to its happy ending, with Cassio and Desdemona strolling off the stage arm in arm, while Iago and Othello lay dead. Apparently, nobody had told Miss Mayton what she was to be doing at this moment of the play, so she just turned and left.

It was certainly a night to remember.

The applause was hearty, as everyone had a delightful story to tell in their drawing rooms on the morrow—poor Lady Rawley's physician had thought Lady Agatha and Mrs. Robinson had stabbed one another.

The acting troupe had all curtsied and left the stage to receive their congratulations.

Lady Cordelia was surrounded by her family and so he could not see a way to politely barge in.

His aunt seemed not at all shaken by the interruption to her play. He'd just heard her say, "That is the skill of an acting troupe, Mrs. Renway. One must stay in character regardless of what occurs. The stage is an unpredictable taskmaster."

Conbatten had just retrieved a glass of wine from the sideboard and stood next to him, admiring his wife as she congratulated Lady Cordelia.

"One of the things that has always charmed me about the Benningtons," the duke said, "is that they are all so approving of one another. If one of them does a thing, the rest pronounce it marvelous. Just this moment, Lady Cordelia will be compared to Sarah Siddons and found superior, though her only line was 'my dearest Desdemona, let us marry.'"

That might be so, in fact Percival was certain it was so. Enough had been said of the sisters' accomplishments to confirm the idea. Everybody knew of the duchess' odd style of playing the pianoforte, which was likened to a cat falling on the keys. And then it was said that Lady Viola had painted a wedding present for the couple that was so ghastly that Conbatten had built a special room to keep it from public view. The youngest sister wrote odes to trees and fences.

But how could they be so wonderful to one another if they allowed the likes of Lord Darling and Chester to lurk around their house?

"Your Grace, I am sure it is not my business, but if I might inquire—why does not the earl do something about Lord Darling?"

Conbatten laughed. "It has always seemed to me that Lord Westmont is helpless against the doings of that house."

"But then, what of Darden?" Percival asked.

"Darden?" the duke said. "Darden is a particularly easygoing sort of man. I imagine he just views the whole thing amusing."

The duke wandered away.

Amusing? How could he view it amusing?

Percival was beginning to wonder if he'd ever known Darden as well as he'd thought he had.

The circle round Lady Cordelia and Miss Mayton was not as tight as it had been. Darden had turned to talk to Mr. Reardon. The earl was congratulating Lady Agatha. The duke had retrieved his bride and brought her the glass of wine. Lady Baderston and her husband had drifted into a corner, heads together as the newly-wedded couple that they were.

Percival set his wine down and strode over.

"Lady Cordelia, Miss Mayton," he said, "my congratulations."

Lady Cordelia nodded her acknowledgment, and Percival noted a faint flush. Miss Mayton said, "We've come through it, Lord Harveston, despite the setbacks."

"Yes, well, my aunt will discover it sooner or later," he said. "I am afraid I am the author of the setback. I ordered the butler to have Lady Rawley's doctor on hand, as real swords would be used."

"Oh!" Lady Cordelia said, unable to hide her surprise.

"I simply did not wish anyone to be hurt, and if they *were* injured I wished they received prompt medical attention."

"That was very kind," Lady Cordelia said.

Miss Mayton was nodding her head. "Ah well, sometimes a kindness goes awry, does it not? I do not suppose anybody was ever in any real danger."

Percival looked Lady Cordelia in the eye. "But if you were to discover yourself in danger," he said, "you could call on me."

Lady Cordelia appeared taken aback by that statement. He was rather taken aback himself.

Percival bowed. "Ladies," he said. He then quickly left the house.

⫸⫷

CORDELIA LAY AWAKE in the early morning hours, that time of day when the sun was not yet up but darkness had fled. She had not been able to sleep at all, so busy was her mind.

So busy was her heart too.

The play had taken a turn, what with Lady Rawley's doctor imagining that Lady Agatha and Mrs. Robinson were dying. Lady Rawley had been a complete professional, clearing up the matter speedily and encouraging them to carry on.

Cordelia had made the most of her one line. She'd worked on it every which way and had finally decided to put the emphasis on two words—dearest and marry. Desdemona *dearest*, let us *marry*. She'd carried it off just as she'd planned.

The audience had seemed very pleased with the play. Of course, her wonderful family had heaped praise upon her. Rosalind had even said that Sarah Siddons would be envious of her performance.

But then, Lord Harveston.

He was what really was taking up her thoughts. That one sentence—if she ever felt in danger, she ought to call on him.

The look in his eyes when he'd said it!

It had been the most impossibly romantic thing she'd ever heard or even imagined.

She had, of course, imagined all sorts of things a gentleman might say to her. Such things as her eyes penetrated the depths of his soul, or her voice was a silken balm to his heart, or her person inflicted deadly longing upon him and he was considering doing a violence to himself.

But that phrase, that had been…she was not certain what it had been. It felt as if that one sentence had moved her closer to him, though the distance between them had not changed.

It had almost felt like a kiss, or at least what she imagined a kiss would feel like. It had marked her out as someone particular to him. Someone he worried about.

She did not know why he should worry, but it was exceedingly gratifying that he did.

That was the thing that was on her mind. How gratified she was to know she was worried about by Lord Harveston.

In the beginning, they'd got off on such the wrong foot! Now, though, there was something between them. She could feel it. She also noticed that she was fast becoming less concerned about finding her Corinthian.

Though, if there *was* something between them, something that could lead to…

Each time Cordelia got to that point in her thinking, her mind clouded over.

What was she to think of it? That it could be possible that someone like Lord Harveston wished to pursue someone like herself? He was an intellectual, she was decidedly not.

Oh, she had proved her womanly judgment well enough, but he knew piles and piles of facts she'd never even heard of.

And then, what of herself? Could she really be satisfied with the differences between them? Would she always feel a bit outclassed? Would she, sometime in the future, regret that she'd not married a Corinthian?

Married.

She'd thought it. The word her mind kept clouding over. There it was.

Cordelia did not know if he would ask. She did not know if she were completely wrongheaded in even imagining it. But her womanly judgment said that he very well might.

If that was so, she must be prepared with an answer. When one was proposed to, one could accept or decline. She had not ever heard of a lady saying she did not know.

She must begin to know her own mind more clearly.

"Do not go out there, Mr. Tattleton," Mrs. Huffson said, holding him back by the sleeve with one hand while her other hand held the door to the garden shut.

Tattleton could not quite discern what had occurred, but he could deduce two things: one, something had happened in the garden, and two, Cook was distraught over it.

The fellow was head in hand, weeping and banging his fist on the counter, while Charlie patted him on the back to console him.

"It's the goat, isn't it?" he asked.

"Aye, I'm afraid so," the housekeeper said.

"Is he dead?" Tattleton asked, a glimmer of hope in his voice.

"Oh no, definitely not dead," Mrs. Huffson said.

There was a sudden pounding on the door, though there was no person to be seen through the glazed window.

"Was that the goat, Mrs. Huffson?" he asked gravely. "Is he having the temerity to bang on the door with his uncouth hoofs?"

"Um, yes, that would be him. Now, remember we did agree that we'd try him out in the garden this morning?"

"Step aside, Mrs. Huffson," Tattleton said.

The housekeeper reluctantly stepped out of the way. Tattleton pushed down the latch and opened the door.

Lord Darling, or Lord Worst-goat-in-England as he would have been better named, trotted through the door with a bunch of peonies drooping from his mouth.

Tattleton looked out to the garden. Surveying the carnage that had been done there, he was no longer in doubt over what Cook was crying about.

The whole place was torn up!

Flowerbeds lay demolished. If a flower had not been ripped up by its roots, then it had been trampled upon or its head was missing and a forlorn stalk left waving in the breeze. The vegetable garden was no more—just dug up dirt left in its stead. The charming, white-painted wood bench that was meant for quiet reflection in the midst of nature had been overturned and its arms chewed on. The fountain with the blue-tiled bottom meant to make the water seem as the sea now only halfheartedly dribbled what looked as if it had come from a sediment filled canal.

"Now, Mr. Tattleton," Charlie said in a soothing voice, "as I told Cook, I know it looks mighty terrible—"

"Mighty terrible? That would be one way to describe the wasteland I am currently viewing."

"But I reckon it can be put to rights quick enough," Charlie said.

"He reckons it," Cook sobbed, "but I just don't know!"

Though Tattleton would like to sob himself, there was no such luxury for a butler. He was the senior-most servant and if he collapsed, the whole house collapsed.

"And what, young Charlie," he said, "would be your plan to put things to rights?"

"My uncle, he's got a farm just outside of Town and he's handy as the day is long. I could write to him and offer to pay if he brings in vegetables and flowers, and all the herbs Cook needs. He could fix the place up. I know 'im, he'd have his cart hitched in a trice."

"A trice?" Cook said, wiping at his eyes. "He really would come in a trice and fix my garden?"

"In a trice, sir," Charlie assured him.

Well, why not? That they had come to requiring somebody's uncle to repair the desolation inflicted upon them by a goat they kept in the house should come as no surprise at this point.

Tattleton supposed he should anticipate that next season they would have a herd of horses in the house and then they could all seem surprised when every stick of furniture was kicked to pieces.

Maybe Charlie's uncle could help with that too!

PERCIVAL PACED HIS drawing room. The investigator, Mr. Rembric, was to come at two o'clock and he expected answers from the fellow. He'd written that he'd begun to make headway. Percival would demand the details of the headway. He wanted answers about this Lord Darling character.

Makepeace fussed with the coffee things. He'd brought out an old service, which Percival presumed was his comment on having the likes of Mr. Rembric in the drawing room.

"He was to be here at two," Percival said. "It must be two by now. I do not like it that he is late!"

"It is five minutes to the hour," Makepeace said, after having glanced at the clock on the mantel.

"I can read the time myself," Percival answered. "I just doubt it is right."

He stopped talking, as even to his own ears, he was beginning to sound like a lunatic. Makepeace only nodded and left the room.

Percival felt driven by a single-minded purpose. He must know about Lord Darling.

He must know what Lord Darling was to Lady Cordelia.

Percival had been up half the night sorting through his thoughts. The more rash side of his temperament, which he rarely allowed any freedom, had wished to ride over to the earl's house and rescue his daughter from whatever untoward situation she was in.

His more rational thoughts told him otherwise. For one, Lady Cordelia had not even hinted that she needed rescuing. For another, if she did, she had not indicated that he would be her chosen rescuer. And for another, if he enacted such a mad plan, he would have turned himself into a perceived danger, on top of the one already there.

Wherever his thoughts took him, they all included Lady Cordelia. How had it happened? He'd gone along keeping an eye out for his lady intellectual, and now all he thought about was a lady quite the opposite.

Finally, as the clock struck two, whether it was right or behind time, he heard the door knocker.

Makepeace opened the drawing room doors. "Mr. Rembric, my lord," he said, looking askance at the fellow's ill-fitting coat.

His butler might well look askance—Rembric was a disheveled sort of person. Nothing he wore seemed to fit, his hair looked as if it had been separated from the company of a comb for too long a time, his boots were scuffed, and his skin was rather pasty.

Nevertheless, Makepeace poured the coffee for them both, bowed, and exited with his usual aplomb.

"Let us get right to it, Rembric. You said you had made headway, tell me everything."

Mr. Rembric had sat himself down before being invited, which Percival assumed must be common in his milieu. The fellow took a long sip of coffee and set down his cup.

"To say I made headway, Lord Harveston, is to paint the thing weak. More like I bored through an Alp and rode my horse straight through it. In these kinds of cases, it is often like that— one goes along inch by inch, creepin' through mud, then all of a sudden-like, one bores through the mountain. In my experience, it always comes down to a person who will tell some tales. Findin' the tale-teller is my specialty, as it were."

Mr. Rembric looked entirely satisfied that he'd explained everything. Percival did not have the first idea of what he was talking about. What did he mean, he bored through an Alp?

"Lord Darling, Mr. Rembric. What have you found out about Lord Darling?"

"Ah, yes, the lord in question. And that Chester you were interested in too."

"Yes, both of them," Percival said, feeling his patience wane, "but especially Lord Darling."

"I don't mind sayin' it, the identity of that fellow took me back. I didn't see that coming in a thousand years."

Identity? Was he some sort of fraud, merely posing as a lord? Did the earl know?

"I done my usual operation, gettin' acquainted with the low-liest of the staff through various means. Kitchen maids in particular are helpful—they don't get paid much, they're grateful for some extra, and they do like sharin' an opinion. Nobody ever asks a kitchen maid nothing, so when you do ask, they're as accommodating as you please."

Percival had a great urge to pull Rembric to his feet and shake him to the point.

"Now then, my lord, I'm leadin' up to the thing all slow-like as it ain't gonna be what you were expecting. I don't know what you were expecting, of course. But what it is, isn't what you were expecting."

"Mr. Rembric," Percival nearly shouted.

"Aye, I see you're gettin' yourself anxious. Well, here it is— Lord Darling, Marquess of Basingstoke, ain't a real lord."

"I knew it!"

"He's a goat that they got livin' in the house. I could never discover why he's livin' in the house, but there you have it. The youngest, Lady Juliet, named him Lord Darling, Marquess of

Basingstoke as that's where they found the little fella. Basingstoke."

Percival sank into a chair. "That cannot be right," he said quietly.

"Oh, it's right," Mr. Rembric said. "I confirmed the thing backwards and forwards."

"And Chester? The fellow who screams all the time?"

"A parrot they done left in the countryside. 'Parently, the creature shouts murder at everybody. I shouldn't like to live with that myself, havin' to think of murder all the time—'tis a bad business."

Could it be true?

It was true that there was a goat in the house—he'd seen it with his own eyes. But could that really be Lord Darling?

The various conversations about Lord Darling presented themselves to him. Lady Cordelia's description of him—he had been met with on their travels. The earl claiming he could not get him out of the house. Darden saying he would eat everything on Lady Rawley's sideboard and then destroy her possessions.

My God. Lord Darling was the goat.

Mr. Rembric rose. "All I know past what I told you, my lord, is that Lord Darling has gone and destroyed the garden. The butler was verging on some sort of apoplectic fit over it, but then it was decided that Charlie's uncle would fix it up in a trice and they're all countin' on him."

The investigator bowed and wished him good day.

Percival still sat, stunned by the realization that his supposedly intellectual mind had led him to think that a kid goat was some roguish gentleman set on seducing Lady Cordelia.

Where had that wild imagination come from? He generally did not have a wild imagination. He left imagining to composers and authors—his was a world of facts.

Makepeace came in and said, "I have shown Mr. Rembric out, but not before him pressing me to find out if we have any other mysteries that needed solving."

Percival nodded. "He told you about Lord Darling, then?"

"He did not. I presumed whatever you discovered, you would be marching that information directly to the earl."

Percival erupted in laughter. "No, not in this case. Lord Darling is the goat they have in the house."

"The goat they were all chasing the night you wandered onto their street? They keep it in the house? Why? Why do they have a goat in the house?"

"I do not know, really," Percival said. "They are the Benningtons, I suppose that is why. They are very charming and original people, very charming indeed."

CHAPTER SEVENTEEN

SEVERAL DAYS HAD passed since Cordelia's triumph as Cassio upon Lady Rawley's stage. The lady had been so kind as to send both her and Miss Mayton flowers, which had been lovely until Lord Darling had somehow got to them.

Poor Tattleton was exceedingly distraught by Lord Darling's mischief in the garden and so they did not mention it to him and just quietly put away the vases and mopped up the water on the floor.

Cordelia's father had also been rather distraught over the destruction of the garden, or at least as distraught as he ever was outside of a housefire. He had been soothed by the idea that Charlie's uncle was to have it sorted in a trice.

Charlie's uncle, who refused to be called Mr. Hanson and would only answer to Farmer Hanson, had since arrived. Tattleton had found him a spare room somewhere and the fellow had set to work. Nobody was quite sure what a trice amount of time would actually be, as Farmer Hanson had shaken his head gravely at the situation.

Lynette said he was not making himself popular with Tattleton as he kept saying things like, "Ya can't never allow a goat into a garden like that" and "I'm still a-head scratchin' as to why ya got a goat in the house."

Everybody else liked him well enough though.

Despite the entertaining doings of the house, Cordelia's

thoughts kept running in the same direction. Lord Harveston.

Certainly, the fates must be trying very hard to tell her something. Certainly, a person did not think of another person night and day without it meaning something particular?

That thing he'd said—if she were in any danger, she ought to call on him—would not leave her. She replayed it and replayed it.

And that was just one thing said! What else might he say?

She did not know, but she was certain she would see him this night, the night of Lady Bloomington's masque.

She and Miss Mayton had eaten a whole plate of biscuits before getting dressed, as they knew Lady Bloomington had some particular habits. As a sort of thumbing of nose at the patronesses of Almack's and their dreadful offerings, Lady Bloomington offered the moon and the stars.

Trays of little bites she called entremets would come round between every dance. Following those trays would be trays of champagne, and many a guest had left Lady Bloomington's rather worse for wear on account of it.

Van Doren had once been a victim of it and had managed to insult the duke in the process. He'd been lucky to not find himself on a green the next morning, answering the insult.

Miss Mayton's remedy was to go into the whole thing with a stomach well lined with biscuits.

Her aunt came into her bedchamber, looking as spectral as she had in other years. She would wear her widow's weeds but had added a long black veil that completely covered her from head to toe. Having had experience attempting to wrangle food and drink beneath the veil, she had since had a seamstress modify it to have armholes and a hole around her mouth cut out. The effect was no less eerie though.

Lynette was laying out her own costume, which was not what she had at first thought it would be.

Miss Mayton examined it. "I think Darden did rather well," she said. "The headpiece is marvelous."

Cordelia nodded. She'd had her heart set on going to the

masque as Desdemona, but then Darden had rightly pointed out that as Lady Rawley had just played Desdemona on the stage, she was likely to appear as that ill-fated lady herself.

She would not for the world wish to step on Lady Rawley's toes.

Rather, Darden had found a very ghostly sort of costume, the appeal of it being the headpiece. It was shaped rather like an old nun's headdress, but then there was a thin veil covering the face. Cordelia had tried it on and it was fascinating—she could see out very well, but her face was blurred in the looking glass.

The entire costume was white, but for the black lace of the veil.

Juliet bounced into the room as Lynette was helping her into the dress. "You shall look a pair," she said, "one ghost all in white, and another all in black."

"Just think, Jules," Cordelia said, "next year you will go yourself."

Juliet hopped on the bed, despite Lynette's warning scowl not to wrinkle anything. "Yes, but unlike anything happening here, I will come into my season searching for my poet and I will go to the masque still looking for my poet. Or, I will have already located him and he will be waiting there for me."

"I cannot help that I do not know what I look for," Cordelia said.

"You do, though," Juliet said. "It's Harveston, is it not?"

Cordelia sighed. "Yes, I think it is, though how I ever arrived at this circumstance, I am sure I do not know."

"Well, now," Miss Mayton said, "Beatrice was rather flummoxed over how she came to love Lord Van Doren."

"We were *all* rather flummoxed," Juliet said, "and some of us still are."

"But look how happy they are together."

"That is true," Juliet said grudgingly. "For all Van Doren's scolding of us, he treats Beatrice as the best thing living. I give him credit for that at least. Do you suppose Harveston will treat you as the best thing living?"

Cordelia could feel her face set afire at the very thought of it. She said, "I do not yet know if he will treat me as anything at all."

"Well, I suppose at the heart of it," Juliet said, "I wish you to be happy and so I'll put up with whoever you bring home."

Lynette had set Cordelia's headdress on her head, adjusted the veil, and pinned it in place.

"You are a very dear sister, Jules," Cordelia said.

Juliet hopped off the bed. "Don't I know it. Now, once you are all out of the house, I shall convince Tattleton and the footmen to play cards with me and Lord Darling will act as our chaperone. Perhaps we will even bring in the farmer—he drives poor Tattleton wild with wondering why anybody allowed a goat in the garden."

She skipped from the room and Cordelia and Miss Mayton were not long behind her.

It was time to depart. It was time to see Lord Harveston. It was time to see what he would say to her, and Cordelia knew what she would say back.

PERCIVAL'S LOGICAL MIND had entirely lost the fight. It had attempted to present all the reasons why Lady Cordelia would not suit. She was not an intellectual and he had long planned to wed an intellectual. She might not view him with the slightest interest.

That was really all that was against it. As for what was for it, well, all he need do was think of her, which he did frequently. His heart had raised its sword to his logical mind and slayed it.

Several times, over days of thinking, he would propose to forget all about Lady Cordelia. That idea had gone down in flames each time.

He realized that he had made some mistakes in how he'd

chosen to carry on with life. His early experiences, and seeing what had happened to Dora, had convinced him to live in a world of facts and figures. They had been the armor round his heart, never allowing him to be destroyed as Dora had been.

Then had come Lady Cordelia.

He could not forget about her. How could he, there was nobody like her.

Though, he could not forget that she'd outright said she was looking for a Corinthian.

He was not a Corinthian. He was not even a little sporting.

Percival was working to rectify that deficiency with Hamill's help, and it was exhausting.

How many mornings would Hamill send a footman up to inquire why he was still abed and that he'd better get up as they had something to get to. Boxing, swordplay, carriage driving. There had even been one morning when they had run through Hyde Park. Barefoot on the grass. Just running around.

Hamill was of the opinion that simply running would increase stamina. Privately, Percival thought one ought to only run around the grass barefoot if one was being chased by a murderer.

But run he had done.

Now, he'd entirely changed his costume for Lady Bloomington's masque. He had planned on wearing a simple domino, as he always did. Instead, he'd had Makepeace search high and low for a costume Shakespeare would have worn in his day.

Lady Cordelia admired Shakespeare, and so he would go as Shakespeare.

He strode through Lady Bloomington's doors feeling that he looked slightly ridiculous and shrugging off the feeling. Why should he care, as long as Lady Cordelia understood the compliment of it?

He'd already spent a morning running around barefoot in the park. Ridiculous was nothing to him.

He spotted Darden quick enough. He already knew that Darden and some of the other YBC members were going as the seven deadly sins. Darden was gluttony, was looking very round, and held something in his hand that resembled a felted turkey leg.

He hurried over. "Darden," he said.

"Harveston!" Darden said. "I'd offer you a piece of this large turkey leg, but as I am gluttonous, I must keep it for myself."

"Very well done costume. By the by, what costume does Lady Cordelia wear this night?"

"Ah, well she was to go as Desdemona, but then we thought maybe Lady Rawley would come as that lady in celebration of her recent performance. So now, Cordelia has come as a ghostly figure. She's dressed all in white and the headdress is shaped rather like a nun's would be. Perhaps a mother superior—it's very distinct. Oh, and there is a veil too."

Percival nodded. "Enjoy your turkey leg," he said, and set off in search of his ghostly figure.

He located Lady Cordelia in a moment. She was, for some reason, standing by the bishop, who had come in his regular bishop's attire.

He approached and bowed. "Bishop," he said.

The bishop eyed him in what felt like a suspicious manner. He could not account for it at all.

He turned to Lady Cordelia. "My lady, may I put myself down on your card?"

Lady Cordelia glanced at the bishop, who nodded solemnly. It was very odd, almost as if she had sought approval from him. Was he a great friend of the family?

No matter, he had given his approval for whatever it was worth. Percival took the card and felt a great amount of relief that the last dance had not yet been taken.

There was no proper supper at Lady Bloomington's masque, as she would be sending round trays of food all evening, but there always were a number of sideboards set up for the end of the night and people were expected to linger. That would give him the time to say everything he wished to say.

The bishop still stared at him. He did not at all understand why but he got the distinct feeling he should be off, having accomplished what he wished to.

He bowed and moved away.

One of Lady Bloomington's footmen handed him a glass of champagne. He gladly took it and felt exceedingly satisfied with how the evening progressed so far.

He supposed he ought to go round and add his name to other lady's cards, but he was not very inclined to it. Perhaps he would skip it altogether and simply be on hand to escort any lady sitting out once the ball began. Hostesses always appreciated that sort of chivalric rescue and as for himself, he did not really care who he danced with but for Lady Cordelia.

Percival spotted Hamill across the room, talking with a group of other sporting men. They were probably discussing some upcoming horse race and how the betting would shape up. He supposed it would not hurt to know more about it than he did.

He set off to join them in a very good frame of mind.

CORDELIA REALLY COULD not understand what was happening. Her card was fast filling, and yet Lord Harveston had not yet approached.

In fact, he'd spent some minutes speaking with the bishop and his daughter, Miss Bretherton, and then made his way to Lord Hamill and some other gentlemen. There he'd been for the past quarter hour!

What was so interesting about Miss Bretherton? She had, according to Rosalind, who found it a very good laugh, come as Mary Magdalene.

It was a very bold sort of thing to do. Did she claim she was more pious than anybody else?

Cordelia admitted to herself that while she did not know how filled up with piety Miss Bretherton was, she *did* know how filled up with facts she was.

Had she been wrong about Lord Harveston? Had she allowed her imagination, her hopeful, wishful imagination, to take her places she was never meant to go?

After all, he was an intellectual, and Miss Bretherton was too.

Gentlemen approached, they were all very pleasant, and they put themselves down on her card. None were Lord Harveston, however.

Lord Hamill had left the group and was very sensibly making the rounds. Lord Harveston remained right where he was, talking to other gentlemen.

She could hardly fail to take the hint.

If Cordelia had been in any doubt of her feelings before, now that what she had considered seemed to vanish in a puff of smoke, she was no longer in doubt.

She loved Lord Harveston, but he did not love her.

Lord Hamill approached. He bowed very gallantly and said, "Lady Cordelia, I believe, is under that veil?"

"Yes, Lord Hamill," she said, working to keep her tone very pleasant.

"May I?" he asked. He took her card and then he paused. "The final dance is still open?"

"Indeed yes," she said, hoping it did not sound like a sigh.

"Odd," Lord Hamill said. He put his name down for it.

That was it. Her card was filled. And, not one of the names was what she wished for.

All those stories of heartbreak Miss Mayton had told she and her sisters made sense now. Where once she could only squint and imagine it, now she felt it. Of course Hans had thrown himself off the side of a cliff, of course Gregorio had run himself through. Who would wish to feel as she did this moment? Who could bear it?

Worse, she was very afraid it would be a permanent condition. The color had drained from the world and it seemed very gray.

⫸⫷

PERCIVAL HAD MADE himself useful at Lady Bloomington's masque, keeping an eye open for ladies sitting out who would rather not find themselves in such a situation.

He'd only needed to step in twice and so had occupied himself with sporting talk with sporting gentlemen and perhaps a little too much champagne.

He was restless; he wished to get to the final dance. He'd even gone out to the balcony for nearly an hour, just to pass the time.

Finally, the moment had come. He searched the room, his eye briefly catching on another lady dressed as a ghostly figure, but that was not Lady Cordelia. That lady had a black veil, where Lady Cordelia's was white.

There. There she was. He hurried over, barely cognizant that the bishop was hovering nearby. So strange, but he had little time to examine it.

"Lady Cordelia," he said, putting out his arm.

"Lady Cordelia?" a voice from under the veil asked.

Percival felt the blood in his veins grow cold. It was not the voice of Lady Cordelia. He was very afraid of whose it was.

He was an idiot! It was Miss Bretherton. That's why she seemed to always be standing next to the bishop. He was her father.

What had he done?

"Lord Harveston," Miss Bretherton said, "if there has been some mistake or confusion…"

"No, of course not," he said gallantly as the bishop eyed him. "Yes, a bit of confusion, but a happy one, naturally. There are two of you dressed as ghostly figures."

"I am come as Mary Magdalene," she said.

"Oh, I see, yes, how stupid of me, my apologies."

As Percival spoke, it was as if somebody else spoke. That part of him that had been trained as a gentleman thought of what to say in this ghastly moment.

His other self, his true self, wished to shout that it had all been a mistake. He'd wasted his time hanging about Hamill and his friends, talking about bets, when he should have been looking for Lady Cordelia.

As he led Miss Bretherton to the ballroom floor, he searched the room for the real Lady Cordelia.

There she was, escorted by Hamill.

Hamill, the *real* Corinthian.

Did Hamill mean anything by it? He did not know, but if he found something out, he would dismiss the fellow as his sporting trainer. He would not have a viper in his very house!

Percival took a deep breath and told himself not to be stupid. This was not a disaster that could not be got over.

The next time he could have a private conversation with Lady Cordelia, or even a not so private one, he would tell her what happened.

It might even end as a funny story they might laugh about.

Maybe.

For now, he would lead Mary Magdalene through the changes while the bishop looked on.

CHAPTER EIGHTEEN

CORDELIA HAD GONE from one dance to another, smiling and making pleasant conversation. Whatever deficiencies had recently presented themselves regarding her education, a lack of manners had not been one of them.

She and all her sisters had been strictly schooled on the niceties and if sometimes they chose to ignore a rule of two, making innocent gentlemen uncomfortable would never be one of them.

Lord Hamill had come to collect her for the final dance.

He was dressed as a proud peacock, as he was one of Darden's group of seven deadly sins.

"Lady Cordelia," he said genially.

"Lord Hamill," she said pleasantly. "As always, the YBC has done a remarkable job with costumes."

She said it as a thing to say, as one rarely went wrong in delivering a compliment.

"Careful, Lady Cordelia," he said, "do not make the peacock prouder than he already is."

She laughed, because she knew she should. It was a clever jest.

"By the by," Lord Hamill said as they waited for their turn at the changes, "did you notice that Lord Harveston comes as Shakespeare? I understand you particularly admire Shakespeare."

Why was he mentioning Lord Harveston? What could he mean by it?

"I cannot claim to be singular in that admiration," she said. "I suppose it would be more unusual to discover that a person did *not* admire Shakespeare."

"Perhaps," Lord Hamill said. "It is a strange thing I noticed this evening," he went on, "your costume and Miss Bretherton's are so similar. Darden described your attire to me and, at first, I did think Miss Bretherton was you. I suppose I am not the only one to make that mistake."

What did he say? Did he mean that Lord Harveston engaged himself to Miss Bretherton for the last dance when he thought it was herself?

If it were a usual circumstance, Cordelia might think of a subtle way to inquire further. It was not usual though and, at this moment, she had little patience for subtlety.

"Lord Hamill," she said boldly, "do you claim that Lord Harveston meant to ask me for a dance and has mistakenly asked Miss Bretherton?"

Lord Hamill smiled. "That is my guess at what has happened."

That was his guess at what happened! He did not know for certain, but he did have reason to think that Lord Harveston would have preferred to be dancing with her right this minute.

That was something, was it not?

It could be true. Her and Miss Bretherton's costumes were very similar, but for the color of the veil and the shape of the headdress.

How had Lord Harveston even known what she wore? He'd probably got the information from another gentleman, and everybody knew they could not be relied upon to describe clothes in any detail. For heaven's sake, her own brother, Darden, lumped together violet, lavender, lilac, and plum and called them all purple, as if they were the same.

Her spirits were buoyed by the idea.

It must be true that Lord Harveston had been confused by the costumes. She would believe it true until somebody could prove to her that it was not true.

⫸⫷

PERCIVAL SIPPED HIS coffee. What a night he had experienced the evening before. He'd had it all planned out—he would secure Lady Cordelia's last dance and he would ask the momentous question.

However, as Burns had so aptly pointed out, the best laid plans of mice and men often go awry.

They had gone awry, alright.

He'd ended the night dancing with Miss Bretherton. Then, he'd thought he could at least catch Lady Cordelia before she departed the ball. He would explain what had happened.

But no, the gods were against him on that idea too. As soon as the dance was over, the bishop had pulled him aside and interrogated him regarding his intentions.

It was pointed out to him that the bishop was aware that he had escorted Miss Bretherton home after Lady Hightower's musical evening. Now, he had secured the last dance. What did the lord mean by it?

Then had ensued a remarkably uncomfortable quarter hour, as he tactfully expressed his lack of any designs on Miss Bretherton in the softest and most complimentary tones possible. The bishop was left satisfied that a match could never be, as Lord Harveston had deemed himself unworthy of his remarkable daughter.

By the time he'd extricated himself from that fiasco, Lady Cordelia and her family had left.

If there had been any bright spot, it was that Hamill had questioned him about the evening, got the truth of it, claimed he had thought the very thing, and had told Lady Cordelia just that.

He'd even said that Lady Cordelia had seemed pleased to hear it.

His valet, Jameston, came in carrying one of his coats. Percival glanced at it and said, "No, not that one. Get the blue one that just came in from the tailor's. I will be calling on the Benningtons this afternoon and wish to have a better coat."

It was the Benningtons' at-home day and he would go. It would make a statement and, if the room were not too crowded, he might have a moment to say his piece.

In fact, even if the room was crowded, he would say what he wished to say.

CORDELIA HAD WOKEN in very good spirits, now thoroughly convinced that Lord Harveston had meant to engage on her card, not Miss Bretherton's.

She had been disappointed that he had not sought her out before she left, but on the other hand, it had seemed as if he wished to.

The bishop had cornered him and Cordelia could not help but notice that while he talked to the gentleman, his eyes were nearly always on her.

His eyes followed her as her father and Darden escorted her out.

In the end, it was probably good luck that such a mix-up had occurred. It had worked to firmly cement her feelings. The world had seemed gray when she'd thought it was all to come to nothing, and then it was full of color again when she realized her mistake.

Now, she was in the breakfast room with Juliet and Miss Mayton, they having lingered over their tea.

"It is odd, though," Juliet said, "that you seem so happy about the evening when you did not speak to him at all."

Cordelia shrugged. She could not properly explain her feelings, they were too on the move, riding up hills and flying down them again.

The earl, who had left the room a half hour before, came back into it. Cordelia started. He held a letter in his hand and appeared almost ill.

"Oh dear, oh dear, oh dear," he said.

"Papa! What is it? What has happened?"

Seeming to come to his senses, the earl took in a deep breath and said, "Beatrice writes that Lily has come down with a croup. The poor little mite runs a high fever and Beatrice says the cough is quite terrible. They are all frightened out of their wits."

Juliet jumped from her chair. "What are we waiting for? We must go to her at once!"

"Yes, yes, of course we must go. Now, I did think about it. Cordelia, you may stay here with Miss Mayton. I should not like to drag you away from your season."

"No, Papa!" Cordelia cried. "Beatrice needs us all there. If something were to happen…"

None of them could bear to say what the something was that Cordelia referred to.

Their dear Lily might die. It would not be unusual, many children did die. It was just that it was their Lily. Nothing could happen to their little niece. None of them would be able to bear it. Beatrice could not bear it.

They were each up out of their chairs and running to find a valise. They must go in all haste.

NEVER IN THEIR lives had the Benningtons set off on a journey as quickly and with as little fuss as they did that day.

The earl gave over all the arrangements to Tattleton, who moved heaven and earth to get them packed and rent an extra carriage and coachman. They were only to take what was needed; the rest could be sent on by their butler.

The rest that would be sent on had, necessarily, included Lord Darling. However, Tattleton swore he would take good care of him. He did not look enthusiastic over the prospect, but

Cordelia knew he would be as good as his word.

As the butler issued orders this way and that, the earl fired off letters to Rosalind and Viola. Cordelia had no doubt the duke and Lord Baderston would escort her sisters home. Darden had been called back from his club.

They were off in two hours, speeding their way back to Somerset. Sandren had been given leave to make the journey as speedily as possible, changing horses at strategic stops. A basket had been packed in each carriage and there would be no stopping but for the horse changes.

The earl had been grim as he spoke to them before they set off. He'd said, "This trip must be different. We are on a serious errand and cannot dally for a moment."

"Papa," Juliet said, "if I leave my book behind somewhere, it is gone forever. If I wish to write an ode, then I will do so from what I see passing by a window. There will be no stopping at all—we must fly to Beatrice and Lily."

The earl nodded approvingly. "And Van Doren too."

He stared at his youngest daughter until she finally whispered, "Yes, and Van Doren too."

It had all happened so fast that Cordelia had not had a moment to think of what she was leaving behind.

As the carriage raced along the road, leaving London in the distance, Cordelia's thoughts bounced back and forth—where she was going and what she was leaving.

"You are thinking about Lord Harveston," Juliet said as Miss Mayton snored next to her.

"I am thinking of Beatrice and Lily, and then Lord Harveston, and then Beatrice and Lily."

"If he loves you, if it is meant to be, he will wait. He will be there, waiting for you, next season."

Cordelia hoped so. She hoped Miss Bretherton did not get her fact-filled claws into him somehow.

"I know you imagined that you would be married by the end of this season," Juliet said, "but it is perfectly fine that you are not.

You will lead me into my own and we will have a jolly time together."

Cordelia nodded. "As long as Lily comes through it."

"Yes, as long as Lily comes through it, else I cannot see how we will ever be jolly again."

PERCIVAL HAD DONNED his best new coat and set off to the Benningtons. This was it. He did not care how many people were crowding up her drawing room.

First, he would relay his ridiculous mistake of last evening. Then, he would very boldly request that he and Lady Cordelia step away for a private moment, as he had something very particular to say.

Then, if she accepted, he would seek out the earl and lay out his case.

He planned on being exceedingly generous when it came to pin money and the jointure, beyond what would be expected from the amount of her dowry. He would even settle a small estate in Hampshire on his new bride that she might use as she saw fit. Nothing was entailed and he could do what he liked. What he liked at this moment was to not give the earl one reason to hesitate in condoning the match.

Though, first he must get Lady Cordelia to agree to it. He planned to outline his plans to become a Corinthian. Of course, he could not lay claim to the title at this moment, but he had made a beginning. He had taken steps.

Painful steps that he did not particularly enjoy. But what was that compared to Lady Cordelia's happiness?

Certainly, she would see that he was on his way to becoming a Corinthian. And in any case, was there not room in his life for both his intellectual pursuits and a sporting life?

Makepeace did not think so, he thought the whole idea a bit

of madness. He also was living in terror that Lady Cordelia's acting troupe would be arriving day and night and examining his sideboard if she agreed to become the mistress of his house.

Percival supposed he could not condemn Makepeace for his very forward opinions. It was not usual that a butler would make comment on his employer's decisions, especially personal decisions, but then he and Makepeace had grown a friendship from the seeds of intellectual curiosity. And from the seeds of his own household.

Makepeace had seen what he had seen all those years ago. He'd been a footman at the time, forever slipping books out of his father's library. They had only spoken of it once years later, when he'd hired the investigator to attempt to track down Dora, but it had established an understanding between them. Makepeace would never countenance acting as butler for a man like his father, a man who would casually ruin a young girl and think no more about it. He was satisfied that Percival would never be that man.

Now, as he turned down Portland Place, he felt his stomach tightening. This was the moment that would set the course of his life, for good or ill.

He was surprised to see a farmer's cart out front. Then he was even more surprised to see a farmer, escorted by a footman, leading Lord Darling to it.

Could the Benningtons really have sold Lord Darling? It did not seem very like them.

The footman stopped short at the sight of him.

Percival reined in but instead of the boy coming to take the reins from him, he'd turned on his heel and raced back through the doors.

He could hear the footman calling for the butler from the front hall.

Percival walked his horse to the cart, just as the farmer picked up Lord Darling and placed him on the hay that padded the cart.

"Did you buy that goat," he asked.

"Buy 'im?" the farmer said, seeming very amused. "I'm to take him all the way to Somerset. This little lord is to get to his estate at Westmont House, don't you know."

Of course, he did not know, but it made sense. Keeping a goat in the house had finally worn the earl down and now it would go to the environment it had belonged in all along.

The butler, Tattleton, came rushing out as if his very hair was on fire. "Lord Harveston!"

The fellow appeared nearly in a panic. Had something happened beyond the goat going to the country?

"Mr. Tattleton, I understood this was the house's at-home day. Is something amiss? I get the distinct feeling I arrive at an inconvenient time."

The footman was just at this moment fanning the butler as Tattleton himself mopped his brow.

"Not so much inconvenient, my lord," he said. "You find us topsy-turvy as the family has recently departed for Somerset."

They were gone? *She* was gone? Why? Why had they gone?

"A family emergency has called them thither."

"I see," he said, though his thoughts were jumbled. "I am sorry to hear it. But Lady Cordelia, she is well?"

"Quite well, my lord."

"Everybody has gone? Darden too?"

"Yes, my lord, and we expect the duke and duchess and Lord and Lady Baderston to be soon on their way. I have been left behind to close the house."

Percival hardly knew what to say. He should not inquire further, but he burned to know the cause. Whatever it was, it was grave indeed if all extended family were rushing to the scene.

"Mr. Tattleton, it is not any of my business, but might I ask…"

He trailed off, knowing he had no right whatsoever to ask. It was just that, he really wished to know what Lady Cordelia was facing just now.

"Lord and Lady Van Doren's daughter, young Miss Lily, has

come down with a croup," the butler said. "It seems to be serious and the family are all making their way there to do what they can, whatever that may be."

The butler sighed and said quietly, "Another letter from Lady Beatrice to her father has just arrived. I dare not even contemplate what it says."

That *was* grave. If he understood it correctly, the child would not even have reached two years. The diseases of childhood were cruel indeed. Percival had even heard of women in his village who would not allow themselves to love a child until they were deemed hearty enough to survive the ever-present dangers.

What could he do about it though? He was helpless in the situation. He could not even write a letter to Lady Cordelia—it would be far too forward before being accepted and it would be graceless to send any sort of communication without knowing the situation the lady faced. Lady Van Doren's child might have passed even now. That was what Tattleton was afraid was in the letter that had missed the earl.

He could write to Darden though. Not this minute, not until time had passed and he understood whether condolences were in order.

What could he do now, though? He wished to do something now!

Percival swung himself down from his horse. To the footman he said, "Take Pericles to the stables." He turned to the butler. "Mr. Tattleton, you will have a thousand things to arrange, I am at your service."

The butler seemed rather taken aback, though the footman clearly approved of the idea. He nodded vigorously as he took the reins.

"My lord," Tattleton said, "we are busy indeed, but all of our tasks are, well, they are to be done by servants!"

"Nonsense," Percival said. "At a time like this, one man's arms are as strong as the next. Now, I imagine there are piles of things to be packed."

Mr. Tattleton rubbed his chin. "I should not like to find the earl did not approve, though."

"He will have more weighty ideas on his mind," Percival said firmly. "Come, I will pack Darden's things. He shan't mind at all."

"Lord Darden. You *are* in the same club…" Tattleton said, trailing off.

"It's settled. Direct me to his room and his trunks. As he mostly lives in Town, he will not want all his clothes—I can sort out what he will require and pack it up to send on."

Yes, that was what he needed to do this minute. He needed to be of use and keep himself engaged. After he had assisted Tattleton in getting the household sorted out, he would redouble his efforts with Hamill.

God willing, Lady Van Doren's child would come through it. All would end happily and then, by next season, Lady Cordelia would return and find herself faced with an intellectual Corinthian.

He did not suppose the world had ever encountered an intellectual Corinthian.

CHAPTER NINETEEN

CORDELIA GRIPPED JULIET'S hand. They had made the trip in two days. Considering their prior trips, neither of them had imagined it could be done so quickly. However, they never stopped but to change horses and speedily use the facilities. Only once did they stop for a few hours for the coachmen to sleep. Sandren had been a man possessed and had driven the hired coachman to keep up.

Now, they were going straight to Beatrice, straight to Faversham Hall. Now, they would discover what they all faced. They would discover what poor Beatrice had already faced.

The carriage wheels thundered down the drive, Sandren determined to do the last mile with all speed.

He reined in, the carriage slowed to a stop, and there was a sudden silence, but for the heavy breathing of the horses. It felt as if nobody could move.

Cordelia peered out the window as Darden helped their father from the second carriage.

"There is no hatchment," she said, examining the doors of Faversham Hall.

Those doors swung open and Van Doren's housekeeper stood there, looking exceedingly surprised.

"She wears no black ribbon on her cap!" Juliet whispered.

Before the housekeeper could say anything at all, the earl said, "We received word about Lily. What is the news?"

"Ah!" the housekeeper said, as if it had been cleared up suffi- ciently as to why she was seeing the family on the drive. "The little lady did very poorly for twenty-four hours, I can tell you it was a fright, but she turned a corner and she is as jolly as she ever was. We're still being careful, mind, but the doctor says she is firmly on the mend."

The earl nearly sank to the drive. Darden held him up.

"She's all right!" Juliet cried.

They tumbled from the carriage and all of them surrounded their father. "She's all right, Papa," Juliet said, as if to be sure her father understood the matter.

"Let us get you indoors, Father," Darden said, lending the earl his arm.

They headed toward the doors en masse just as Beatrice came down the stairs.

"You are all here!" she cried.

"Of course, we are here, my dear," Miss Mayton said. "Where else would we be at such a moment?"

The sisters and their aunt threw themselves at one another as Darden helped the earl to a chair in the drawing room and ordered the footman to fetch him some ale.

The next minutes were a flurry of news back and forth.

"I did write again," Beatrice said. "After the first letter, I wrote a day later that the danger seemed to have passed."

"I suppose we missed it," the earl said. "We set off not two hours after receiving the first."

"You would never believe how fast we were off," Juliet said. "There was nothing like it."

"And we came straight through," Cordelia said. "We only stopped to change horses—no admiring vistas or ordering plates of ham or anything. I think Sandren rather enjoyed it."

"Indeed," Miss Mayton said, "we even ate our meals in the carriage as that fellow barreled along. Quite the mess we made at it too."

"Do not attempt to spread mustard on bread in a moving

carriage," Juliet said sagely.

"I shouldn't have written at all until I knew more," Beatrice said. "But it was so frightening, and I did think she might…you know. I could not talk about it with Van Doren, he just would not hear of the possibility. He was up at all hours walking her back and forth as if his strength would keep her going."

"Where is he, by the by?" the earl asked, looking a bit restored by a glass of ale.

"In bed with a cold," Beatrice said with a smile. "He positively wore himself out. Naturally, he argued from here to Sunday about taking a rest but I convinced him to be abed by telling him my nerves could not hold up under another dangerous situation."

"I'll bet he's a cranky patient," Juliet said.

"The crankiest," Beatrice said with a laugh.

"Well, if he stayed up all the night long with Lily, I cannot fault him for crankiness," Juliet said begrudgingly.

"I have sent Genroy to bed as well," Beatrice said, "as I do not think our butler has properly slept in days."

"Can we see her?" Cordelia asked. "Would the doctor say it's all right?"

"Oh, I think so," Beatrice said. "He's given me leave to bring her out of doors when the weather is fine and we no longer need isolate her from other people. Though, perhaps this is an awful lot of people at once."

The earl said, "Beatrice, take the girls and Miss Mayton to the nursery. I feel I must write to Tattleton before another moment has passed. He will have been staring at that second letter and fearing the worst."

"Poor Tattleton," Juliet said. "His nerves were stretched enough over Lord Darling."

"Lord Darling?" Beatrice asked.

"The goat," Juliet said. "I did write that we'd adopted a goat."

Beatrice laughed. "Indeed you did. I did not know you named him Lord Darling."

"Lord Darling, Marquess of Basingstoke," Juliet said.

"That particular marquess is to be on his way here shortly," the earl said, "by way of somebody's uncle."

Before Beatrice could ask how somebody's uncle had got involved in Lord Darling's future, the earl said, "Darden and I will wait our turn to see Lily and we will have a second glass of ale to restore ourselves, if one of the footmen will be so good."

"That is a fine notion, Father," Darden said. "And I will write to Hamill about club matters—I left some things up in the air on account of our speedy departure. In any case, far be it for us men to try to get ahead of a pile of women when a baby is involved."

That was all the convincing anybody needed, though Cordelia privately thought Darden dead wrong in his ideas. As far as she could see it, Van Doren had been a veritable mother hen during Lily's illness and she very much approved of it.

They had all leapt up and run up the stairs to the nursery.

Beatrice had been nesting in the months leading up to her confinement, but it perhaps came as a surprise the exact extent of that nesting. They had all seen the piles of clothes embroidered and the stuffed toys made and they'd been perfectly aware that she had grand plans for a nursery.

However, when they'd left for Town, Lily had been still in a small set of rooms next to Beatrice's bedchamber. Now, the nursery had been finished and the nurse and Lily had made their move there.

It was entirely charming. There were soft colored forest scenes painted on the walls, filled with fairies peeking round leaves and an owl on a high branch overseeing it all. The crib was painted white and intricately carved with flowers and greenery. There were two large dressers to contain all the embroidered clothing Beatrice had worked on. Felted animals to play with sat in every corner and airy white crepe curtains let the sun through. Two large chairs in pale blue velvet sat on either side of the fireplace.

It was a magical little place.

The nurse curtsied as they came in and stepped aside to reveal Lily determinedly holding herself up on her feet by way of one of the chairs.

Her round chubby cheeks dimpled at seeing she had visitors. She boldly took steps away from the chair, wobbled, and collapsed on the rug. She laughed and seemed delighted with herself.

Lily promptly got on hands and knees, as that was still her speediest mode of transportation, and got to a stuffed sheep. She gamely held it up to show to everyone as if it were the crown jewels.

All was well. Though she'd known it from hearing it, Cordelia felt as if she *really* knew it from seeing it.

Her niece was just as cheerful as she had been when last they'd seen her.

Lily had come through.

Beatrice picked up her daughter and her stuffed sheep. "Now, my dear Lily, we shall like to hear all about Aunt Cordelia's season. It has been cut short on account of your croup, but we will be interested to know what has happened so far."

Nobody could be sure if Lily was in fact interested, but she did drop the sheep and clap her hands rather enthusiastically.

A sound behind them made Cordelia turn.

"What are all of you doing here?"

There was Van Doren, looking as cranky as ever, and looking quite ridiculous in his nightdress and a bright red nose to go with it.

"They have come to check on Lily, my darling," Beatrice said, laughing at the sight. "Back to bed with you before you come down with a fever."

Van Doren sighed. "I was rather hoping this *was* a fever dream," he said, wandering back down the hall.

Everything was just as it ought to be. Lily was well, Van Doren was cranky, and Beatrice was delighted with him.

Only a few hours ago, Cordelia had feared such a happy outcome would never be.

"Let us all arrange ourselves on the carpet and admire Lily while you tell me everything, Cordy."

"You will not believe the everything, Bea," Juliet said, throwing herself down.

Ah yes. The everything. Lord Harveston.

As Lily wobbled on her fat little legs, tipped over, bravely got up again, shoved her stuffed sheep into their faces, and used any chair she could grab to steady herself, Cordelia told Beatrice all about Lord Harveston.

⟫⟫⟩⟨⟪⟪

PERCIVAL HAD SEEN Tattleton and the rest of the Bennington household off on their way back to Somerset. He'd convinced the butler to give him a key to the back garden gate and then brought his own gardener to Town to rectify what Lord Darling had put asunder.

After that, he'd waited impatiently for three days for Hamill to return from racing his carriage somewhere or other. The fellow was forever racing his carriage!

Finally, Hamill had turned up and Percival had acquainted him with his ideas. Their work was to be redoubled. They would go at it night and day.

"You see what I say," Percival said as Hamill sat on his sofa, looking bemused. "I'll do whatever you ask—we'll run round in our bare feet all day long, we could even swim the Serpentine, I'll box until I'm unconscious on the ground. Nothing is out of bounds!"

"For you, maybe," Hamill said, laughing. "By the by, Darden wrote to me—Lady Van Doren's child has recovered."

Percival sank into a chair. "Has she? That is good, very good. Now, I wonder, does the family return to Town now that the danger has passed?"

"No, they do not," Hamill said. "Apparently, moving the

Bennington household from one place to the next is a bit of a palaver."

"Yes, I can see how it would be," Percival said thoughtfully.

"Darden says the duke and Baderston have arrived to Somerset with their wives in tow and will stay for some months. They are a rather united group, I think."

Yes, they were united. It was part of their charm.

If he were lucky, and turned himself into a credible Corinthian, he might find himself a part of it all.

It was strange to think about. He did not himself have much of an extended family. He was an only child, as was his mother. His father had a brother, but he'd died before marrying. Percival did of course have more distant cousins. It was England, everybody had those. But they were the sort one exchanged Christmas greetings with, little more.

A darker thought occurred to him. "Um, what sort of gentlemen are lurking round that neighborhood in Somerset? Do you happen to know?"

The idea of some fop riding over to her house every day was, well it was not to be borne.

"I do not happen to know, though Darden has never mentioned anybody in particular."

"Well now, good news all round. As to our plan, we'd best get started mapping out a schedule," Percival said. "A tight schedule, mind you."

Hamill had roared with laughter over the idea. "My friend," he said when he could catch his breath, "you are coming at this like you are writing a paper for the Royal Society. The thing with various sports is, it is supposed to be fun, not work."

"Fun?" Percival said, entirely unsuccessful at keeping the incredulity from his voice. There had been nothing fun about his outings with Hamill.

"Yes. Fun. Amusement. Enjoyment of competition. A diversion," Hamill said.

The last thing he would have called running round the park

was diverting.

"What do you advise then?" Percival asked. "As I cannot claim to yet see the fun in any of it."

"Relax. That's what I advise. Tomorrow morning, we will box until we drop. Other days, we will do other things. In a month, you can come home with me and continue on at my estate. My mother and father are jolly as anything, we have a bowling green, tennis green, loads of trails to ride out on, hiking, billiards, and we even have a lake and one-man sailboats. Then, of course, the shooting."

"Well, I do not know, I would not like to be an imposition to the duke and duchess."

"They won't see you as an imposition. Of course, my sister might, but Theodora has always got her nose in a book and is complaining about the noise."

Hamill paused. "I suppose the two of you will have a lot to talk about, she considers herself quite the intellectual. We do not encourage her at it, though. It makes for tedious dinner conversation. Do any of us wish to know the reproductive habits of frogs? No, Theodora, we do not."

Percival laughed at the idea, though he also found himself a bit embarrassed over it too. He did know the reproductive habits of frogs, it had been a Royal Society paper, and he would not mind discussing it.

He had bigger things to do though. By next season, he must be a seasoned sportsman. The frogs could manage themselves.

"I'd have to make arrangements with my steward," he said quietly, "though he is a reliable fellow—"

"It's settled then," Hamill said.

THEY HAD BEEN at home in Somerset for a month and as the fear of Lily's illness faded, the idea of Lord Harveston took over

Cordelia's thoughts.

She had thought long and hard about him. Cordelia was near certain that he felt something for her. Some sort of feeling that was stronger than his interest in intellectual matters. Some feeling that would cause him to cast aside any ideas he may have had about choosing someone as deep into facts and information as he was.

However, that might not hold through a lifetime.

She would not take the chance that it would not hold.

When Cordelia had been buoyed by her success at the literary salon, she had been encouraged to take her education in hand. She wished to know more than she did. Dear Mr. Lackington had found her all sorts of interesting books—histories of Shakespeare, flora that could be found in her neighborhood, and a variety of books about the kings and queens of England.

After serious thought on the matter of her mind and the knowledge it currently stored, compared to Lord Harveston's mind, she realized that these pleasant meanderings on subjects that interested her would not be sufficient.

She must turn herself into a proper intellectual. Cordelia was certain she could do it. All her tutors had said, one way or another, that she was capable of learning anything if she would just apply herself.

So, she would apply herself.

During the day, she very determinedly locked herself away in the library and read books and papers. Her mind was getting filled with all sorts of information.

Though, she did notice that it was far easier to remember what the information was when it was a subject she was interested in. Those subjects tended to have people involved in them. Some of the non-peopled facts only seemed to make a brief stop in her mind, rather like a change of horses at an inn. There for a quarter hour and then speeding off into the distance, never to be seen again.

She admired her own discipline, though. It was no small thing to ignore the laughter from the drawing room, or to see everyone marching off to Faversham Hall or to a picnic.

Nevertheless, she was determined.

Not so determined that she would miss dinner though. The house was exceedingly lively with Conbatten, Rosalind, Viola, and Lord Baderston in it, and then Beatrice and Van Doren so often walking over from the Hall. And then of course, there was Bess and her pup, who they'd since named Princess Imogen, and the cats—Cupcake, Mischief, The Duchess, and Pandemonium—ranging round everywhere, and then their dear parrot Chester, who carried on shouting murder at anybody who passed his cage in the drawing room.

Lord Darling had arrived safe and sound, thanks to the good care of Charlie's uncle. He'd since been introduced to the dairy cows and had hit it off terrifically with them. Clara, a dear old thing, had taken him in hand the same day he arrived. When Lord Darling got too energetic for the cows' liking, Clara would gently knock him on the head.

"How goes your studies, my dear?" the earl asked from his end of the table.

"Very well, Papa," Cordelia said.

"I could not do it, Cordy," Juliet said. "I should fall asleep with a book in my lap."

"Dare I ask what it is you are studying?" Conbatten asked.

"I am looking at a wide range of subjects," Cordelia said. "For example, today I read a Royal Society paper about volcanoes. A Scot has been studying them and the Earl of Buchan has recommended him to the society. The gentleman hopes to provide information to people so they will not be killed in an eruption."

"As we do not have any volcanoes in England, may I ask what collecting this information is for?" Van Doren asked.

"To inform my mind, for my own edification," Cordelia said, glancing at her sisters and her aunt. They might know why she was spending all her days in the library, but nobody else did. She planned to keep it that way.

"Some of us care about what happens to people living next to a mountain that might blow up at any moment," Juliet said, narrowing her eyes at Van Doren.

"I will eat my boots for breakfast if you care about it," Van Doren said.

"Tell your cook to heat up a frying pan," Juliet said in a rather frightening tone.

"I can't think when was the last time I thought about volcanoes," Darden said. "Dashed inconvenient to live nearby one of them."

"I can tell you from firsthand experience," Miss Mayton said, dabbing her lips with her napkin, "when I was in Italy, I often feared some fellow would throw himself into Mount Vesuvius over me. There *were* threats. Though, I understand it would have been a long walk up, so that was always comforting."

"Well now, if Cordelia wishes to explore any suitable topic to enlarge her mind," the earl said jovially, "she has my full approval."

"Thank you, Papa," Cordelia said.

"Yes, *thank you*, Papa," Juliet said, staring at Van Doren.

Beatrice, looking vastly amused, said, "Dear Aunt, will you be reading to us this evening?"

She ignored her husband's groan over the idea.

"I do hope so, Miss Mayton," the earl said. "We are so close to the denouement, and I cannot imagine what will happen."

"I will be positively bereft if I do not hear the denouement of this remarkable tale," Conbatten said, smiling at Van Doren.

Darden snorted. He was always very much amused when the duke teased Van Doren.

"Never fear, Your Grace," Miss Mayton said condescendingly, "I will catch you up to where we are so far before reading the shocking conclusion."

"Shocking!" the earl said, seeming delighted. "Now I am on tenterhooks over it."

And so they'd gone merrily on and Miss Mayton did read the shocking conclusion to *The Dreadful Doings of Dembric Hall.*

Amidst Van Doren's shifting in his chair, pained sighs, and staring at the doors as if he wished he could go through them, Miss Mayton explained to the duke what had happened to that point.

Mr. Denbrow had been considering marrying his decidedly pregnant kitchen maid, though he was not the father and did not know who was. The maid attempted to convince him that a son would nullify any arrangements he'd made with the duke, he could keep all the duke's money, and he would not be murdered by the villagers if they moved to sunny Spain.

The poor duke and Mr. Denbrow's daughter, now the duke's beloved duchess, remained poor as church mice in their ducal residence. They were still chopping their own wood and living on raw eggs, as neither of them knew how to cook anything. They had made attempts, but they'd all gone up in smoke. A villager sometimes brought a piece of roasted meat and the couple were very careful to eat it bit by bit.

It would turn out that Mr. Denbrow could not face leaving for Spain without seeing his darling daughter once more. He arranged to stop by the duke's house very casually, without saying he was going anywhere.

The duke, being accustomed to acting the host extraordinaire in days gone by, would not countenance his father-in-law failing to be fed during the visit. He cracked a few raw eggs into a bowl. Then he gamely fetched the last of the pork that Mrs. Willow had brought them three weeks prior, which had been stored in a cabinet in the drawing room.

The whole thing smelled like sulfur and death, but Mr. Denbrow ate it out of guilt.

He was dead not three days later.

At that very opportune moment, Chester had jumped round his cage and cried, "Murder! Murder!"

"Oh no," Miss Mayton had said to the parrot, "you see, it was just that the duke was so used to entertaining properly and he had to make do with what he had."

As it *was* an accident, and as Mr. Denbrow had seemed very miserable to be rich, he was fondly missed, but not overly mourned.

The duke and his duchess were restored to their wealth and the duke spent the rest of his life dousing his lady with presents and jewels. The duchess, for her part, planned elaborate dinners of twelve courses—they would never eat raw eggs again.

The earl had been delighted with the story, exclaiming, "So Mr. Denbrow does himself in by the very hardships he'd forced on the duke and his own daughter! If he hadn't taken the money, he wouldn't have been served raw eggs and the pork that had gone off. Well, it just goes to show."

"I had hoped they'd all be dead thirty pages ago," Van Doren muttered.

Conbatten had raised a brow. "For myself, I am rather cheered that the duke was restored to his fortune."

"If we ever find ourselves in such a situation, Conbatten," Rosalind said, "I would sell off my jewels before I would allow you to eat raw eggs."

"You will do no such thing," her duke assured her. "I would hire myself out as a laborer before one diamond departs your neck."

"What about you, Baderston?" Darden asked. "Are you to hire yourself out as a laborer in such straights?"

"I rather think I'd hire myself out as an accountant," Lord Baderston said. "I'm very good with managing the account books and, in any case, I imagine Viola would prefer it."

Viola nodded. "He always does wish to know what I would prefer."

"What of *you*, Van Doren?" Juliet asked. "What will you be doing once your estate hits the rocks?"

"My estate will never hit the rocks, as you phrase it. I am very careful to protect me and mine, as everybody well knows."

Beatrice patted her husband's hand.

"Yes, yes," the earl said. "My daughters have all married very fine husbands, indeed. I am well pleased."

Cordelia had gone to bed laughing over the improbable demise of Mr. Denbrow and the even more improbable second careers of her brothers-in-law.

CHAPTER TWENTY

THE MORNING FOUND Cordelia hard at work, ignoring Chester's shouts of murder from the drawing room. It was a bit harder to ignore Tattleton's retort, which was along the lines of, "Do not tempt me, you heinous bird."

Tattleton himself knocked on the library door and entered. "Lady Cordelia," he said, "a messenger has brought this for you and claimed he must wait for an answer. It is very untoward, I think, to demand an answer. He would not be moved though and the earl is not in the house to ask his opinion of it."

"Do give it over, Tattleton," Cordelia said laughing. She could not imagine who would have written requiring an answer right away, but for Miss Anne Garrow, a neighborhood spinster who looked upon the scheduling of a sudden afternoon tea as a countywide emergency.

She tore it open. It was not from Miss Garrow.

It was from two people as yet unknown to her—the Duchess of Castleton and her daughter, Lady Theodora Highbury.

Goodness, this was Lord Hamill's mother and his younger sister who was due to come out next year.

Cordelia scanned the letter.

Lady Cordelia Bennington—

I and my daughter, Lady Theodora, have been assured by my son, Lord Hamill, that we are not too forward in this invitation. We are planning a house party for the 14th, scheduled to run a fortnight, and Lord Hamill singled you out as a lady it would behoove Theodora to know.

Were you to be so gracious as to accept our invitation, we would quite naturally expect you to bring along someone of more mature years to supervise your visit, whether that be the earl or Lord Darden who I am both acquainted with, or Miss Eloise Mayton, who I understand is a very pleasant lady. Quite naturally, bring your maids and valets—we have ample accommodations for them.

We do hope you might condescend to attend us. We will have all sorts of activities to entertain the ladies, while the gentlemen will have plenty of sport to engage in. I will personally plan for the ladies, and the duke, my son, and his friend Lord Harveston will plan for the gentleman.

We are not so very far from your estate, being at our summer estate in Devonshire, just north of Thorverton. We would send one of our carriages and the trip could be done in a day.

Respectfully, we have directed our groom to wait for your answer.

Lady Theodora and I do hope we will see you in our house very soon.

Georgianna Castleton

Cordelia reread the letter. No, she did not reread it exactly. Rather, her eyes were glued to the one phrase—"my son and Lord Harveston."

"Goodness," she said to herself. "Lord Harveston is there."

"Is he still at the house, then?" Tattleton asked. "I did not think the garden would take as long as that."

"The garden?" Cordelia said, not having the first idea of what the butler was talking about.

Tattleton nodded. "After the family departed Portland Place, he turned up for your at-home day. Certainly, Lord Harveston does not write to you directly?"

"No, of course not. But he was there? At Portland Place? Just after we left?"

Tattleton nodded. "After being apprised of the circumstances, he helped pack up Lord Darden's things, then insisted on having the key to the garden gate so he might bring in his own fellow to repair that goat's…modifications. I was not so certain I ought to have given the key to him, but the earl saw no harm in it when I told him of it."

Cordelia smiled. He'd fixed up the garden after Lord Darling's rampage. That was a very singular thing to do.

"I have since had a letter from Mr. Bramwell," Tattleton went on. "He is the butler next door on the right. He says the garden is looking very well and a fellow comes by once a week to do the weeding and pruning."

She leapt up. "Where is Papa?"

Tattleton seemed very taken aback by her swift reaction to hearing the neighbor's assessment of the garden. "My lord has gone to the south field to check on how that goat is getting on with the cows," Tattleton said.

"Tell that messenger to wait, Tattleton. I must see Papa and get permission to go to a house party. Do not allow him to leave. Give him ale, or biscuits, or…you will know best what to do with him, but do not let him leave!"

On her way out the back doors that led to the fields, Cordelia stopped at the bottom of the staircase. "Aunt! Aunt, where are you?"

Miss Mayton came hurrying to the top of the stairs. "Goodness child, I am just up here, assisting Juliet in organizing her odes into a book."

"Would you go to a house party with me?"

"A house party? Goodness, I've never been to a house party."

"You will go, though? Lord Harveston is there."

"Ah! I see. Of course we must go then."

Having that confirmation in her pocket, Cordelia fled the house in search of her father.

PERCIVAL HAD SUPPOSED he had not known what tired really was before coming to Hamill's house.

How could so many activities take place on one estate? Why were the family all so active?

The duke and duchess rarely sat down. They were always off riding, or they played lawn tennis, or bowled, or sailed. They had all looked positively fidgety the day it had rained so hard it really had been impossible to do anything out of doors. After grimly staring out the windows, they had finally settled on a billiards tournament.

He should not lump them all into one basket, of course. Hamill's sister, Theodora, was not at all like them. She could participate in whatever they were up to well enough, but she only did so when she felt like it. Very often, what she felt like doing was closeting herself in the library.

There was no such repose for Percival. He'd told Hamill he must be turned into a Corinthian and Hamill was doing his level best to accomplish it.

There was no hiding from the truth, though—it was slow going. Just this afternoon, Hamill had taken him down to the lake and attempted to teach him how to sail.

Oh, he got the gist of it, he supposed. But it was a rather confounded thing. When one wished to go right, one must push the tiller left, and vice versa. If one wished to change direction, one had best consider the swinging boom a deadly weapon. One was meant to be sailing close to the wind, but that also meant one was on the verge of tipping over.

Hamill had said that if he did tip over, he was to just hang on to the overturned hull until somebody rowed out to get him. It usually was not more than a half hour.

Percival had stuck his hand in the water, he knew how cold it was. That was to be a long half hour!

It seemed he would not be bound for the Royal Navy any-time soon.

If there was any rest to be had in Hamill's house, it was at dinner. Even this energetic family must sit down to accomplish it.

Blessedly, that was where he found himself this moment. The duchess always arranged a very fine repast that would go many courses.

As far as Percival was concerned, the more courses the better, as those courses would all be had sitting down. He just hoped the duke was not set on bowling by candlelight afterward, as he had last evening. Every servant in the house had been out there, chasing balls with their lights.

"Castleton," the duchess said to her duke as the first course came round, "the house party is all arranged for the fourteenth."

House party? Percival glanced at Hamill, who only nodded. Lady Theodora sighed just the smallest sigh.

"Excellent!" the duke said.

"I will arrange for the ladies," the duchess said, "and you will arrange for the gentlemen. As always, my dear, do not forget about us ladies. We will wish to observe you at your sport from time to time. I myself would prefer to be a part of it, but we must accommodate the more staid activities that a usual lady will like to do."

"Are we to spend our time in the library, then?" Theodora asked.

"Certainly not," the duchess said. In a kinder tone, she said, "Now I know a house party will not be one of your favored activities, but you are out next season. You must become accustomed to meeting people and making connections. I have invited a very suitable young lady for you to know."

Percival examined his soup. Now he was to have an audience while he attempted to make himself a sportsman?

The duke said, "I am ahead of you on the planning, my dear. I've been thinking it over for months and have the thing all worked out. We're to have a regatta!"

"Wonderful!" the duchess said. "You really are so clever. How did we not think of it before?"

"We did not have enough boats for the thing," the duke said. "Now we do. Plenty of boats to go round, plenty of sails. I've even got different colored flags so the onlookers can easily identify who is who as we round the buoys. I've put our crest on Hamill's."

Catching Percival's eye, Lady Theodora said quietly, "A regatta is not so bad, you can bring a book with you and read it under a tree—nobody will notice."

"What's that?" the duke said. "Do not imagine our Harveston shall be stuck on the sidelines, Theo. No, he will be in it with the rest of us. Hamill has already taken him down to the lake to show him what's what."

"A very brief introduction, I'm afraid," Percival said. "I could not claim the skill to participate in a race."

"No, of course not yet," the duke said jovially. "Hamill will take you down again on the morrow. You'll pick it up in no time at all and you've got a full three days. You'll be a regular Francis Drake by the end of it."

"And you'll have the advantage of the other gentlemen," Hamill said. "They will not have been sailing in ages and will not be familiar with our lake or our boats."

Three days. Three days to turn himself into Sir Francis Drake. And sailing was not even all. There would be all sorts of sports played.

The only thing that would not be done was the only thing he was actually good at—sword play. There was a logical elegance to swords that had always interested him, and since he was interested he'd worked at it. Short of a duel, though, there was not much opportunity to show it off.

A sudden and awful thought came upon him. "There will not be boxing, will there?"

He prayed the answer was no. Each time he'd got into the ring in London, he'd been pounded out of his wits. Jackson, who really was a kind and thoughtful fellow, encouraged him no end. He was convinced that Percival should have a breakthrough any moment and really get the hang of it.

The duke had laughed heartily. "Boxing? Indeed, no," he said. "That's hardly a country sport. In any case, I do not imagine the ladies would like it."

"Absolutely not," the duchess confirmed.

That was something, anyway. He would at least not be walking round with a black eye anytime soon.

"Mama," Lady Theodora said, "who is this paragon of a young lady it will behoove me to know?"

"The Earl of Westmont's daughter—Lady Cordelia Bennington."

Percival's spoon clattered into his empty soup bowl. Hamill winked and nodded.

Lady Cordelia! She was coming here!

Of course, Hamill had arranged the thing. Good old Hamill!

"Is she likely to share my interests?" Lady Theodora asked, glancing at Percival's spoon come to rest in his bowl. "Please do not tell me she is some silly creature who hasn't looked at a piece of literature lest it be *The Lady's Magazine*."

"I adore that magazine," the duchess said.

"She is a great admirer of Shakespeare," Percival said. "*Othello*, in particular."

"That is something, at least," Lady Theodora said.

"Lady Cordelia has attended my literary salons," he continued, "and has made her mark there."

Lady Theodora laid down her spoon. "Now that is *really* something," she said. "Well done, Mama."

The duchess nodded graciously, if not a little confusedly.

Lady Cordelia was coming. She was coming to a house party where there would be no end of opportunities to display sportsmanlike skills.

Percival was bone-tired, but this was not the moment to slow down. In three days, he must appear the Corinthian. The *sailing*

Corinthian, no less.

"Hamill, we should go down to the lake first thing," he said, "and carry on with our lessons."

"The wind won't be up until the afternoon," Hamill said.

"Then we will do something else in the morning. The point is, we ought to be doing something."

Hamill smiled. "Right you are."

"Cordelia Bennington," the duke said thoughtfully. "Is that, what I say is, did not…one of the other sisters arrange her own…ah, never mind, she's a duchess now. But what about the one who…I do not know how to even describe it…there were three proposed duels and then somehow a caravan…?"

The duchess nodded, seeming to understand perfectly well that the duke alluded to the Duchess of Conbatten, née Lady Rosalind, arranging her own kidnapping so the duke might rescue her and Lady Baderston, née Lady Viola who had…well, Percival was not certain what that had been about. There was a meeting on a green between Baderston and three other gentlemen, one of which had been his own cousin, and then the entire family eloped to Scotland.

The duchess said, "All the old and great families have their idiosyncrasies, my love. Do not forget about Freddy."

The duke nodded, seeming rather regretful to be reminded about that individual. He shook his head. "Nobody told him to drink himself silly and go into that cage!"

Percival looked at Hamill inquiringly. Hamill said, "A distant cousin. You will know Lady Castlereagh keeps a tiger? *That* cage. It was all hushed up, of course."

The duke sighed. "Though people do continue to ask him what happened to his hand and he tells the most ridiculous stories about it."

"He was always too much of an optimist," Lady Theodora said.

The duke snorted. "Attempting to pet a tiger and imagining you will leave with the body parts you came in with must be the height of optimism."

"Poor Freddy," the duchess said.

Poor Freddy indeed. Percival thought they must be talking about Lord Frederick Germaine, who was forever drunk and forever telling people that Napoleon himself had struck off his left hand. Percival did not think Lord Frederick had ever set foot in France. He had presumed the missing hand had been lost in some careless accident.

Which, he supposed, had been entirely right.

Well," the duke said, "I suppose the Benningtons could not be worse than Freddy."

"The Benningtons are everything genial," Percival said, attempting to keep the defensive tone from his voice. "I have grown to know the earl, and I have spent an at-home evening with the family—they are very closeknit. I quite admired it."

"Anybody can see that, Lord Harveston," Theodora said in a teasing voice.

Percival did not answer. Really, he did not care a jot what anybody could see or not see. It was what Lady Cordelia would see in three days' time that mattered, and what she must see was a Corinthian.

⇻⇉⤏⤎⇇↤

NOW, MR. TATTLETON," Mrs. Huffson said, sipping her brandy, "you really cannot have cause for alarm if the earl does not."

"Oh, can't I?" he said gravely. "The two of them, setting off to a duke's county seat? A duke, mind you."

"Lady Cordelia is equipped to encounter any family, whether it be a grocer's or a duke's."

Tattleton shook his head sadly. It forever amazed him that Mrs. Huffson never saw trouble coming. He, himself, could feel it in his bones. It was his particular gift, and his particular curse. He often could not identify the exact trouble that had taken flight and was winging its way in their direction, but he could feel it coming.

"I thought you'd find yourself in a very cheerful frame of mind these days," Mrs. Huffson went on. "We are in the peace of the country and Lord Darling is out of the house and into the fields—he will trouble you no more."

Tattleton glanced meaningfully at the shredded sofa, courtesy of the cats, and the muddy paw prints running across the floor, courtesy of the dogs, then pointed his finger toward the ceiling to the far-off cries of murder from the parrot.

He noticed Mrs. Huffson had no retort to *that*.

"It is not Lady Cordelia I worry about," he said, "at least, not if she were to be escorted by the earl or Lord Darden. It is Miss Mayton. Those young ladies think of a terrible idea and then Miss Mayton says, 'Give me a moment, I am certain I can think of something worse.'"

He could not know what worse than terrible idea Miss Mayton had thought up this time, but he did know that Lady Cordelia had been a veritable Hun about her studies.

Tattleton had known those young ladies since they were born! Not a one of them willingly found themselves in a library. They'd ventured in after that first literary salon and had not lasted a morning before they gave it up. They'd very cheerfully informed him that they were casting aside the earl's books and would rely on their own judgment.

Couple that with Lord Harveston being of an intellectual frame of mind, and Lord Harveston fixing up their garden, and now Lord Harveston also attending this country party...well, he could only assume the worst.

"I am very afraid, Mrs. Huffson, that Lady Cordelia is going to attempt to pass herself off as a bookish lady and she is going to try it with Miss Mayton's help."

Mrs. Huffson laughed at the notion. "Goodness, I suppose that would not be the worst thing in the world."

No. Not the worst thing in the world. Until Lord Harveston

discovered the ruse. Until he discovered that Lady Cordelia Bennington had only very recently become acquainted with books on shelves.

He had a sneaking suspicion that Lady Cordelia was partial to Lord Harveston. Very partial. He could not account for what had happened to her idea of finding herself a Corinthian, but there it was.

"If Lord Harveston breaks that young lady's heart, or if he mocks her sudden entry into the world of attaining information, I will...well I do not know what I will do, but it will be very awful."

"Goodness. That was sudden turn, Mr. Tattleton."

CHAPTER TWENTY-ONE

Cordelia had so little time to prepare for departing for the Duchess of Castleton's house party—primarily the question was, what she would pack to wear. After informing the duchess' groom that she would attend with Miss Mayton and a maid, that groom had handed over a list of suggested wardrobes.

She would need to be dressed for picnics, riding out, a trip to the local village shops, lawn bowls, dinners, and a ball at the end of it, to name only some of the activities listed.

Amidst sorting through her clothes, which Lynette referred to as a frenzied parade of mind changes, Cordelia did of course think of Lord Harveston.

She thought of Lady Theodora too. She thought of Lord Hamill describing his sister as an intellectual. Then she imagined Lady Theodora and Lord Harveston having an intellectual conversation.

Lady Theodora's penchant for knowledge had not seemed as if it carried much weight within the family. But how much weight would it carry with Lord Harveston?

How long had he been in that house, in close quarters with knowledgeable Lady Theodora?

Lady Theodora was very terrible to think about. She had everything—an intellectual bent, the highest of connections, she must have an outstanding dowry, and there was every chance that she was pretty. Cordelia supposed she was amusing too!

It seemed very unfair that such a paragon should be just now conversing with Lord Harveston.

Cordelia attempted to soothe herself by remembering that Lord Harveston had brought his personal gardener to Portland Place to repair their garden. Another point that buoyed her was thinking of all the studying she had done since she'd left London.

Did Lady Theodora know anything about the current work being done regarding volcanoes? She rather wondered about that.

For all her fretting and frenzied packing, she, Miss Mayton, and Lynette had been got on their way. The duchess had sent two carriages—one for herself and Miss Mayton and the other for the luggage and Lynette.

They could not, of course, leave Lynette to fend for herself with only hatboxes to keep her company, so she was relocated to their own carriage. Cordelia hoped she did not shock the duchess with such an arrangement, but it would have been too cruel to abandon Lynette alone.

As they drew ever closer to their destination, a new worry presented itself to her thoughts.

"Aunt," she said, "this must be a very great house. It is the duke's seat and I have never been inside of such a one. Well, except for Conbatten's of course, but he is different—he is family."

"I do not suppose anybody could out-duke Conbatten, dear," Miss Mayton said, not appearing the least flustered. "Will the Duke of Castleton be bathing at precisely ninety-eight degrees with chilled champagne as Conbatten does? Will he have an absolute madman of a French valet who is always threatening to throw himself into the Thames? Will he have built a special room for the gifts he receives from relatives, that nobody else is permitted to see?"

"I rather doubt it," Cordelia said. "All those things seem peculiar to Conbatten."

"Just so," Miss Mayton said. "If we can manage Conbatten, and we have, then we can manage any other duke with ease.

Simply depend upon your good instincts."

Cordelia was much reassured by these ideas.

"I hope I am not to be lorded over by lady's maids who think they are better than me, just because they serve a duchess and her daughter," Lynette said.

Lynette was forever worried about being lorded over. She probably had good reason to chafe under the idea. Miss Mayton's maid, Fleur, threw round French words that Lynette did not understand, even though there was not a drop of French blood in the maid and her real name was Flora.

Fortunately for Lynette, Fleur/Flora was just this moment attending a sick aunt and so must miss the trip. It was supposed that Lynette would make fine use of the circumstance in future.

Cordelia said, "Lynette, I am certain you can hold your ground without giving offense."

"I never give offense," Lynette said, as if the idea was preposterous. "I just won't be lorded over by some who pretend they can speak French is all."

The coachman made a turn and it was clear enough that they were on the duke's land. They stopped at a gatehouse and the coachman had a brief conversation with the man who came out to meet them. This man had obviously been waiting for them. He tipped his cap, mounted his horse, and set off at a gallop to alert the house to their imminent arrival.

The avenue was lined with old oaks and went on for what seemed like two miles at least. On either side, green fields and apple orchards gently rolled off into the distance. Finally, a colossus of a house came into view. It was not so much long as it was tall. Grey stone built into four storeys—a giant surveying its land.

Beyond the house, Cordelia caught sight of a very large and brilliant blue lake.

"Goodness me," Miss Mayton said quietly.

The doors to the house were thrown open as the carriage came to a stop. A butler, housekeeper, and bevy of footmen hurried forward, followed by an elegant lady and her very pretty younger companion.

That must be Lady Theodora! Cordelia had nursed a private hope that she would come with some defect—a humped back or squinty eyes would not have been unwelcome.

But there she was and looking rather perfect.

They were helped down with quiet efficiency, Lynette coming out last and standing to the side.

"Lady Cordelia, Miss Mayton," the duchess said, coming forward. "How pleased we are that you have accepted our invitation."

Cordelia curtsied low and said, "Your Grace."

"Goodness, we are in the countryside, let us not have that sort of formality, Duchess will do very well. Here is my daughter, Lady Theodora."

"You are both very welcome," Lady Theodora said prettily.

Blast it. She was so charming!

"Now, I will not have you standing on the drive a moment longer," the duchess said. "My housekeeper shall show you to your rooms where you can rest and change from your traveling clothes."

"Oh Mama," Lady Theodora said, "do allow me to show them the way. I do know the ins and outs of those rooms. Mrs. Blowton can show the maid, what is your name?"

Lynette bobbed a curtsy and said, "Lynette, my lady."

"Mrs. Blowton can show Lynette to the servants' quarters," Lady Theodora said. "Mr. Graves has put aside two of our best spare rooms for her use."

The duchess nodded her assent. Lynette appeared positively delighted and rather reassured that she would not be lorded over. She was also probably filing this moment away for a future communication with Fleur.

Cordelia really wished Lady Theodora would stop being so utterly charming. She did not suppose it was every duchess' daughter who would inquire into a maid's name.

"We meet in the drawing room at seven," the duchess said. "By then, the duke, my son, and Lord Harveston will have returned from their manly pursuits."

"We are to be a small party, then?" Miss Mayton asked.

"For tonight," the duchess said. "The rest of my guests will descend like pigeons to roost on the morrow. I did so wish to give Lady Cordelia and my daughter some time to become acquainted with one another beforehand."

This was rather marvelous. Not so much because Cordelia wished to become acquainted with Lady Theodora, she was already almost sickened by how charming the lady was, but because it would be a small party with Lord Harveston. She supposed there was every chance she would be seated next to him at dinner.

They were led into the house and Lady Theodora showed them up the stairs.

"As you might guess," she said, "this is a very old house, full of…well, I would call them quirks, though others might call them oddities and deformities."

Cordelia could see for herself that the house had passed down through many hands. The very staircase showed it. The dark wood had been worn smooth, a testament to all those generations who'd run their hands along it.

"You have probably also noticed that we have an excessive amount of floors," Lady Theodora said. "At a party such as this, one might expect the unmarried ladies to be in one wing and the gentleman in another. In this house, the ladies are on this floor and the gentleman on the next up."

They had come to a landing, and indeed Cordelia could see the staircase running up another two floors. The servants would be at the very top, which must be a long climb for them.

"Goodness, your servants must be run off their feet," Miss Mayton said, speaking precisely what she had been thinking.

"It is a defect of the house, to be sure," Lady Theodora said. "To remedy the situation, each servant has two rooms—one on the top floor and one on the basement level. They move between them as they like and sometimes they do get the better of us. If it is very hot, they are cool in the basement, and if it is very cold, all the heat of the house goes right up to their accommodations."

"I applaud your care of your servants, Lady Theodora," Cordelia said, hardly able to imagine Lynette's delight with the circumstance.

Cordelia did not wish to applaud the lady, but what could she do?

"My father says that in a house like this everybody must all pull together—if people are unhappy, they will no more pull for you than a bad-tempered pony will pull a cart."

"A man of good sense," Miss Mayton said.

They had come to the first room and Lady Theodora opened the door and showed them in. "These rooms are connected to one another, by that door there."

Miss Mayton bustled over to confirm the idea. Upon opening the door, she found a long dressing room with ample closets that led into a charming sitting room and then on to another bedchamber.

"I chose this especially for you, as it does have that lovely little sitting room and the view is of the lake."

Cordelia went to the windows. The view was spectacular. It was also highly interesting. She could see two men just pulling their boats up on the banks as a third looked on. Though it was at a distance, she would recognize Lord Harveston by his height anywhere.

"Now, you are not to worry that the place is haunted by ghosts if you were to suddenly hear voices coming from somewhere and seeming very far away. It is a quirk of the chimneys that carries the sound from one place to another. Anything you hear will come from above and will be no more ghostly than a valet informing his gentleman of what coat he is to wear."

"Goodness, I'm glad you said, I imagine that would be rather alarming," Cordelia said.

Confidentially, Lady Theodora said, "One time, I heard from two floors up. Two maids were comforting each other over our housekeeper's stern words to them. I told them of it and now they only gossip in the basement, where they cannot be over-heard."

As Miss Mayton went through the connecting doors to view her own bedchamber, Lady Theodora came beside Cordelia.

"That is my father, my brother, and Lord Harveston at the lake," the lady said. "They have been practicing like madmen for the regatta."

"There is to be a regatta?" Cordelia said. What she really thought was how interesting that Lord Harveston knew how to sail. She would not have thought it.

"May I tell you a secret?" Lady Theodora said.

Cordelia's heart sank. The only reason a lady wished to tell another lady a secret was a gentleman. Was she poised to hear that there was something between Lady Theodora and Lord Harveston?

Her heart felt as if it were being squeezed by a fist.

"It was not my mother's idea to invite you early," Lady Theodora said. "It was my brother's idea. He convinced Mama that it would be better for the two of us to have a quiet evening together before the other guests arrived. But, I think he really meant that you and Lord Harveston should have some time together."

Lady Theodora looked at her intently to see what she would say to it.

"Did he?" she said weakly. She was delighted that Lord Hamill should have had such an idea, but she did not dare admit it.

"I am certain of it," Lady Theodora said. "Lord Harveston dropped his spoon when he discovered you would come."

"Dropped his spoon?"

"At dinner. It positively clattered. Then, he went to great lengths to sing your praises. Your family is a delight and you have made your mark at his salon."

"Did he say that?"

"Indeed he did," Lady Theodora said.

Cordelia was most gratified, but there was still this niggling idea about how charming Lady Theodora was.

"I suppose, though," she said slowly, "that Lord Harveston must sing your praises too. After all, Lord Hamill has told me you are a very great intellectual."

"Has he?" Lady Theodora said, with peals of laughter. "Goodness, how did I ever land in such a family? The truth is—I adore poetry and novels and read the occasional treatise on some subject or another. My brother thinks anybody who steps foot into a library is bookish."

"So then…you are not…" Cordelia hardly knew how to ask such a question. She hardly knew because there was not a way to answer such a question.

Nevertheless, Lady Theodora understood her meaning.

"Not a jot," she said. "My particular interest lays elsewhere. He is a neighbor and will come on the morrow. Do not say a word of it, though. He is only a baron and my mother and father are determined I have a season, so we will not say anything until I have gone through it. Then, they shall hear the awful truth."

"The view is heavenly!" Miss Mayton called from the other room. "And look, Cordelia, mark me that is Lord Harveston."

Both ladies giggled. Lady Theodora said, "I will leave you on your own now, your maid and your luggage should be up shortly. By the by, do call me Theo."

"Call me Cordelia, or Cordy for short," Cordelia said.

PERCIVAL HAD WISHED to be on the drive when Lady Cordelia arrived, but Hamill had convinced him otherwise. For one, Hamill said he needed every spare moment to prepare for the regatta. He understood the mechanics of it well enough, but he was so uninterested in the whole thing that his mind was forever wandering, and then he'd make a mistake.

He'd already run his boat into the shore, making a horrible scraping sound and damaging the centerboard, almost knocked himself out when he'd changed direction and nearly forgot to duck, and he'd come close to tipping over twice.

For another, Hamill said if they got their timing just right, Lady Cordelia might be able to spot him down at the lake, engaging in a sport.

Percival had gone along with it, as he really did need all the practice he could get. In any case, Hamill was to be trusted—he'd arranged for Lady Cordelia and Miss Mayton to come a day early.

He would spend this evening acquainting her with this new, Corinthian-like figure he was turning himself into. Then, in the days that followed, he would *show* her the various strides he'd made. On the night of the ball, he would ask for her hand.

Now, he hurried down the long flights of stairs from the second floor to the ground floor. It was his understanding that the ladies traveling without husbands would be housed on the first floor.

As he reached the first-floor landing, the swish of silk caught his eye.

Lady Cordelia.

She was escorted by Miss Mayton and she looked marvelous. Lady Cordelia was in an elegant deep blue silk dress with no adornment but for a sapphire necklace of the same hue.

He bowed. "Lady Cordelia, Miss Mayton. Very good to see you again."

Lady Cordelia curtsied. Miss Mayton did too, then the matron suddenly said, "Gracious, I quite forgot, I was meant to…see somebody about something or other."

She then squeezed by him and set off down the stairs at a record pace.

It could not have been more awkwardly done and Percival

found himself very fond of her for it.

"Lady Cordelia," he said, putting out his arm, "may I escort you down?"

The lady nodded and laid her hand on his arm.

"I find my family must thank you, Lord Harveston," Lady Cordelia said. "Tattleton has made me aware of the efforts you have taken to restore our garden at Portland Place."

"It was nothing at all," Percival said, very gratified that Tattleton had seen fit to tell his secret.

"I do not think you can claim it as nothing," Lady Cordelia said. "Our neighboring butler has made regular reports and says your man comes by weekly to do the weeding and pruning."

"I hope Lord Darling has settled into country life?" Percival asked, even more gratified that the nosy butler next door had been sending reports.

Lady Cordelia laughed. She had such a charming laugh.

"Lord Darling has been taken in hand by one of our oldest dairy cows. Her name is Clara and he follows her round very dedicated to her. When he becomes too rambunctious, she knocks him with her head."

"I am glad to hear it," Percival said, taking the steps very slowly so they might prolong the conversation. "And Lady Van Doren's child, I am sure Tattleton ought not have told me, but I did press him on it. I understand she is well."

"Lily is very well indeed. In fact, she was on the mend by the time we arrived home. Now she is getting places as fast as her chubby little legs can carry her."

Percival nodded. "I did think, even though the danger was past, that it was very well done for the entire family to decamp to Lady Van Doren. Really very good."

"What else can a family be counted on for, if not to rush to the one in need?" Lady Cordelia asked quizzically. She seemed not to have considered that other families did not perhaps inconvenience themselves so much.

They had reached the ground floor and found the butler, Mr.

Graves, ready to lead them into the drawing room.

"You will know everyone but for the duke, I think," Percival said.

Lady Cordelia nodded.

"You will like him, he is a genial fellow."

"By the by, Lord Harveston, have you been following the scientific discoveries regarding volcanoes?"

That caught Percival entirely off guard. "No, I have not. Have *you*?"

"Indeed, it is all very interesting. Gracious, I do worry about the people who live next to them. They must be terrified for their children."

Percival smiled to himself. His intellectual cronies would be throwing facts at him just about now, none of which would include the slightest interest in the people within range of an active volcano beyond figures and amounts.

It was very like Lady Cordelia to worry about them.

CHAPTER TWENTY-TWO

CORDELIA WAS WELL-PLEASED with the evening so far. Really, it could not have gone better. Lord Harveston had met her on the stairs, almost as if he'd been waiting for her. She'd taken that opportunity to casually mention her interest in the current work being done about volcanoes.

All her hard work was showing—he'd seemed mightily impressed by it.

And, just as Lord Harveston had said, their host was a genial fellow and had at once pressed her to address him as duke. He was not at all as prepossessing as Conbatten could be when he had a mind.

Now, at dinner, she was not, as she had hoped, sat next to lord Harveston. However, they were a small party and he was just across from her.

He did keep looking at her when he thought she did not see. It was very marked, she thought.

"Lady Cordelia," the duke said, "do you enjoy a regatta?"

"I have never had the pleasure of witnessing one, Duke," Cordelia said. "Though it sounds rather thrilling."

"There now," the duke said jovially, "you've hit the thing on the head. It is sure to be a nailbiter. The men will be pulling in the sheets and sailing close to the wind to round the buoys and make a mad dash to the finish."

"Lady Cordelia," Lord Hamill said, "you are to know that

Harveston has picked the thing up in record time. You'd think he'd served in the navy."

"That is more than a step too far," Lord Harveston said.

Cordelia was rather surprised that he'd just learned the skill.

"Nonsense, Harveston," Hamill said. "It's been just like the boxing ring. Jackson said he'd never witnessed a fellow come so natural to the sport."

Now Lord Harveston was boxing? Lord Harveston?

Cordelia was entirely perplexed. About the last thing she would imagine Lord Harveston doing was boxing.

Lord Harveston looked embarrassed to be noted so. Goodness, he was a natural at boxing, and modest about it too.

"Ah well," Lord Hamill said, "Harveston does not like to be singled out about his various skills. I suppose he's told nobody that we raced our phaetons on the way here and I was beaten handily."

Now Lord Harveston was racing a phaeton? She would not have imagined the lord even owned a phaeton.

"I certainly did not tell anybody such a story," Lord Harveston said, staring at Hamill.

"Modest as the day is long," Hamill said, looking very satisfied with himself.

It occurred to Cordelia that Lord Hamill had noted all of this for her benefit. Yes, of course that must be it—Lady Theodora had said that it was Hamill who had suggested she come early. He was attempting to play the matchmaker.

It was a very nice thing for him to do. Though, she was still trying to reconcile the Lord Harveston she thought she understood to the Lord Harveston that had just been described. Who was this person who was boxing and racing and sailing?

"If we might change the subject," Lord Harveston said, "Lady Cordelia has informed me that she is looking into the current work being done regarding predicting volcanic eruptions."

"Thank heavens we do not have them here," the duchess said. "I should be frightened out of my wits."

"That is just what I thought," Cordelia said. "It must be a constant worry over one's family."

"But what is being done to stop them?" the duke asked.

"It is not so much what is being done to stop them," Cordelia said, "as it is to find out why they erupt so they might predict when next it might occur."

Though Cordelia was certain on that particular point of the paper, she realized that she was not at all certain about the rest of it. What, particularly, was being studied? Was it the soil round the volcano?

That sounded vaguely familiar, though there were no associated facts coming along with the idea.

She realized that though she'd read the Royal Society paper, once she'd understood the gist of the problem, her mind had flown off to imagining the people faced with such a problem.

Cordelia had spent a deal of time thinking of one family in particular—a mother, father, son, and daughter living very nearby a smoking volcano somewhere in the South Seas. But that family was not actually in the paper.

"I always did worry about Vesuvius during my time in Italy," Miss Mayton said.

"Ah," the duke said, "forever wondering when you were going to have to run for your life, eh Miss Mayton?"

"Oh dear no," Miss Mayton said. "It was the gentlemen of my acquaintance I worried about. Might one throw themselves into it over unrequited love? Several of my suitors made threats about it."

"Chucking themselves into a volcano over disappointed hopes?" the duke asked. Cordelia thought the duke, while exceedingly genial, was not of a particularly romantic temperament.

Miss Mayton nodded. "Though, it was only Gregorio who was to suffer a tragic fate and he did it by dealing himself a deadly blow. In the end, it was nothing to do with a volcano—ironic, is it not?"

Cordelia could not tell if the duke saw the irony in worrying about a volcanic end and then getting an entirely different one.

The duke looked at his duchess and said, "We ought to introduce Miss Mayton to Freddy. Lord Germaine, Miss Mayton, I think you might enjoy his company."

"If you are not opposed to a missing hand," the duchess said.

"A tiger took it," the duke said, shaking his head. "One ought not go into a tiger's cage while the tiger is still in it."

"Was it a case of unrequited love?" Miss Mayton asked, seeming very interested to hear more about Freddy.

"It was a case of *something*," the duke said.

The dinner went on very well, with much spoken of regarding Freddy. Cordelia found herself relieved that the subject had been changed to that individual and his mishap with a tiger.

She was not so relieved to find that she really recalled very little about the paper on volcanoes, so rapt had she been in considering the imaginary family that lived next to one.

It did shake her confidence in her studies. Especially when she realized she'd done that quite often. She'd struggle through some treatise or other and then her mind would go flying off to the people involved in the situation.

She'd read one about frogs in a pond and their life cycle, though she only vaguely remembered the lifecycle and mostly remembered the little girl she'd pictured who'd sat by the pond and watched it all happen. The girl's name was Penny and she'd named all the tadpoles. Then Penny had a charming conversation with her father about how the tadpoles were getting on.

Cordelia had a sinking feeling that her mind was not equipped to keep up with Lord Harveston's mind.

His mind would not go gallivanting off to invent young Penny watching the tadpoles.

After dinner, Cordelia had thought they would retire to the drawing room. She supposed she would be asked to play. Perhaps there would be cards.

She'd been very surprised to hear of lawn bowling by candlelight.

Though Lady Theodora had counseled against it, they all very soon found themselves out of doors and the men engaged in a tournament.

Cordelia could not say who had won. She could not *see* who had won.

Though, as they retired for the night, Lord Hamill made a great show of claiming that Lord Harveston had trounced them.

It seemed he was to be good at everything now.

Cordelia was not certain she could like that. Particularly when she'd just discovered that she'd been fooling herself about the success of her studies.

He was to be good at everything and she was to be good at…imagining people who did not exist.

What a useless talent.

THE DUKE AND duchess' guests had arrived all morning. There were quite a few of them Percival knew, and a handful that were local to the neighborhood that he did not.

He'd wished to find a moment with Lady Cordelia. He'd thought to inquire more into the people living nearby volcanoes that she worried about.

It had occurred to him that her way of thinking was a thing he would likely never master. He'd spent far too long ignoring the human condition to focus his attention on facts and lists.

Had he been reading the paper on volcanoes, he might not have given a thought to who lived nearby them.

It was a defect, he knew. A defect he probably would never be able to entirely remedy.

But was that not the beauty of Lady Cordelia's mind? That she did think of such things very naturally?

He did not have such a moment to speak to her, though. The

duke had rounded up all the gentlemen to choose their boats, while the ladies were off in carriages to shop in the local village.

The morning had been spent examining the boats, ensuring all equipment was on board and in good order, listening to Lord Poppin's harrowing account of sailing in high seas off the coast, and endless conversations about the nonexistent wind. Mr. Bedminster, in particular, seemed to think if one licked one's finger and held it up in the air, the wind would take the hint and pick up.

Despite Bedminster's hints, the wind did not pick up until the afternoon, after they'd been sent sandwiches and ale from the house that they ate at the water's edge. Then, it was time to put all the talk to the test.

The palaver that had followed did not give Percival very much confidence concerning the upcoming regatta.

Gentlemen, as they were always so prone to do, had confidently claimed their skill at the tiller, even when they had very little acquaintance with it. Or any at all.

After what he'd witnessed, very few of them had ever sailed the ocean, never mind any high seas they'd mentioned.

Near misses, entanglements on buoy lines, run agrounds, sails flapping in the wind, and Lord Bertram capping the whole thing off by tipping over were the scenes of the day.

Hamill, the duke, and a baron who lived on a neighboring estate had their hands full racing from one disaster to the next.

The regatta was on the morrow and Percival was just hoping to get through it with nobody drowned.

Finally, the duke had called it a day and they were released to change for dinner.

Percival had held on to very little hope that he'd be seated next to Lady Cordelia, not with so many people arrived to the house, but Hamill had pulled him aside and said he'd arranged it with his duchess.

Hamill was really turning out to be a stand-up friend.

Percival paced the drawing room, saying hello to this person or that, but always with his eye on the doors.

Finally, Lady Cordelia entered.

She was entirely smashing. She wore a silk dress the color of claret. The cream colored ostrich feather in her lovely hair was a picture of restraint—not like some other ladies' feathers that reached for the sky and waved dangerously close to the candles in the chandeliers.

He made an effort to not think too deeply about her companion, Miss Mayton. That lady was forever dressed in her widow's weeds, though pity would go to the person who offered their condolences and heard of the husbands who had never been.

He hurried to her side. "Lady Cordelia," he said with a bow.

"Lord Harveston, how did you get on with sailing today?" she asked.

"We did see just the end of it from our windows," Miss Mayton added. "It was hard to make out where everybody was hoping to go. I do hope Lord Bertram did not catch a chill. He seemed to be treading water for quite some time."

"Yes, there were some mishaps," he said, not wishing to outline the full scope of what had transpired. "I understand the ladies went shopping in the village?"

Both ladies nodded, and he said, "One hopes a sufficient amount of ribbons and bits and bobs were located?"

"Indeed," Lady Cordelia said, "we felt it a duty to put some money into the villagers' pockets, as we do at home."

Her tone was rather sharp, though he could not account for it. He'd only asked about ribbons, after all.

"It was well we did," Miss Mayton said. "Were you aware that Mrs. Macklethorpe has just lost her husband and now runs her shop alone?"

Percival, of course, had no way of knowing who the lady was or what her situation might be.

"I am afraid I am not."

"Oh yes, Cordelia and I had a long talk with her," Miss Mayton said. "Very sad thing, really. She was fond of Mr.

Macklethorpe."

How like Lady Cordelia to have a talk with a shopkeeper and discover the woman's personal circumstances.

"Lady Cordelia," the duchess said, "Do meet Lord Poppin."

Lady Cordelia turned round to meet the said lord, who Percival thought was not aptly named. He'd have been better to be named Lord Popinjay. This morning he'd claimed to have mastered ten-foot seas off Brighton; by the afternoon he was floundering on a lake.

Percival was left with Miss Mayton.

"Now mind," Miss Mayton went on, "Mrs. Macklethorpe was a bit standoffish in the beginning, but Cordelia could see well enough that the lady was in some sort of straits. After the other ladies had left the shop, she said to me, "I do believe that lady is near tears."

"Was she?" Percival asked.

"Oh yes, we got to the bottom of it quick enough. She was frightened over whether or not she was capable of running the shop on her own. We assured her she was and had a comfortable tea together until one of the duchess' footmen came to fetch us away. Cordelia bought the very feather she wears tonight. It was overpriced, we both knew it, but in the circumstances…"

Percival found the tale strangely touching. He did not suppose any of the duchess' other guests had noticed Mrs. Macklethorpe's sad demeanor.

No, of course they would not have. *He* would not have. Only Lady Cordelia would have comprehended the situation.

"Oh goodness," Miss Mayton said, "there is Theodora. She wished me to tell her more about Mount Vesuvius."

Miss Mayton hurried in Lady Theodora's direction. To Percival's surprise, Lady Theodora appeared delighted to note it.

The world, at this moment, seemed topsy-turvy. What he'd thought it was, it wasn't. At least, not entirely.

His rationality, his pursuit of knowledge, had only taken him so far. It had been like a dead-end road that went nowhere. All along, hiding behind his facts and figures, there was this whole other world of people and their feelings.

Again, Lady Hightower's words came back to haunt him—there were more types of intelligence than he'd been aware of.

He'd been a shell of a man and had not known it.

All that would change, though. He would act the Corinthian and he would learn from Lady Cordelia.

Assuming she would accept him.

And assuming he could drag her away from Lord Popinjay, who was just now droning on about his harrowing ordeal at sea.

The duke's dinner gong sounded. Conversations quieted and everyone began to organize themselves by rank to be ready to file into dinner.

The duchess stood at the doors and said, "We are a country party and need not be formal, so I will pair everybody off in some amusing fashion."

And so the duchess did pair her guests off.

Lord Popinjay appeared disappointed to understand he would not be escorting Lady Cordelia in, but Hamill had been as good as his word.

Percival held his arm out to Lady Cordelia.

CORDELIA HAD BEEN rather stung by Lord Harveston asking her if she'd bought sufficient bits and bobs from the village. It had struck her to mean that she was a silly creature who would be entirely entertained by ribbons and feathers.

Worse, she generally *was* entertained by shopping for ribbons and feathers.

The way he'd said it had felt a bit…condescending. As if her mind were not capable of more than choosing between a blue or green ribbon.

She was cognizant of the fact that she was particularly sensitive at the current moment, as she had so recently come to the realization that she'd not got nearly as far in her studies as she thought she had.

Now, he'd taken her into dinner, which had been wholly unexpected. She guessed it must have been Lord Hamill's arrangement somehow.

"Miss Mayton relayed the rest of the story regarding Mrs. Macklethorpe," Lord Harveston said.

"Poor lady," Cordelia said.

"Yes, indeed," he said. "And I think not many ladies would have known it, as they would not have asked."

Cordelia nodded. "I did of course wonder if it were my place to inquire."

"No, no, that is not it," Lord Harveston said. He looked rather intent and his tone was insistent. "That is not it at all. Not many ladies would have even noticed something was amiss."

Cordelia wrinkled her brow just a little. "Anybody must have seen it."

"No, I do not believe so. Furthermore, I do not think just anybody would have even looked. I am certain I would not have, and ashamed to admit it too."

At the head of the table, the duchess turned, signaling all to turn to their other seatmate.

Lord Harveston looked almost stricken and reluctantly turned. Cordelia turned as well to speak to Lord Poppin.

She did not really hear much of what the lord said. Something about how the shore receded in the distance and a whale circled the ship and it seemed all was lost.

She was far too busy attempting to unravel what Lord Harveston had just said.

Cordelia could not entirely understand his intense interest in Mrs. Macklethorpe and her unfortunate loss, nor why he thought it was somehow singular that she and Miss Mayton had a conversation with the lady.

He did think it was something fine, though. That was clear

enough.

It cheered her to think so. And after all, just because her studies had not been what she would wish up to this point, that could change. Could it not?

Of course it could. Now that she knew her habit of allowing her mind to wander and invent people who did not exist, she could fix that particular failing.

She could take in everything that had been done about the volcanoes and speak about it knowledgeably.

There really was not anything to prevent it but her own determination.

Further, should she not rise to the challenge? Lord Harveston was a noted intellectual, and now apparently he was a sailor and a boxer and a carriage racer.

If something were to come of whatever was between them, she must measure up.

"And so," Lord Poppin said, "we barely made it out with our lives."

"Goodness," Cordelia said, feeling that comment was almost always sufficient when a gentleman relayed some sort of derring-do.

"What shall us men face on the morrow?" Lord Poppin mused. "The waves will not be as high as some I have faced, but the danger will be in so many boats near one another. Collisions, Lady Cordelia. Dangerous collisions."

"Gracious," Cordelia said, using the second preferred phrase in her arsenal of supposed admiration. She hoped she would not be pressed to use her third word, which was "heavens" because after that she had no more and Lord Poppin would be left adrift without further buoying up.

Privately, she was beginning to find Lord Poppin rather ridiculous and was not at all certain the stories he told were true.

From the end of the table, the duke used a spoon to ding on his glass. He rose.

"My dear guests," he said, "on the morrow, the gentlemen

will go forth on a regatta, wind willing. They will round two buoys set in a classic triangle from the start line, the last leg being the downwind."

"Danger will abound," Lord Poppin whispered.

Cordelia suppressed a giggle. "Heavens," she said softly.

"The neighborhood has been invited to view the spectacle and there will be plentiful food and drink for those good people," the duke said. "Our esteemed lady guests will have a special viewing area with chairs for their convenience, set apart from the milling crowd."

"Ah, very good," Lord Poppin said quietly. "There may be ruffians in the crowd and I cannot be in two places at once."

Ruffians from the village? What an idea.

"This is to be the start of a grand tradition," the duke said. "I have already arranged for a plaque to be hung in the billiards room that will one day house dozens of brass plates naming the winner of that season's race. Will *you* be named on the first brass plate?"

"Undoubtedly," Lord Poppin said to her right.

"Unlikely," Lord Harveston said on her left.

"I raise my glass to the competitors," the duke said, "and let the best sailor win."

There were loud 'hear hears' from the gentlemen at table.

Cordelia was grateful to turn to Lord Harveston and leave Lord Poppin to overwhelm his dinner companion with tales of high seas adventure.

"Why do you say it is unlikely you will prevail, Lord Harveston?" she asked.

"Because it is," he said with a laugh. "Despite Hamill's claim that I might be taken for a navy man, I would not be taken for a navy man."

"I do not suppose any of the gentlemen competing would be taken so," Cordelia said. "At least, that is my impression."

Lord Harveston glanced over her shoulder at Lord Poppin's profile. "Some less than others, I imagine."

Cordelia stifled a laugh, as Lord Harveston had seemed to rightly take Lord Poppin's measure.

"Now, Lady Cordelia, tell me more of Mrs. Macklethorpe," Lord Harveston said. "I understand from Miss Mayton that she is worried about running the shop on her own."

And so they went on very genially discussing Mrs. Macklethorpe's case, Lord Harveston having the idea that it was keeping the books that likely troubled the lady. It was the sort of thing Mr. Macklethorpe had likely done on his own.

If they had missed a cue to turn to their opposite seat mates and left those two persons adrift for a time, that could not be helped. Not when Mrs. Macklethorpe had such a thorny situation to unravel.

In any case, when she was forced to turn to Lord Poppin, all he had to talk about were the various dangers surrounding them. Cordelia was staying in a duke's house; she thought it likely she had never been more safe in her life.

If Mr. Poppin had contributed to her happiness at all, it was that it felt such a delight to turn to Lord Harveston.

The dinner ended far too soon, and the duchess had risen to lead the ladies out while the men were left to their port. Cordelia was certain Lord Poppin was poised to recount his harrowing days at sea.

All was lost, indeed.

CHAPTER TWENTY-THREE

I N THE DRAWING room, Cordelia and her aunt found a quiet corner. There, she relayed all that had transpired at dinner and how interested Lord Harveston had been regarding Mrs. Macklethorpe.

"I wonder if he is not interested because *you* are interested," Miss Mayton mused, "it would be very promising if that were the case."

"I do think he likes me, I really do," Cordelia said. "But Aunt, I have recently realized that my intellectual studies were not perhaps as intellectual as they should have been."

"Oh dear, I know so little about that sort of thing I hardly know how to counsel you on it. I have far too many feelings to make time for facts."

Cordelia nodded vigorously. "It is all right, I know what I must do. Now that I know my own proclivity for mind wandering, I must just use discipline to stop it."

"I see, yes, that does sound very good. You girls are always so clever."

"I only wish I had more time to do it! I wish I had realized this when I began my studies."

Miss Mayton tapped her chin. "It seems to me, now that you have set your course, you might rightly claim your destination. After all, you know where you are going, I see no reason you might not act as if you are already there."

Cordelia shrugged. "I believe that is what I have been doing in mentioning the Royal Society paper on volcanoes. Thank goodness I was not asked a slew of questions, as I remember little about the actual facts of it."

"Yes, but there is one thing you have not considered," Miss Mayton said. "You are an actress, Cordelia. In your heart and soul, you are a born actress. Take on the part, really throw yourself into it. *Be* the intellectual, as if you were treading the hallowed boards."

Cordelia looked inquiringly at her aunt.

"As a beginning, perhaps you might stage a bit of a tableau for Lord Harveston to view."

"A tableau?" Cordelia asked.

"Oh yes," Miss Mayton said, seeming as if she were bursting with an idea. "What if I were to go and get my reading glasses? You might perch them on your nose. And then, there are several heavy tomes on that bookshelf there, one of which must be suitably intellectual. You might casually walk by Lord Harveston's view, glasses on nose and book in hand."

"I see, Aunt. A tableau!"

As PERCIVAL LISTENED to Lord Poppin drone on about his alleged adventure at sea, which now included a whale though no whale had been present in the version told earlier in the day, he could not be opposed to the fellow.

Was there any other gentleman at table who could have been more preferred as Lady Cordelia's other dinner companion?

No, Poppin had been perfect in his ludicrousness and could only raise Percival's estimation in Lady Cordelia's eyes.

What a conversation he and Lady Cordelia had! He thought he'd begun to understand how Lady Cordelia's mind worked. At least, the overarching framework of it.

He had thought it quite usual to carefully curate those let into one's sphere using cautious consideration over time as a yardstick. His own sphere had been defended by a veritable moat, with murder holes manned with archers—always at the ready to pull up the drawbridge.

Lady Cordelia's worldly sphere was very different. Her castle gates were thrown open and absolutely anybody might walk through them—welcomed as a friend until proven otherwise.

This, he supposed, was the real thing one gained from a family such as the Benningtons. It was a blithe confidence in the good of the world.

When one was not so caught up with defending the castle, one might notice a person such as Mrs. Macklethorpe.

He'd already determined he would do something for the lady. Percival would send Jameston into the village and offer to pay the local schoolmaster to provide a service. If Mrs. Macklethorpe could be taught to manage her own books, she would proceed on firm footing.

"And so," Lord Poppin said, downing his port, "we barely escaped with our lives."

"Yes, a whale, they can be dastardly," the duke said, rising. "Well gentlemen, we should not keep the ladies waiting longer. In any case, it ought to be an early night for our sailors—a regatta awaits."

Percival had not needed to be told twice that port was at an end and the ladies were to be joined. He smiled as he thought that even the duke, genial as he was, had heard enough of Lord Poppin's alarming sea voyage.

He entered the drawing room, searching it for Lady Cordelia. She was not at the pianoforte, nor did she sit with the cluster of ladies round a teapot.

Out of the corner of his eye, he saw her.

She had just come from a bookshelf set to the side of the drawing room doors. The lady carried what looked to be an exceedingly heavy book and had glasses perched on her nose.

He had not known she wore glasses, but then so many people did for close reading he supposed he should not be surprised.

She looked rather charming in them. He could picture her wearing them by his fireside on a cold afternoon, curled up with a book or magazine.

As she made her way forward, Lord Poppin somehow came round him and said, "Ah! Lady Cordelia wishes to read."

He grabbed at an ottoman and pulled it forward. "Allow me to assist you to a seat."

Lady Cordelia looked vaguely in Lord Poppin's direction, almost as if she were attempting to locate where his voice was coming from. Seeming to home in on it, she smiled and said, "That is quite all right, Lord Poppin."

Then she walked right into the ottoman.

Or over it, as the case really was.

She stumbled, then tumbled onto the ottoman, before rolling to the carpet and coming to a stop.

Percival pushed Lord Poppin out of the way. "Lady Cordelia! Are you hurt?" he said, propping her up.

Naturally, when one tripped over an ottoman in a duke's drawing room during a country party, every person in that room must gasp and hurry forward.

"Stay back and give the lady air," Percival said in a sharp voice.

Lady Cordelia looked somewhat dazed and her glasses rested askew on her nose.

"Goodness, where did that piece of furniture come from?" she asked.

Nobody answered, least of all Lord Poppin, who was just now slipping to the back of the crowd.

"Allow me to help you to your feet, Lady Cordelia."

"Yes, do, thank you," she said.

Percival lifted her up, freeing her from her encounter with the blasted ottoman, and set her on her feet.

As soon as her two feet landed on the floor, she cried out and picked up one of them.

"I am afraid you have hurt your ankle," he said.

The duchess had pushed through with the duke close behind. "Gracious, you poor dear. I will send for the doctor this instant."

"Oh no, I am sure it must be all right," Lady Cordelia said.

"Can you put any weight on it?" the duke asked.

Lady Cordelia gingerly put her foot down, but it was not more than a second before she pulled it up again. "I am afraid not."

"That's settled," the duke said. "Graves, send for Doctor Raythorn. Drag him from his bed if necessary. Harveston, carry the lady to her rooms. Miss Mayton? Where are you, good lady?"

Miss Mayton pushed her way forward.

"Miss Mayton, you will follow Harveston and see that Lady Cordelia is comfortably settled as we await the doctor. Raise the ankle with pillows and I will send up a strong drink to assist with the pain."

"I am not in that terrible a pain," Lady Cordelia said.

"Nonsense, my lady," the duke said, "you are as white as a sheet."

It was true. Lady Cordelia was looking very pale. That idiot Lord Poppin! What was he about, dragging furniture in front of people?

"Harveston?" the duke said.

Percival swept Lady Cordelia up in his arms while the duke cleared the path forward shouting, "Make way, we are coming through."

As he made his way to the staircase with Miss Mayton fluttering round him like a panicked bird, Lady Cordelia said, "Goodness, I do not like to make so much trouble."

"Nonsense, it was Popinjay's fault. He might talk a good story about a murderous whale, but it is *he* who is the real menace."

Lady Cordelia laughed at the idea, which he thought was a very good sign.

As he carried her up the stairs it began to dawn on him how personal it was for her to be in his arms.

He'd planned on her being so sometime very soon, but could not have imagined the current circumstance.

She gazed up at him as he traversed the stairs and Percival had a very great wish to bend down and kiss her.

He would do no such thing of course, not until the question had been asked and answered. It would not do to put the lady in a compromising position and he did not yet know if the lady even wished to be compromised.

"Just here, Lord Harveston," Miss Mayton said, running ahead of him and throwing open the door.

Percival carried her through it.

Good lord, now he was in her bedchamber. And carrying her to the bed.

He was not certain when last he had to exert as much self-control as he did at that moment. He'd very much like to throw Miss Mayton out the door.

Lady Cordelia's maid came hurrying in. "What has happened?" she cried, staring at him.

"Your lady has injured her ankle," he said by way of explanation.

"I heard that part from the butler," the maid said. "What I didn't hear was that she was in a lord's arms!"

The girl was rather saucy.

"You ought to put her down, the earl shan't like it!" the maid said.

"Do be quiet, Lynette," Lady Cordelia said. "I have injured my ankle and could not put weight on it."

"Pull the bedcovers back," Percival said, hoping his face had not tinged red from saying it.

"What?" the maid cried.

Really, this Lynette was a bit of a hysterical sort of person.

"I cannot lay her down until you move the covers," he pointed out.

"Go on, Lynette," Miss Mayton said. "Do stop being such a booby about it."

Lynette, seeming to realize the fastest way to get her mistress out of his arms was to do as she was asked, hurried round him and pulled down the blankets.

Percival laid her down gently, her head on the pillow. "Fetch me those other pillows," he said, pointing to the other side of the bed.

For once, Lynette followed a direction without shrieking about it.

"Now," he said, "I will lift Lady Cordelia's ankle, keeping it straight and steady, as you slide the pillows underneath. Do you understand? We do not yet know if it is broken—all care must be taken."

Lynette gulped and nodded. "Aye," she said.

Percival carefully and gingerly lifted Lady Cordelia's ankle, supporting it from underneath to keep it still.

She winced just a little as he laid it down.

"Thank you, Lord Harveston," she said, looking up at him.

"Yes, thanks much, my lord," Lynette said, pulling him by the sleeve. "We will take things from here."

The maid was literally pushing him toward the door.

At least the outrageous behavior of her maid had brought a smile to Lady Cordelia's face.

Lynette gave him one final push into the corridor. "Thanks much!" she said, and slammed the door in his face.

Percival sighed. That was the last of the lady he would see tonight. All he could do now was wait for the doctor to do his assessment and hear the report.

Please God let it only be a sprain. Else, Lord Popinjay might discover that Lord Harveston was the new murderous whale in his life.

AFTER LYNETTE HAD thrown Lord Harveston from the room, Cordelia had smiled ruefully at her aunt and said, "Not the tableau we were hoping for."

"That Lord Poppin is a confounding sort of creature," Miss Mayton said.

Indeed, he was very confounding. All would have gone smoothly if he had not pushed that ottoman into her path. She had a book in hand and glasses on and was feeling very scholarly.

Though, her aunt's glasses were rather stronger than she'd imagined they'd be. They'd turned the whole room into something that looked as if it were being viewed inside an aquarium. Everything had been blurred and wavy.

Even so, she'd mapped out her marks, just as if she were on the stage, and had been poised to pass close by Lord Harveston so he might view the tableau.

"I don't see why the housekeeper couldn't have carried you up," Lynette said. "Or I could'a done it."

"Do not be ridiculous, Lynette," Cordelia said. "There was no impropriety in Lord Harveston carrying me up and neither you nor Mrs. Blowton would have made it up two steps before dropping me."

Lynette shrugged, as she knew that was perfectly true.

And how lucky it was true. How interesting it had been to be carried by Lord Harveston.

He had very strong arms, as it happened. She was not certain she would have thought it, but he'd picked her up as if it were nothing at all.

It really had been rather glorious.

After a half hour of considering Lord Harveston's arms, there was a sharp rap on the door. Mrs. Blowton bustled in with an older gentleman following her.

"We were in luck," Mrs. Blowton said. "Mr. Graves recalled that Doctor Raythorn was to be at a card party at the Hendersons' not a half mile down the road. Lady Cordelia, this is Doctor Raythorn."

The doctor came forward. "Let us see what has torn me away from a winning hand. It's the ankle, is it?"

Cordelia nodded and said, "I am very sorry to hear of that, Doctor Raythorn. I suppose you are a very good card player?"

This little bit of soothing seemed to go a long way in Doctor Raythorn's books. As he examined her ankle, feeling along the bones and then moving it this way and that, he said, "Well, there will be other card games, I suppose."

"Is it broken?" Lynette whispered. "Will you have to set it while my lady screams?"

Doctor Raythorn knit his brows at Lynette. "I cannot tell if you are horrified or interested in the idea. No matter, it is not a break. It is a bad sprain, though."

He turned back to Cordelia. "I am afraid it is bedrest for the next few days, at the very least. Keep it elevated as you have done."

While Cordelia was grateful that there were no broken bones, she was less grateful over the idea of staying abed. How was Lord Harveston to say anything, to declare anything he might be thinking of, when she was abed?

"Mrs. Blowton, I will leave you a poultice for the injured area. First, bathe it in cold water, ice if you have it. Then the poultice."

The housekeeper nodded.

"For all that, Lady Cordelia, the only real cure is rest. Do not fool yourself into thinking you can get on your feet for at least three days."

Three days!

"Oh dear," she said, "I shall miss the duke's regatta."

The doctor snorted. "If my sources told no tales, what you will miss is the great crashing of boats. I'm quite looking forward to it."

"But Doctor," Miss Mayton said, "certainly there would be no harm if Lady Cordelia were to watch the regatta from the window?"

The doctor considered the idea. "It could be done, but carefully. If she were helped there, hopping on the good foot, and then using that ottoman over there to prop it up. Well, for a limited time, I suppose it could not hurt."

"I will arrange it all," Miss Mayton said. "I will stay up here and provide company."

Cordelia sighed. Watching from the window would not be ideal, but at least she would be able to see Lord Harveston.

Perhaps he might see her too. She could wave to him.

In the meantime, she would direct her thoughts away from her injury. Though really, they did not need to be directed. Even as the doctor spoke, Cordelia could think of little beyond having found herself in Lord Harveston's arms.

With any luck, she would find herself there again sometime soon.

CHAPTER TWENTY-FOUR

PERCIVAL HAD BEEN up early. He'd been dressed and sent Jameston to the village to see about a teacher for Mrs. Macklethorpe.

He understood from the doctor that Lady Cordelia's ankle was sprained, not broken. That was very good news.

On the not so good news front had been the doctor's orders that she must be abed for at least three days.

As he sat in the drawing room with a book, he'd almost managed to forget about that blasted regatta. Though, he had been gratified to know from Miss Mayton finding him there that Lady Cordelia would be watching from a window.

Now, crowds of villagers had begun to gather on the edges of the lake and the ladies were led to their viewing spot on a gently rising bank.

He turned to look up at the house, attempting to spot Lady Cordelia's window.

The sun was against him and all he could see was a glare on the panes of glass.

It was no use, he wouldn't have a chance to spot her until the sun moved behind the trees or some of the fast-moving high clouds ran over it.

The duke had gathered all his sailors together. Behind him, Percival could hear Lord Popinjay come to the conclusion of his whale story. Or, he should say whales, as now there were *two* of the behemoths attempting to kill him.

Percival turned and stared at him and the tale came to a rather abrupt end.

"My friends," the duke said, "we are poised to have a roaring regatta. As you can see for yourselves, we are in for a real spot of luck—the wind is absolutely cracking today.

Unfortunately, the duke told no tales. The wind had been picking up since noon.

Percival could see small white caps on the lake, which he certainly had not seen on the other days.

Though the duke was delighted about it, Percival was not.

At least the rowers, those hardy fellows who would row out and pick somebody up who'd landed in the lake and eventually tow their boat back to shore looked unconcerned with the state of things.

Percival suspected they were on the verge of a busy day.

The duke was helped onto a stage that had been hastily constructed at water's edge. "People of the county," he said loudly, "welcome to the first Castleton Regatta!"

There were the usual enthusiastic shouts from men who were happy to drink the duke's ale for whatever reason.

"As you can see, we have marked out the course with the starting line at this end of the lake, going round the two buoys there, and then turning back for a race to the finish! While I do not condone betting, I understand Mr. Kretcher has got something going."

Percival watched in some amazement as the men of the neighborhood turned on mass and besieged Mr. Kretcher and his bet book. How on earth would they know who to bet on?

"Gentlemen!" the duke cried, now looking rather red in the face. "To the boats!"

Percival trudged toward his boat, which flew a purple flag just now snapping in the wind. Other of the gentlemen raced ahead, but he did not see the point of it. Everyone would need to be sailing behind the start line before the duke would ring a cowbell as the start. He need not be sailing back and forth and dodging other boats for longer than was necessary.

After all, there might be whales out there. Lord Popinjay had already explained the danger they could incur.

As men struggled to get the sails raised and centerboards pinned at the half up, Percival went through the task methodically. It really had helped to have Hamill as a guide.

Hamill himself was first out into the lake and speeding along at a terrific pace. Others were not so fortunate.

Lord Bertram had managed to fall over the side of his boat and into the water already, but it was only a foot deep so he did not require rescue this time.

Popinjay had pushed off and shouted victoriously, until he suddenly came about and ended up beached again.

Lord Wosley could not work out why his centerboard would not go down the slot, somehow failing to realize that he was attempting to push it into earth.

Percival did his best to ignore the chaos and just do what Hamill had showed him to. His sail was up, he pushed off, and found the wind. The moment he hit the deeper water, he released the centerboard from its peg.

God help him, he was sailing.

Worse, he was sailing far too fast for comfort.

He let his sail out and luffed into the wind to slow himself down and was rather proud of himself that it actually worked.

Percival steered the tiller to keep himself out of the way of the other boats who were heading toward the starting line.

Boats were going this way and that, coming about at inopportune times or suddenly turning and luffing in the wind.

It was absolute chaos and Percival dearly wished the duke would ring that cowbell already.

The duke shouted, "Come on, Bertram, get out there!"

Percival looked to see what Lord Bertram was doing. He was rolling himself back into his boat, so presumably he'd fallen in again.

Bertram gamely got behind his tiller and pushed off, heading for the start.

The duke clanged on the cowbell, which only seemed to increase the confusion. It was as if everybody had forgot where the start actually was.

Everyone except Hamill, who had shot off toward the first buoy.

Boats were going round in circles and tipping this way and that as men dove under their swinging booms and came up the other side.

Percival attempted to sail away from the confusion, gradually angling toward the start. The sun, whose glare was not helping the situation, was dimmed by a grouping of clouds moving overhead.

Percival stood up and shaded his eyes, seeking out Lady Cordelia's window.

There she was! She was waving!

He waved back.

Behind him, Popinjay shouted, "Out of the way!"

His stern was struck, heaving his boat to the left. The boom swung, he felt a sharp crack on the back of his head, and he saw no more.

CORDELIA HAD HOPPED to the window with the assistance of Lynette and Miss Mayton and settled there, eager to view the regatta.

Or eager to view Lord Harveston, as the case actually was.

"Ah look, they are going to their boats," Miss Mayton said.

"Yes, I see! Lord Harveston's boat waves a purple flag, that's how we will know him as he goes round the buoys," Cordelia said.

Lynette was engaged in straightening the room. She said, "I

understand when a person goes a floatin' on the water to get somewhere. Like, if a person's got to leave England. I'd never do it myself, but it's understandable. I don't understand this though."

"It is a race, Lynette," Cordelia said.

"A race for what?"

"For a brass plate that is to be in the billiards room," Miss Mayton said, as if that would explain all.

"Drowning for a piece of brass," Lynette said shaking her head. "Don't seem worth it."

Ignoring Lynette, Cordelia said, "Look, Lord Hamill is off the banks already. Oh goodness, Lord Bertram just fell in."

"Told ya!" Lynette said.

"He's perfectly fine," Cordelia said. "Oh, there goes Lord Harveston! He is rather good, do not you think?"

"I wouldn't know," Lynette said with a sniff.

Of course, Cordelia was not asking Lynette in the first place, but did not scold her as her maid was still shaken to have found her in Lord Harveston's arms.

Cordelia was rather shaken herself, but it was a more pleasant sort of shaken than Lynette experienced.

"Good Gracious," Miss Mayton said, "that Lord Poppin seems more of a menace on the water than he is in a drawing room."

Her aunt was right. Lord Poppin was barreling through the other sailors with near misses everywhere.

Even at this distance, they heard the duke clang the cowbell for the start. Cordelia leaned forward in her seat, her eyes firmly on the boat with the purple flag.

It was thrilling.

Suddenly, the sun raced behind clouds. Lord Harveston stood in his boat and waved.

He waved to her.

Cordelia waved enthusiastically back, so he could be in no doubt that she'd seen him.

"Oh dear," Miss Mayton said. "What is Lord Poppin doing now?"

Cordelia squinted against the sun that had reappeared.

"He's heading right for Lord Harveston!" Cordelia waved wildly. "Get out of the way, Lord Harveston!"

Lord Harveston did not get out of the way. Lord Poppin's boat crashed into his stern and his boat swung sideways.

It seemed as if he'd almost had time to duck the swinging boom, but not enough time.

Lord Harveston dropped in his boat to be seen no more.

Cordelia jumped to her feet and then immediately collapsed back down from the pain in her ankle.

Miss Mayton grabbed her arm. "Look, the rowers have seen it and are racing to him. Don't worry, my dear, they will see that he's all right."

Cordelia watched in both horror and anger as the rowers approached Lord Harveston's boat and Lord Poppin reset his course and crossed the start line.

The rowers peered into the boat, but Cordelia could not see. What were they seeing? Was Lord Harveston dead?

One of the rowers signaled to another of the row boats and it made its way over. They tied Lord Harveston's boat to their sterns and towed it the short distance to shore.

"Why are they not helping Lord Harveston?" she cried.

"I reckon they've got to get him on land first," Miss Mayton said. "I'm sure he's all right, he is young and strong and has just taken a bump on the head."

"I knew it," Lynette muttered. "I knew it from the start."

"If he is not all right," Cordelia said, "if Lord Poppin has caused him a mortal injury, I will, well I will...I will take one of Darden's pistols and shoot him!"

"Here we go," Lynette said with a sigh.

"Let us not get ahead of ourselves," Miss Mayton said.

Though her aunt remained calm, Cordelia could see she was just as worried.

The boat reached shore. Two men ran to the rowers with a wooden door between them and Lord Harveston was gently lifted from the boat and placed upon it. The lord did not move. At this distance, Cordelia could not see his face clearly, but she thought his eyes were closed. The men carried Lord Harveston up the bank and headed toward the house, pushing their way through curious onlookers.

"Aunt, you must go and find out his condition. And the doctor! He said he would be here, do be sure they have found him quickly. Oh, how I wish I had use of my own two feet just now!"

"Stay right where you are," Miss Mayton said. "I will discover what has happened and return as soon as I have news. Lynette will remain behind to comfort you."

"I knew it would go bad," Lynette said, by way of comfort.

Miss Mayton hurried from the room. Cordelia was left to view the regatta and the stupid Lord Poppin making a fool of himself. If there was any comfort at all to what she viewed, it was that he'd lost total control of his vessel and was just going round in circles.

From the corridor, she heard feet pounding up the stairs until they were over her very head.

Lord Harveston was up there somewhere. Please God, let him be all right.

PERCIVAL AWOKE IN a very confused condition. One minute he was sailing in that cursed regatta, and now he was in his bed.

Even more alarming, Miss Mayton was in his bedchamber peering down at him and the doctor had just pierced his finger with a needle.

He yanked his hand away.

"You felt that," the doctor said. "Good, very good."

The doctor then waved a candle in front of his eyes. "Pupils even and reactive, excellent. Not any permanent damage done that I can see."

"Very well," Percival said, attempting to rise.

"Oh no, you don't, Lord Harveston," the doctor said, gently pushing him back down. "You've had a commotion to the brain, thanks to Lord Poppin."

The doctor sighed. "So many of those poor sots out there bet a week's wages on that fool to win after hearing his cockamamie story about three whales attacking his boat off the coast of Brighton."

"He did not win, please tell me he did not win," Percival said.

The doctor went to the window. "Ah, he's tipped his boat over and is shouting to the rowers."

"Good."

"Lord Harveston, you are to stay abed for at least three days, then I will assess your condition. You must take this very seriously to avoid any long-term effects. If I deem you fit in three days' time, your recovery is not ended. You must proceed carefully. If you have ridden here, you must depart in a carriage. Do nothing that would involve violent jostling or the risk of another hit to the head. Really, it would be best if you could stop here for some weeks."

"Weeks?" Percival asked.

"Weeks. Your brain has been shaken around and brains do not like to be shaken around. If you like, I can bleed you, though I do not think it will do a thing for you."

"A stupid practice," Percival said.

"Indeed, in most cases," the doctor averred.

"Now, Doctor," Miss Mayton said, "if Lord Harveston was to be very, very careful, might he not descend to the drawing room of an evening?"

"Is Lady Cordelia to descend to the drawing room?" Percival asked.

"She is not and you are not," the doctor said sternly. "You both have the sort of injuries that are not life threatening, but if not treated properly may carry life-long effects. I do not suppose Lady Cordelia would like a permanent limp and you should wish to be addlepated, all to hear the latest gossip? You would make a very fine pair."

"Nobody said we were a pair," Percival said.

"No? I had thought…"

"As had I," Miss Mayton said, staring down at him.

"That is, nobody said we were *not* a pair either," Percival said. "The thing has not been discussed."

Miss Mayton looked very satisfied with that response. She rose and walked to the window. "Ah, Lord Hamill has seized the day, I think. And Lord Poppin is soaking wet."

She walked to the fireplace mantel and straightened a picture frame on it. "Perhaps the whales capsized him."

This made Percival laugh despite himself.

The doctor rose. "My work is done here for now. Lord Harveston, I will leave your valet with tincture of laudanum to treat the headache that is likely to result from your adventure and will return in three days' time unless you take a turn. Do follow my advice and do not venture out just because you feel you can—your brain needs time to settle."

The doctor bowed. Then he stared at Miss Mayton.

She stared back at him.

"Miss Mayton," he said, "I hesitate to leave you in a man's room?"

Miss Mayton seemed to come to her senses. "Goodness, no, you had better not."

Jameston took the vial from the doctor and showed them out.

What a day.

CHAPTER TWENTY-FIVE

C ORDELIA HAD BEEN waiting anxiously and staring at the door. She'd also been determinedly ignoring Lynette's various comments on the day, which tended toward not being surprised to find out somebody was dead.

She must know if Lord Harveston was unharmed.

There had been footsteps overhead, and muffled talking. But then in a clearer sound, she was certain she heard Miss Mayton say "the whales capsized him."

It made no sense whatsoever, but unless she was beginning to experience false delusions, she was very sure she'd heard it.

Lynette had been no help to confirm it, she'd been too busy muttering to herself.

Finally the door opened.

Her aunt hurried through it. "Lord Harveston only has a commotion of the brain and the doctor says if he will rest for a few days and be careful a few weeks longer the commotion will subside and he will be right as rain."

Cordelia breathed a sigh of relief. He would be all right. They both would be.

Lynette looked a little annoyed to hear it and Cordelia supposed she had been counting on being right in her prediction of disaster.

"I'll go see what's to be done about your dinner, Lady Cordelia," Lynette said. "I'd like to hear what they're saying about all this in the servants' quarters."

Her maid closed the door behind her.

"Aunt," she said, "while you were above stairs, did you happen to say something about whales capsizing his boat?"

"Whales? Goodness, I suppose I did. Not his boat, though. Lord Poppin ended up in the lake and I joked that perhaps the whales he's always going on about put him there."

"I heard you say it," Cordelia said. "Lord Harveston's room must be just above us."

Miss Mayton tapped her chin. "Let us see, yes, three doors down from the landing. Yes it must be. But goodness, in an old house like this I am surprised you can hear anything from above."

"It is the fireplace," Cordelia said. "Remember, Theodora told us of the sound traveling through the chimneys so we would not be alarmed if we heard something."

"Oh I see," Miss Mayton said. "Yes, indeed, I was standing by the fireplace when I mentioned the whales. Shall you talk to him through the chimney, then?"

Cordelia had been thinking that very thing, but it seemed an impossibility. What on earth was she to do—just call into it?

"I do not know," she said. "I would like to, but he might think it very forward. He might not like it. And then, what would I say? He likely does not even know I can hear anything. It might feel an invasion of privacy."

Miss Mayton shrugged. "If anybody wanted their privacy invaded, I think it would be Lord Harveston just now. You saw how careful he was to carry you up the stairs last evening. I think he is...on the verge."

"On the verge?" Cordelia whispered.

"On the very verge," Miss Mayton said.

Cordelia's aunt hopped up and went to the mantel. She bent down and said loudly, "Now Cordelia, this is a very pleasant spot just here next to the fireplace, away from the draft at the window. After Lynette has brought your dinner, I will have to go down for my own and you will be quite alone for a few hours. Alone, at least a few hours starting at seven. I suggest you sit here, right by the fireplace, with that intellectual book you are reading."

Miss Mayton rose and said, "That ought to do it, I think."

"I would say so," Cordelia said, laughing.

Now, if only Lord Harveston had heard, and would say something.

If only he really was on the very verge and would say something.

PERCIVAL HAD TAKEN the laudanum as, just as the doctor had predicted, his head had begun to pound.

He lay back and tried to empty his mind of the various irritations that were currently haunting it. He would like to throttle Poppin, who he was certain was even now explaining that he was not at fault.

He would like to speak to Lady Cordelia. He *should* be speaking to Lady Cordelia, had Poppin not tripped her with an ottoman and then run his boat down in the lake.

Now they were both confined to their rooms and he had no chance at all.

The duke had been in and made light of the whole thing, but then admitted he could not like Poppin. The fellow had injured two of his guests and he just could not like that at all. He'd also grown weary of hearing about whales.

The duchess was in a right temper with the fellow and said she would like Lord Poppin to be popped right out of her house.

If it was any consolation, Lord Poppin would not be invited back.

Percival had supposed that was the only consolation he would get, but then the duke had sent up a very good bottle of wine, a plate of excellent cheeses, and a loaf of fresh-baked bread. That, combined with the laudanum, soothed a little.

But not entirely. All his plans had gone up in a puff of smoke. He must have a new plan, but when would the two of them be able to leave their rooms?

He still had time, he reminded himself. The house party had only just begun and was to go on for a fortnight.

As Jameston fiddled with this thing and that, he updated Percival on the Mrs. Macklethorpe situation, which he'd all but forgot about.

Jameston had located the local schoolmaster and made arrangements there, then went to visit Mrs. Macklethorpe and informed her of the arrangements.

Jameston said the lady was very grateful, but as much as he said Lord Harveston had made the arrangements, he was sorry to say the lady insisted on giving Lady Cordelia all the credit.

Percival wasn't sorry for it—he'd done it on her behalf.

Quite suddenly, they both heard Miss Mayton talking as if she was in the very room.

They looked at one another, Jameston raced to the door and peered out, then came back.

Then they both stared at the chimney.

"Away from the draft at the window," he heard Miss Mayton say as clear as if she were very nearby him.

"After Lynette has brought your dinner," Miss Mayton went on, "I will have to go down for my own and you will be quite alone for a few hours. Alone, at least a few hours starting at seven. I suggest you sit here, right by the fireplace where I am speaking now, with that intellectual book you are reading."

"She's talking next to the chimney," Jameston whispered.

They heard no more after that. Nevertheless, at seven o'clock, Lady Cordelia would be seated near the chimney.

He was fairly certain Miss Mayton wished him to know it. Did Lady Cordelia know about the chimney?

"Jameston," he said quietly, "I do not wish to be disturbed after seven."

"But my lord, dinner has not yet been sent up. I really do not think it should be skipped, in your condition I mean."

"I have a bottle of wine, good cheese and excellent bread and I have a conversation in a chimney that needs to be had. That will do quite well."

⇛⇚

IF CORDELIA COULD pace her room, she certainly would be pacing.

Her ankle would not allow it though.

After her dinner, Lynette and Miss Mayton had helped her to a low, cushioned chair by the fireplace.

Lynette could not understand the point of it. Why was she to sit there of all places. If she did not wish to be abed, then why not sit by the window and watch the fireflies?

Miss Mayton had hushed her questions and given her the night off.

Lynette said she did not want the night off.

Miss Mayton ordered her to take the night off.

Lynette had left deeply suspicious, but she had left.

Cordelia watched the clock strike seven. She held her breath.

Not a moment later, she heard his voice.

"Lady Cordelia, I wonder if you can hear me? It is Lord Harveston."

Cordelia bent closer to the hearth. "Yes," she said, "I can hear you, and of course I know it is Lord Harveston." She paused, then said, "I would always recognize your voice."

"Would you? Excellent, yes, good," he said. "This might seem very untoward, but I happened to hear from Miss Mayton, inadvertently through the chimney you see, that you would be on your own. At seven."

"Yes," Cordelia said. "It is seven now. I am quite alone."

"Ah, yes it is seven. I also am alone. Now that it is seven."

Cordelia leaned forward. Her instincts told her that Miss Mayton was right—he was on the verge. She could hear it in his voice.

"I wonder, Lady Cordelia, if you have ever thought, that is, I am aware that we got off to a rocky start, on the wrong foot, as it were. But then, it seems to me we have got on rather better footing since then."

"Very good footing, I think," Cordelia said.

"Yes, very good footing indeed. And I have noticed things and learned things that I did not know before. I have come to see that I was very narrowminded in my thinking and, well, as Lady Hightower has pointed out, there are all sorts of intelligence."

It was a sort of a jumble of thoughts and Cordelia was not certain what he meant. But she suddenly realized she must be honest with Lord Harveston. He must know what she really was and not be fooled by any tableau she'd attempted.

"Lord Harveston," she said, "I have a confession to make. That paper on volcanoes I mentioned? I really do not remember much about it. I was far too busy thinking about the family who might live nearby. It is a habit of mine."

There. She'd said it. If he wished to go forward, he now knew that she was not the intellectual that he was.

"Yes, I know!" he said. "That is precisely it. That is what I did not see before."

"But what I am saying is," Cordelia said slowly, "I am not now and probably will never be an intellectual."

Suddenly, she heard Lord Harveston laughing. He said, "That is nonsense! You are an intellectual, and a far greater one than myself. I may be an intellectual of books, but you are an intellectual of hearts."

"Am I?"

"Yes. And really, what are books to that?"

"I hadn't thought…"

"And, you've touched my own heart. Deeply." There was a pause, then he said, "It's funny, I hadn't really thought it could be touched."

Cordelia clutched her robe tighter round herself. Say it, she thought. Say it, say it, say it.

"Now, I know you had hopes for a Corinthian sort of fel-low—"

"No, I do not!" Cordelia shouted at the chimney.

"No?"

"No, absolutely not."

"Because I am not. You must know that upfront."

"You carried me up the stairs, Harveston," Cordelia said, "that is quite enough athletic prowess for me."

"So do you say then…"

"I can say nothing until I've been asked something," Cordelia said, hands on her cheeks.

He's on the verge, the verge, the very verge.

"Lady Cordelia Bennington, I am hopelessly in love with you—a thing I never thought possible. I was right to think it, as it would not have been possible had there not been Cordelia Bennington in the world."

He could not go back now. The verge had been reached.

"Lady Cordelia, would you consent to be my wife?"

It was said! He'd said it!

"Yes!" she shouted at the chimney.

"Yes, you do say yes?"

"Yes, I said yes."

"I would have Popinjay run me down a hundred times over to hear such an answer."

"Yes, and he might push all the ottomans at me that he likes. But what are we to do now, though?" Cordelia asked. "At such a moment, it seems as if we should…"

"Yes, we should. And yet we are confined."

"I can hop," Cordelia said.

"You can hop? Well I can walk slowly, as long as I do not jostle around too much."

"We can meet halfway," Cordelia said. "On the stairs, I am sure we can both get there."

"You are sure? Your ankle?"

"I am sure, Harveston," Cordelia said, laughing. "I am hopping now."

"I am coming."

PERCIVAL WAS NOT certain if his head was spinning from his very recent brain commotion or from the idea that he'd just proposed to Lady Cordelia through a chimney and been accepted.

She was on her way to the stairs and brain commotion or not, so was he.

He grabbed a candle from a side table and staggered out of the room, holding on to walls as he went.

Percival got to the landing and saw Lady Cordelia at the next landing down. She hopped and he staggered to meet one another halfway.

She threw herself into his arms. He had not been ready for that and fell back, with her atop him. He held the candle away so as not to set her hair ablaze.

It should have been a shocking situation, but it felt entirely natural. She leaned down and kissed him.

Percival threw the candle away and held her tight.

"My perfect Lady Cordelia," he whispered. He softly kissed her.

She nuzzled his neck and said, "I am not so perfect, but I hope your affection will make you blind to my faults."

"You are perfectly perfect and I will not have the point argued," Percival said. "You have made me join the land of the living again. Out of my books and into the world."

"You are really very handsome, Harveston," she said, tracing her forefinger down his jaw.

He kissed that charming finger and said, "But I am no Corinthian," he said with a laugh.

"I don't know about that. After all, when I think of it, I was most looking forward to my Corinthian carrying me up the stairs. You did that remarkably well."

"Which I will happily do all of our lives."

He kissed Lady Cordelia once more and the kiss went on for…how long? He did not really know. It was as if all the world had very conveniently faded away and they were just on their own. There was nothing but her and him on the stairs.

Somewhere outside of this lovely interlude, Percival vaguely smelled smoke. It did not entirely penetrate his thoughts until he heard someone yell, "Fire!"

Cordelia's head snapped up. So did his own, just in time to see a footman running toward a section of burning carpet just below them.

The footman doused the flames with a sand bucket.

"Was that the candle you came with?" Cordelia said.

"I'm afraid so. I have a brain commotion, you know."

Not a moment later, those people who had been in the dining room, which was most of the people in the house, were upon the stairs in a crowd.

Percival sat up with Cordelia in his lap.

"We are engaged, if that is at all helpful," he said to the on-lookers.

THE DAYS THAT followed comprised perhaps the most unique engagement the duke's house had ever experienced.

Cordelia would be carried down to the drawing room, while Lord Harveston's valet would lead him down the stairs to avoid any jostling.

There, they found their preferred corner, the view of its sofa blocked by the hulking pianoforte.

It turned out very convenient that the duke and duchess were such active people. They nearly always had their guests engaged in some sort of activity and the drawing room was theirs alone.

The couple would laugh and think of their good luck on the occasions when some of the exhausted guests would stagger into the drawing room looking for quiet refuge away from the storm of things to do.

They'd had to cover their mouths to stop their laughter when Lord and Lady Ledwellen had collapsed on chairs, entirely unaware of their presence.

Lady Ledwellen had said, "How many days left, Ledwellen. How many days?"

Her lord had answered, "Six. Six more days. We must just survive it, then we will return home and rest a month."

"We should hide after dinner," Lady Ledwellen said. "I positively refuse to lawn bowl in the dark again."

Though it had at first seemed highly inconvenient that Cordelia had sprained her ankle and Harveston had jostled his brain, they were happy to be just where they were.

Whether there was any jostling done in the drawing room…well it seemed there were no lasting ill-effects from it.

Though Lord Harveston would have, in any other circumstances, ridden to the earl's estate to ask for his daughter's hand, it was not possible at that very moment.

Instead, he wrote a long letter outlining his case. Cordelia wrote her own letter and enclosed it within. Her father was to know that it had recently been pointed out to her that she was an intellectual of the heart.

The earl's approval came a few days later, along with a note from Juliet that said she wished for her sister's happiness and if it must be Harveston, so be it.

They were married three weeks later, at the first opportunity that their injuries allowed.

For a wedding trip, Harveston told Cordelia nothing was out of reach. Wherever she wished to go, they would go.

Rather than setting off to Timbuktu or Bombay, Cordelia chose a small cottage that the lord owned in the Cotswolds. He had described it to her during their long hours together in the duke's drawing room and it seemed precisely where they should go.

And so it was.

Nestled in a pine forest and miles away from any other being, sat a thatched cottage that only had a caretaker come twice a month to keep it up.

They hauled in everything they would need on a farmer's cart and settled in for a month.

Amidst the quiet of the forest, where even their footsteps were silenced by a carpet of pine needles, Cordelia and Lord Harveston lolled in bed and had shockingly late breakfasts.

It turned out Lord Harveston could manage cooking eggs and could even get bread toasted sometimes. The rest of the meals were more a roll of the dice and they had smoked themselves out of the cottage on more than one occasion. The lord admitted to thinking the duke and duchess of Dembric Dale had been ridiculous in their inability to cook for themselves, but now he saw the veracity of the situation.

When they were not busy nearly burning the cottage down, they wandered the pine forest and stopped by a favored stream and watched quietly as the small forest animals went about their work. They rather felt like forest animals themselves, as they roamed with Cordelia only in a shift and the lord in just his breeches.

They came to know each other in both mentionable and unmentionable ways and came to know better who and what they were. There were long and languid conversations about histories and views.

Upon hearing of her lord's childhood household, Cordelia glimpsed a frigid world she could never have imagined. What would she have been, had she been raised in such a house?

Makepeace greatly grew in her estimation, when she was apprised of his opinion of the old baron and his treatment of poor Clara.

Percival, for his part, heard of Cordelia's household, full of children's running feet and laughter and Miss Mayton surrounding them with unwavering approval.

It was very difficult to imagine such a situation, but Percival had seen the result of it and was determined his own family would have just the same.

Miss Mayton grew in his estimation, when he understood that she'd been all of the Bennington sisters' bedrock of constancy. The lady was eccentric in the extreme, and likely a very great liar, but when one of her girls fell down, her hand reached out to pull them back up.

In the end, they concluded that Cordelia was not unintellectual. Harveston was not unemotional. They simply had different strengths.

After their month in the pine forest, they made the obligatory visits.

Lord Harveston's mother had been informed by letter that her son had wed Lady Cordelia Bennington at the Duke of Castleton's residence. The dowager had not had the first idea that a marriage had been in the works. In fact, she had been rather despairing of her son's marriage ever being in the works. She had not been able to understand why, until Cordelia explained the matter to her.

The dowager and her husband had not provided a very comforting or loving home for their son, which the lady had at first been affronted to hear. But, she had the good sense to not only face it, but to regret it. She had been pushed into a marriage that had never suited and had allowed an ice-cold house to be the result. She rejoiced that the family Cordelia would create would be far different.

Cordelia's father, for his part, had long got over any surprises his daughters might provide him. He took the whole thing in stride—his daughter had sought a Corinthian and then brought home an intellectual. It really mattered very little to him. He respected Lord Harveston and had every confidence in the lord's care of his daughter, and that was quite enough.

OVER TIME, THE couple would come to some satisfactory arrangements regarding their particular strengths. Percival read to Cordelia about facts, but he worked hard to make them interesting and ask her about what she thought of the people who might be affected by the topic.

Cordelia enacted her Desdemona final scene often – sometimes Desdemona would live and go off happily with Cassio, and sometimes she died very dramatically. Whatever her fate, Desdemona was generally carried up the stairs afterward.

Cordelia also educated her lord on when he might be feeling the effects of love, particularly if he felt as if his hair had been struck by lightning, to which he invariably claimed it had burst into flames the moment he'd met her.

If a question arose whose answer might lie in a book, Percival found it. If a question arose that might be found in a heart, Cordelia provided the guidance.

Makepeace, as might be imagined, was not over the moon to understand a mistress was coming into the house. Cordelia was able to soothe his bruised feelings by assuring him that his sideboards were excellent and that she did not require an outrageous amount of flowers in the drawing room.

The literary society carried on, with Lady Harveston on hand to deliver a heart to heart with one of its members when it was deemed necessary.

Surprisingly, it was often necessary.

The men, and eventually the women, of the society were made better for it.

Though Cordelia's season had ended abruptly, it had ended happily.

The earl had one more daughter to go—the youngest, Lady Juliet. She would arrive in London armed with the hundreds of odes she had written, and she would find her poet.

At least, that was the plan.

The End

About the Author

By the time I was eleven, my Irish Nana and I had formed a book club of sorts. On a timetable only known to herself, Nana would grab her blackthorn walking stick and steam down to the local Woolworth's. There, she would buy the latest Barbara Cartland romance, hurry home to read it accompanied by viciously strong wine, (Wild Irish Rose, if you're wondering) and then pass the book on to me. Though I was not particularly interested in real boys yet, I was *very* interested in the gentlemen in those stories—daring, bold, and often enraging and unaccountable. After my Barbara Cartland phase, I went on to Georgette Heyer, Jane Austen and so many other gifted authors blessed with the ability to bring the Georgian and Regency eras to life.

I would like nothing more than to time travel back to the Regency (and time travel back to my twenties as long as we're going somewhere) to take my chances at a ball. Who would take the first? Who would escort me into supper? What sort of meaningful looks would be exchanged? I would hope, having made the trip, to encounter a gentleman who would give me a very hard time. He ought to be vexatious in the extreme, and *worth* every vexation, to make the journey worthwhile.

I most likely won't be able to work out the time travel gambit, so I will content myself with writing stories of adventure and romance in my beloved time period. There are lives to be created, marvelous gowns to wear, jewels to don, instant attractions that inevitably come with a difficulty, and hearts to break before putting them back together again. In traditional Regency fashion, my stories are clean—the action happens in a drawing room, rather than a bedroom.

As I muse over what will happen next to my H and h, and wish I were there with them, I will occasionally remind myself that it's also nice to have a microwave, Netflix, cheese popcorn, and steaming hot showers.

Come see me on Facebook! @KateArcherAuthor